THE SILVER SHIPS

S. H. JUCHA

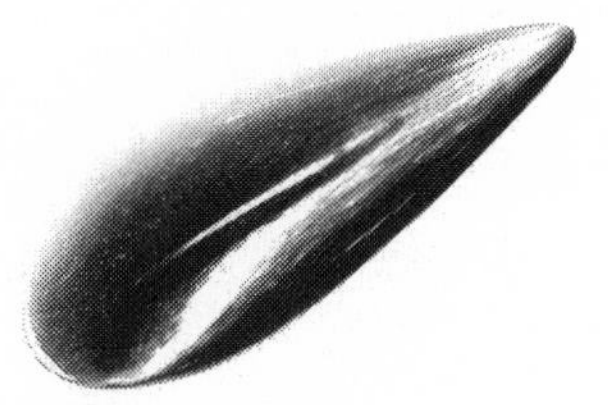

Published by S. H. Jucha
www.scottjucha.com

ISBN: 978-0-9905940-1-7 (e-book)
ISBN: 978-0-9905940-2-4 (softcover)

First Edition: February 2015

Cover Design: Damon Za

For my wife, Peggy, who has stood by me
and lent me her love and support
for thirty-four years.

Acknowledgments

There are always people who help you reach your goals. For me, these individuals made significant contributions that enabled the publishing of this book. My deepest thanks go to Jan Hamilton, Barry Jucha, and Dr. Kiyan Mehdizadeh.

A special thanks to my independent editor, Angela Polidoro, whose suggestions and guidance made this a much better story. And yes, Angela, Julien said the words *my friend* first – just like you wanted. In addition, my thanks to Joni Wilson, who assisted me in polishing this book.

As this is my first novel, I would ask you for your patience with any errors. They are all mine.

Glossary

A glossary is located at the end of the book.

-1-

"Anomaly detected," Tara's dulcet voice announced.

Alex sat upright in his pilot's seat. "Show me." On the navigation screen, a thin red line encircled a tiny dot. "Any telemetry available?"

"The object is headed in system at 13 degrees below the ecliptic. Distance is 388 million kilometers."

"Velocity?"

"It's constant at 0.02c."

His heart skipped a beat. "That's too fast for an asteroid. So what are you?"

New Terrans had ventured no farther than the ice fields, a dense ring of asteroids circling beyond Seda, a gas giant and their system's ninth and last planet. Since their colony's founding 732 years ago, there hadn't been any outside contact ... human or otherwise.

"How soon before it reaches the ice fields?"

"At its present velocity, it will enter the rings in five days."

"When will it intersect our system horizon?"

"Two days later, it will cross the ecliptic near Seda."

At present, he was headed for Sharius, one of Seda's moons, for refueling. The *Outward Bound*, under its 1g acceleration, had achieved a velocity of 0.01c. In seven days, his path would intersect with the anomaly.

Thirteen days earlier, Alex had piloted his explorer-tug next to a dark, craggy, 580m long asteroid, whose thick layer of ice covered a small, solid core. Using beams, he'd pinned it to his ship then fired a 2-meter long metal shaft into the ice. An electronic beacon housed in the shaft switched on and began broadcasting. Encoded with Tara's telemetry, it did double duty as information for bidders and as a tracking signal, broadcasting the asteroid's tag and his ship's ID.

Tara recorded the claim with the Ministry, initiating the bidding. All the mining outposts on Ganymede's frozen, rocky moons and the government habitats on Niomedes were bidders, as none possessed a natural source of water. Days later, the Niomedes Gordon Habitat was confirmed as the highest bidder and the new owner of Alex's latest haul.

With the asteroid firmly tethered in place, the *Outward Bound*, with engines blasting, had slowly redirected the mass from its ancient orbit into a new trajectory. Running Alex's proprietary g-sling program, Tara had tightened their arc until the desired course was achieved. Alex, in the meantime, had endured the heavy acceleration reclined in his pilot's couch and eating prepackaged rations.

When Tara announced the exit point, Alex had freed the asteroid, slinging it on a ballistic course, system inward. This was the beauty of his innovative, mathematical model. While other explorer-tug captains were forced to haul their asteroids to a destination – Sirius, Ganymede, or Niomedes – Alex slung them directly to the buyer's planet or moon.

It had taken nearly three years and a perfect record before the Ministry of Space Exploration had deemed his program viable and approached him with an offer. Alex knew that once the Ministry owned the application, they would distribute it to every government-contracted tug captain. The moment it did, his exclusive and lucrative edge would come to an end. So he drove a hard bargain for its sale and won three years of bonus payout on top of the Ministry's original offer.

He was returning for another haul from the ice fields by way of a refueling stop when Tara had informed him of the strange object.

Alex had spared no expense for Tara, his bridge computer, and had patterned her voice synthesis program on recordings of his college advisor, Amy Mallard. The striking brunette's orbital mechanics class was one of the most popular courses at Ulam University, especially among the male undergraduates. She was also one of the university's most brilliant professors.

He passed the days exercising, reading, and watching vids on his reader as he closed the distance to Sharius. If Tara had been human, his unceasing information requests would probably have earned him a slap upside the head. Eventually, as the distance closed, she was able to display a dim outline of the object. It was slender and symmetrical with no heat signature.

"So ... we have what ... an alien vessel on a cold coast coming from outside the system?" Alex mused out loud. Tara didn't respond – she was programmed to ignore rhetorical questions. With no one else aboard, Alex had fallen into the habit of sharing his thoughts with her.

The image changed the nature of Alex's curiosity. Before, he'd wanted to see it; now, he wanted to touch it. But he and the alien ship were on opposing trajectories. Even if he reversed course, it was moving at twice his velocity and would pass him by with a delta-V of nearly 3K km/sec.

He debated comming Sharius, the government outpost for explorer-tug support and refueling. Ultimately, he decided against it since he hadn't made his own decision about the ship. He passed the time in his chair, idly calculating intercepts, discarding one plan after another. One plan he concocted had the slimmest possibility of working, although its initiation window was closing fast. Despite the hazards, his curiosity had begun to consume him, forcing his decision – he would risk it.

He leapt up, grabbed the rungs of the bridge ladder and slid down into the central living hub, which rotated around the tug's spine, providing gravity when the ship coasted. In his tiny galley, he grabbed a handful of meal bars then changed into an acceleration suit.

Jumping back into his pilot's chair, he stashed his meal bars and hooked his suit into the ship's cleanser system, which processed his sweat and wastes. He loaded the flight plan into Tara's navigational sub-system, shifted the chair into its horizontal position, strapped himself in, and executed the program.

Long plumes of incandescence bloomed from the *Outward Bound*'s engines, accelerating the ship toward Seda. His plan was to sling around the gas giant and come to a nearly parallel course with the vessel.

Uncertainty haunted Alex as he gritted his mouthguard. If the latch was solid, his ship would be yanked forward and twisted onto a new trajectory, even if only by a few degrees. The force could damage his ship ... and maybe him. And he wasn't ready to die, not at twenty-eight years old, the youngest captain in New Terra's short, eighty-three-year history of space exploration.

Alex wasn't only the captain of the *Outward Bound*; he was its sole owner. Other explorer-tugs had a minimum crew of four, mandated by their government contracts. Alex, as an independent owner-operator, chose to go it alone. He preferred his own company to that of strangers, and he'd never been one to have many friends.

His late teenage years were spent on his parents' explorer-tug, the *No Bounds*, mining the system's great asteroid belt. With their efficient engines and powerful beams, the tugs were designed to be the perfect crafts to harvest the ice fields.

After university, Alex had spent three more years with his family on their tug, employing his new g-sling program with great success. The inventive approach to harvesting had guaranteed his parents met, then exceeded, the conditions of their government contract. On completion of the contract, they were awarded the ship's title and had sold it. They'd retired and invested their profits with Alex in the *Outward Bound.*

Throughout his ship's design and construction, he'd pushed the engineers to build a one-of-a-kind explorer-tug. And with it, he'd delivered 60 percent more asteroids annually than his parents had been able to sling with the *No Bounds*. In two years, he had repaid his parents with interest.

As he accelerated toward Seda, pressed deep into his couch, he mused that he was about to find out if he'd gotten his creds' worth.

Hours into his burn, he received an emergency comm from Sharius Tracking Control requesting his status and asking if he needed assistance. Normally, ships nearing Sharius were decelerating to dock for supplies and refueling, not shooting past for the great dark. Alex managed a chuckle even through the heavy pressure on his chest. He was nearing 0.012c. "Just how would you catch me if I *did* need help?" he wondered out loud. Instead, he asked Tara to send his prerecorded message.

"Message sent, Alex. Your vital signs indicate extraordinary stress. It is recommended that you reduce acceleration."

"Negative, Tara, remove medical safety locks."

"Confirmed, Alex, medical safety locks have been removed."

He wished he had a vid link to Sharius' control room to watch the tracker's faces when they played his message. His reputation and g-sling's perfect record meant they wouldn't dismiss a message from him offhand, no matter how crazy it sounded. They'd monitor his approach, confirm his slingshot trajectory, and swing their tracking dish to the coordinates he had shared. Once they verified the alien vessel, they'd relay his comm to the government tracking centers on Cressida, Niomedes, and New Terra. A priority message would be sent to the minister's office, adding substantially to Alex's notoriety. He had been quite the media sensation after his first slung asteroid arrived on target. This message, as soon as it leaked to the news media, would make that story pale by comparison.

As he accelerated around Seda, his vision tunneled, threatening a blackout. Bright pinpoints of lights danced in the corners of his eyes. He concentrated on mathematical computations, a trick he used to help him focus. When he cleared Seda's gravity well, his vision slowly cleared.

"Update," he requested.

"We are on course," Tara replied. "Velocity is 0.018c; acceleration is holding at 4.3g; engines are within operating parameters; reaction mass is at 38 percent. Estimated time to intercept is 3.42 hours; velocity at intercept will be 0.0198c; delta-V estimated at 0.0001c; delta trajectory will be 2.2 degrees."

"Object on screen," Alex coughed out and sipped from his water tube. He stared at the image. The vessel was an order of magnitude larger than the *Outward Bound* and unlike any ship of his people. New Terrans had built tugs, fuel haulers, shuttles, and small freighters that carried passengers. This multi-decked, slim-lined, 300-meter long ship, distinctly free of gravity wheels, was much more technologically advanced. Telemetry still detected no heat signature and the ship's aft end silhouette appeared to be distorted or damaged. "No doubt about it, Tara. It's an alien ship."

"Spectrographic return on the hull is an unknown alloy," Tara added.

"Okay," he mumbled, "not only an alien ship, but an *advanced* alien ship. But the real question is whether this is salvage or rescue."

As he waited out the few remaining hours, his mind whirled with more questions. If this was salvage, would he be awarded the rights to sell the ship? On the other hand, what if it was a rescue? Who would he be rescuing? And his last and strangest thought was whether any survivors would be grateful for their rescue ... or was he about to be a snack for starving aliens.

* * *

The starship and the tug crossed bows so close that any tracking center observer would think they'd collided. Just before interception, Tara energized the beam engines to full power and fired them at the hurtling derelict. The tug's hull groaned under the sudden acceleration and the small but significant 2-degree course shift. Alex's body was jerked within his restraints and he blacked out.

As he came to, the dim light he perceived grew brighter, the black edges fading to gray before his vision finally cleared. He called out, "Are we latched on?"

"The target has been acquired. Drive engines have been shut down," replied Tara, her melodic voice a pleasant balm to his bruised mind and body.

Alex unstrapped himself and activated the chair's upright position. The weightlessness was a relief after the crushing acceleration. The alien hull captured in the tug's exterior vid cam filled his display screen. He murmured, "Look what I found, Mom. Can I keep it?"

In that moment, Alex urgently wanted to share his success with someone, anyone – jump up and down with a friend, hug a woman. But, he acknowledged, this was the sore point of going it alone. He didn't regret the way he'd chosen to spend the past three years. The creds he'd accrued would allow him financial freedom to pursue other projects. But he'd come to understand one thing; his difficulty forming meaningful relationships wouldn't be solved by self-imposed isolation.

He shook his head to clear his thoughts and belatedly remembered his blackout as stars twinkled at the corners of his dimmed vision. "Idiot," he announced. "Tara, what's the status of our reaction mass?"

"The tanks are at 23 percent."

"That's not good." At those levels, he should be headed for Sharius, not shooting above the ecliptic. He checked his chronometer and was shocked to realize he'd been out for almost five hours. "Display the planet positions," he requested.

He groaned as he realized Ganymede and Niomedes, the only two planets with fuel services that might have stood between him and New Terra, were passing on the far side of Oistos, their star. His only viable target was New Terra. "Tara, plot the most efficient burn to rendezvous with New Terra."

It was quiet while Tara calculated the added mass of the new ship, the required deceleration curve, and the required delta-V. When completed, she announced, "We have insufficient reaction mass for a zero-velocity rendezvous with New Terra."

"Black space," Alex muttered. "Calculate a deceleration burn to put us on course for New Terra until reaction mass is at 5 percent."

After a couple of moments, Tara responded. "A course change for rendezvous must be initiated within 92 hours. Shifting the start time will create a deceleration variable of 0.25g to 3.3g.

"Estimate velocity at time of shut down with the most efficient burn."

The question wasn't only whether he had enough reaction mass to head back into the system, but if he had enough to reduce his speed sufficient to enable a fueling tug to rendezvous with him. They were traveling close to 0.02c, and their velocity would need to be far below 0.01c. Otherwise, he would have to cut his prize free, and that was an unthinkable loss.

"Most efficient burn of 0.25g requires initiation within the next three hours. Estimated velocity at 5 percent reserves will be 29K km/sec to 30K km/sec."

Alex's breath blew out in a whoosh. He had enough reaction mass to keep his prize even if it resulted in a cold coast toward New Terra, *and* he could decelerate sufficiently to match a refueling tanker's slower velocity. Although, a rescue refueling would mean owing the government before negotiations over the alien ship even began. This would be the same Ministry he'd gone head-to-head with for the sale of his g-sling program only two months ago – but there was no avoiding that. "This is going to cost me," he mumbled.

He was in parallel with the derelict, bow to bow, and would have to reverse this orientation before Tara could initiate their course change. "Switch off bow and aft beams," he ordered. "Rotate us around the central beam until optimum position is achieved for the deceleration program."

Alex monitored his display screen as the derelict's hull rotated past. The smooth surface was marred by holes varying from half a meter to a meter in diameter. "It looks like they ran afoul of an asteroid storm."

Tara signaled the rotation's finish. "Optimum position achieved."

"Re-engage bow and aft beams. Initiate course change for rendezvous with New Terra with most efficient burn. Shut the engines off when reaction mass drops to 5 percent."

"The deceleration program has been initiated. Fuel reserve status set."

At only 11 percent power, the *Outward Bound*'s engines supplied 0.25g, decelerating their coupled crafts and curving them back toward the ecliptic and New Terra.

Alex climbed down into the central hub. He took out two synth-meals, added water, and popped them into a heater. He wasn't any taller than most of his people at 1.8 meters. But his 146-kilogram frame of heavy muscle, courtesy of a 1.12 grav-world and years spent helping his father offload space junk, demanded more than a single synth-meal at a time. Reaching his arms overhead, he could feel his shoulder muscles roll and pop. While waiting for the food to heat, he spent the time stretching sore muscles.

When the heater chimed, he grabbed an oversized tray, loaded it with the meal pouches, utensils, and a sealed juice carafe then climbed back to the bridge. Settling into his chair, he placed the food tray in his lap and quickly consumed the meal. He let the desserts cool in their pouches while he checked his comm board.

A priority message from Sharius Tracking Control was listed at the top of the display. Another tap and Colonel Damon Stearns, commander of Sharius, appeared on his vid screen. "Captain Racine, at the time of this message, you are about to attempt an interception of an alien ship. If you have been successful, you are requested to stay in your ship and redirect to New Terra. Arrangements will be made to relieve you of the craft before you enter orbit. Please acknowledge soonest."

Alex replayed the message twice more as he finished his desserts. "Did you notice, Tara, the colonel did say requested, not ordered?"

"Affirmative, Alex."

It seemed the colonel had recalled that Alex didn't report to Terran Security Forces (TSF) or the Ministry of Space Exploration. He was an owner, who had to report to no one. On the other hand, he didn't want to anger those in power.

In the end, he decided to borrow a favorite ruse of his kid sister, Christie. She had the frustrating habit of pretending she didn't know her unapproved adventures were off limits. The colonel would later receive a message saying that Alex had already been on an extravehicular activity (EVA) when the request arrived. Alex knew if he followed TSF's or the Ministry's guidance, he'd never get a look inside the ship. "I ran it down, and I'm getting first peek," he mumbled.

Alex ordered Tara to cut the aft beam and tied two directives to his deceleration instructions. Setting *no watch* and *EVA* conditions on the control board, he grabbed his tray and climbed back down to the central hub, recycling his empty food pouches and heading aft through the spine tube to the rear airlock.

It took time to climb into his 85kg-EVA suit with its mag-boots, armored gloves, tool belt, and oxygen tanks. He snapped his helmet into place, checked his oxygen read out, and cued Tara with *engines off.*

When he felt the engines shutdown, he depressurized the airlock, which recycled the air back into the ship's reserve tanks. Then he released the outer hatch's locking mechanism and swiveled the hatch aside. The derelict was oriented upside down. He regarded the 55 meters separating him from the huge ship and searched for a point of ingress. Odd symbols in two columns left and right of an area seemed to indicate a hatch, but the hull was in shadow, and a hatch wasn't visible.

He pulled a grappling pistol from his belt and clipped its safety line to the retaining ring on the tug's hull. Aiming at the symbols, he fired the pistol's mag-clamp. It sailed across the gap, the line paying out behind it, but the mag-clamp bounced off the hull.

"Well, she said it was an unknown alloy," he mumbled.

He reeled the line back onto its spool and reattached the pistol to his belt. Then, before he had time to argue himself out of it, he wrapped stik-pads over his boots and gloves, aligned his body with the derelict, and triggered the suit's jets. He floated across the gap, the safety line paying out behind him as his heart thundered in his chest. When he struck the hull, 4 meters to the left of his target, the impact jarred his teeth, but his stik-pads anchored him in position.

Now, he could just make out the hatch. "That's some great craftsmanship," he murmured, admiring the exquisitely fitted metal surfaces.

* * *

Small sensors, embedded in the ship's hull, had relayed the contact of the *Outward Bound*'s beams. Subsequently, other sensors relayed the impacts of the mag-clamp, then Alex. The signals were transmitted to the ship's bridge, initiating a wake-up routine.

As the derelict ship drifted through space, power had become a premium, and the bridge computer, managing what little energy remained in its power-crystals, had shut down its sub-routines and later its primary routines in an attempt to preserve its existence for as long as possible.

Utilizing the barest amount of energy, the wake-up routine ended the entity's time-dilation program. Restored to real time, the self-aware digital entity (SADE) studied the sensor logs and the small, odd craft holding it in traction. It monitored the progress of the humanoid figure walking across its hull. When the figure crossed into shadow, its tinted visor cleared, providing an unobstructed view of its face. In response, the SADE signaled the airlock's exterior hatch to open.

-2-

Alex knelt beside the hatch, the *Outward Bound* floating above him. He'd searched for an access panel without success and was rethinking his approach when the hatch recessed a half meter into the hull and slid aside.

"Yeah, just ask," he said to himself. He switched on his suit lights, illuminating the darkened interior, released one boot, then the other, and used his jets to glide inside. The outer airlock hatch promptly closed behind him, but before he could panic, the interior hatch slid open. No attempt was made at atmosphere replacement. There was no air, but there was power. "So is this automation or a welcome?" Alex murmured.

Alex tested his comm to Tara and received a response. He signaled *engines on* to reinstate the decel program and steadied himself with an outstretched arm against a bulkhead as the *Outward Bound*'s engines ignited.

The interior corridor was anything but utilitarian. It was spacious and clean-lined, without pipes or ducts running overhead. Doors were evenly spaced down the corridor. An odd thing though – there were no numbers, letters, or labels of any kind – causing him to wonder how anyone knew where they were going.

Dust motes, floating throughout the corridor, and a fine sheen of ice crystals coating every surface reflected his lights back to him. The debris was settling toward the bow under the deceleration. A piece of delicate, multihued, faded fabric caught on his shoulder as it drifted past. He'd never been on a dead ship before; never had to recover the bodies of those who'd died in space. The thought made him shudder.

Down the corridor, a small light blinked on. Then a second and a third light followed suit, blinking on and off slowly and rhythmically, 3 meters apart from one another. As Alex stared, more of them joined the pattern, like nightlights guiding a shuttle landing. He recalled one of his father's favorite comments: "Anything done by half measure is done half-assed."

So Alex took a deep breath, blew it out slowly, and let loose of the bulkhead. Having removed the stik-pads from his boots, he used the *Outward Bound*'s momentum to drive him down the corridor toward the bow, following the lights. They led up a wide, vertical chute located inside the bulkhead wall. He halted his motion by bracing a boot in the shaft's opening and slapping a stik-padded glove against a bulkhead. The shaft was empty, so he crawled on his hands and knees along its forward face. Even though the engines only generated 0.25g, his combined mass pressed him forward with 56 kilograms of force.

The chute opened into another corridor and Alex followed the lights to a wide accessway. A double set of split doors, spaced 2 meters apart, were open. Beyond the doorways lay an extensive bridge with enormous vid screens. Two large command chairs, centrally located, were elevated on a pedestal and surrounded by small vid and control panels. Despite the bridge's impressive appearance, Alex's first reaction was one of relief. The chairs were shaped much like his pilot's chair, a sign that the occupants are or were humanoid.

A small vid screen on one of the command chairs lit up. "Uh, oh ..." he whispered. He released his hold on the doorway and floated across to the chair, bracing a hand against its back. The screen was obscured by a film of ice crystals, which he carefully scraped away with a stik-pad, surprised that it could operate in the cold vacuum.

Character groups scrolled up the screen, but he couldn't read them. As the letters Sol-NAC appeared in his own alphabet, he flexed an EVA-encumbered hand toward the screen and the rolling list froze. The hairs on the back of his neck stood up and he glanced around the bridge. Turning back to the screen, he positioned an armored finger over Sol-NAC.

The screen went blank then refreshed with words in his language. "Hello. I'm Julien, this vessel's SADE, a self-aware digital entity. How are you called?" The screen went blank, replaced by an alphanumeric keypad.

Alex carefully typed out his first name.

"Hello, Alex," scrolled the response, "I'm in need of your help. Are you the captain of the ship that anchors us?"

Alex typed in his reply, "Yes," and then, "Are you an AI?" New Terrans had yet to develop AIs or artificial intelligences, but that hadn't stopped computer scientists from postulating myriad possibilities.

In response to his question, he saw, "As you might define artificial intelligence, I'd answer yes, Captain."

"Wow," Alex exclaimed to himself, then typed, "What help?"

"Our ship has been heavily damaged, Captain. The bridge has been cut off from its primary power supply and my backup power is extremely limited. A new power source is required immediately."

Alex typed, "Want to help. No means of transferring power."

"I have a means in mind, Captain," appeared on the screen.

For the next half hour, Alex responded to the SADE's questions about his ship's manner of propulsion and how he managed a supply of energy while in dock. Then he turned and exited the bridge, headed for the chute that led down and out to his ship.

* * *

The SADE watched Alex leave and pondered his abrupt departure. No agreement had been reached. He reran the exchange, hoping to discern whether the individual was choosing to help, leaving them adrift, or allowing him to expire so the ship could be claimed. He couldn't reach any conclusion. His only option was to do what he had been doing for years: wait.

* * *

Alex navigated his way back to the derelict's airlock and signaled Tara with *engines off*. The AI operated the airlock hatches for him, allowing him to leave. For Alex, this was an important test as to whether he might trust the entity or not. The thought made him laugh. "I'm debating whether to trust an alien computer!"

As he looked above his head to judge the leap back to his own airlock, the darkness lit up beside him. A section of hull glowed around a ring extruded from the ship's skin. It hadn't been there before. He was sure of that.

"Convenient," Alex murmured, "and oh so clever." He pulled the safety line from the stik-pad that had secured it to the hull and locked it onto the ring. Saving his suit jets, he returned to the *Outward Bound* by pulling himself hand over hand along the tethered line, his suit's safety ring sliding along the line.

While cycling through his own airlock, he considered his next move. He wanted to think through his decision logically, weigh the pros and cons, and come to a mature decision. Instead, and without much further consideration, he gathered a long length of power line from a storage locker, dropping it on the airlock's deck, then dropped the jet pack and changed out his oxygen tanks. There wasn't time to ponder the risks and potential benefits of aiding the alien ship. That could take forever, and the AI said it didn't have much time left.

A memory from childhood surfaced in his mind. He'd come home with a bleeding face and torn clothes one day, embarrassed to be seen by his mother. Three boys had beaten and kicked another boy to the ground. After jumping in to help the injured boy, he'd suffered the same fate. His mother had tilted his bloody face up to look into her eyes and said, "You have a choice in life, Alex. You can help someone in need or stand back and do nothing. And the choice you make determines the person you are." Then she had kissed his dirty forehead and told him to wash up.

When it came down to it, it wasn't a choice at all.

He cycled back through his airlock. Outside, he attached the power line to his ship's dock receptacle and uncoiled the line as he made his way back across the safety line to the derelict. As his boots' stik-pads hit the hull, a small panel beside the airlock hatch slid open. He peered into its interior and saw nothing – no connectors – just a dark funnel extending into the hull. Dubious though he was, he followed the AI's instructions and pushed his power cable into the funnel's throat. To his utter astonishment, the funnel's sides closed around his line's connector.

The power line was designed to transfer dock power *to* the *Outward Bound.* Despite Alex's efforts to convince the AI that the line limited the flow to one-way, it had assured him that the line would work for their purpose.

The line's telltale green flashed, signaling current flowing, but the power meter wasn't registering, which didn't seem possible. The meter's circuitry prevented power discharge from his ship, or, at least, that was its purpose. Yet, power was flowing ... out of his ship, bypassing the meter's control circuits.

He broke out of his reverie and commed Tara. "Limit the discharge on this line to 20 percent of our generator's output. Set an alarm for the charging capacitors. I don't want any drain on them. Cut the power to this line if the alarm is activated."

"Orders received," Tara responded.

Then he slid back into the derelict's airlock. As the AI operated the hatches for him, he signaled *engines on* to Tara.

* * *

The brief time Julien waited for the captain's return felt longer to him than all the years of isolation he had spent waiting for rescue. Just when he was starting to wonder if he had been deserted, the small ship's rear airlock reopened. The captain uncoiled an armload of cable, plugging one end into his ship's receptacle before making his way back.

Julien opened the charging receptacle hatch for him and signaled the funnel nanites to engage the power-line connector. It took only a moment to detect the primitive flow switch, analyze its circuitry, and reverse its polarity. Current immediately flowed into his power-crystal banks. It compared poorly to his ship's overall energy needs and ultimate capacity, but if Julien had been capable of shedding a tear of relief within his metal-alloy case, he would have. His primary question was answered – the human was *not* a scavenger.

As the ship drifted, Julien had been dependent on the bow's power-crystal bank, which allowed the bridge to operate its redundant systems in isolation from the remainder of the ship during emergency conditions. With a renewed power supply, he would be able to resume control of any bridge systems still operational. He closed the double set of access doors behind Alex as he entered the bridge and flashed the command screen to gain his attention. Across the screen, he sent, "Captain, there are decompression openings in the bridge bulkheads that must be fixed. If you would continue to help, please locate the supply cabinet to your left, with the blinking light, and remove two plates."

* * *

When Alex finished reading the instructions, he scanned to his left and spotted the cabinet door. Inside, stacked on edge, were plates about half-a-meter square and two centimeters thick. He pulled two out and returned to the vid screen.

"Excellent, Captain," he read. "You must apply them to the two openings you see in the hull, one high to starboard and the other low to port. The plates will self-seal once provided with sufficient heat."

Heat, Alex thought and considered his options. "I'll be back," he told the AI, then retraced his steps back to the *Outward Bound*. Once aboard, he stopped for some water and a meal bar. He considered checking his messages, but he figured it was better not to know who had commed what to him.

Back on the derelict's bridge, Alex unloaded two full packs of tools. Whatever this AI, Julien, required next, he was prepared to deliver. He pulled a compact welding canister out of his pack, grabbed one of the repair plates, and made his way to the more accessible portside hole. It was perfectly round, about 32 centimeters in diameter, with smooth edges. He twisted his body around to look at the other hole, which appeared the same. A hole had been punched completely through the bow. The decompression would have been powerful enough to suck anyone on the bridge into space. It explained why there weren't any bodies.

Putting aside the unsettling mental image of the bridge crew's demise, Alex returned to his work, lighting the welder and dialing it to its minimum output. He positioned the plate over the hole and applied the torch to the far edge of the plate, gawking as the edge became liquid and spread out to merge with the bulkhead. In his surprise over the life-like movement of the metal, he had pulled the torch away before the edge became seamless. So he waved his torch over the edge and watched it disappear. Then he applied his torch to the other edges, following the flow of metal until all signs of the plate disappeared. When he finished, he stood up and examined the bulkhead. If he hadn't applied the seal himself, he wouldn't have known it existed.

Suddenly, a touch of vertigo overcame him. The ship's advanced technology surpassed anything his people had ... seamless repairs that took only moments to apply, a funnel that could mold itself to fit a power line, and a self-aware digital entity that could converse in Alex's language or many others, for that matter. He felt strange and out of place, like a child left to fend for itself in an adult world.

He mentally shook himself and tackled the second hole on the bridge's starboard side, its repair just as simple, then returned to the chair's vid screen. The screen switched to the keyboard and he typed, "What next?"

"Allow me a few moments, Captain," was sent back.

After nearly a quarter hour, Alex wondered if something had happened to the AI. Then his suit's audio pickup relayed the soft hiss of air, and his helmet readouts displayed increasing air pressure. When the hissing ended, his helmet registered an acceptable air mixture for breathing, though with less oxygen than was found on his world. The air temperature was acceptable so he broke his helmet seal and tested the air. Satisfied, he removed the helmet completely.

With air present to transmit sound waves, a pleasant male voice came over the bridge speakers. "Hello, Captain. It's a pleasure to speak with you."

"Julien?" Alex asked tentatively.

"Yes, Captain. May I know your full name?"

"It's Alexander Racine. Black space! I don't know where to start. I have so many questions."

"As do I, Captain Racine, but I must ask you to wait. There are emergency repairs that must be made to restore minimal functionality to the ship."

When Alex failed to respond, Julien perceived an important facet of the young captain's personality – he would help, but he wouldn't be directed. "What questions might I answer for you, Captain?"

Alex understood the AI would have his own agenda, but he couldn't continue without at least some answers to the questions swirling in his head. He decided it would be best to compromise and save most of his curiosity for later. "Two questions, for now, Julien. Are your people human or something else?"

"They are human, descendants of an Earth colony ship as I imagine your people are also. And your second question, Captain?"

Humans, Alex thought. *Well, at least I probably won't get eaten.* "Is there anyone else alive on this ship?"

"And that's my greatest concern, Captain. Due to our damage, I have little access to most of the ship, so I don't know. If they are alive, they are in stasis and as much in need of power as was I."

"You should have said that in the first place! What do I need to do first? I haven't a clue about your technology. You'll have to show me what to do," Alex blurted out.

Despite the calamitous circumstances, Julien found himself amused by the captain's exuberance. "I will be pleased to guide you, Captain."

Alex admitted he was definitely willing to be guided. He couldn't wait to learn more about the ship's technical marvels. "If I could but discover this world's wonders ..." he murmured, quoting an early colonist's poem.

"Is that an affirmative, Captain?" Julien asked, unsure of his response.

"Yes," Alex laughed, breaking the tension, "yes, it is."

"And your efforts are much appreciated, Captain."

A light blinked on a small cabinet door and Alex walked over to it without prompting. It opened to reveal a set of tiny devices stored in slots.

"Captain, these are comm devices. Please take the one next to the blinking light and place the contact end to the inside of your ear."

Alex picked up the device, which looked like a short, dark, thin stick attached to a piece of sealant. Intuiting which end was the contact end, Alex pressed the daub of sealant into his right ear. It was cool to the touch but warmed instantly and suddenly the little mass of sealant flowed into his ear. "Whoa," he yelped as he tugged the comm device out of his ear. "What just happened?"

"My apologies, Captain," said Julien, realizing he would have to give more consideration to the technological gap going forward, "the contact end is a small patch of audio-integrator nanotech that conforms to your inner ear on contact with your skin. When you wish to release it you only need to pull gently on it."

Alex eyed the sealant end dubiously, but then pressed it back into his ear, allowing the daub of material to warm and flow into his inner ear.

"How does it feel, Captain?"

"Fine ... as if you're speaking inside my head. Will this allow us to communicate when I'm aboard my ship?"

"Once the repairs are further along and a ship-link has been strung, it will be possible. While on the bridge, I might respond via the bridge speakers or comm, depending on your preference. When you are off the bridge or your EVA helmet is sealed, we must depend on the ear comm."

"What about recharging?" Alex asked.

"Your body heat charges the nanites."

"Of course," Alex mumbled quietly, "alien miracle technology."

Julien decided it would be better not to explain the ear comm's complete capabilities. The fact that he could monitor Alex's blood pressure, pulse rate, and other physiological parameters through his inner ear might be more than the young human was prepared to handle.

-3-

Alex worked for many more hours on bridge repairs before deciding to call it a day. "Julien, I'm tired and hungry. If your conditions are stable, *I* need to recharge," he said, chuckling at his own joke.

"I'll be well until your return, Captain. Your efforts have been greatly appreciated ... more than you know."

"Will the people in stasis be all right for now?" Alex asked, concerned that he might be deserting them.

"My people have been in stasis for a long while, Captain. If they still live, another day or two will not make any difference. Your well-being is important too."

"One more question. If your power supply had been exhausted before I could help you, couldn't you have just been rebooted?"

"No, Captain, I'm not a computer. I'm a self-aware entity that has been created ... born, you might say. While I have the ability to minimize my processes and applications, I would cease to exist if I lost all power. I'd be dead."

Many more questions occurred to Alex, but he was too tired to think straight, so he said good-night and retraced his steps back to his own ship. Out of the thirty-hour New Terran day, he had logged more than fourteen hours in his EVA suit. He paused in the galley for food, this time deciding on three synth-meals, and carried them to the bridge to check messages.

As he expected, his message board was brimming. Several vid messages were from Colonel Stearns. He skipped to the latest one and the colonel's rather stern face appeared on screen. "Captain Racine, Tracking Control has confirmed that the *Outward Bound* is tethered to the unidentified vessel. This unknown vessel is now under the auspices of the Ministry of

Space Exploration, which has ordered it quarantined. Continue on course for New Terra and remain in your ship."

Alex spied a vid message from The Honorable William Drake, Minister of Space Exploration. The minister's face, which was very familiar to Alex, also carried a stern expression. "I seem to be upsetting a lot of people lately, Tara."

The minister began, "We were copied on your original message, Captain Racine. You are to refrain from boarding the alien ship. Send detailed images of its exterior and remain on course for New Terra. My tech advisors estimate you will be low on reaction mass, and a tanker has been dispatched to assist you. Once refueled, you will settle the vessel into an orbit 250K km from New Terra. Under no circumstances are you to bring the ship closer than this distance."

Alex played the message again and considered his reply. "Tara, send the following message to Minister William Drake, New Terra. 'Sir, before any messages were received requiring me to remain in my ship, I was granted ingress to the vessel by the ship's artificial intelligence called Julien. There is extensive damage to the ship, especially to the stern, and the ship's engines are offline. At his request, I've provided a temporary power source to the vessel's bridge to keep him alive. Your advisor's estimate of my reaction mass is correct. I'm at 18 percent capacity now and will shut down engines when I reach 5 percent. One last thought for you, Minister Drake. I'd deem my actions a rescue. Will you grant that Julien has the rights to this ship?'" He tapped off the recording and hit send.

Brevity appeared to be his best defense. The government had drawn a hard line and he'd already crossed it. The less he communicated; the less he exposed himself.

* * *

The double bridge doors were cycled for him the next morning, allowing the bridge to maintain air. As he entered, he heard, “Careful of your step, Captain.”

Before Alex could puzzle out Julien’s meaning, he stumbled forward but managed to regain his footing. It took a moment to register that he was standing upright, with no hint of the decel force. “Okay, I’m impressed.”

“My power reserves are still minimal, but I thought it would help you, Captain, if I balanced the inertia of your ship’s propulsion. This will only be in effect on the bridge until my power reserves grow.”

Balanced the inertia – just how in black space do you do that? Alex wondered.

The next two days passed in a blur of repair work for Alex. He put in as many hours as he could until he was hungry or exhausted or both and returned to his ship for recharging. Always, in the back of his mind, he worried that he wouldn’t complete the repairs in time to be of help to the people still in stasis. Each time he asked if there was a way to speed up the process, Julien counseled patience.

Alex knew he wasn’t making much of a dent in the ship’s repairs – one person working alone couldn’t hope to restore a multi-decked vessel of this size. At one point, after some effusive praise from Julien, Alex told him to stop *cheerleading*, a term Julien tagged for future research once his entire functionality was restored.

After completing as much bridge repair work as possible, Alex, under Julien’s direction, proceeded aft. He would seal a corridor’s or compartment’s bulkheads then attempt to restore power, comm, and environmental services to the area.

The repair process continually fascinated him. He questioned Julien about the technology, learning along the way that the people called themselves Méridiens. They employed microscopic machines called nanites in a variety of processes, including seamlessly repairing damaged ship components in moments – repairs that New Terrans would take hours to duplicate as they cut out damaged sections and welded or spliced in new components.

To fix a severed power cable, he squeezed a thick, viscous material from a tube on to one end and slowly drew the loop of nanites to the other end of the cable then watched in wonder as the dangling loop of nanites, warmed by his torch, tightened into a straight line, reconnecting the cable.

At one point, Alex repaired a hole in the overhead of the top deck, the same deck as the bridge. The matching exit hole was in the compartment's bulkhead wall. Alex laid his tools and repair plates down and followed the hole to the deck below. An opening in a corridor was matched to one through a nearby storage compartment. He descended the next two decks, following the holes, until one cut through the hull.

His thoughts tumbled over one another. An asteroid might pass through both sides of the relatively slender bridge, but it couldn't possibly do this – passing through multiple decks of a ship as if the walls were nothing more than foil. He'd seen what meteor strikes did to a ship. They left messy damage, a ragged collision of ice, ore, and metal. This was something else, something manmade. That meant there had been a fight, which begged the question: which side was he helping?

It was obvious the Méridien ship was a luxury passenger liner, which had placated his concern that he was restoring a fighting ship. But he didn't know what trouble had found these people, or, if it followed them here, how his technologically inferior planet could hope to defend itself.

Near the end of his third day aboard, he heard from Julien that there were sufficient reserves in his power-crystals to activate the grav-plating and inertia systems in the repaired sections. Alex seated himself at a table in a cabin he had recently restored and waited out the transition. As the plates were slowly activated, he watched the loose materials in the room, layered against the forward bulkhead, slowly sink to the deck.

"Captain, are you all right?" came Julien's concerned voice.

"Fine, Julien."

"Is the gravity level comfortable?" Julien asked.

Alex chuckled. "Is this normal gravity for your people?"

"Yes, Captain, it is."

"It's about 80 percent of our New Terra gravity," Alex replied as he stood up and tested his weight. "So your colonists found a world with slightly less gravity than Earth?"

"Yes, by 11 percent, Captain."

"Has it affected your people, the way our heavier gravity has affected us over the centuries?"

Julien compared Alex's stature to his people. The difference was considerable – more than considerable, if Alex was the norm. "I would say, yes, to a degree, Captain, it has."

At the end of the day, Alex climbed back into his bridge chair aboard the *Outward Bound.* "No grav-plates here," he groused to himself as he strapped in. Tara had shut down the main engines when the 5 percent reaction mass reserve had been reached. The remaining fuel was needed to continue powering his ship, the beams, and the derelict. Aboard his ship, Alex would have to work and live in zero gravity until he was refueled.

Each evening, he had found his message queue filled, and tonight was no different. The critical ones got responses. The others received auto responses or were deleted.

Minister Drake's response to Alex's discovery of Julien had been that he would discuss the subject further with his advisors. In the meantime, advisors and scientists alike had flooded him with questions – the great AI debate had been resurrected. The scientists wanted to know how he knew for certain it was an artificial intelligence. What could it do that a smart computer couldn't? Then there was the greater question. What were the rights of an artificial intelligence?

Alex paid particular attention to the comms of the Honorable Darryl Jaya. As Minister of Technology, his questions were more pointed. Alex enjoyed sending back short, succinct answers to the minister's perceptive questions about the composition of Julien's memory components, his ability to relocate or even co-locate, and his responsibilities aboard the ship.

The good news … Colonel Stearns' strident messages had ended when Minister Drake assumed control of communication. Alex was fairly sure that he hadn't made a friend of the colonel. Not a good thing for an explorer-tug captain who depended on the *last outpost* for support and, if he was unfortunate, for rescue.

One vid message caught his eye. He tapped his comm board quickly, anxious to hear from his professor, Dr. Mallard. "Your old friend, Minister Drake," she said, "has invited me to his office to discuss, of all things, you. Since the two of you have such a pleasant history," she said, laughing, "he must be after something specific, but, for the life of me, I can't figure out what that might be. I'll be sure to keep you apprised. Alex, I always believed you would do great things. I just didn't think that would extend to snatching alien ships flying through our system." She laughed again – that wonderful, rich sound he loved. "I'm proud of you. Please take care of yourself. Comm me when you reach orbit." Then her expression had changed to that of his lecturing professor. "And you *will* make orbit ... hear me?"

He'd played the message several times. Tara's voice synthesis was a pale imitation of the real thing.

-4-

Julien had guided Alex to restore power, bridge control, and environmental systems to the stasis suite located near the ship's bow, all while keeping Alex out of the suite. He couldn't risk the safety of his charges to a stranger, no matter how appealing he found the young captain, who had exerted himself for days in an effort to save people he had never met. It was Julien's hope that the suite itself wasn't damaged, which would necessitate Alex entering it.

During their third morning together, Alex's repairs finally allowed Julien to communicate with the stasis suite's controller, the highly sophisticated sub-station responsible for monitoring the stasis pods. He was devastated to discover only eighteen pods remained viable. The suite could have accommodated over 300 pods. It meant most of the passengers and crew hadn't been able to reach this inner sanctum and secure themselves before their surroundings were holed to space or their inertia compensation was lost.

Anyone who had safely reached a pod would have had to wait for the crew to revive them. But the crew and passengers who hadn't made the pods were lost, and Julien's access to the suite had been cut off.

Each pod had its own power-crystals and operating system to ensure maximum stability. However, when the pods developed faults, there was no one available to respond to the controller's maintenance requests. Viewed through their crystal covers, the faces in the failed pods were peaceful. Eighteen occupied pods still functioned, so Julien triggered their resuscitation routines.

* * *

When the eighteen were completely restored, the crystal covers of the pods unlatched and slid open. With no one available to assist them, the occupants fended for themselves, climbing from their pods, naked, shaking, and disoriented. Two males, in better condition than most, prepared injections of nanites, electrolytes, and nutrients to restore the survivors from the effects of such a long, unintended sleep. After a couple of hours of rest, they took turns standing in front of a fabricator, which scanned them to assemble wraps and ship suits.

At the same time that Alex's repair had supplied power to the stasis suite, the food tanks were activated. While the ship had drifted, the stock had been preserved by the absolute cold of the surrounding vacuum. As the tanks warmed, the heat activated the nanites, which maintained the viability of the food stocks.

Julien monitored the survivors via their implants, the tiny electronic device embedded in the cerebral cortex of each Méridien. The implants were capable of transmitting comms, recorded memories, thoughts, and physiological data. In the adroit user, software applications, mathematical research, and engineering formulas could be manipulated without an external electronic device. However, their most common use was for communication, enabling private conversations even in a crowd.

Renée de Guirnon finished her hot thé and slowly sat the empty cup down. All eyes swept to her. <Julien, status?> she sent via her implant on open comm, so that all of her people could monitor the exchange.

<Ser, I'm pleased to find you and your companions alive and well.>

<Your sentiments are appreciated, Julien. Please update me.>

<Ser, the ship was severely damaged in the attack. The engines are offline. I have limited access to the ship's primary systems and nearly no knowledge of the ship's condition aft of your location. Grav-plates are active in some forward compartments, your stasis suite, and in two corridors connecting your suite to the bridge. It appears that nearly every

compartment has been exposed to vacuum. The eighteen awake in the suite are the only survivors.>

There were cries of anguish as the survivors surveyed the room, taking stock of who was not there. One of Renée's companions wailed. Her husband and young son weren't among the survivors.

As the others comforted one another, Renée thought of elderly Captain Jacque de Guirnon, her *grand-oncle*, who had been so kind to her throughout her life. The realization that he was gone was a knife in her heart. She looked over at the other individuals frozen in the failed pods. <Julien, how long were we in stasis?>

When the others heard her query, they all quieted to hear the answer. Family and friends still waited for them on their home world and colonies.

<Seventy years, Ser.>

Julien's pronouncement was an emotional blow. Stasis was an emergency option to be used for a year or two at most before rescue. The survivors' implants communicated their extreme stress reactions. While he could conceivably live forever, a thought he tried not to dwell on, Julien knew they were immersed in thoughts of mortality – elder generations lost forever, families aged into the next generation, and lovers who would have moved on.

<Ser,> he continued on open comm, <we haven't traveled far. We were in FTL flight for only 14.4 days before we dropped into sub-light at .02c, but our last bearing took us out of Confederation space. Communications and emergency beacon systems were offline, eliminating the possibility of our rescue by our ships.>

<But we've been rescued, yes?> Renée asked.

<Yes, Ser, a single ship, originating from the present system, has locked its beams on us, and its captain has provided us with power.>

Étienne, one of Renée's escorts, started to speak, but she raised a hand to stop him and overrode his comm. <Tell us more about this captain. Does he know our tech?> Then she added, <Is he one of us?>

<Yes, he is human, Ser.>

Many mumbled thanks to good fortune. Rumors of other intelligent life forms had often circulated through the Confederation, but no other star-faring civilization had ever been discovered by the Méridiens ... until their attack.

<I would surmise, Ser, that his people came to this system on an Earth colony ship near the same time as your ancestors settled Méridien. However, for some reason, his tech is well behind ours – not far advanced over the tech of the colony ships themselves. I've been guiding him through the repair processes and have adapted an ear comm for his use.>

<Is the captain armed?> Étienne asked.

<He came aboard with a weapon on his waist, but he hasn't been wearing it for the past two days.>

<Very trusting of him,> Étienne's twin brother, Alain, sent him in a private comm.

<Julien,> Étienne sent back. The one word was explanation enough. They knew well the persuasive skills of their SADE.

<And our next step?> Renée asked Julien.

<When Captain Racine returns tomorrow, I'll seek a suitable time for an introduction.>

<We'll await your comm,> Renée replied.

-5-

Driven by his burning curiosity, Alex had risked his life to discover the secrets of an alien ship. Now, four days later, his life was about to take a turn that he could never have imagined.

After the day's work, he had stripped off his EVA suit on the bridge and now sat in one of the command chairs, sipping a hot vita-drink from a dispenser, the liquid's electrolytes working to revive him. Even though he credited Julien with openly communicating about his technology, little to nothing had been said about his people, their world, or the damage done to the ship.

"Julien, did you know my government gave me strict instructions to remain in my ship? And the leaders were more than upset when I provided you with power without their approval."

"Those would have been wise precautions to take with a strange vessel," Julien agreed. "But you helped us nonetheless. Why, Captain?"

"Good question." Alex continued to sip on his drink, wondering if Minister Drake might have been right. This ship could represent danger. "Julien, do you have priorities, imperatives?"

"Yes, don't you, Captain?"

"Yes, I suppose I do," agreed Alex. "One of which is to help others in need." They shared a quiet moment then he asked, "Can you lie to me?"

"I'm self-aware, Captain. And, it is my duty to protect my charges and my citizens at large."

"So you could lie to me," Alex pressed.

"Yes, Captain, I could."

Both of them pondered the exchange. Alex wondered once again if he'd been foolish. He was aiding a battle-damaged ship from an advanced civilization he knew little about, without any knowledge about the conflict. For all he knew, the Méridiens might be the aggressors.

* * *

After so much time spent alone, Julien was enjoying his exchanges with Alex. The captain reminded him of the ship's first mate, who had often engaged him in discussions of philosophy and societal trends. It felt wonderful to converse once again with an intelligent and good-natured human.

Still, it didn't escape his attention that their rescuer wasn't in a positive mood now. There was a frown on his face and his gaze was distant. He was lost in thought, perhaps dwelling on his efforts to restore the ship in contravention of his government's directives.

Julien signaled Renée. <Ser, it's time to meet the Captain. He requires information that would be more appropriate coming from you.>

Renée and her two security escorts, Alain and Étienne de Long, exited the stasis suite, and were directed by Julien through the restored corridors. <A visual of Captain Racine, please,> she requested.

Julien sent an image to her and her escorts. Captured from behind the command chair, it showed an immense pair of shoulders and the back of a head with short, dark brown hair.

<Is this the best angle?> Renée inquired.

<Repairs are still underway, Ser,> Julien responded, evading the question.

As she navigated the corridors, she wondered why she hadn't been able to monitor comms between Julien and the captain. Fear gripped her. If Julien had been damaged by the ship's sudden loss of power, they might never return home.

* * *

"Julien, I need answers to some questions," Alex challenged. "I've decided I can't continue to help you resurrect this ship to its full capabilities and potentially hazard my people. I hope you understand."

"I do, Captain."

"Good, good," Alex murmured, wondering what to ask first.

"Perhaps, Captain, it would be best to introduce you to my people," Julien offered.

"When they're revived, I would be pleased to meet them," he said, rising from the chair and pacing to ease his frustration. "But that's my point, Julien. I'm helping you revive them without knowing if that's good or bad for my people. It's obvious you've been in a fight. But whom were you fighting with – other humans? And you have this technologically advanced ship, superior to any of our craft, but I have no idea of your intentions toward my people." He fell silent after his outburst.

"My pardon, Captain, I was proposing that you meet my people now."

At that, Alex heard the whisper of the bridge access doors opening. He turned to regard the three people who walked through it. Later, he would realize that his first thought should have been devoted to his pistol, locked aboard the *Outward Bound*, especially since the two males flanking the woman had their side arms. Instead, he was transfixed by the young woman, who stood staring at him.

As Julien observed the two of them, mesmerized by the sight of each other, he was reminded of Renée's fascination with their founding colonists. The Méridiens' colony ship had been launched nearly a millennium ago by Earth's European-Indian Enclave, an amalgam of the old European Union, India, Singapore, and Thailand. The contributions of each country – in terms of funds, technology, and services – guaranteed that country a proportional number of seats for its people aboard the ship.

The Méridiens' ship was one of five launched from Earth. Three great space-capable multinationals had planned to launch a total of forty-two massive colony ships. The North American Confederation, with Israel and Japan, ultimately launched two ships, while three were launched by the European-Indian Enclave. The Russian-Chinese Concord, which had set the most ambitious goal of all, never launched a single ship. Too many squabbles due to the ills of a dying Earth – resource wars, sea coast flooding, and violent weather conditions from rising greenhouse gases – had broken down the international cooperation needed to build and launch the ships.

The colony ships targeted Goldilocks planets, which had been identified by probes some two centuries earlier. By design, the colossal ships achieved their final velocity over the course of several years. Once launched, there were insufficient resources to reroute them. Thus whatever qualities the colonists discovered on their new planets, good or bad, they would have to make do.

Renée's ancestors were on Earth's last colony. It targeted the G-type, white star, called Mane and safely achieved orbit around the planet previously designated GL-137. The colonists had renamed their new home Méridien.

Stories of the founding colonists, especially those portraying their struggles to overcome their planet's challenges, had occupied hundreds of her reading hours. In front of her house stood a larger-than-life-sized statue of the captain of their colony ship. Alex could have posed for that heroic sculpture. Although, his world's greater gravity had driven the people to develop even heavier statures than those of either of their colonists. In contrast, Méridien's lighter gravity was emphasized in its peoples' slender builds.

<You're an Ancient,> Renée sent, eyeing Alex's powerful frame.

In preparation for their introductions, Julien had engaged his translation program to manage instant voice and implant communication between his people and the captain.

"Uh, Julien," Alex stammered, receiving the translation. "Did she just call me old?"

"No, Captain. Ancients were the original Terran colonists, who founded our home world of Méridien. It's a term of honor."

Alex traded stares with the woman. She appeared to be in her mid-twenties. Her slender figure was wrapped in a short garment of swirling and shimmering colors. Her eyes glowed softly with colors as well, a light palette of blues and grays. Shoulder-length, wavy black hair framed her ethereal face.

"Captain, I'd like you to meet your host, Ser Renée de Guirnon, of House de Guirnon." <Ser, this is our rescuer, Captain Alexander Racine.>

Alex hoped he didn't appear as dumbfounded as he felt as the young woman crossed the bridge to him. Her eyes looked him up and down and then settled on his face.

<May I greet you, Captain Racine?>

"Julien, sorry, what is she asking to do?"

"She wishes to extend her formal House greeting to you. She is grateful for what you have done. It won't hurt," he added, a trace of humor in his voice.

"Then, yes."

When Renée received Alex's affirmation, she said a silent *thank you* to her House ancestors, who had preserved so much of their colonists' culture, including their intimate form of greeting. She tried to observe the solemnity of the occasion, but his clean-cut features and muscular frame called to her. Gripping his upper arms, she sent, <Captain Alexander Racine, I greet you and give you my thanks for your efforts on behalf of our people.> She leaned in and kissed him on each cheek. In her mind, she might have been kissing the 3-meter statue in front of her father's home, although this warm-blooded human, was, as she had hoped, much nicer to touch.

As Renée stepped back, Alex responded with, "It's a pleasure to meet you, Ser de Gurr-non."

"Captain, that's de Guirnon," said Julien, pronouncing the first syllable as *gear*.

Alex observed the woman smile softly at the same time. "Julien, will my conversations with the Méridiens always be through you?" he asked, embarrassed by the lack of privacy.

"Yes, Captain, for now. Once I've provided the *Rêveur*'s survivors with a translation program, you'll be able to communicate with them directly."

The *Rêveur* ... it was the first time Alex had heard Julien say the ship's name. He also noted Julien's choice of words. He'd said *survivors*. It meant there might be more than just these three.

Renée introduced her companions. <These are my escorts, Alain and Étienne de Long.>

Alex looked from one to the other. Dressed in identical dark blue ship suits, he couldn't tell them apart. They were male counterparts to Renée, with sculpted, symmetrical faces, aquiline noses, and dark eyes – handsome in appearance and far more lithe than New Terrans.

Belatedly, Renée realized that without an implant, the captain wouldn't receive simple IDs. She indicated the twin on her right and said, <Étienne.>

"A pleasure to meet you, Étienne," Alex said, extending his hand.

Étienne looked at the outstretched hand in confusion.

<It was a traditional Earth greeting,> explained Julien, and he sent Étienne a vid of arms extending, hands clasping, then shaking.

Alex watched the hesitation in the young man's stance. He kept his hand up to prevent the armed stranger from taking offense or offering him the same greeting delivered by the young woman.

Étienne stepped forward and initiated the captain's greeting. His hand was promptly closed on and shook along with most of his upper body.

Renée hid a brief smile behind her hand. The captain, wearing an earnest grin, was shaking her escort as one would air out a bed covering. In the middle of his greeting, he suddenly stopped. His expression became apologetic, and, in concession, he gently clasped Étienne's hand with both of his.

"And it's nice to meet you too, Alain," said Alex, releasing Étienne's hand and extending his hand to the other male.

Alain, who had witnessed the unfamiliar ceremony, joined hands with some abandon. But he needn't have been concerned. While he could detect the young captain's tremendous strength, his hand shook with the most considerate of motions.

As Renée watched the captain greet the twins, she recalled the bulk and hardness of his arms. Her fingers still tingled.

<Captain Racine, would you share a meal with us?> Renée inquired. <There are others I'd like you to meet.>

As Alex hesitantly followed Renée into the ship's interior, he whispered, "Julien, any conversations between you and me will still be private, yes?"

"Yes, Captain. However, if I believe the information has a bearing on the well-being of my principal, then I will share it."

"I can understand that. And your principal would be Renée, correct?"

"That's correct, Captain."

"And, Julien, you also said there was a *degree* of difference in our stature," Alex challenged, as he eyed Renée's slender figure from behind.

"Did I err in translation, Captain?"

"Julien, I think there is much more to you than meets the *ear*," Alex murmured.

Renée approached the double doors of a large room of tables and chairs that Alex had restored just a day ago. He stopped her with a soft touch on her shoulder, causing her escorts to stiffen in response. "Excuse me, Renée. I've been working all day and I'm not really fit company."

<Nonsense, Captain, we would be poor hosts indeed if you weren't honored properly. Your present attire is of no concern to us.>

With that, the doors slid open and Alex followed her into the room, coming to a halt in front of a small assembly of people. Like Renée and the twins, they were slender, graceful people with pale, attractive faces. They were all dressed in a similar fashion, in clothes whose colors shimmered, glowed, and danced subtly around their bodies. Little was hidden by the delicate fabrics.

<Captain Racine, may I present the survivors of the *Rêveur*, who wish to extend their thanks and honor you,> Renée announced.

The Méridiens had witnessed, via their implants, Renée's view of the meeting on the bridge. Each man, determined to honor the captain by imitating his tradition, stepped forward and shook his hand. The women copied Renée. Each introduced himself or herself by name.

For Alex, whose usual human interactions were limited to Sharius TSF personnel or vid messages, the focused attention of so many exquisite people was more than a little overwhelming, not to mention the intimate greetings from the exotically dressed young women. He wondered at the group's youthfulness, as the oldest appeared to be no more than in their late thirties. Then again, it made sense that during the emergency only the young and fit might have reached the stasis suite in time.

After greetings were exchanged, a woman with fiery red hair and bright green eyes stepped up to Alex. <Your arm, please, Captain,> she sent.

<Captain Racine,> Renée sent, <Terese is a medical specialist. She wishes to ensure our food will be safe for you.>

"What does she need to do?" asked Alex, concern evident in his voice.

Renée laid a calming hand on his other arm and said, <It won't hurt, Captain. We,> she said emphasizing the word, <wouldn't hurt you.>

Terese placed a small device on his inner wrist, and the object immediately molded to his skin. He twitched at the intimate connection. She examined her handheld reader, which beeped softly, then nodded to Renée and carefully detached the small device from his wrist.

<Our food is safe for you, Captain, although all might not be pleasing to your palate,> Renée told him. <Come join us.>

She led him to a rectangular table with two chairs. The stem of the table and chairs blended seamlessly into the deck, as did all the ship's furniture he'd seen. He suspected that it involved the same principle he had used in his repairs – position the furniture, warm the central stem, and *instant connection.*

The others chose to sit at tables close to Renée and him, preserving the intimacy of the gathering. Observing the small group of Méridiens occupying so few tables in a room capable of seating 300, it struck Alex how many lives had been lost in the fight.

As he sat beside Renée, his chair seat warmed and broadened to accommodate his bulk. All the ship's chairs had this feature, he'd learned, and given that each part of him was larger than that of a Méridien, it was immensely appreciated.

Alex watched as the survivors walked up to a line of dispensers at the rear of the room, returning with covered food dishes and pitchers. Several people served his table, removing the covers to release tantalizing scents. Terese poured a glass of water for him and a dark red liquid for Renée.

Alex looked over the dishes of food. The enticing aromas made his mouth water, but he couldn't wrap his mind around how it had been done. The Méridiens hadn't even touched the dispensers, just stood waiting patiently, and then opened small cabinets to extract the dishes and pitchers.

Observing the way the captain was staring at his food, Renée sent, <Julien, are you aware of any dietary limitations of the captain?>

<Considering his size, Ser, I believe that the captain probably consumes everything in sight.>

As she regarded the captain out of the corner of her eye, she decided Julien was probably right.

<Captain, is the food unappealing to you?>

"Umm ... no ... it's just that ..."

<Please, Captain, feel free to be forthright with us.>

"It's just that I'm wondering how you did his," he said, indicating the dishes of food with a wave of his hand.

<Tanks of organic food stocks, nanites for preservation, and a controller programmed with recipes, through which we direct our orders.>

She had said it simply as if he only needed to be reminded of the components to understand the process. He felt dizzy, but he wasn't sure if it was from failing to eat since morning, except for a little vita-drink, or this overwhelming glimpse into a strange new world. As he slowly sipped from his glass of water, his lightheadedness faded. It was replaced by the awareness of a gnawing hunger.

Renée saw the captain glance at her glass. <This is the juice of a fruit, the *aigre*, native to our home world, Captain. It's an acquired taste, and you'd need to build a tolerance for it even if you did like it.> She picked up her glass, signaling the beginning of the meal.

Alex tentatively sampled various dishes in front of him and found many to his liking. He abandoned his fears and dived into the food, hoping the rumbling of his stomach didn't reach Renée's ears. He was starving and the serving dishes were tiny compared to just one of his synth-meals. To his delight, as fast as he emptied the serving dishes, they were whisked away and replaced with fresh ones.

<Captain Racine seems to have an appetite that befits his size,> Terese sent to Renée.

<Julien reports that the captain performed repairs at a rate equal to a crew of three. When the grav-plates were turned on, he was still carrying hull plates, up to seven at a time, 84 kilos, while wearing that awkward EVA suit and carrying bags of tools.> She forwarded a vid from Julien of the captain, fully encumbered and under gravity, advancing down one of the ship's corridors.

When the short vid finished, Terese stared at the captain for a moment and then stood and headed for the food dispensers for more dishes for him.

Belatedly, Alex noticed that Renée had finished her food and was sipping her drink. In fact, when he looked up, he saw that all the Méridiens had finished and sat waiting for him. He eased his utensil, overflowing with a spicy dish he had found particularly tasty, back down to his plate. Julien translated Renée's murmur of *good appetite*, and he felt his neck and ears warm. He wiped his mouth with a fabric napkin, and the serving dishes, some still with food, were cleared away. He winced as they vanished, wishing he might have kept the food for later aboard his ship.

Étienne rose and addressed him. <Captain Racine, would you tell us the story of our rescue?> All heads nodded in agreement.

Renée indicated her fellow survivors and said, <Oral storytelling is prized by our people. Your story would become part of our history. It's how we honor a person and his deeds.>

Solemn faces regarded him from each table. A sense of an important, perhaps even critical, moment prompted Alex to set aside his usual reticence. He took a moment to gather his thoughts, straightening in his chair. Then carefully, succinctly, factually, and without blandishment, he recounted his story.

Rather than begin with the discovery of their ship, he told them how he had come to be out here, capturing ice asteroids, choosing to work by himself. When he reached the part about detecting an object moving too quickly for his ship to catch, he was honest about his near decision to ignore it. His curiosity had won the day, he told them.

He detailed his plan to accelerate around a gas giant and snag the *Rêveur* with his beams. He didn't hide the fact that the violent lurch of his ship, at the moment of capture, caused him to blackout for hours, and he felt fortunate to be alive. Finally, he told them how he'd made the EVA trip across the 55 meters separating their ships, even though he couldn't detect an entrance and credited Julien with opening the ship for him.

When he finished his story, they asked questions but not about his strategy or the mechanics of his approach. They asked how he felt and why he did it. Their inquiries were gentle, searching, and he heard himself sharing more intimate thoughts with these strangers from another world than he'd ever done with his university peers. He related his moments of fear and of triumph, of the requests and then orders of Colonel Stearns and Minister Drake to remain outside the ship, and of his desire to see their ship despite the prospect of earning the government's ire.

The last question answered, he regarded the faces of his audience. Their eyes were on him, and, as one body, they stood up, crossed their forearms, placing their palms against their chest, and bowed their heads. When he turned to Renée, he found her searching his face.

<They are deeply moved by your story, Captain Racine, and will keep it to share with others while they live,> she said.

"Keep it?" Alex asked.

<Yes, Captain,> and she pointed to her temple. <It will be shared with others in honor of what you have done for our people.>

Alex watched as Renée stood and adopted the same pose as her people. All of them stayed that way, appearing to wait, and Alex, allowing intuition to guide him, stood and inclined his head in a solemn nod. Their salute complete, they smiled at him, broad smiles ... smiles that celebrated their resurrection. He felt the blood rush to his face, embarrassed by such fierce attention. Making his apologies to Renée, with mumbled excuses about messages to review back aboard the *Outward Bound*, he quickly fled the meal room.

As the captain left, Renée queried Julien. <What message do you think he will send to his people this evening?>

<An excellent, question, Ser, and as I'm unable to monitor his ship's communications, we might never know.>

<Are you able to verify his story?>

<Ser,> Julien responded, <I've worked closely with the captain for days now. I've found him to be refreshingly forthright and an honorable young man.>

Her implant showed Julien had closed the connection. *Curious*, she thought. Julien hadn't answered her query.

* * *

After his EVA trip back to the tug, Alex stored his suit in the cleanser and floated up to his pilot's chair to check his comm queue. There was still no slowing of the message onslaught. Even his auto responses hadn't dented the deluge.

Tara had prioritized his queue based on his assigned values, and a message from Minister Drake's office administrator was near the top of the list. Now that his drive engines were shut down, New Terra Orbital Tracking Control was able to determine his approach course. The administrator had provided coordinates for a tanker rendezvous, so he sent a quick acknowledgment.

Next, he opened a message from Minister Drake, who relayed the general opinion of his advisory staff and scientists that the alien bridge computer was a nonentity. Therefore, the minister concluded, the ship would be considered salvage. A formal decision, he said, would require the Assembly's approval, and, of course, he hastened to add, Alex would be well compensated by the government for his efforts.

It was with a certain perverse pleasure that Alex recorded his response. "Tara, message to Minister William Drake, New Terra. 'Minister Drake, as to Julien's rights, the question is moot. For the record, I strongly disagree with the advice you've been given. It's the eighteen Méridiens, who've been awakened from stasis, who would refute your claim to the *Rêveur*.'"

He ended the message and sent it, laughing to himself. After answering his other priority messages, he found one from his father and mother. As he listened to their voices and their words of encouragement, his eyes filled with tears. He missed them. They were his anchor. Then his thirteen-year-old sister, Christie, jumped into the comm screen, demanding that he bring home an alien to show her school friends. He laughed so hard he started choking. He sent a reply telling them that all was well and he'd made some new acquaintances.

-6-

In the morning, Alex fixed himself a hot meal. The reconstituted synth-meals were a poor substitute for the Méridiens' food, but at least they were filling. After a quick cleanser, he donned his EVA suit and made his way back to the *Rêveur*.

Not knowing where to start, he made his way to the bridge and found Renée and five others waiting for him. Instead of the eye-catching garments most had worn the previous night, they were all dressed in utilitarian ship suits, although nicer than any Alex had ever possessed.

"Greetings, Captain," Renée said. "We have further work assignments for you."

"Good morning, Renée," Alex replied. "I notice your voice is emanating from you this morning and not the bridge speakers or my ear comm. What's changed?"

"Yes, Captain. Julien has created a translation program for us. We are now able to communicate with you through our harnesses," she said, indicating the streamlined belt around her waist, paired with a strap that ran from the belt's right front over the opposite shoulder to the back of the belt. The others had identical set ups, he noticed. "Now, as for your work assignments –"

Alex interrupted her in mid-sentence. "Good morning, Julien. How are you today?"

"Good morning, Alex. I'm well. Thank you for asking," Julien replied. "The bow's primary power-crystal bank is fully charged. It appears the secondary bank isn't recoverable and will need to be replaced." Julien surmised Alex's intentions. With Captain de Guirnon's demise, Ser was now the House representative aboard the *Rêveur*, and, as such, she expected Alex's deference. But he wasn't Méridien and his nature favored independence. Julien had heard Alex's story last evening and was surprised, as they all were, that Alex was alone on his ship, something no Méridien would contemplate doing. He urgently wished Ser to understand that they needed Alex's goodwill. A ship without power in a foreign system was at the mercy of others, and those others waited at the end of their journey. Without Alex to represent them to his people, to stand for them, if he would, they might lose the opportunity to return home.

Rather than reacting adversely to Alex's dismissal, Renée considered the exchange between Julien and the captain. As her father had often said, "Know whom you're contracting with before the deal is negotiated." *Perhaps, I know too little here*, she thought.

"Captain Racine," she said, trying a different tack, "Julien has shared with us your efforts to restore our ship, and we are truly grateful. We," she swept an arm around to encompass the others, "wish to work with you on the continued repairs."

Alex noticed the change in her demeanor. He hadn't meant to be rude to her, but something in her earlier mien had reminded him of the snobbish university peers who'd come from well-to-do families. *If she can reconsider her approach, so can I*, he thought and relented. "I'd be pleased to work with your people, Renée, however I can."

Renée re-introduced her companions, whom he had met the previous evening, explaining how they might help. Edouard Manet was a navigation specialist and could continue the intricate work on the bridge. Claude Dupuis, the engineering technician, could work with Alex to open new areas of the ship. It appeared Claude was the only Méridien qualified for EVA work. The twins, Alain and Étienne de Long, would provide support for them.

"The others can't help?" Alex asked.

"It has perhaps not escaped your notice, Captain, that the *Rêveur* is a passenger ship. In fact, it is one of my House's premier liners. The others aboard are House support staff with little skill in repairs. Over time, this could be rectified, but for now, these people," she indicated those standing behind her, "will be effective immediately."

"When you recover crew or passengers," Renée continued. "Alain and Étienne will care for the bodies and take them to Terese Lechaux in Medical. She will see to them."

This last statement sobered Alex, banishing the remainder of his petty feelings.

When Renée finished, they separated to attend to their respective tasks, and she stayed behind to speak with Julien. <You have developed a rapport with Captain Racine. I wish to hear your thoughts.>

<It would be my pleasure, Ser. The captain, different as he might be from our people, chose to intercept us at the risk of his life. Whether it was out of greed for a prospective bounty, curiosity about our technology, or the desire to aid any survivors are questions you might ask. However, the moment he learned there might be survivors in stasis, he devoted every moment aboard this ship to your recovery, constantly worrying that his efforts would not be adequate. Recognize that at any time before you were awakened, he might well have claimed us as salvage, but he didn't. And he accepted me as an equal.>

<Julien,> Renée exclaimed, <the captain isn't your equal.>

<Ser, consider this. Our people have had SADEs for more than two centuries. The captain has never met one. Why should he consider me anything but a bright computer? Yet, he treated me with respect and courtesy. Our people will undoubtedly see his people as technologically primitive. Yet this *primitive* person met something for which he was totally unprepared and came to a mature conclusion. I believe that we've been rescued by an extraordinary young man, extraordinary under the definition of both his people and ours.>

Renée pondered Julien's statements, but rather than comment, she closed her comm and left the bridge.

* * *

As Alex walked through the corridors with Claude, he noticed that the Méridiens were coordinating their efforts without speaking to one another. "Julien," he commed, "when Renée pointed to her temple last night and said my story was recorded, did she mean it literally?"

"Yes, Alex. Méridien children receive an implant and are trained extensively in its use – open comms to a group, maintaining privacy when they wish, recording and transmitting sensory input, and many other capabilities."

"Incredible," was all Alex could think to say.

The first task for Alex and Claude was to build a temporary airlock that they could attach to a hatchway or doorway to reclaim a new area that might be exposed to open space. It was the only means by which they could ensure the safety of everyone else.

They sealed the airlock in place with nanites, then entered the space to cover holes, repair power and comm, and restore environmental systems, if they could. Not all spaces could be recovered completely, and Julien, monitoring their efforts, catalogued repairs to be completed at a later date. Claude commed the twins for additional materials, and they, in turn, would stack the needed supplies inside the makeshift airlock. Julien would complete their efforts, if possible, by powering the grav-plates, inertia compensators, and environmental controls.

As they recovered a crew member or passenger, they'd take the body or, in some cases, body parts and leave them in the temporary airlock for retrieval by Alain and Étienne. Alex couldn't imagine anything worse than finding the body parts until he found his first child. She lay in her bunk. He unstrapped her tiny, desiccated body, still clothed in her brightly printed sleep shift, and carried her to the airlock.

The twins, alerted by Claude, waited on the far side of the airlock's transparent panel as the captain entered the airlock, the child cradled in his arms. His massive EVA suit dwarfed her tiny remains. They could see the tears streaming down the captain's cheeks as he gently lay the little girl down and retreated back through his side. Alain carried the child to Medical, where Terese reactivated her implant to identify her. She suffered a pang of guilt over her relief when she realized she wouldn't have to notify the parents. They too were among the missing.

As Alex and Claude passed people in the corridors after mid-meal, he often felt a comforting pat on his arm or shoulder. He glanced at Claude once or twice for an explanation, but just received the universal response of a shrug. A simple implant error had been committed earlier.

Étienne was on open comm with his companions, updating them on cabins coming available and requiring cleaning, when Alex entered the airlock with the child. The grief etched in the captain's face had halted his message and the vid of the captain cradling the remains of the little one had streamed to his people.

Julien had instantly detected the comm error, but it wasn't his place to censor his people's communications. And had it been, he would have chosen to allow the vid's transmission. His people, especially Ser, needed to understand Alex's nature and embrace him as an ally.

At the day's end, Claude led Alex to a Méridien refresher. It wasn't fully functional, but it was a place to clean up. A utilitarian Méridien ship suit had been prepared for him. When Alex asked how they knew his size, Claude laughed and just pointed to his head. It had become a running joke between the two of them. It seemed to Alex that almost everything they did was accomplished with the use of their implants.

Claude led him to the meal room by a different path than he had taken earlier for midday meal. Alex, attempting to build a visual map of the ship, had an epiphany about the implant's power. It was the reason for the lack of labels on the doors, which he'd noticed the first time he boarded the *Rêveur*. Méridiens, he realized, could instantly locate rooms and one another throughout the ship. They might even be able to navigate it with their eyes closed, he hazarded to guess.

Another concept clicked for Alex. His ear comm was powered by his body heat, so it probably was the same for their implants. It answered a delicate question that had perplexed him, but one he'd chosen not to ask. The Méridiens couldn't locate their dead comrades, because those implants were inactive – their environment cold.

The evening meal was a subdued occasion compared to the previous evening. The recovery of their comrades' bodies had dropped a gloom over the small group.

* * *

After evening meal, Alex quickly headed for the bridge. He was more comfortable talking to Julien while he sat in the command chair, and he was anxious to have an overdue conversation.

"Julien, I've been wondering about the ship's damage. Can you tell me what happened to the *Rêveur*?"

"Yes, Captain. Edouard has reinstated the bridge's holo-vid projector. Allow me to show you." Suddenly an image of space and a distant ship appeared in mid-air in front of Alex's command chair, a hovering, frighteningly, life-like miniature.

"Captain Jacque de Guirnon, Renée's uncle, was responding to an emergency distress beacon from the freighter *Celeste*, which had taken on a load of ore mined in a barren system. Within a day, we exited FTL near the freighter's location and decelerated to rendezvous."

Alex watched the freighter's image expand in front of him. While he was fascinated by the holo-vid's quality and the story unfolding, he hadn't missed Julien's words, *exited FTL*. He was rapidly collecting intriguing yet frightening new terms.

"As we closed on the freighter, I was able to examine in detail the ship's condition, and remarked to the captain on the holes in the freighter's cab and the ship's cold engine cones. The *Celeste* didn't respond to comms."

The view expanded until Alex could see the now-familiar holes. Holes he knew would extend entirely through the freighter. As he leaned forward to view the image more closely, he noticed Renée slip into the second command chair.

"A strange craft rose from behind the freighter," said Julien, as he activated simultaneous comm threads – Sol-NAC to Alex via his ear comm and Con-Fed to Renée via her implant.

Alex stood up and walked into the holo-vid to better view the small craft. It was shaped like a gourd seed, a shallow convex silhouette, the front pointed and the rear ovoid. Its hull was a polished, dark silver and unbroken by protrusions.

"The captain ordered me to hail the alien ship on all frequencies, but there was no response. Instead, an energy beam speared out from the small craft and penetrated the *Rêveur*'s aft dorsal hull."

Although the beam that had been fired wasn't visible, Alex asked his question anyway. "Julien, can you back it up to the point when you think the ship fired its weapon?"

"Certainly, Captain," Julien agreed as the holo-vid display reversed.

Alex studied the silver ship. He peered closely at the silhouette, and Julien obliged him by expanding the view further. "Strange."

"How so, Captain?"

"There's no protruding weapon, no barrel. Unless … unless the entire silvered hull *is* the weapon," Alex said, pondering the image,

"That's an interesting observation, Captain."

The holo-vid rolled forward and Julien continued his narrative. "Captain de Guirnon ordered evasive maneuvers and I attempted to keep the freighter between us and the silver ship, but the attacking craft was highly maneuverable, and it struck us many more times. All passengers were ordered into the stasis pods. Unfortunately, in the short time available, most didn't reach the suite. The captain ordered the crew, who were assisting passengers, to join them in stasis. Then he ordered an emergency jump to FTL. As I altered our course toward open space, the silver ship continued to strike us with its energy weapon. In the moments before we entered FTL, a beam struck our engine compartment. Another beam holed the bow, and all bridge personnel were lost."

Julien was silent for a long moment, as if reviewing his memories of that moment. Alex, for one, was glad he wasn't shown the vid of the bridge event. The discovery of the child still haunted him, and he didn't need any more images like that in his head.

"With the bridge crew lost, I assumed command. Unfortunately, I detected no active implants on the ship. The stasis pods had been sealed, and I'd lost contact with the suite. My navigation and FTL comm access were gone as well."

They lapsed into silence again as Julien closed the holo-vid.

"There was the distinct possibility the silver ship might follow and complete our destruction, but as you can see, it never did. Though we managed to enter FTL, I had lost control of the engines after the bridge was damaged. We were in FTL for 14.4 days, when we inexplicably exited FTL and resumed our originating sub-light velocity of 0.02c, drifting until you found us. My presumption is a beam damaged some portion of the engine support systems. Undoubtedly, safety protocols cut in and shut down the engines when the operating parameters were exceeded."

"Without access to our FTL transmission system, I had no way of detecting whether our emergency beacon was broadcasting. After the first year, I calculated the probability of a rescue at less than 32 percent since our last maneuver had taken us on a tangent away from Confederation space. After the fifth year, I deemed the probability of a rescue so low the number isn't worth mentioning. When my power-crystal banks reached 11 percent, I shifted my clocking routine to a ratio of 1 to 500 to slow my kernel and set routines to wake me if our hull sensors were triggered."

"How long ago was this attack?" Alex asked.

"Comparing our time to the internal chronometer in your EVA suit, it would be seventy-two of your years, Captain"

"What?" Alex exclaimed and whirled to face Renée. "Seventy-two years?" he asked.

"Seventy years of our time, Captain," Renée spoke quietly. "That's how long we've been gone from our people."

He watched as tears formed in her eyes. He wanted to console her, but before he had the chance, she stood up, wished him a good sleep, and left the bridge without another word. Alex felt deflated.

"Were you able to do any damage yourself … I mean to that silver ship?"

"That would require weapons, Captain, and we have none."

"That's because you're a passenger ship, correct? But you have ships that can fight?"

"No, Captain, we have no fighting ships or offensive weapons. We are a peaceful society with a single home world and many colonies, under one government, the Confederation. We've had a few minor conflicts during our first several hundred years, nothing significant or recent. Even a successful trespass against one of our citizens by another is improbable today, if not impossible, with our implants. The hand weapons you see on Étienne and Alain are for personal protection. They can do no more than stun and are more likely to be used against aggressive fauna than anything else. It is against our laws to have a weapon that can cause harm, much less kill any being."

After a few moments of reflection, Julien added, "We've never had a need for a weapon that could incapacitate a ship ... until now."

Alex continued to sit in his chair, imagining such a peaceful society suddenly attacked by alien ships. He recalled a vid of a wild diablo, a vicious species of New Terran fox, invading a den of Earth rabbits introduced by the colonists. The slaughter was quick and thorough, even though the diablo couldn't consume even half the small rabbits it killed. The similarity between the two images was frightening. Even more frightening was the thought that his people were just as defenseless.

He climbed out of the command chair to head back to the *Outward Bound* for the night, but stopped in the bridge's accessway. "Julien, I'm sorry."

"Sorry for what, Captain?"

"I'm sorry for all those years you spent alone." Alex stood with his hand braced against the bulkhead, waiting for Julien's response.

"You are the first to offer me that sentiment, Captain."

"Then I'm sorry for that too," said Alex as he left.

Into the silence of the bridge, Julien said, "Good evening, my friend."

* * *

Later that evening, Renée was in her House suite, one of the few relatively undamaged cabins, when she commed Julien. <Has the captain retired for the evening?>

<He is gone, Ser. I take it you wish to discuss him.>

<Yes, I have concerns, yet I know that you like him.>

<There is much to admire in the young man, Ser.>

<He is courageous,> she admitted.

<His courage is not to be doubted, I agree. Still, it's his compassion that I find most laudable, Ser.>

<Yes, I received the vid of him and the child. But how could you not be moved by the death of one so young?> she argued.

<Admittedly, it was a harsh moment that would crumble the strongest person,> Julien agreed. After a pause, he continued, <Tonight, the captain apologized to me.>

<Apologized? Whatever has he done?>

<He said he was sorry for the many years that I spent alone.>

Renée sat on her cabin's bed, unable to respond. By law, SADEs were endowed with basic rights and were treated with courtesy. *But have we treated them as equals?*

Finally, she admitted the truth that had occurred to her. <Then, technologically advanced or not, our captain is a better human being than I am, for I haven't thanked you for preserving this ship. If not for your sacrifice, those of us who survived wouldn't be able to warn our people.>

<You have suffered a great loss, Ser. It's understandable that you were preoccupied.>

<Understandable, perhaps,> agreed Renée, <but not forgivable. It appears our captain has more to recommend him than courage and a stalwart frame,> her last words were accompanied by a soft laugh. The silence between them extended until Renée said, <Julien, I'm concerned about the status of the *Rêveur* and its command.>

<Yes, Ser, now that my databases have been unpacked, I've been reviewing legal precedents. In the event that a ship's officers are lost and the ship is recoverable, responsibility passes to the ship's SADE to return the ship to Méridien or, if that isn't possible, to seek the nearest colonial port and request instructions of the House. In the event a House representative is aboard, the SADE will take direction from the representative, providing the SADE deems such instructions don't endanger the passengers and crew.>

<What discretion does the House representative have in determining where to take the ship?> she asked him. <And as the House representative can I enter into a contract with others?>

<As to the first question, you may choose any destination that you feel protects the interests of the House. Although any and all steps you take will be reviewed by the House Leader … your father, in this case. As to the second question, any contract entered into with a House or colonial representative must be reviewed and approved by your father before it can be consummated.>

<So the language is specific to House and colonial representatives?> she confirmed.

<Most assuredly it is, Ser.>

<Then these Ancients …>

<They refer to themselves as New Terrans, Ser.>

<Then these New Terrans aren't covered by the articles,> Renée completed her thought.

<No, they aren't, Ser.>

<So under the present circumstances, I'd be free, as a House representative, to make any agreement with these New Terrans that

benefits us, and this agreement wouldn't be subject to overrule by my father.>

<I would concur, Ser. Edouard restored comm reception today and I've begun monitoring this system's broadcasts.>

<Tell me about them.>

<They have one organization, the Terran Security Forces, responsible for maintaining order on their home world and outposts, and a second organization, the Ministry of Space Exploration, responsible for habitat development on their fifth planet and space works within their system. Each organization is required to report to the New Terran leader, called a president.>

<Are these organizations similar to our Houses?> Renée asked.

<It doesn't appear so, but my research has just begun.>

<Do they have these fighting ships that the captain asked you about?>

<I'll attempt to determine this. At present, it doesn't seem likely.>

<And their government?> Renée asked.

<It's a democratic form with a representative assembly and an elected president. As a whole, they appear to be a well-adjusted society, peaceful and supportive of their populace.>

<A critical question, Julien,> Renée continued, <do these New Terrans have the technology to complete the repairs on the *Rêveur*?>

<If Alex's ship and equipment are typical, the answer is no. They've just begun to explore space and have yet to travel outside their system. However, with their cooperation, we would be able to elevate their technology sufficiently to enable the repairs.>

<Elevate their technology? That's a dangerous concept.>

<I concur, but it's the only resource we have to exchange … our technology for their material and services.>

<A workable plan to ensure they don't flounder with the knowledge would be formidable since we know so little about them and have so little time to learn. On the other hand, we have no way of preventing them from taking our ship and learning our technology for themselves, if they

wished.> Then she questioned her own statement. <Could they learn our technology for themselves?>

<That is a point of leverage for us in the initial negotiations, Ser. Without my assistance, it would take decades for them to reverse engineer our basic technology, and they have no means by which to force my cooperation. Yet, if they choose to bargain with us, they could have our technology immediately. Our first step will be critical in that regard. We'll need someone who will speak for us, someone …>

<Someone such as the captain?> Renée completed his statement for him. <Is this why you're so supportive of him?>

<I'm not attempting to foster the captain as our champion, Ser,> Julien said firmly. <It's not necessary. I believe our champion has found us.>

<Let's hope so, Julien.>

<I'll continue to monitor their communications to form a better understanding of their technology. Then I'll be able to devise a means of elevating it sufficiently to manufacture the materials for our repairs.>

<Last question, Julien, what about that silver ship? How will we or these New Terrans, for that matter, defeat it, especially if there is more than one?>

<To that question, Ser, I have no answer.>

* * *

Alex floated over to his pilot's chair, physically and emotionally exhausted after his first day with Claude. The repair work was grueling, particularly given the mass of his EVA suit. He was used to wearing it for a few hours at a time, once every twenty to thirty days, not for five full days in a row. But the intense labor was nothing compared to the recovery of the Méridien bodies. That part of the work had become a wakening nightmare.

"Messages, Tara," he requested, too tired to examine the queue himself.

"You have a priority message from Minister Drake."

"Play it."

"Captain Racine," Minister Drake began, "perhaps we've attempted to micromanage the man-on-scene, so to speak, and our choice of action or inaction might not have been entirely appropriate." Alex snorted at the minister's opening statement, which was as close to an admission of wrongdoing as he was ever going to get.

"It appears that you are our defacto representative," Drake continued, "and as such we need you to consider the wishes of your government in your communications with these aliens. In addition, we need detailed daily briefings. Learn their technology, learn what they might offer us, and discover what they might request in exchange. This is an opportunity that must not be squandered. Please adopt this position with the great responsibility that it entails."

"Message ends," Tara stated.

This message, as did the others from Minister Drake, rubbed him the wrong way. Despite his reaction, he argued his own counterpoint: wasn't what the minister said true? Shouldn't he be working to make the best deal for his people? But somehow that didn't seem right. He liked the Méridiens, and they were human too, just different ... and beautiful, come to think of it.

"Tara, message to Minister Drake, New Terra," he began and then gave the minister as much detail as he could fit within the message's buffer limit. He had to send four messages to complete his brief.

He knew the day that had just passed would be the template for the next seven days until the refueling rendezvous. With little to do aboard his own ship, he would continue working with the Méridiens to restore the *Rêveur*, while seeking answers to the tragedy that had befallen them.

-7-

Minister Drake strode along the well-appointed Government House corridor, lined with its magnificent vid displays of New Terran landscape and, recently added, vids of space. He stopped in front of an administrator, who gave him a professional smile.

"President McMorris is waiting for you, Minister," she greeted him. "The rest of the attendees are already there."

The double doors of the president's office slid open at his approach, security identifying him in advance. Arthur McMorris was seated behind his intricately carved, guriel wood desk, crafted by the twenty-third president's son for his father. The task had taken the son almost three years to complete, the wood more akin to metal due to its high mineral content. No president had ever replaced the desk as it had become a symbol of the office.

General Maria Gonzalez, head of Terran Security Forces; the Honorable Darryl Jaya, Minister of Technology; and the Honorable Clayton Downing XIV, District 12 assemblyman were already seated in the matching antique, brocade-covered, guriel chairs arrayed in front of the president's desk.

"Ah, Will, come in and have a seat," the president greeted him, "We are all anxious to discuss Captain Racine and hear your thoughts."

"Good morning, Mr. President, Maria, Darryl, Mr. Downing," he greeted the assembly then took a seat on one of the centuries-old, hand-carved chairs himself.

From the moment Will Drake had received Alex's latest set of messages, he'd been planning how best to present the situation to the president. He'd hoped for a private meeting, but the president had beaten him to the punch, announcing this meeting and his choice of participants.

He'd wrestled with the quandary of how to make the most of Alex's find from the moment he learned of it. Their relationship had become fractious during their protracted negotiations for Alex's g-sling program, so he sought an edge in his dealings with the captain. He had contacted the university chancellor, who had first brought Alex to his attention years ago. The chancellor had referred him to Dr. Amy Mallard, Alex's advisor.

The professor had been kind enough to visit him in his office. Her entrance was a pleasant memory that he'd replayed more than once. In his own university career, there hadn't been any professors who looked and sounded like Dr. Mallard. But if the visuals were pleasantly stimulating, the discussion was anything but. The professor rebuffed his every attempt to gain advice on how to get what he wanted from the young man. He was told, time and time again, that he shouldn't attempt to order or manipulate Alex. In the end, she'd become frustrated and taken charge of the discussion, delivering some strongly worded advice.

"Minister Drake," she had begun, "let me tell you about Alex. When he came to our university, he was a socially undeveloped person. His late teenage years were primarily limited to interactions with his father, mother, and younger sister, on his parent's explorer-tug, the *No Bounds*. We had several discussions concerning his inability to form partnerships. It wasn't that he was unattractive, quite the contrary. However, our young female undergraduates are accustomed to more socially adept young men. They offered quick dalliances with whispers of the exotic items available to our youth … mood enhancers, pleasure toys, and multiple partners. Most were surprised, some offended, by his polite refusals and, unfortunately, they often told him so."

"While he was at university, he earned both his ship operator's and pilot's licenses, recording the TSF's highest scores for both written tests and operational field tests. If I would guess, I'd say he was probably competent in those areas before he left his parents' ship."

"But that would be highly illegal …" Will had started to object.

"That's neither here nor there, Minister," Professor Mallard had stated. "My point was to bring to your attention the incredible scores he earned for a young man his age. I'm telling you this, Minister, so that you understand Alex is a set of contradictions. But make no mistake, Sir, he's one of the most brilliant students I've ever taught. And this isn't just my opinion; ask any of his professors. We cherished him. He pursued interstellar navigation and applied gravitational forces with the passion and skills of a researcher twice his age.

"He developed the mathematical algorithms that predicated his g-sling program while at university. We both know similar efforts had been attempted in the past, none of which had proved successful. Alex's model was inventive and sophisticated compared to the crudity of the earlier versions.

"In his second year, I introduced Alex to Mr. Sorensen, a CEO who was searching for a more efficient means of navigating his ships through shifting ocean currents. It was Alex's first real-world application of his predictive mathematical models. The company supplied him with years of data on wind, currents, and ship locations, notated by date and time. In the first year of his model's implementation, he realized the company a 3.2 percent fuel savings and a 2.8 percent reduction in delivery time. His first real-world job, a difficult one at that, and Alex was wildly successful. Do you realize the odds against that, Minister?"

Since her question was clearly rhetorical, Drake had refrained from speaking. The professor seemed intent on having her say, and he thought it wiser to sit back and let her speak. Professor Mallard's impassioned delivery was revealing the fierce mind beneath the waves of dark hair.

"And, Mr. Sorensen was only Alex's first client. Before he left us, Alex had fourteen more. He made money for every one of them ... every one of them. When he completed his undergraduate work, the faculty did everything they could to entice Alex to stay for his postgraduate work, including a full scholarship and some perks," and she'd smiled as she said *perks*.

Will Drake had refused to ask what she meant, lest he place his very large shoes in his mouth.

"Alex came to me one night, wrestling with his decision," she'd said, looking wistful as she recalled the evening. "He wanted to return to space, despite being intrigued by our offer. I asked him if he needed funds and he shared with me that he had over 788K creds in his account."

Drake had nearly choked on that piece of news. It was more than twice his annual ministerial salary.

She had laughed at his expression. "Yes, Minister, that look you're wearing is the same one I wore after he told me. But what convinced me that all of us were wasting our time was when Alex said two things. The first was that he wanted an opportunity to prove his mathematical model using a tug to project a passive body through our system to a target, and we both know how that turned out. He said the creds he'd make, if successful, would be used for his family. The second was that he missed the *No Bounds* and the beauty of space, cold and dark though it was.

"What I'm trying to communicate to you, Minister Drake, is that you have on your hands a socially inexperienced genius with a proclivity for helping others. You do with that information what you will. But, I can tell you this, you should under no circumstances cajole or order him. He can be very stubborn when confronted, especially if the pressure comes from a position of authority or privilege. You'll do better if you entice him or offer him something he can't resist, a puzzle to solve or a cause to aid."

And he had ignored her advice, much to his detriment. She'd been very prophetic about what Alex would do if he attempted to dictate to him. Now his only recourse was to change his ways and fast.

He'd copied Alex's recent multipart briefing to all of the meeting's participants. His prior ill-managed communications with the captain, he kept to himself. At this point, he could see no upside to sharing it.

The senior assemblyman, the Honorable Clayton Downing XIV, who represented one of the most financially affluent districts, chimed in first, "Damned ridiculous having our first alien contact managed by a child, prodigy or no prodigy."

"That child, as you put it," shot back Maria Gonzalez, the head of the system's police force, "attained 0.02c to catch that ship. No other ship of ours has ever reached that velocity. Without him risking his neck, we wouldn't be talking about Méridiens or AIs."

"And you make my point, General Gonzalez," the assemblyman rejoined, "Reckless! Not what we need at this critical juncture."

"Assemblyman Downing," Will Drake eased into their debate, "I know Captain Racine is young, but I don't believe he's reckless. According to his advisory professor, he's a brilliant mathematician and navigator. When confronted with a challenge, he has the ability to examine the parameters involved and calculate the best course of action that will allow him to achieve remarkable results. The rest of us might consider these results to have been achieved by fortune simply because we can't perceive the logic behind the decision-making process. To him, he's simply following the numbers." Drake knew he was dancing here, but he was quoting Professor Mallard in the hope the others would listen to reason where he had not. He'd edited her comments and included them with Alex's messages.

"Fine, I'll admit this rendezvous couldn't have happened without him," Downing relented, "but now we need a seasoned negotiator to communicate with these Méridiens. Who knows what they're planning? What are they capable of? Are they even safe to be near, diseases and all?"

"Pardon me," the president interrupted, drawing their attention to him, "the time for debate about Captain Racine as the appropriate representative is past. He's there now, and it isn't as if we have a simpleton standing in for us. Our captain has an impressive record, if I read Professor Mallard's synopsis of him correctly. What we must do now is make the best of it. What are our priorities?"

Darryl Jaya, who was seated on Will's left, spoke up quickly. "Look at what Alex said about their technology in his third message. It's mind-boggling ... grav-plates." He looked around the room, adding, "Nano-technology repairs squirted from a bottle! We could jump our technology hundreds of years if they're willing to share it."

Will looked over at Maria, who was lost in thought. He valued her opinion above the others. She truly cared for the people under her command and was passionate about the safeguarding of their planet from industrial plundering. One of the foremost instigators of the Niomedes Experiment, the habitats developed on the next planet outward of New Terra, she had recommended him to the president as the man who should fill the new position of Minister of Space Exploration. He looked up at the president and tilted his head toward Maria.

Downing attempted to take control of the conversation again, but Arthur held up his hand and said, "Maria, you appear to have something on your mind."

She slowly looked up at him. "Mr. President, we do indeed have a singular opportunity. But it would appear that Captain Racine is already pointing the way for us."

"How so?" the president encouraged her.

"Review the fourth message," she explained. "He reminds us that these aren't aliens but humans, technologically advanced, yes, but humans nonetheless. These are our cousins from Earth, descendants of a colony ship such as ours. He describes them as gracious and gentle. And he states that these Méridiens have had their ship severely damaged by an alien ship, a truly alien ship. So, I'd ask, what is our duty to fellow humans in trouble, humans who have been attacked by an alien ship that fired without any provocation?"

"But these aren't our people!" Downing nearly yelled into the quiet following Maria's words, "You can't ascribe our values to them!" His face reddened with outrage as he looked around for support.

As the president leaned back in his great, carved chair, Downing knew that he had lost support for his position. He decided to engineer a quick and graceful exit. "Mr. President, perhaps after reviewing Captain Racine's message in more detail, my industrial advisors will have recommendations for your office."

"Downing, that's a marvelous idea," said the president, seizing the offer. "How soon could you have their feedback for me?"

"I can get started right away, Mr. President," Downing said, rising, "and I'll keep you apprised of our progress." Downing said his goodbyes and decorously exited the room as if he'd won a great concession.

Minister Jaya said into the room's quiet, "The consummate assemblyman."

"All right, people!" the president said, clapping his hands, "We have a preeminent and possibly one-time opportunity that has just been handed to us by our tug captain. The three of you are now my Negotiations Team. Congratulations!"

Focusing on Maria, he added, "What you said makes sense to me. They're human and they were attacked. So our position will be that we are here to help them. Let's see what they're willing to offer us in exchange for our commitment to help them in whatever way we can."

"Will," he said, "as Minister of Space Exploration, this is your area of responsibility. You're team lead. And, as you have the most history with Captain Racine, your advice will be invaluable here. If I understand you correctly, he already has a very favorable position with them."

"It would seem so, Mr. President," agreed Drake.

"And Darryl, you're our technology expert. You'll know best how to prioritize whatever technology we might be offered during negotiations. So what's the timetable?" he asked looking earnestly at his newly formed team.

"The refueling tanker," Maria said, "will rendezvous with the *Outward Bound* in seventy-two hours. Thirteen hours afterward, we should have nearly lag-free comms with Captain Racine and presumably with the Méridiens as well."

The president regarded the comm-band on his wrist. "So you can be communicating real-time with them in about three days?"

"Yes, Mr. President," Maria affirmed.

* * *

The Negotiations Team stood in a circle down the hall from the president's office.

"Well, fearless leader," said Maria, addressing Will Drake, "what's your plan for taking this singular, world-shattering, one-time opportunity and making the most of it so that the three of us don't go down in history as three prime idiots?"

Drake met her gaze without flinching, though it was the very question he'd been dreading. He had always depended on his intellect to win the day, but deep in his gut, he felt that it might not be enough ... not today. Then a simple answer came to him. "I'm going to take the advice of a woman," he said, then smiled at her and Jaya and set off down the corridor with a jaunty stride.

-8-

Ambassador, the word had echoed in Alex's head ever since he'd played Minister Drake's message. He wasn't one for center stage, and, despite his famous reputation, he'd always envisioned himself as the man behind the curtain. But now, in the minister's words, he was the *ambassador for his people*. He wondered exactly what that meant. Did it mean promoting the interests of his people over those of the Méridiens?

His Uncle Gerald often said that the best agreement was an honest contract that benefited both sides. "That way," he'd said, "the two parties are earnest in their mutual participation because each sees the advantage to adhering to the contract." He decided to take his uncle's advice and broker a mutually honest agreement, but with one significant addition. The recovery of the Méridiens' dead had left him with an intense distaste for their defenselessness. He vowed that under no circumstances would he allow them to go home without finding a way to give the *Rêveur* some teeth.

Alex finished his morning meal and, after his EVA trip, found Claude waiting for him at the *Rêveur*'s airlock. They were scheduled to conduct repairs in Medical, where Alex had already sealed off the leaks, so he was able to free himself from his cumbersome EVA suit. In Medical, he and Claude helped the twins move equipment to provide access to interior walls. Conduits and comm lines had been sliced in two.

As they worked, Terese educated him on Méridien biotech, explaining how deeply nanotechnology was embedded in the fabric of their society's health system. Medical nanites were used for everything from making repairs at the cellular level to programming the DNA of eggs and sperm.

Ah, thus all the beautiful people, Alex thought, noting again Terese's luxuriant red hair, bright green eyes, and perfectly sculpted face and body.

The thought that he could banish all his people's ills staggered him. *All I need to do to bring Méridien technology to my people,* Alex thought, *is ensure that both sides get what they want.*

Terese was reconnecting a med-bay imaging station that Edouard had repaired when she asked, "Captain Racine, are you designed or are you a natural product of your parents?"

Alex regarded her for a moment, pondering the ramifications of being *designed,* then responded, "I'm natural. My parents created me as do all our parents." He blushed as he said this. "And my mother brought me to term," he added to clarify his response.

Terese stared at him, incredulous. "She carried you inside herself ... no artificial womb?"

"That's correct," replied Alex, smiling at Terese's wide-eyed expression.

Terese continued to stare at him, murmuring something Alex didn't receive in translation. Then she moved on to help Claude reposition a medical rehab chamber.

"Julien," Alex commed, "I didn't get Terese's last comment. I think my comm failed."

"It was a Méridien expression that doesn't translate well," Julien temporized.

* * *

After the work in Medical and a midday meal, Alex found himself back in his EVA suit. The group proceeded aft to reclaim more spaces. They reclaimed a storage room that contained 2-meter square repair plates, which were needed for the larger holes, as well as a stockpile of the Méridien equivalent of Alex's welding torch, which was a good thing, because Alex's torch fuel was nearly exhausted.

They also located some Méridien lightweight, zero-G, environment suits for Étienne and Alain. These were particularly useful because Alex and Claude had found holes exceeding 1 meter in diameter and they needed help with the plates. It was Julian's hypothesis that these larger holes had been burned through the ship when the *Rêveur* was closer to its silver nemesis. Alex filed that important piece of information away for later – wider when closer; narrower when farther away – a point-focused beam.

The same storage space contained small grav-lifters to transport the larger plates through the corridors and hoist them into position. Despite the weight-canceling capability of the grav-lifters, the bulky load of plates made them awkward to manage. Three of them guided the lifter, which in addition to the plates carried their tools and spare tanks. The fourth went ahead, manually opening hatchways and accessing their temporary airlock.

They continued to find the remains of Méridiens as they progressed through the inner spaces and cabins. Alex found he was managing his emotions better. The anguish he had felt when he discovered the first child had turned to sadness. Now, he found his sadness turning to anger.

After wrestling and welding a plate into a ceiling corner, which had required them to cut out an overhead brace in order to access the hole, they took a break in the temporary airlock for water. Alex used the opportunity to ask the twins about their duties.

Étienne and Alain happily discussed their lives as *escorts* to Ser. The more they chatted on about their companionship with Ser, the more confused Alex became. Jealousy crept into his thoughts as the twins discussed the necessity to remain close to Renée at all times and the satisfaction and pleasure they found in her company, and vice versa.

Julian was fully engaged in multiple projects, especially in monitoring all the New Terran comm traffic his bandwidth could handle, so the changes in Alex's physiological readings, transmitted to him via the ear comm, didn't catch his attention immediately. When it did, he replayed the conversation, a sub-routine having been assigned to record any conversation with their all-too-important rescuer. Correlating the twin's use of Méridien terms with those same words in Alex's language, Julien, via priority override, interrupted Alain mid-sentence.

<If I may,> Julien announced privately to the three Méridiens, <a communications error has occurred. The translation program has

unfortunately allowed a match of our term *escort* to the same word in Sol-NAC, which has an entirely different meaning. While we use it to define security duties, New Terrans use it to describe the paid services of a sexual partner.>

Julien's words caused more than one heartbeat to skip. The twins realized they had been explaining to Alex how much they enjoyed bedding Ser and how pleased she was with their performance. Their faces reddened with embarrassment, and they began apologizing profusely, talking over each other until Alain quieted, allowing his crèche-mate to take up the explanation.

It was Claude, standing behind Alex, who sent Étienne and Alain the image of the crushed, empty water bottle in Alex's hand. A Méridien would have had to jump on the metal-alloy container several times to equal the damage done by Alex's hand.

Absorbing the inherent message behind the image, the twins carefully resumed their clarification, ensuring that Alex fully understood the miscommunication. They protected Ser from over-casual contact with citizens, they explained. They also accompanied her to meals when she was away from the House or the ship, deterred the wild fauna of the colonies, and managed the transport-delivery of materials that Ser contracted for on the spot.

Later, Alex wondered about his reaction to the translation error. It was an uncomfortable reminder of his abysmal track record with university women, which is why he decided not to dwell on it.

When they resumed their work, he asked the twins about their weapons, which he hadn't seen them wearing since their first meal together. They launched into a detailed explanation, describing the model's mechanical-electronic components, the stun levels, and the crystals that fed the energy spooling process, allowing for multiple shots with no recharge time. What Alex took away from the conversation was the extreme care that had been taken to interweave safeguards to ensure that the weapon could only incapacitate another being or creature. He was once again struck by how vulnerable the Méridiens were to malevolent external forces.

Alex discovered that the twins had used their side arms only once, when they were forced to stun a Bellamonde herbivore that had charged them. They said Renée had cried over the creature's huge, prone body and insisted they remain with the animal until the stun wore off because predators were in the area. They had never had an occasion to fire them at a Méridien.

* * *

Renée was in her suite when she reviewed Alain's vid of the stun gun discussion with Alex. The vid reminded her to query Julien for an update of his monitoring efforts. <What more have you learned about their society, Julien? Are they aggressive? Do they require the use of weapons against their own people?>

<They do carry personal weapons, but these individuals are authorized by their government to do so. Apparently, some of their citizens transgress against others and their property. From what I understand, the individuals who transgress are detained, forcibly if necessary.>

<Forcibly?> queried Renée.

<Yes, Ser, some individuals, who have committed a transgression, resist or flee the authorities, either because they believe they were justified or because they wish to avoid punishment, thereby necessitating their apprehension.>

<And is this common?> Renée asked.

<No, and the transgressors rarely commit violence against their compatriots, more often it's against property.> Julien explained. <And, as to their vessels, they have explorer-tugs, such as Alex's ship, small freighters, which also act as passenger transport, and shuttles. None of them have large-scale weapons. They'd be as defenseless against a silver ship as we were.>

Renée considered the information she was gathering on the New Terrans. Alex's stature was probably typical of his people because, according to Julien, his ship's central hub, while in rotation, delivered 24 percent greater gravity than the *Rêveur* maintained. Terese had shared that their mothers endured natural childbirth. Summarizing, she had sent, <They are a robust people, much more acclimated to trials and suffering than our people.>

The New Terrans were very different from her people, but, through Julien's insights, she was realizing there was value in those differences. And while she was reluctant to use her one example, Captain Racine, as a general indicator, they wouldn't be able to return home for years, if ever, without the New Terrans' help.

So much rode on Renée making the right decisions in the coming days – not just for their immediate needs, but for her people's future. She wasn't consoled by the fact that the attack of the *Celeste* and, subsequently, the *Rêveur* had occurred far from the Confederation's major space lanes. A great deal of time had passed, and odds were good that the silver ship or one of its comrades had discovered her people's colonies. In her heart, she believed danger was coming to the Confederation. *If there was to be a clash with the silver ships*, she wondered, *who is better equipped to defend our worlds ... Méridiens or New Terrans?*

-9-

In the evening, one day short of the scheduled refueling rendezvous, Alex was seated on the *Rêveur*'s bridge when he heard the double doors whisper open.

"Good evening, Renée," he greeted her with a smile. "Would you like the lights up?"

"No, please, Captain, this is fine." She knew Alex enjoyed the darkened view through the bridge's plex-crystal shield, which offered a 150-degree panorama of the stars from the ship's bow. Julien had shared with her that Alex's ship had no such view, only external vid cameras relayed to small bridge screens. She slid into the command chair next to him and it transformed to cradle her body. They sat in companionable silence, enjoying the stars – something that as a young girl she'd done with her father and uncles, all captains of their House ships.

After a while, she broached the subject that had been preying on her mind. "Captain, Julien has learned that your home world was settled 732 years ago. He calculates from your calendar and planet's solar orbit that this happened at about the same time my ancestors landed on Méridien."

Alex looked over to her, "Yes, he shared those calculations with me. Our colony ships probably left Earth within a decade or two of each other."

She struggled with how to ask her question. Finally, she said, "What happened to your people?"

"You mean how is it we appear to be your backward cousins?" he replied, offering her a lopsided grin.

She reached out and rested a hand on his forearm, intending to lessen the awkwardness of the moment, but pleased to have an excuse to touch him nonetheless. "It's only technology, Alex."

The touch of her hand and the use of his given name, a first for her, softened his discomfort. "To answer your question," he said, and he related the story of his people as he had been taught it.

Their colony ship, the *New Terra,* was one of the two ships launched from Earth's orbit by the North American Confederation (NAC), Israel, and Japan. The *New Terra* carried 52,000 passengers in deep sleep modules with 1,200 crew members rotating in shifts of 100, one year on and eleven years off.

En route to their chosen star, Cepheus, they ran into an enormous asteroid field, their huge ship unable to dodge the wide swath of oncoming pebbles, stones, and boulder-size space rocks. Penetrated in hundreds of places, the ship sustained major damage to its engines, environmental support and deep-sleep module bays. More than 28,000 men, women, and children died in their sleep.

Their original destination was now beyond reach. They had one option – Oistos, a yellow star that had been an alternate choice in the original mission planning. Probes had graded the system's goldilocks planet only seven points less, on a scale of 100, than their original destination. They'd pass near it. It required they hold the ship together for seven months and then abandon it, launching shuttles loaded with food, supplies, and the few colonists they could carry.

Once the decision was made by the *New Terra*'s captain, Lem Ulam, the crew sealed off many portions of the ship, preserving air and environmental services for a small living and storage space. Six crew members crammed into cabins designed to accommodate two people.

The captain and officers planned the shuttle trip – best exit time, trip requirements, planetfall requirements, and the maximum number of people that could be carried. Unfortunately, the *New Terra* carried just twenty-two shuttles. Once the extensive supplies necessary for a successful colony landing were loaded, they only had air and space for 2,400 passengers and crew. The fact that less than a tenth of the remaining survivors would be able to make the trip was a difficult concept for the crew to absorb. Arguments often broke out as opponents of the present plan pushed forward alternatives, although none of those proved feasible.

The captain, first mate, and the chief medical officer formed a committee to select the colonists who would be given space on the shuttles. Healthy families, comprised of young parents and children older than seven, were given priority, especially if the parents possessed multiple skills – combinations of mechanical or chemical engineering, manufacturing, applied physics, biotechnology, medicine, law, celestial navigation, or crop and livestock cultivation.

All of the heavy terra-forming equipment and large-scale manufacturing machinery had to be left behind. Premium space was allotted for small items – computers and their libraries, navigation and comm equipment, medical diagnostic equipment, laboratory test equipment, hand weapons, human and animal ova-sperm stock, seed stock, and tool and circuitry production machinery.

When the time approached, the crews readied the shuttles, knowing that only half of them had been selected by the committee. The captain waited until two days before the exodus to wake the 2,347 sleepers who would join the fifty-three crew members. The sleepers, groggy from their recent awakening, were told that an accident had necessitated that they abandon ship. When the shuttles were filled, they exited the landing bays and set course for nearby Oistos.

The colony ship, with air and power running low, was left to glide on into the dark, its crew of forty-seven, led by the second mate, monitored the 21,000-plus humans still in deep-sleep.

Originally, the captain had announced he would remain aboard the *New Terra*, but it was the opinion of the crew, to a person, that their journey and their survival, if they made planetfall, would require a strong leader, and the captain was an imminently respected man. So, at the crew's near maniacal insistence, the captain joined the first mate, the *New Terra*'s primary navigator, in the lead shuttle when they set course for Oistos, their last hope.

Additional oxygen tanks, CO_2 filtration units, and racks of algae tanks had been crammed into each of the massive shuttles to bolster their chance of making landfall. Though each shuttle had been designed to seat 340 passengers, all the seats had been torn out before the exodus. The approximately 100 passengers and crew, traveling in each shuttle, slept on the equipment crates.

Of the twenty-two shuttles that launched, twenty-one successfully reached Oistos. One unfortunate shuttle suffered an engine malfunction soon after launching. While the senior officers were examining their rescue options, the troubled shuttle exploded in a massive fireball.

When the shuttles passed a gas giant, now called Seda, as they entered the Oistos system, wild cheering and celebration broke out. The back slapping, hugs, tears, and kisses doubled when they made orbit around their target planet. To the survivors' amazement, the original probe's information appeared accurate. The planet had many similarities to Earth – 1.12 gravity, half the planet covered in ocean waters, large lakes dotting the continents, and abundant tall trees. Later they would discover the darker realities of their world, but from orbit it appeared as if fortune had smiled on them. They called their home New Terra, in memory of the tens of thousands of passengers and crew still aboard their colony ship.

The oxygen and fuel in the shuttles were nearly exhausted by the time they reached their new home, forcing them to land within days. And while the world looked picturesque from on high, it held some nasty surprises, which eventually cost the *New Terra* survivors more than half their paltry number.

Botanists, analyzing the plants and soil, announced the bad news that the flora was inedible. Alkaloids in the plants made them poisonous. Even worse, bacteria and other bioforms in the soil consumed their precious stock of Earth seeds before they could sprout. The colonists built elevated sheds, cleansed the soil of microbes, pail by pail, and planted their remaining seed stock. Their food supplies dwindled while they waited for their plantings to bear fruit. An enterprising biochemist discovered she could remove the alkaloids from several varieties of local mushrooms and fungi after they were pulverized into a mush, and starvation, if not completely averted, was slowed.

But the most heartbreaking trauma the colonists endured was the loss of every baby. Most were miscarried or stillborn. A few mothers, who were able to give birth, lost their children within months. It would be years before biochemists and doctors identified the problem as a subtle disruption of the fetal hormonal levels. Then more years would pass before they identified the responsible pathogens and found a way to protect the growing fetuses.

An auspicious day arrived when a newborn reached her first birthday. Mothers had given up naming their children, the names only adding to the pain of their loss. Now, the little girl, named Prima on her first birthday, became a moment of great joy and celebration. Hope, so long buried and forgotten, rose again. Of the 2,291 castaways who had landed, 938 colonists saw the beginning of their new society.

Later generations came to love their second home despite the tragedy that had befallen the colonists. Theirs had been the second colony ship launched from Earth, so they expected many more intrepid adventurers to populate their corner of the galaxy. They never learned that Earth, continuing to succumb to systemic pollution, global climate change, coastal city flooding, droughts that killed crops and animals, and unceasing regional wars for dwindling resources, especially for clean, fresh water, would launch only three more colony ships.

On the eve of the population surpassing one hundred million, legislation was passed by the Assembly authorizing the funds for the Niomedes Experiment. Although their footprint on the land was still minimal, the populace remembered why their ancestors were forced to abandon Earth. They would conquer space *before* they exhausted their planet's resources. Eighty-three years ago, under the government's supervision, science and industry had produced a plan to construct self-contained habitats on the next planet outward of New Terra, Niomedes, a large ball of rock and frozen gases.

The habitats were designed as experiments to test various construction processes, energy systems, life environments, and methods of food production, attempting to find the cheapest yet safest ways to build self-contained and self-supporting habitats, while ensuring the mental well-being of the inhabitants.

As the history of his people came to a close, Alex continued with his family's story. His parents, with the aid of government funding, had joined the Niomedes Experiment, contracting to supply ice asteroids for the Niomedes habitats and the mining companies on Ganymede's moons, which supplied much of the processed metals needed to build the habitats.

While their ship, the *No Bounds*, was under government contract, his parents earned salaries, and all their reaction mass and supplies were provided by the government. After their eight-year contract was up, the ship was granted to them.

When Alex completed university and rejoined his family aboard their tug, he sold his parents on his g-sling program despite the early failures of so many explorer-tug captains. Their greatest initial challenge was finding a buyer who was willing to take the same gamble. Alex's thought was to enlist his staunchest supporter, Dr. Mallard.

According to Professor Mallard's story, which she later relayed to him, she'd listened to his message and immediately met with her dean. Moments later, the two of them made their way to the chancellor's office. The chancellor, convinced by the dean and the professor, had commed his friend, the Honorable Mr. William Drake, the new Minister of Space Exploration and the individual in charge of the Niomedes Experiment.

Dubious though he was, the minister accepted the chancellor's recommendations. He, in turn, contacted the CEO of Purity Ores, Samuel B. Hunsader, at his fishing retreat. Hunsader wasn't as quick to acquiesce. So a deal was struck. Purity Ores would contract with the Racine family at a discount and the ministry would cover any losses, at double the creds.

Duggan and Katie Racine received a message several days later from the Purity Ores general manager on Cressida stating, "We will contract with the *No Bounds* for six ice asteroids to be delivered within a 200-day period, following the arrival of the first delivery, on passive approach. In recognition of the risk we're taking, we will pay 75 percent of market price for each. Ten percent will constitute a nonrefundable down payment and the remainder will be paid on delivery within a 100K-km approach."

Alex grinned as he told Renée of his parents' shock when they received the GM's comm. No longer would they have to waste precious time hauling their cargo inward to Cressida, Ganymede's moon, or the Niomedes habitats. Instead, they'd only need the outpost at Sharius for supplies and reaction mass, providing, of course, that Alex's program worked.

Nearly a year passed before the asteroid had arrived at its destination, during which time they had launched nine more, four of them to a competitor of Purity Ores. The long time frame was the essence of Alex's program. Previous explorer-tug captains attempting the same feat had launched their asteroids directly at the future position of their target, but their tugs' inferior tracking equipment invariably created substantial errors, including sending one ice asteroid on a collision course with New Terra. His parent's tug, being the exact same government model, was no better, which was why Alex took a different tack. First, he used Sharius' Tracking Control Center to establish his ship's and his target's exact positions. Then, rather than launch at the target, he sent the asteroid inward at an angle that placed it in the target's path, using decades of historical planet and moon rotational data. In essence, the target body and asteroid approached each other at a shallow angle. It took over twice as long as a direct delivery, but after the first asteroid arrived, the others quickly followed.

That first asteroid was good-sized at 2,400 meters in length. He recalled his parents' anxious monitoring of the daily telemetry updates from the Tracking Control Center. His mother was amused by his lack of concern and his father wasn't.

The news media carried the story of the system's first accurate passive ice asteroid delivery and an interview with Timothy Greene, the GM of Purity Ores. Apparently, he'd been surprised to learn from Cressida's

Tracking Control Center that his delivery was in the moon's immediate path and he needed to dispatch a tug forthwith.

Alex laughed at the memory.

"You did this without a SADE?" Renée marveled.

"That's what fingers and toes are for," said Alex and mimed counting on them.

She smiled at his humorous remark, but wasn't fooled by his self-deprecation.

His story finished, he turned to watch the stars twinkle and dance, alone with his thoughts. A little while later, he said good evening to Renée and left for the *Outward Bound.*

Renée remained on the bridge, observing the stars, and contemplating fate, luck, or the old Earth gods, whichever people believed in. One or more of them had orchestrated very divergent histories for her people and Alex's.

Julien observed Renée, who remained on the bridge for more than an hour after Alex's departure. Suddenly, her right fist closed and pumped once. He knew the signal, which had been a habit of hers since childhood. A decision had been reached on a subject that she'd probably worried about for much longer than the past hour.

<Julien,> she announced, <we will put everything on the table in our negotiations, our entire libraries. We must credit that this planet's leaders understand their own people and will know how to deal with the introduction of our technology.>

Following another long silence, she asked, <If our people had witnessed the arrival of an alien ship, what would they have done?>

<They would have attempted communication and prepared a welcome,> he responded.

<And if they knew that the aliens had ship weapons, what would they have done?>

<They would have attempted communication and prepared a welcome,> he said, using repetition to drive his point home.

<Precisely, they would have prepared a welcome,> she agreed, drawing out the words slowly, as if the statement agreed with the conclusion she'd reached.

Moments later, she picked up the conversation again. <And if an alien starship had entered the outer edge of our system on a cold coast but at nearly twice our ship's cruising velocity, which of our young men would have risked their lives to rescue the craft?>

<A moot question, Ser, since, as you well know, the onboard SADE or controller wouldn't have allowed such an unsafe maneuver.>

<Yes, unsafe,> she murmured, <so unsafe.>

<It appears, Ser, you have come to the conclusion that our people aren't prepared to respond to the danger we've encountered. And, while we might have the more advanced technology, we don't have the mindset to apply it to our defense.>

<Yes, Julien, that's precisely what I've been thinking.>

<And what, may I ask, Ser, has guided you in this decision to share our technology?> Julien asked, curious to understand her motivations, although he had come to this same conclusion in the early days of his interaction with Alex.

<We've learned that these New Terrans have lived through a much more difficult history than we have. Through their struggles they've developed great personal strength. Captain Racine is a prime example of those strengths.>

<I had the impression that you were not convinced of the captain's motivations or his character, Ser,> Julien persisted. He had perceived her reticence with Alex, but had been unable to understand her reaction. His personality analysis programs indicated a very high probability of an excellent match between the two. But, he had to admit, this was the key difference between him and humans ... they weren't always logical.

<It might be I offered resistance without cause.> She didn't want to admit to her powerful visceral reaction to the captain on their first meeting. Since then, she had invented excuses to keep him at arm's length. But every day that passed, she was less successful at maintaining the façade.

<Take my word, Julien. I don't hold the captain in disregard.> *Perhaps, just the opposite,* she thought. <We need these New Terrans. Our technology and their strengths might be the answer to conquer these silver ships.>

Julien heard her use of the plural – *ships.* It was a conclusion that he had reached seventy years ago, during the first hour of FTL following their attack. It was inescapable. Such an advanced and dangerous craft would not exist alone. Where there was one, there had to be many more. The question that plagued him was where had *they* gone after the attack?

-10-

Alex hailed the approaching fuel tanker. "*Thirst Quencher, Outward Bound*, Captain Racine here," He was stationed on his bridge to coordinate the maneuver.

"*Outward Bound*, this is Captain Osara. We are 23K kilometers out and approaching from one-seven-zero degrees, down five degrees. Well, that's one-seven-zero degrees from the ass end of that big ship. You appear to be bow on to us, in inverse orientation. I'd appreciate any suggestions you have for this hook up, Captain Racine," he requested with more than a little concern in his voice.

"If you will approach my starboard side, parallel to my craft, I'll stabilize you with my beams," Alex replied confidently.

"You can do that in addition to holding that huge ship?" Captain Osara queried.

"There is more here than meets the eye, Captain," Alex assured him. "Trust me. We'll manage it."

During the next two hours, Captain Osara carefully maneuvered the *Thirst Quencher* to match the *Outward Bound*'s velocity and course. He'd been in transit to Sirius with a load of reaction mass when he received the priority call to reverse course and catch the *Outward Bound.* He cut his main engines 2 kilometers out and used his maneuvering jets to slowly close the distance, still traveling at nearly 29K km/sec.

When the *Thirst Quencher* came parallel to Alex's ship, only 45 meters separating them, he called out, "Beams on." He and Claude had spent the entire day in EVA suits preparing for this moment by rigging Méridien power and comm lines between the *Outward Bound* and the *Rêveur.* And the plan worked. On Alex's call, Julien reversed the energy flow between their ships, and Tara powered up the starboard beams. The sudden dump of power from the *Rêveur* enabled the tug to pin the tanker while maintaining its hold on the *Rêveur*.

The first on comms was Captain Osara. "That was a most impressive display of power, Captain Racine. Pilot reports zero delta-V. We had no idea you had so much power."

"Thank you, Captain. But this was a joint effort with the Méridiens. They transferred additional energy to my generators to enable the grab."

"So, it's true, Captain. These Méridiens are the aliens you found."

"Did I let that slip, Captain?" Alex deadpanned back.

Osara's chuckle was heard over the comms.

"Let's just say that I've found some lost *human cousins*," Alex replied. He let Osara absorb that comment. "Captain, I'm cutting power to my stern beam and will meet your refueling crew at my aft airlock."

"Acknowledged, Captain, the crew is standing by with a hose."

After the tense moments of the docking maneuver, the refueling was anticlimactic. A crew of four, housed in EVA mech-suits and hooked to safety lines, hauled the tanker's fuel hose to Alex's aft airlock, where an access port was embedded in the hull.

Tara managed the flow of reaction mass, topping off the ship's primary and auxiliary tanks, which were attached to the spine of the tug. Alex had added the extra tanks despite his design engineer telling him repeatedly he'd have little need for them given his oversized main tanks. "Thanks for the excellent advice," Alex murmured to himself as the *Thirst Quencher*'s crew finalized the refueling process.

Julien, monitoring comms, smiled to himself. He often heard Alex speaking or mumbling to himself when no one else was around and understood that the captain was comforted by the sound of a human voice, even if it was his own. *For one so young, you have been alone too long – we both have.*

The tanker crew retreated to their ship, hauling in their hose and safety lines. The captain hailed Alex and offered some parting words. "Captain, it's taking all my self-discipline to keep from requesting a visit. But I've been advised, in no uncertain terms, that my contract would be voided if I stepped aboard either of your ships. So, let me just say, it would be my pleasure to buy you a drink, make that several drinks, and hear your story someday."

"The offer is appreciated, Captain," Alex said. "If the opportunity presents itself, I'll be happy to accept. Safe voyage, Captain!"

"And to you, Sir, safe voyage! It appears you have the greater need."

After the tanker's departure, Alex reprogrammed his deceleration burn to bring their ships into a close orbit about New Terra. Tara would monitor their progress and alert him in case of difficulties. He climbed back into his EVA suit for the return trip, which had become a daily drudgery, morning and evening. He had considered asking Renée for a sleeping space aboard the *Rêveur*, but he didn't want to be an imposition. Once he was safely inside the *Rêveur*'s airlock, he requested Tara initiate the engine burn.

An odd feeling overcame him as the airlock cycled. The *Outward Bound* had been his dream, and he'd worked for years to earn the creds to make the ship's final payment only months ago. He thought he should feel disloyal for focusing his efforts elsewhere. But as the inner door slid open and he stripped off his suit, a smile crossed his face at the thought of joining his new friends for evening meal.

-11-

The evening after refueling, Alex sat in his pilot's chair reviewing his message board. The top one from Minister Drake, addressed to both him and Renée, announced the minister's appointment as head of the president's Negotiations Team to *assist* the Méridiens, as he put it. His initial request was for an audio conference, as a vid conference's greater bandwidth required the ships were closer to New Terra.

Rather than wait until the following morning, Alex used the intership line to notify Renée. The line terminated at Julien, who relayed his comm to Renée, in her cabin.

<Greetings, Captain. Didn't you get enough food at our evening meal?> she teased.

"A person could starve to death if they depended on those tiny plates you serve," he teased back.

<Perhaps I'll have special plates fabricated just for you. A half meter across should do nicely. I'm sure the twins will be able to carry it to your table.>

Alex chuckled over the exchange. They were both greatly relieved by the refueling. As long as the *Rêveur* was coupled to Alex's ship and he could control their course, it allowed the Méridiens a semblance of sovereignty, an important distinction in the upcoming negotiations with the New Terran government.

"The news is that the president has appointed a Negotiations Team and they want a conference call."

<Good. I'd like it soon.>

"Your wish is my command, my lady," Alex said gallantly and closed the connection.

Alex responded to the administrator's office, suggesting a conference call at 13 hours the following morning. He was surprised to receive an acknowledgment, a quarter hour later, confirming the call time. For years, his messages had sat at the bottom of queues. It was unnerving to discover his comms were now priority tagged, and at the Ministry level, no less.

A sudden thought occurred to him, inspiring him to comm his parents. Despite waking them up, they were overjoyed to hear from him and had a slew of questions for him about the ship, the aliens, his health, and many more. After satisfying their curiosity, he explained the reason for his call. While he had a history with Minister Drake, he didn't know the other team members or how, as individuals, each would approach their responsibilities.

Duggan and Katie eased his mind by telling him he couldn't have asked to work with better people. In his father's opinion, it was exactly what he would have expected of President McMorris. "He's chosen the three people who have done more for New Terra's space program than anyone else. They tend to be very progressive thinkers," he said.

"I'm a fan of General Gonzalez," Katie added. "In the years that she has been in charge of the TSF, the negative incidents have fallen to nearly zero."

* * *

Edouard had restored Julien's comm reception days ago. Unfortunately, the FTL transmission center was located in the stern and Julien still had no access. However, with the intership line, New Terran-*Rêveur* comms could be managed, albeit through a patchwork process. An added benefit of the intership line was that Alex could manage his message board and comms from the *Rêveur*'s bridge, provided he didn't mind sharing with Julien. In preparation for the conference call, Alex gave Julien Tara's access codes.

Early that morning, Alex tapped on the door to Renée's cabin suite. When no one answered, Alex called Julien to ensure that Renée was in her suite.

"One moment, Captain," Julien replied.

<Ser, you have a guest at your cabin door.>

Renée stepped out of her refresher, confused by Julien's comm. <At my cabin door?> Then it dawned on her – only one person would be unable to signal her. <The Captain?">

<Yes, Ser, he waits outside your door.>

<What does he want?> she asked, grabbing a wrap and tucking it around her. As she signaled the main salon door open, she thought to snatch her ship harness.

<I imagine he wishes to speak with you,> Julien replied, the humor evident in his tone.

Before she could deliver a retort, Alex was standing in front of her. He wore the same expression as when they'd first met on the bridge, and she self-consciously tucked a lock of moist hair behind her ear.

"Is something wrong, Captain?" Renée inquired.

"Umm, no, I wanted to talk to you before the conference call. Is now a good time?" he asked, trying not to stare at the shimmering, short wrap that barely covered her from breast to hips.

"Yes, please come in, Captain," she said as she led him into her sitting room.

<Ser, please be aware, the captain's heart rate has accelerated to 83 percent above rest levels,> Julien sent, his tone deliberately dry and matter of fact, despite his desire to laugh.

<Is he ill, Julien?> Renée sent. <Should we inform Terese?>

<I believe the captain's biorhythms will return to normal when you change your attire, Ser.>

Renée turned around and found Alex's gaze fixed on her bare legs, and Julien's advice sunk home. "If you'll take a seat at the table, Captain, I'll return as soon as I finish dressing." As she entered her sleeping quarters to change, she was aware of the rapid beating of her own heart.

Alex's view of Renée was cut off as she entered her sleeping quarters. He didn't know whether to be upset or grateful, but he settled for grateful since he couldn't afford to be distracted. "Méridiens," Alex spoke sotto voce to Julien as he sat down, "seem to be very comfortable with their bodies."

"Indeed, Captain," Julien replied, and confirmed the drop in Alex's heart rate.

<Ser,> Julien signaled Renée, <the captain will be fine. It was as I expected. Our captain is very body conscious, but whether it's of his body or yours, I can't determine.>

Dressed in a ship suit and about to return to the sitting room, Renée was stopped in her tracks by the facetiousness of the remark. <Julien, I believe the captain is corrupting you.>

<Yes, Ser, I agree that he proves to be a most invigorating influence.>

Renée heard Julien's laughter as he closed the comm. She stepped back into the sitting suite to join Alex at the table, aware of a change in him. His expression was stern, his hands clasped firmly together – the shy, young man who had come to her door had left in her absence.

"Renée, you know the value of what you have to offer. Your technology is centuries ahead of ours, and you're asking very little in exchange for your repairs. You know this, correct?" asked Alex.

"Yes, Captain, this is understood."

"Good, but I urge you ask for one more concession. Ask our government to help arm the *Rêveur* with weapons so that you can protect yourself."

"Does your government know how to do this, Captain?"

"No, it doesn't, but we can figure it out together; just make it one of the conditions," Alex said and leaned across the table to take her hands. His eyes were locked on hers, pleading, "Please, Renée."

She had been expecting him to ask for a reward, which any Méridien citizen would consider their due for extraordinary services rendered. That his first request wasn't for himself but for them surprised her, but his request had struck a chord with her. She squeezed his hands in return. "I will, Captain. I don't know how this will be done, but I'll request it." She watched him deflate, pulling back across the table, the reason for his visit accomplished.

As he rose to leave, Alex tried to express the fears he harbored. "I have no idea what you'll find when you return home. But I have this unsettled feeling that won't leave me. And, if I'm being forthright, I've had the strangest dreams about the silver ship. In my dreams, I don't see one ship; I see hundreds."

What he didn't tell her was that twice before ugly images of death and danger had plagued his sleep until reality supplanted the nightmares. One early morning, he'd stopped his best friend from taking their elementary school transport. Later at school, they heard that the driver and three children aboard the transport had died following its collision with a hover car, whose guidance system had inexplicitly failed. Death and destruction had come to pass as it had been in his dreams.

Three years later, nightmares of his father's shuttle plummeting to the planet plagued him. He broke down sobbing when he told his parents of his fears. They knew Alex and his friend had chosen not to take the school transport on that tragic day, but they had considered it a fortunate coincidence. Still, Alex continued to plead with his father to stay home until Duggan called his boss and told him of the dreams, pretending they were his and not his son's. Mr. Clancy, knowing Duggan was one of the most levelheaded men he had ever met, chose to ground his shuttle service the following day. Later, people on the planet's dark side were treated to a dazzling meteor shower of space dust and pebbles that swept past their planet. The two rocks that struck the Joaquin orbital station did minor damage, but no one was killed.

Renée sent Julien the vid of Alex's visit. She added no comment, unable to voice her own fears ... or tell him of her own haunted dreams.

<One would hope, Ser, that our young captain isn't prophetic. But, as I've never met his like before, I certainly cannot postulate what capabilities he might or might not have. I must confess that after accepting the loss that has befallen us, I've been energized by recent developments. Perhaps I might have been too exuberant in my wish for the excitement to continue.>

<Indeed,> she replied wryly, <perhaps you should wish for less, should we receive more than we can manage.>

* * *

At the conference call's designated time, Alex and Renée settled into the bridge's command chairs. After Julien opened a connection to Tara, Alex directed her to open a comm to New Terra, Minister Drake's office.

"Comm engaged," Tara replied. "Connection established."

A friendly, male voice answered. "Minister Drake's office."

"This is Captain Racine and *friends* for the scheduled conference," Alex replied, passing Renée a quick grin.

"Yes, one moment, Captain Racine!" the administrator replied excitedly.

"Minister Drake here, Captain Racine, with General Maria Gonzalez and Minister Darryl Jaya."

"Hello, Minister Drake. With me is Ser Renée de Guirnon. Also present is Julien, the *Rêveur*'s SADE."

At the start of the conference, questions flew back and forth, clarifying titles and responsibilities. The Negotiations Team wanted to understand Renée's position as a House representative, confirming she had authority over the *Rêveur* and was empowered to act on behalf of her people. To Renée, the ministers mirrored Confederation Council members, so she understood their purpose. Alex had described the TSF and a general's duties, but Renée was curious about the woman, whose role had no Méridien equivalent. She chatted briefly with Maria, while the others waited patiently.

There were even more questions for Julien. At first the questions were tentative and simple, but when Minister Jaya asked Julien how he was *born*, Minister Drake interrupted. "I believe there will be time for more detailed discussions later. Captain Racine, let me begin by saying that the president asked me to relay his profound thanks for your efforts on behalf of all New Terrans."

Renée glanced at Alex, wondering how he would react to praise from such an important figure, and was mystified by the frown on his face.

"Thank you, Minister," Alex replied dryly. "Please relay my appreciation to President McMorris for his kind words."

Despite his office's cool temperature, Minister Drake could feel the sweat forming under his arms. He wanted to bring the president something solid from their first conversation and was trying to put his best foot forward with Alex. But, he could tell he was getting a cool reception. "Ser de Guirnon," he started, his team having received Alex's messages concerning titles and manners of address, "the president of New Terra wishes you to know that we will offer whatever help you need. You have only to ask."

"Excellent, Minister Drake," Renée replied. "Then I believe I can make this a short but quite valuable conversation for us all."

Alex could just imagine the expressions on the other end of the comm.

"We deeply appreciate your assistance, Minister Drake," she continued. "Julien will provide all the technical specifications you require to produce the grav-plates, crystals, FTL engine repairs, nanotech material, service goods, and anything else we require."

"Pardon me, Ser de Guirnon, but we can't make those things," Minister Jaya interjected.

"We're aware of that, Minister. We've studied Captain Racine's ship and equipment," Renée explained. "What we propose, Sers, is that we give you the manufacturing technology to make these items for us. Julien has designed three generations of machines you will need to build in order to produce our material. New Terra provides the raw material, the fabrication plants, the labor, and absorbs the cost. We provide the technology."

There was dead silence on the comm for so long that Alex wondered if they'd lost the link.

Then Minister Drake said, "FTL drives, grav-plates, nanotechnology, crystals … anything that you need us to make, you'd give us the science to produce these things for ourselves?"

"Yes, Minister Drake, we would give you that and more … our starship specifications, our navigational data, and the history of our people after landing. Julien would create a clone of his data banks and a librarian program to navigate it."

Stunned, Alex stared at Renée. He heard whispered exclamations among the team members, indicating they shared his surprise, before the link was silenced.

When the comm opened again, it was General Gonzalez who addressed them. In the early moments of their conversation, Renée had developed an instant affinity for the woman, who was forthright and engaging.

"Why would you do this for us, Ser de Guirnon?" the general asked. "And what would you want from us in return?"

"Excellent questions, General," Renée laughed. "I might say it's because we're cousins and should be helping each other. However, my father taught me that the best contracts exist when both sides have a vested interest in the trade. I know what I'm offering is an enormous boost for your technology. The stars could be yours in two years instead of 200. But the items I require in exchange are no small requests either."

"And what are they?" she asked.

"The first is the repair of the *Rêveur* to our specifications, along with a quantity of reserve materials."

"Understood."

"The second is a refit of the *Outward Bound* with our technology and again to our specifications."

"But, I didn't …" Alex interrupted.

Renée silenced his objection with a hand on his arm and continued, "If not for Captain Racine's efforts, which nearly cost him his life, all of us and our technology would be far outside your system, lost to you. This is the least we can do for him."

Drake added, "Yes, we are very grateful to Captain Racine for his efforts as well. We can appreciate the reason for your request."

"Before I make my final request, I'd have you know this. The first foreign starship to enter our space in the more than 700 years of our existence attacked us when we came to the rescue of one of our freighters, which it had just crippled. It fired on us without warning until we escaped into FTL, never responding to our communications attempts."

"In order to protect ourselves from such an attack again, we wish to form a contract with you that you will use our technology to arm the *Rêveur.*" She gave Alex a quick smile of her own. "We understand you have no concept of arming a ship. I can tell you that our Confederation, which is a conglomerate of our home world and colonies, has none either. The attack on our ships took place seventy-two of your years ago. Perhaps, a fighting ship is something we both need before this species finds either of our inhabited worlds."

They heard Minister Jaya whisper, "They were in stasis for seventy-two years," before the comm went quiet again.

After a few moments, Drake responded, "We are pleased to be able to help your people, Ser. The gift of your technology represents a great boon to our society, which will be well worth the hardships of integration. And while we could grant your first two items, the question of weapons will require further discussion. I'll present your requests to President McMorris for his consideration. In the meantime, I'll have a summary of our conversation worked up for your records."

"That's quite unnecessary, Minister Drake," Renée said. "Julien has informed me that he's transmitting a draft of our proposal and a record of our conversation to your readers even now."

"But how would he get access to our readers?" Minister Jaya sputtered.

"Never mind, Darryl," they heard the general say, "check your reader. It's a done thing."

"We'll await your response, Sers." Renée continued. "You may communicate with the *Outward Bound.* Alex has programmed his Tara to transfer your comm requests to me. *Rêveur* fini," she said and cut the link.

Renée turned in her bridge chair and looked at Alex, a smile stretching across her face. "How do you think I did, Captain?"

-12-

The *Rêveur*'s repair progress came to a halt with the exhaustion of its nanotech and circuitry stock. Much of the ship was still in need of reclamation.

Alex monitored their flight path from the *Rêveur*'s bridge. Its expansive information displays and augmented telemetry made his job much easier. And it was where he most enjoyed conversing with Julien. The Méridiens, recognizing his affinity for the space, politely avoided venturing unnecessarily onto the bridge.

One evening, Renée approached Alex as he left the meal room. "Captain, if I might have a moment of your time? Would you walk with me?"

"Certainly," he said and fell in beside her, walking to a cabin located just behind the bridge.

The door slid open at Renée's approach and she stepped through it, announcing, "This is the captain's cabin, which we wish to offer for your use. Your daily journeys back and forth to your ship are an unwarranted risk, and I must apologize to you for not considering it sooner."

He gazed around the well-appointed sitting room. It was furnished with a conference table and chairs, a lounger, and a work desk with an intricately etched metal surface. He activated the vid display and discovered the bridge's telemetry data could be at his fingertips.

"Renée, this is very nice, but Julien told me your uncle was the captain of this ship ..." He stopped as she held up a hand to silence him. A door opened behind her and she gestured toward it. Curious, he stepped through it into the adjoining sleeping quarters. The amount of space staggered him. A large bed was situated against a bulkhead. Display shelves, lining one wall, held a personal collection of Captain de Guirnon's mementos.

"I believe this bed is big enough to accommodate even you, Captain."

"Plus a companion or two," he said absentmindedly, staring at it. Then the implication of his words dawned on him and a blush crept up his neck. A quick glance at Renée revealed she was smiling, whether from his statement or his embarrassment, he wasn't sure.

Renée watched Alex struggle with his decision. Her people would have simply accepted the gift as the honor due them. In many ways, New Terrans, or at least this New Terran, continued to baffle her. Yet, he cared for the well-being of her and her people as no Méridien ever had – save one whom she had previously underestimated – Julien.

"This is but a small gift, Alex. A gift you deserve. My people owe you our thanks." Then she added, "*I* owe you my thanks." And she kissed him as she had the first time, her lips lingering on his cheeks.

* * *

The next morning, the cabin chime slowly penetrated Alex's consciousness. He struggled to remember where he was and place the unfamiliar sound. He spotted his comm device on the sideboard and restored it to his ear. "Julien?" he croaked.

"Greetings, Alex," Julien responded, "Your morning meal is ready. Shall I allow them access to your cabin?"

"What time is it?"

"It's 10.75 hours, by your ship's clock. No one wished to disturb you earlier … so, they have brought morning meal to you. Shall I admit them?"

The long sleep was what he had needed. The continuous days of heavy work, most of which he'd spent in his EVA suit, had taken their toll. Barely awake, he could already feel hunger gnawing at him. "Yes, please let them in." As he sat up, he heard people moving about in the main salon. The events of the previous evening slowly returned to him. The private refresher, once he'd mastered its operation, had been pure bliss. The Méridiens used an ingenious mix of pulsing air and some sort of liquid for washing. Whatever the process, the refresher had left him feeling clean and massaged.

He'd discovered the cabin's self-guiding garment cleaner. Following Julien's directions, he'd thrown in everything he was wearing, allowing the device to autodetect the fabrics. Then he'd climbed into bed, the surface reforming beneath him, and slid into oblivion with a smile on his face, savoring the unaccustomed comfort.

Now, as he struggled up from the bed, he realized his clothes were still in the cleaner. So he wrapped the bed's coverlet around his waist and listened at the door. Hearing nothing, he tapped the door control and stepped into the sitting room, discovering not only a well-laid table of food but two women standing patiently behind it.

"Good morning, Ser," they said in unison.

"Good morning, Geneviève, Pia," replied Alex, nodding to both. "My … my clothes are in the cleaner."

"No difficulty, Ser," Geneviève said enthusiastically, and moved past him into the sleeping quarters.

"Ser, will you wish to change before your meal or begin now?" asked Pia, gesturing to the trays.

Before Alex could respond, Geneviève whisked back into the room and laid his clothes across the back of the lounger. With a hand indicating his clutched bed coverlet, she offered, "May I assist you, Ser?"

Alex glanced between the women's faces and saw nothing but innocence. His sister's face often wore a similar expression during one of her pranks, and the recognition of the similarity cleared the mental cobwebs. "I think I can manage, Geneviève, thank you," he responded politely, refusing to play their game. "In fact, that will be all for now," He walked over to stand by his cabin door.

"Yes, Ser," they replied in chorus as they exited, their gazes lingering on the wide expanse of his exposed chest.

Alex smacked the door control. As it slid closed, he heard a chorus of giggles echoing down the corridor. "Oh, black space!" he sighed. Then, he headed for a quick change before sitting down to devour everything on the table.

* * *

Renée was helping Terese review the medical equipment that required repair or replacement when she accepted Julien's comm. <Are you laughing?>

<My pardon, Ser, but if I'd known our rescue would be this entertaining, I might have disabled the engines myself and coasted us here. Except,> he added sobering, <without the death and destruction.>

<Don't dwell on the past, Julien. I, for one, take heart in hearing you laugh again … something I think we all need. What has humored you?>

<Our captain has had a memorable introduction to his new accommodations. Geneviève and Pia took it upon themselves to service our captain this morning.>

Renée felt her heart skip a beat at his words, which didn't go unnoticed by Julien. <That is,> he continued, <they brought him meal trays while he was still in bed. He answered the door wrapped in his bed coverlet, so they offered to dress him.>

<And did they?> she asked.

<Our captain managed to blush, stammer a thank you, and guide them out his door. His last utterance was, I believe, a common New Terran expletive.>

Renée smiled as she visualized the scene. <Seems our captain has the courage to face death but might not be so brave with the women.>

<Or perhaps the difficulty lay in who offered to dress him,> Julien added. He waited, but Renée chose not to respond to his provocation. *One small step at a time*, he thought.

-13-

As they approached New Terra, Julien accumulated information on the New Terran solar system and local astronomy charts. Using the data, Julien and Edouard worked to determine their present position relative to their home world.

Tara's interception telemetry provided their starting point. The calculations and mapping took hours, but they finally pinned down the information they needed.

<Ser,> Edouard signaled Renée, <we've backtracked our position. The local star charts refer to a star called Mane, which, according to Julien, was our star's original name before the Ancients changed it to Oikos. We are only 23.6 light-years from Méridien.>

<So, if our negotiations are successful and we can repair our ship, home is attainable,> she said, her excitement rising.

<Yes, Ser, most certainly,> Edouard agreed.

* * *

From the *Rêveur*'s bridge, Alex used his link to Tara to maneuver both ships into a mid-level orbit around New Terra.

Julien interrupted his efforts. "Your pardon, Captain, Minister Drake is calling for Ser. She is on her way to the bridge."

"Thank you, Julien," Alex managed to say before the accessway slid open, admitting Renée.

"Minister Drake, a pleasure to speak with you again," she said, activating her harness audio.

"Ser de Guirnon, we are overjoyed to see you make New Terra safely."

"We have a remarkable Captain, Minister." Renée glanced quickly at Alex, but he was concentrating on his telemetry boards. "What update do you have for us?"

"Ser, it's our president's opinion, and we concur, that prior to entering into an agreement we must personally view your technology. If you'd allow a small group of visitors to examine your ship, speak to Julien, and see a demonstration of some of your technology, this would satisfy our first requirement. And, second, after verifying the superiority of your technology, the president wishes you to personally present your request to arm the *Rêveur* to our Assembly for its approval."

<Wise precautions,> Julian sent privately.

"May I presume, Minister Drake," Renée responded, "that your team will be the visitors?"

"We wish to bring five visitors, our team and two others, if you'd agree."

"Please communicate the names and titles of these other members to Tara, Minister. When would you like to schedule your visit?"

"We will forward the requested information immediately," Drake acknowledged. "We can be aboard the *Rêveur* in thirty-three hours, Ser."

"Quite acceptable, Minister Drake, we will see you tomorrow. *Rêveur* fini," Renée said as she ended the comm. She sat for a moment, thinking through the concept of a tour, trying to imagine her ship as an entertainment center instead of its current state – a wreck. And then there was the request to present to the New Terran Assembly. She would be a junior woman asking senior leaders to arm a foreign ship against an alien invasion that might or might not have happened. It sounded ludicrous when she stated it so simply. Yet, she couldn't shake the feeling that the survival of their civilizations was inextricably linked. Whether it was Alex's eerie premonition or her own troubled dreams that fostered her fear, she couldn't say.

While lost in thought, she heard Alex whisper, "Well done, Renée. Don't let them lead you. Request or demand what you need. You have the stronger hand."

She looked over at him, but his eyes were fixed on his boards. Below them floated an enormous orbital station clearly visible through the bridge's wide view shield. Renée had her first unmagnified view of Alex's home world and it was breathtaking. Vast blue waters stretched to the horizon. Tall mountain ranges were sheathed in deep greens and blues and capped in snow. His civilization's footprint was minimal, unlike her home world.

Minister Drake's message identified the two new team members, Assemblyman Clayton Downing XIV and Jonathan Davies, an employee of a space shuttle contractor.

Alex placed another quick comm to his parents about the two new team members. Neither of them knew about the engineer, Jonathan Davies, which was as he'd expected. But he'd heard the name Clayton Downing before ... and not in association with anything good. Unfortunately, his parents confirmed his suspicions.

Forearmed with the update, Renée called a meeting in the meal room to discuss how best to entertain the New Terran visitors. She laid out the visitors' requests, what they wanted to see and learn. Then she told them what *she* wanted their visitors to learn, emphasizing that a successful presentation was a critical step in returning home.

She passed the lead to Alex, who summarized what he knew about the visitors. Julien disseminated images to their implants for easy identification. Alex spent the majority of his time talking about the assemblyman. He summarized the New Terran democratic process, the elections of district representatives and the Assembly, which created the laws that guided his people.

The Méridiens questioned him about the election process, which appeared foreign to them. When Alex explained the juggling of power between the common vote and the industrial captains, who gathered power for themselves, he could see their eyes glaze as they commed one another.

"Perhaps this is too much information," Alex said, regaining their attention. "I understand that our ways are not your ways. Let me summarize. Of the five visitors coming, three will be your supporters. Another is an engineer who will be impressed, rest assured. The fifth, the assemblyman, is neither friend nor enemy. He has his own interests and will do whatever is necessary to further those interests, regardless of what might become of you."

Renée received comms asking why the assemblyman wasn't censured for failing to act in the goodwill of the people. She overrode their comms in priority mode to gain control of the meeting. "I require suggestions that will display our technology in impressive demonstrations."

Several ideas were volunteered and enthusiastically accepted, except for Terese's suggestion that she could examine the visitors and inform them of any life-threatening conditions they possessed.

Before they finalized their agenda, Alex requested a time slot be reserved for him at the end of the tour, then invited Renée and the twins to his suite.

* * *

Alex directed the shuttle pilot of NT-GOV3, carrying the Negotiations Team, to the *Rêveur*'s port side, opposite from the *Outward Bound*.

The shuttle crew deployed a docking collar to *Rêveur*'s midship airlock hatch, allowing the five visiting team members to transfer without EVA suits. Alex stood waiting in his new ship suit of deep, dark, Méridien blue, the fabric subtly conveying deep ocean waters.

Alex had verbally wrestled with Geneviève and Pia when they brought the suit to his cabin and offered to help him change. His timely recollection that his measurements were taken with a laser device had saved him. Assuring them it would fit, he'd ushered them from the cabin with his profound thanks.

It was a snug fit, yet it accommodated his movements more comfortably than any garment he'd ever worn. It was durable too, which proved opportune when he ran his shoulder into a piece of metal protruding from a bulkhead. The Méridien suit not only didn't tear; it didn't even show a mark.

Alex greeted each visitor as they stepped through the airlock hatch: Ministers Drake and Jaya, General Rodriquez, Assemblyman Clayton Downing, and the senior aerospace engineer Jonathan Davies.

Each individual greeted him as Captain Racine, except for Assemblyman Downing, who merely regarded him and said, "Interesting choice of clothing." So he took more than a little pleasure in handing out the Méridien ear comms, deliberately handing Downing the first one, and, without elaboration, instructing him to place the daubed end in his ear. He barely avoided smiling when the assemblyman, with a shout of surprise, yanked the device from his ear and threw it on the deck.

"You came to witness Méridien technology, Sirs, General," Alex addressed them. "You must to be better prepared than this." The assemblyman's reaction – a clenched jaw and pulsing blood vessels in his temples – was what Alex was seeking. It was his intention to prevent Downing from grandstanding and hijacking the tour, which he had been warned the assemblyman would do, if given half a chance.

He continued handing out ear comms, explaining how they worked and why they were required to converse with Julien when off the bridge. Minister Jaya's face stretched into an ecstatic smile as he felt the nanites deploy in his inner ear. The others followed suit with varying reactions.

As the visitors followed Alex to the bridge, the assemblyman snatched his comm device off the deck and hurried to catch up. Finally inserting the device, he winced and his skin crawled as it secured itself.

While they walked the corridors, Alex said, "You'll have noticed that the *Rêveur* bears no resemblance to our ships. For one thing, it has no rotating hubs for gravity, yet you're walking normally." The visitors exchanged a series of glances as if realizing for the first time what he said was true. Alex didn't slow his stride. His plan was to keep the visitors unbalanced while delivering an entertaining peek at the Méridien's technology.

Renée was staged just aft of the command chairs, in full view of the bridge accessway, with Étienne and Alain on either side of her. Both twins were armed with stun guns and displayed the stern expressions that they'd practiced with Alex. All wore Méridien-blue ship suits.

As the visitors stepped onto the bridge, they came to an abrupt halt, looking from one Méridien to another. Alex recalled his initial impressions of these beautiful, graceful people – utterly mesmerizing. He introduced the visitors to Renée, trying his best to imitate a scene from one of his sister's favorite holo-vids of a courtier introducing supplicants to his queen.

Minister Drake stepped forward as he was introduced, his hand extended to Renée.

"Gently," Alex warned. He'd emphasized the Méridien's slighter frames in his messages and again on the way to the bridge.

Renée shook the minister's outstretched hand and gave him a dazzling smile. The other visitors were also careful to shake Renée's hand gently. Alex simply introduced the twins as Renée's security – no names were offered.

"Welcome to the *Rêveur*, Sers," Renée began. "We will tour parts of our ship, demonstrate some of our technology, and then share a meal with you. Let us start our tour here on the bridge. Julien, our SADE, will begin."

In their ear comms, they heard Julien introduce himself and lead them through the ship's capabilities. As he calmly detailed the *Rêveur*'s FTL flight capabilities, the star systems the Méridiens inhabited, their Confederation-wide FTL communications, and their nanotechnology applications in medicine, ship construction, and personal items, Alex watched the visitors' various reactions. The Negotiations Team was clearly in awe, but the quiet look shared by the assemblyman and the engineer bothered him.

After Julien's introduction, Renée led them to where Méridiens waited to demonstrate their technology. The twins flanked Renée with strong, intimidating strides, so unlike their natural, graceful steps.

In the partially recovered landing bay, Claude hooked up grav-lifters to the skids of a damaged shuttle. He used his controller to levitate the 22-meter hulk into the air, then turn it slowly in a circle. The engineer's mouth fell open, and Alex thought the man might have fallen in love.

Another stop was Medical. Thankfully, Terese had been disabused of her notion to diagnose the visitors. She led them through the Méridiens' medical imaging and diagnosis tools, explaining the application of nanites to repair traumatic injuries and their science of genetic manipulation. The last topic had the visitors exchanging significant glances again. Terese ended her demonstration by imaging herself to display her implant.

"That's why none of you have an ear comm," Maria said, looking first at Terese and then at Renée. "You wear your comm on the inside. What else can it do?"

"They are quite versatile," Renée replied.

"Could you give us a list of those capabilities, so that …"

"General Rodriquez," Alex interrupted, "perhaps we should save the in-depth questions for later." He disliked being rude to the general, but he had a date to keep.

Renée led the guests back to the bridge for her own demonstration. She had Étienne step forward and hold out his sidearm for their visitors to inspect. Then she indicated her ship suit's 5-centimeter wide belt and harness strap. "This accessory has several functions, one of which is personal protection. When activated, it creates a field around the wearer. It might be activated by sudden movement, such as one might experience in a fall; by one's biometrics, such as the fear reflex; or by the activation of a stun gun. Let me demonstrate. Étienne, if you will."

Renée stepped back. Étienne thumbed a button on the stun gun and pulled the trigger. To the visitors, nothing much appeared to happen, but a small, blue energy field flared briefly around Renée.

The demonstration was designed to be underwhelming and Assemblyman Downing stepped right into the trap. He looked at Renée and said, "Nice show, but how do we know if anything even came out of the weapon?" To which, right on cue, Étienne turned, pointed his sidearm at the Honorable Clayton Downing XIV, District 12 assemblyman, and pulled the trigger. Alex caught the man as he went limp and slid to the deck. Alain inserted himself in front of Renée and both twins faced the visitors with weapons drawn.

"Stand still, everyone!" Alex commanded to the startled visitors.

"The man has insulted Ser," Étienne declared in a stern voice.

Renée spoke a command in her language, which the visitors didn't receive in translation. They watched as the twins holstered their weapons and stepped back.

"You have my apologies, Sers, for my guard's actions. Such an insult from one of your members was unexpected. Captain Racine has never acted in this manner. Had I known New Terrans capable of such behavior, I would have thought to brief my security detail."

The engineer stared at Downing on the deck and asked, "Is he dead?"

"Certainly not," Renée stated imperiously. "He has merely been stunned; only the primitive kill. Terese has been commed, so he won't remain in this state for long."

On cue, Terese entered the bridge and knelt at Downing's side, running her diagnostic equipment over his head. She tapped the screen twice, detached a small accessory from the side of the device, and touched it to Downing's temple.

Downing's eyes suddenly popped open and he grabbed his chest with both hands. He pointed a finger at Étienne and exclaimed, "He shot me!" The two ministers struggled to help the portly gentleman up as he continued to shout at Étienne, "You shot me!"

As the assemblyman drew breath for one of his infamous tirades, Alex stepped in front of him and commanded loudly, "Downing, stand down!" The assemblyman was taken aback, and before he could regain his inertia, Alex pressed on, "I'm afraid the issue hasn't been settled. You weren't stunned as a demonstration of the weapon, which you doubted, but because you insulted a representative of House de Guirnon. This ship belongs to a Méridien House. It's sovereign territory."

Alex was speaking the assemblyman's language, and he could see it in Downing's eyes as the man looked from one security twin to the other, whose hands rested firmly on the grips of their weapons. Then Downing flicked his eyes to Renée, who stood with her arms folded across her chest and an impatient look in her eyes.

Alex stepped aside as Clayton regained his composure. The other visitors subtly cleared some space around the assemblyman, not wanting to be near him if he was going to incite the Méridiens again.

Licking his lips, Downing cleared his throat and said to Renée, "My apologies if my words impugned you, Ser. That certainly wasn't my intention. Perhaps it was in the translation ..." He stopped short as the twins started to draw their weapons once more.

Renée uttered another sharp command and placed a restraining hand on each of the twins.

Downing looked nervously between the two escorts, and the visitors cleared even more space around him.

Renée looked at him coldly and said, "First, Assemblyman Downing, you insult me by implying I'd attempt to fool you with my demonstration. Now you insult my SADE, implying he's unable to translate your language. Captain Racine tells me you have nothing resembling a SADE in your world, so one might forgive your ignorance. But know this, Ser. Julien's capabilities extend far past any of ours, including the ability to perform a simple translation between Con-Fed and Sol-NAC, one of hundreds of languages in his archives." She stood defiantly, waiting for Downing to speak.

Completely cowed, he stammered out one of the sincerest apologies Alex had ever heard, addressing his comments to both Julien and Renée. Whatever the man's failings, he was good with words, too good.

When the assemblyman finally wound down, Julien accepted Downing's apology. Renée waved a hand in dismissal and said, "We'll speak no more of it," and strode off. "We'll share a meal and forget this nonsense," she added over her shoulder.

Downing nervously eyed the twins, then ducked his eyes away from their cold, hard stares as they passed him.

The party entered the meal room, where they sat with Alex and Renée at an expanded central table. Soon a wide array of dishes and drinks were spread out before them.

"The Méridiens are able to synthesize or prepare their foods on demand," Alex explained. "Apparently, they maintain tanks of what they refer to as base food stocks, which I imagine are complex groups of carbohydrates, proteins, esters, oils, and such. Nanites are employed as preservatives in some manner. Then a controller, for want of a better word, fabricates the dishes. It might sound unappetizing, but the food tastes wonderful. I've been eating it safely ever since I came aboard."

The visitors began to eat, first with trepidation, and then, as the exotic tastes exploded on their palates, with gusto. Downing was quiet throughout the meal, and no one attempted to engage him.

As the dishes were cleared, silence filled the room, and the Méridiens turned expectantly toward the visitors' table. Alex gently cleared his throat. "When Méridiens entertain guests, one of them reciprocates with a personal story," Alex explained. "They record it in their implants and share it with others. It isn't required, but it's their custom."

The visitors exchanged glances. Downing merely stared at his water glass, meeting no one's eyes. Alex was about to thank them for their visit, bringing the meal to a close, when Maria leaned forward in her chair and said, "I gave birth to two beautiful boys, three years apart."

She told the story of her two inseparable sons, the older boy, Dalton, always looking out for his adventuresome younger brother, Tim. As teenagers, they were intoxicated with dangerous sports, riding air currents with their foils and racing the rapids in their glide boats.

On a beautiful summer's day, she'd watched her sons race their glide boats down one of Mt. Carine's fast-flowing rivers, with seven other teens. The river was swollen from recent rains and the usually blue green waters were a muddy brown. At the start of the race, Tim took the lead, his more aggressive style finding the faster path through the rapids. Dalton was third in the pack. Halfway through the race, a large tree branch, swept downstream by the torrents, punched up through Tim's glide boat, capsizing it and throwing Tim into the rough waters. When he saw his brother disappear beneath the surface, Dalton tore off his flotation jacket and dove into the dark roiling waters. Hours later and kilometers downstream, they recovered the bodies of the two boys. Tim's chest had been punctured by the thick branch. He'd died instantly. Dalton had drowned trying to save his dead brother.

When Maria finished, silence held the room captive. "You have all suffered great losses. Your crewmates and friends are dead and a lifetime has passed while you slept. As a mother, who remembers her sons every day, I understand your loss and you have my sympathy."

Her audience rose to their feet and saluted her with heads bowed and arms crossed. Maria glanced at Alex. He signaled her to rise and nodded his head down, implying that she should do the same. She rose and mimicked his action, holding her head down for a solemn moment.

Renée thanked their visitors, motioning them toward the exit. The twins led the way. As the New Terrans filed out, many of the Méridiens brushed a sympathetic hand on Maria's arm or shoulder as she passed them. Tears formed in her eyes in response to their gentle attention. She regained her composure on the way to the airlock and hung back as the others entered before her. Stopping beside Alex, she whispered in his ear. "Good tour, lovely people, wonderful meal. I especially loved the theatrics on the bridge." Then she gave him a wink and joined the others in the airlock.

Once their visitors were safely transferred to the shuttle's airlock, Alex, Renée, and the twins walked back to the bridge, where they found the rest of the Méridiens waiting.

"Did we do well, Ser?" Terese asked Renée.

"Yes, I'm very proud of you all."

"And us, Captain Racine," Étienne asked, "did we perform adequately as you requested?"

The bit of drama Alex had devised for the assemblyman had been a serious gambit. But, in his heart of hearts, he knew that a man like Downing might have easily mistaken the Méridien's gentle ways for weakness, and first impressions, his parents had reminded him time and time again, were critical.

As he thought of the terrified look on Downing's face, he started to laugh and couldn't stop. When he finally caught his breath, he assumed a stern face and imitated Étienne, "The man has insulted Ser," and surrendered to another fit of laughter, releasing the tension he had built up.

He stepped forward and hugged Étienne. "Well done, Étienne, and you too, Alain," Alex said still chuckling. "Well done, everyone," he repeated, turning to face the others. They beamed and clasped hands with one another, basking in his compliment.

Renée watched her people enjoy a moment of contentment. She realized that Julien had been right all along. Alex was much more than their rescuer.

-14-

At Minister Drake's request, Alex settled their twinned crafts into a geosynchronous orbit 70km from the Joaquin orbital station. It was not lost on Alex that the minister was bending over backward to develop a cordial relationship with him, and he considered that a very good sign.

They waited for the government's response to the visitors' tour. Alex split his time between discussions with Renée and Julien, direct vid links with his parents and sister, and work with each of the *Rêveur*'s specialists, cataloguing repairs still to be made.

Claude presented him with a substitute for his EVA suit, a Méridien environment suit that was half the weight and much more flexible. Pia and Geneviève had deconstructed three of their suits to make it for him. Its snug fit was similar to a New Terran ocean dive suit, and even though the air tanks were smaller, they delivered 40 percent more air time than his tanks.

Utilizing the new suit, Alex helped Claude cover the entire interior and exterior of the ship's hull with a laser-scanning transmitter built by Edouard that allowed Julien to catalog three-dimensional views of the hull's damage.

The view of the hull saddened both Alex and Claude as they examined the deadly strikes delivered by a single silver ship. Each energy beam had cut through the entire ship, except for the hardened FTL engine cones, burning through interior bulkheads, energy-storage crystals, cabin furniture, and thousands of other items, vaporizing them on the way from one side of the ship to the other.

Alex asked Claude about the crystal shards they continued to find. He was told that Méridiens grew their crystals as gaseous compounds under pressure, allowing the crystals to incorporate various metals or metallic compounds introduced during the process. The compounds determined a crystal's engineering function: metal-crystal matrices produced capacitors and memory storage; and metal-amalgam crystals, suspended between lasers, were used to send and receive FTL comms.

During their recording process, Alex examined an engine support frame struck by a beam. "Julien, are you seeing this?" Alex asked as he panned the laser tool across the damage.

"Yes, Captain, I'm always recording."

"No, sorry, what I meant is, take a look at the path of this beam strike and the extent of the damage."

"Understood, Captain," replied Julien, taking a renewed interest in the request. "Please step back to cover a wider area first." Alex complied with his request. "Thank you. Now move the transmitter slowly from port to starboard. Now proceed to document the damage as you had been doing. What would you like done with this additional data?"

Claude, having worked closely with Alex since the first day, was well aware when he was on the hunt to solve a puzzle.

"Follow my train of thought, Julien," Alex continued. "With your vids of the attack, you might be able to isolate this particular strike and calculate how far away the alien ship was when it caused the damage. And no one knows better than you how the *Rêveur* was built and with what materials. Now, you also have recordings of the damage caused by this particular beam."

"Yes, Captain," Julien stepped in quickly, "with the assembled data I can calculate the energy the beam carried when it struck the ship. It also might be possible to determine the type of energy released."

"One more thing for you to consider," Alex replied. "I've noticed that the beam strikes vary in diameter but not in strength. They had the same capacity to pass through the hull regardless of the beam's diameter or the distance between the ships."

"If I anticipate your reasoning, Captain, it would appear the silver ship uses a focused beam weapon. It narrows to a point at its farthest range, preserving power by doing so."

"That was precisely my thought."

"I'll begin analysis of this information immediately."

Claude laid a hand on Alex's shoulder and smiled at him through the faceplate of his environment suit.

* * *

Renée had organized her fellow Méridiens into teams to walk every inch of the repaired areas – bridge, corridors, suites, crew and passenger cabins, refreshers, maintenance rooms, and general purpose rooms to catalog the supplies they required to be fully functional. Julien used their lists to extrapolate what might be needed once the rest of the ship was accessible, then added 30 percent more, per Alex's suggestion.

Meanwhile, Terese cataloged the medical supply needs and Edouard did the same for the environmental systems. All lists ended up in Julien's databases.

Alex and Claude continued their damage survey on the engines, inside and out; the two shuttles, both damaged; and the ship's primary and secondary power-crystal banks. Only the bow's primary power bank had survived, a fact that Julien didn't miss.

After the evening meal, Julien requested the presence of Renée and Alex on the bridge. They arrived to find Claude waiting for them. The holo-vid displayed a structural diagram of the aft end of the *Rêveur*. As they took their seats, Julien began. "I've prepared the calculations you requested, Captain. The beam's energy when it struck the port engine frame, section 34D, was 10.7 mega-joules. The nature of the energy is undeterminable at this time. But I've designed a device that, once fabricated, will be able to sample the melted metal alloys and help me make that determination."

"Wonderful job, Julien," Alex declared. "I'm not sure how we'll use this data. But I fear we might find ourselves in need of as much information as possible in the near future. Not to mention that it will help us make our case to the New Terrans about the danger of the silver ship."

The subtle changes in Alex's speech, the longer he was on the *Rêveur*, had not gone unnoticed. He often referred to the New Terrans in the third person, including himself with the Méridiens. Julien had also noted the change in the way his people referred to Alex. He was no longer *Captain Racine* or the *New Terran captain*. He was *captain* or, in the more intimate form, *our captain*.

"So, Julien, do you have anything in those vast archives of yours that would allow us to one," Alex held up a finger, "generate an energy weapon that's equally strong or stronger, and two," he held up a second finger, "design a hull shield capable of protecting us from multiple strikes?"

"I'll begin reviewing my archives for answers, Captain." Julien said.

Renée tried to assume a casual tone but it worried her that Alex's fears echoed her own. "Do you think this work is necessary?" She felt relieved to finally vocalize the concern that had been weighing on her mind for many days.

"An alien starship attacked two of your starships," Alex said, his tone gentle. "There was no prior contact or advanced warning. That small ship had a weapon that punched through your ships with 11 mega-joules of energy, and you had no means with which to defend yourselves. Furthermore, you've been gone from your Confederation for over seventy years. There are five possible scenarios for when you return to Méridien; one, your people won't have had any more contact with the aliens; two, they'll have met them and made peace with them; three, they'll be at war with them; four, they'll have been defeated by them; or, five, they'll have defeated them. Where are you placing your creds?"

Renée was saddened to admit their encounter had probably not been a unique event, especially due to the speed and efficiency with which the silver ship disabled their vessels. She did not want to admit that the answer to Alex's question was that her people were probably losing colonies and space or had already been utterly subjugated by an invading fleet. If the latter was true, the question became: were her people now subjects of this predatory race or had they been decimated, removed to make way for the expansion of an alien civilization?

They were all saved from their dark thoughts by Julien. "Ser, Minister Drake is on comm for you."

"Minister, Renée de Guirnon here."

"Good evening, Ser, I'm pleased to announce that the tour of your ship was a resounding success. President McMorris has scheduled an emergency meeting of the Assembly in two days, with your presentation at 11 hours."

"We are more than pleased to hear of your decision, Minister." Having already considered the next step, Renée requested, "We will need transportation to your Assembly for four, Minister Drake."

"A shuttle has been dedicated to your needs, Ser. I'll send the contact details of the pilots and crew to Tara soonest. It's scheduled to rendezvous with you tomorrow at 14 hours. We will have accommodations prepared for you at Government House."

"My thanks, Minister, we anticipate with pleasure our first visit to your planet. *Rêveur* fini."

-15-

Alex and Renée used most of the evening to prepare their presentation. Julien downloaded the final vids and data to a portable holo-vid projector.

On schedule, their assigned shuttle stationed itself alongside the *Rêveur*. Renée turned over command to Edouard, then transferred to the shuttle with Alex, Étienne, and Alain.

Their flight was quick and relatively uneventful, other than the fact that the three crew members couldn't take their eyes off the Méridiens. When they set down at Prima's main port, a pair of hover cars, flying the president's flags, awaited them just outside the safety zone. The Méridiens dialed up the tiny grav-controllers embedded in their belt harnesses to counter New Terra's greater gravity before exiting the shuttle.

The Méridiens were thrilled with the ride to Government House. Tall, broad trees lined the main boulevards, rugged snow-capped mountains loomed in the distance, and New Terrans rode a variety of vehicles in the lanes beside them. Renée couldn't help comparing the view to her home planet. Her people had spread up and out across the surface of Méridien before establishing their first colony on Bellamonde. Whereas the New Terrans had buildings no taller than fifteen or twenty stories, the Méridiens, with their anti-grav technology, had commonly built two-mile high structures, utilizing underground connectors for all modes of transportation, allowing the development of nearly every square mile of surface space.

Though her people protected the environment in their own way, she appreciated the New Terrans' obvious respect for their planet's innate beauty. The massive trees lining the boulevard, with their thick trunks and wide canopies stretching across much of the lanes, appeared to be hundreds of years old. During the centuries, Alex's people had chosen to preserve them rather remove them to make way for expansion.

At one point, a young couple on a hover bike zoomed up alongside their presidential convoy. While the driver looked for his next opening, the young woman seated behind him, her face decorated with a bright, faux mask, looked into the darkened, security windows hiding Renée's face and waggled her fingers at the glass before her driver opened the throttle and the hover bike disappeared ahead.

"Your people are so expressive, Captain," Renée said.

"Expressive? Yes, I suppose so. But that can be a good thing and a bad thing."

At Government House, President McMorris personally greeted them. Alex watched the experienced politician manage his first in-person view of the Méridiens. He was better than most, but he still hesitated for a second or two, like a vid freezing, before continuing. Then, they were ushered up the front steps, out of the sun, and into the cool interior of the presidential offices and home.

Alex had toured Government House twice before, once after the president gave an important speech to a crowd assembled outside, so he noticed a significant change. The president's security was keeping a very low profile, dressed in casual clothes, with weapons stowed out of sight, and only two agents present. After giving them an opportunity to freshen up in their rooms, the president led them on a tour of Government House.

Renée noticed how the president mixed details of the tour with questions that invited comparison with her people, drawing her out. He seemed genuinely interested in her culture, and she found herself warming to him. If her father still lived, the two men might become good friends.

A statue, more than twice her height, stood in the central rotunda, a man in an Ancient's ship uniform. His physique wasn't as commanding as that of the present New Terrans, but he bore many similarities. His expression was somber, and his eyes appeared to be looking far ahead, perhaps into the future.

"I gather he was an important person to your people, President McMorris," Renée said gazing up to the statue's face. She'd seen the plaque but couldn't read the words. Julien's translation program managed only audio sources, an oversight they would need to rectify later.

"Yes, Ser, he is Lem Ulam, Captain of the *New Terra*."

"I've heard the story of your colony ship, Mr. President. And may I say that despite the tragedy of your beginning, your people have much to be proud of, overcoming such hardships to flourish as you have done."

"It certainly has made us robust individuals, Ser," replied the president.

"Yes, I've observed that firsthand," Renée answered, sparing a glance at Alex. "Did he govern your people after he led you here?" she asked.

"He remained our captain for almost twenty-seven years. Then one day he announced general elections and proclaimed his retirement. From that day, he was always found doing one menial task or another … anything he could do to help. He died four years later."

"He is a man worthy of honor," Renée said solemnly. "His family grieved for him, I'm sure."

Silence greeted her statement. "Ser," the president explained gently, "the captain's family remained aboard the colony ship. He didn't wake his wife and two young children. Later it was argued that he made the decision so that he wouldn't be accused of favoritism; others claimed his wife and children didn't qualify based on the selection board's criteria."

"Then he led a lonely life on your planet," Renée lamented. "I wonder if our people would have fared as well under the same conditions. As circumstances would have it, we weren't so tested."

"We did have our growth pains even after we stabilized the enormous challenges of food and health," the president said as he continued the tour. "Probably one of the most telling moments in our history occurred in 359 AL, that's after landing. Some forty-seven industry leaders banded together to propose a private school for their children and applied for a government permit. The press published their names, their holdings, and every product they had a hand in selling. Business for them ceased overnight. Contracts were cancelled. Drivers of their cargo and harvesters of their crops walked off the job. Days later, the land owners and company presidents made a public appeal, recalling their permit request. The populace paid them no mind and continued to boycott their goods until the forty-seven were broke. The government stepped in and purchased their land and companies at default prices, then sold shares of the enterprises to the employees. The general populace made their point pretty clearly."

"And what do you believe was their point, Mr. President?" Renée inquired.

"Simply this, Ser," McMorris said. "If they wanted an elitist society, they were living on the wrong planet."

Renée wondered if the New Terrans would view the Confederation as elitist. The thought would never have crossed her mind before the attack. But since her revival, she had found herself asking many new questions, ones she'd never thought to ask before.

"The view of your home world from the *Rêveur* is delightful. You have such a small footprint on the land, and yet you've already been in space for almost a century."

"It's true we still have a small population, only 131 million, but our people never forgot why our ancestors left Earth. It shows in the type of representatives our people favor … individuals who believe it's a government's duty to protect our planet and ensure it doesn't go the way of Old Terra. As you've learned, we constructed habitats on the next planet outward, Niomedes. However, I think our experiment is about to change drastically, courtesy of your people's superior technology, if we can come to an agreement."

"That's my wish also, Mr. President."

They continued the tour and their conversations until evening meal was called. As they walked to the dining hall, Alex felt Renée's touch on his arm. She spoke softly, asking if New Terrans cultivated their protein. He was tempted to tell her that his people still enjoyed ripping meat from the bones, but the concerned look on her face gave him pause and he explained they had been cultivating protein for over 300 years.

Renée commed the twins with the news and they visibly relaxed. At the table, she ran a scanner over each dish to test for unsafe substances. Previously, Terese had tested the *Rêveur*'s visitors, scanning for any dangerous microbes that might await her people on the planet. She'd found nothing that their enhanced immune systems couldn't handle.

The Méridiens found the food pleasant if not a little bland. Alex felt the same way, which surprised him, since the president's table offered some of the best food on the planet. It occurred to him that he had developed a preference for the more tantalizing fare of his new friends.

* * *

That night, Alex turned off his room's vid display and was headed for bed when he heard a soft tap-tap on his door. He opened it to find Renée standing there. Without a word, he stepped aside to let her enter, then quietly shut the door behind her.

"Captain," she said then changed her mind. "Alex, I would speak with you of your Assembly meeting tomorrow. I wish to know where you will stand."

"Where would you like me to stand?"

Renée uttered something in her language that wasn't translated, but he got the gist of it.

"Try again," he encouraged.

She took his hands in hers. "These are your people, Alex. Tomorrow, I'll stand in front of them as a representative of Méridien, a stranger to them. I don't want your people to think less of you for standing beside me."

He gazed into her eyes, the soft swirl of colors in her pupils reminding him that she wasn't New Terran. "When I was young, I learned that I was very different from my peers. For years, it hurt, until I stopped caring what strangers thought of me," he told her. "Tomorrow, I'll stand with you."

She let go of the breath she'd been holding. They owed their captain so much, and they continued to need him. She would have let go of his hands, but he carefully held on. Despite his strength, he was always gentle with her and every Méridien.

Renée waited for him to say what was on his mind. But without another word, he released her hands, opened the door, and bid her good-night. She paused in the doorway to offer her thanks. But the words felt inadequate and they weren't what she wanted to say. She blamed the inadequacy of the translation program, but she knew that wasn't true.

* * *

At 10.75 hours, their entourage's hover cars settled on a ramp beside the Prima's great Assembly Hall. TSF troopers, arranged on both sides of the walkway, held salutes as they exited their vehicles to walk a carpet of deep maroon, entwined with delicate, intricately woven swirls of silver.

Inside the Assembly Hall, Renée felt a moment of panic. Over 500 august men and women filled the seats of the main floor and gallery rows. She felt Alex's fingers slip into her hand and squeeze gently. She smiled at him in return and focused on the hall's design rather than the assembled representatives, admiring the seats, built with ancient woods that shone with a soft luster. It was a venerable hall, a fitting place for their peoples to form an alliance.

The president escorted them to the front of the hall and a broad raised dais. He led Renée past Assembly security stationed at the base of the steps. As Alex approached security, a hand reached out and gripped his arm, restraining him. Quicker than the eye could follow, the agent found his hand swiped away, Étienne suddenly standing between him and Alex.

Amid the ensuing commotion, the president's firm command was heard, "Hold." Security for each side froze with hands on side arms.

"Étienne, is there a difficulty?" Renée inquired.

"Ser, this man obstructed our captain."

Before the agent could draw breath to explain, Renée challenged him. "Is this true, agent? Did you impede our captain?" Without waiting for his answer, she turned to the president. "It's a poor beginning for our peoples if simple courtesies are so easily ignored."

The president mentally kicked himself for not preparing Assembly security with the same careful instructions he'd given his own team. And Renée's response cued him to an important sign he'd missed. He and the Negotiations Team had counted on Alex's ties with the Méridiens to enable their agenda. It appeared they had underestimated what those ties meant to the Méridiens. "I must offer my apologies, Ser de Guirnon. It was our error due to customary procedures. No offense was intended."

"Security, stand down," he commanded. "Captain Racine, Étienne, and Alain, if you would please," and he gestured for them to follow him up the steps. Étienne and the security agent exchanged a last look and Alex wondered if he'd rehearsed the twins a little too much. But the speed of Étienne's execution was something he hadn't seen before.

The president gestured Renée toward a tall, ornate, wooden chair beside his own and Alex to a similar chair on his other side. When he shifted his attention to the twins, they had already taken up positions – Étienne standing behind Alex and Alain behind Renée.

An Assembly monitor rose from his desk below the dais and spoke in a deep, strong voice, "Let the Assembly gather and hear. The president of New Terra, the Honorable Arthur McMorris would speak."

The president rose and approached a transparent lectern that rose out of the floor. In his opening remarks, he greeted the Assembly and welcomed them. There was no need to go into great detail as each representative had received several briefs as the *Rêveur* made New Terran orbit.

"It is with great pleasure," the president announced, "on this unique and momentous occasion, that I introduce our first extra-solar visitor, Ser Renée de Guirnon, representative of House de Guirnon of Méridien, home world of the Confederation."

Amid loud stomping, Renée approached the podium, smiling her thanks to the president. Alex had informed her of the Assembly's custom of greeting a speaker with the tapping of their shoes. However, she suspected a mistranslation because the booming echoes sounded nothing like tapping.

When their welcome died down, she said, "Distinguished representatives of New Terra, it's an honor and a privilege to address you today. For more than 700 years, my people have had no contact with other humans. We rejoice to discover that you too survived your exodus of Earth to prosper on this beautiful planet. And we are saddened to discover that you had to struggle mightily to do so. Today, we celebrate the mutual discovery of our civilizations. But I'm afraid I must also mar this wonderful occasion with great and terrible news. We aren't alone and they didn't come as friends, but as foes ... to both of us."

"But before I continue, honor must be paid to one of your own, who risked his life to catch a derelict starship and become the savior of my people. Before this premier body of his people, I would pay honor to Captain Alexander Racine."

Renée turned toward Alex, crossed her arms to her shoulders and bowed her head. Étienne and Alain adopted the same pose. The Assembly broke out in a thunderous roar of stomping and whistles as Alex rose from his chair and inclined his head to her. Renée held her position as the noise of the Assembly slowly died away. When she finally raised her head, her eyes gleamed with unshed tears and she gave him a brilliant smile. She gave herself a moment before turning to face the audience again as Alex seated himself.

The president glanced at Alex and reconsidered his status – not his diplomat – their champion. He looked across the rows of representatives. Assemblyman Downing sat with his conservative cronies who represented many of the wealthier districts. Their expressions were fixed in stone. Not so for the majority of the representatives. He could see it in their faces and body language. They liked this strange, young woman with her exotic features. She didn't threaten them. In fact, she was winning them over by honoring one of their own.

"I've come to offer a contract with you," Renée continued, "and I would not expect this Assembly to enter into this agreement without proof of what we both face."

Alex rose from his seat with a small case. He took out the holo-vid projector and placed it on the lectern, attaching a slender cable to the device. He knelt on the floor and touched the other end to a power outlet, which morphed to fit the connector. He nodded to Renée and turned in time to catch the stunned expression of the president, who had witnessed the cable come alive. Alex offered the president a quick, lop-sided smile and a shrug before returning to his seat.

"Representatives of New Terra," Renée announced, "here is the record of our meeting with our first aliens." Then she signaled the projector to start. New Terrans had holo-vids too, but they emanated from heavy, fixed bases, and produced small, three-dimensional images. The Méridiens had small, portable units that projected huge, three-dimensional images with startling clarity. Gasps sprang from the audience, and hands twitched as people instinctively sought to reach out and touch the images.

Julien's synthesized voice filled the Assembly as he introduced himself and narrated the encounter. The Assembly was mesmerized by the scenario played out by the three ships. Some of the best and brightest minds of New Terra were present, and they absorbed many of the details on display and in Julien's commentary. They were awed by the massive length of the Méridien freighter, which dwarfed anything the New Terrans had. They took note too of the tremendous amount of space, light-years, that the *Rêveur* had crossed in a brief amount of time to answer the freighter's emergency beacon. Méridien technology was evidently hundreds of years ahead of theirs, yet the powerful energy weapon of the alien craft pierced their ships with ease. The holo-vid sold Renée's story as words never could.

When the vid finished, Renée enumerated her points. Their people shared a common ancestry – that of Earth. They faced a common enemy, one who was powerful and offered no quarter. The attack on the *Rêveur* had taken place seventy-two New Terran years ago. So it was only a matter of time before a silver ship found its way to New Terra.

She concluded by thanking the Assembly for its time and President McMorris for the opportunity to speak before the august body. Amid another round of deafening whistles and stomping as the Assembly took to their feet, she returned to her chair.

The president brought the session to a close. He promised the Assembly that the Negotiations Team would soon formalize an agreement with the Méridiens for its ratification. Lauded by another round of Assembly appreciation, the president and his entourage exited the Assembly for the return to Government House.

* * *

But Alex and the Méridiens soon discovered there was one more hurdle to clear before they attained the solitude of Government House – the media.

When word leaked of the *Thirst Quencher* rendezvousing with two stranded ships, telescopes throughout the planet searched for them. The larger telescopes were the first to resolve the images of the damaged, alien craft held in traction by an explorer-tug. The story resulted in tens of millions of flashes to subscribers that clogged the comm networks. Later, when the explorer-tug was identified as the *Outward Bound*, news media producers knew they'd found the story of a lifetime.

Flashes focused on the young, handsome Captain Racine, who was the first man to solve the intricacies of passive asteroid delivery and now the first man to *capture* an alien ship.

When word leaked that there were entities alive aboard the derelict ship, the media became increasingly desperate to gather information on the aliens. News drones followed government officials in the hopes of capturing footage of the visitors' arrival. An enterprising young woman, posing as a terminal employee, gained access to a runway's service apron and managed to snag a vid of the government representatives boarding a shuttle that was tracked to the ships in orbit. The sale of that vid paid for a year of the aspiring journalist's university tuition and brought her to the attention of a prestigious news editor.

Uniformed TSF troopers assembled outside Assembly Hall, forming a protective barrier for the planet's first alien guests. While the enthusiasm of the media was commonplace on New Terra, it was overwhelming to the Méridiens. Reporters jostled one another as they awaited the president's promised statements. Press badges pinned to their shoulders projected small holo-images announcing their media affiliation. Nearly sixty hover-cam drones jockeyed for position above their heads, their operating crews stationed nearby.

As her escort, Alain moved closer to Renée. Instinctively, she had slid behind Alex's shoulder, then chastised herself for her fears and eased out beside him.

The president stepped up to a portable lectern. The vid drones focused on him before rising up for better angles of Alex and the Méridiens. News media had been warned, in no uncertain terms, to maintain a 5-meter distance from the visitors at all times. Any violations would be dealt with severely.

Unfortunately, once vid crews had their establishing shots, they zoomed in for tighter shots of the Méridiens. The producers, viewing the close-ups of the striking faces, forgot all about the warnings and harangued their drone operators to get closer. Even a prominent women's fashion magazine reporter, who had wondered how she'd spin a story about aliens for her readers, was nearly fainting at the sight of the twins. She realized it would hardly matter what words she attached to their images.

The president's message was short and sweet. He summarized the Assembly event and emphasized the momentous occasion for all New Terrans. He promised daily press releases from his office as new information came to light, but emphasized that negotiations were still ongoing. Per both parties' agreement, no mention was made of the silver ship.

Despite the advisement to refrain from asking questions, reporters couldn't contain themselves. Good vids were news and the Méridiens offered the best vid in decades. Reporters shouted questions, and the Méridiens responded as they had been coached. Standing on the Assembly steps, Renée, Étienne, and Alain smiled, waved, and tried to appear as nonthreatening as possible.

When the president ended his comments, General Gonzalez made a call on her tactical comm to a subordinate, Major Tatia Tachenko. The major's reputation in TSF had a curious duality. To the new recruits, who saw her only from a distance, she was a blue-eyed, blonde, buxom beauty – prime fodder for nighttime fantasies. To the veterans, she was "that hard-ass you better not cross."

On the major's order, Terran Security Forces jumped to form a corridor from the waiting hover cars to the president and his guests, firmly guiding the news media out of their path. When the corridor was formed, the president led the way, Alex and the Méridiens following close behind.

As they walked between the rows of troops, a group of attractive young women hoisted a colorful banner on air-floats, yelling out to Alex. "We love you, Captain Racine!" Their banner displayed the same words, but with huge, red lips behind the text.

Renée leaned close to Alex and whispered, "It appears you have admirers, Captain," and smiled to herself as a blush crept up his neck.

-16-

After their return to Government House, the president announced, "My team will join us for lunch shortly. Afterward, we'll have a conference before you depart this afternoon." He escorted them upstairs. An attendant opened the double doors of a suite, and the president waved them inside.

As Alex and Renée walked through the expansive doorway, a young woman squealed Alex's name and rushed at him from across the room, jumping into his arms and wrapping her legs around his waist. Alex held her close, burying his face in the waves of her thick brown hair.

Renée recognized Christie from Alex's family vids. She suffered a moment's pang for her own family, wondering what had become of them.

Duggan and Katie joined their son and daughter. As Alex set his sister down, his mother took his face in both her hands, studying him for a moment before pulling him into a long, tight hug, acting as if he'd been miraculously found after being lost for years. Duggan greeted his son last, delivering a hug and a few hardy back slaps that had the Méridiens cringing.

Watching the family exchange greetings helped the Méridiens understand more about their captain and the New Terrans. Étienne experienced a swell of pride at having been the first to receive the captain's hug on the evening of the visitor's tour. The wash of his emotions leaked to his twin, who smiled in understanding.

The president paused in the corridor when he heard Christie's squeal and grinned, breaking into whistling a tune. The reunion had been planned as a small reward for Alex. But after witnessing the high regard in which the Méridiens held him, he now saw it as one of his more brilliant political strokes, even if it was due more to fortune than planning.

In the suite, Alex introduced his parents and sister to the Méridiens. In the awkward moment of two cultures meeting, Duggan whispered to his son, "How do we greet them, Alex?"

Katie laughed in response to her husband's question. "Duggan," she admonished him and stepped forward to tenderly and warmly hug first Renée and then each of the twins, welcoming them to New Terra. Christie, not be left out, followed suit.

Alex watched Renée as she was hugged by his mother. His concern melted away when Renée, who started tentatively, leaned into his mother's embrace and then hugged his sister as if they were old friends. All the while, Alex reminded himself that many of her immediate family had probably not survived her seventy-year absence.

The twins were pleased by the affectionate hugs of the Racine women, but then they faced Duggan, the reserved one of the family, who extended his hand to them with a quiet smile. The Méridiens eyed his powerful hand, greater even than Alex's, with some trepidation, so they were surprised by his light touch.

The introductions complete, Renée bowed her head and crossed her arms, the twins following suit, "We are honored to greet the family of our captain," she said solemnly. The formal moment over, she lifted her head and smiled, "And now we see from whom he inherited his good heart."

There followed a moment of shared laughter as both Duggan and Katie tried to claim credit for their son's best qualities.

A quarter of an hour later, a polite knock at the door interrupted their conversation. An attendant announced lunch was ready and ushered them downstairs to the dining hall.

Christie grabbed her big brother's arm, bouncing along beside him. "Trust you to be the first man to find aliens ... and for their leader to be absolutely the most beautiful woman in the solar system," she whispered into his ear. At the table, she insinuated herself between Etienne and Alain. Eyeing Alain, she offered him her best teenager smile.

General Gonzalez, Minister Drake, and Minister Jaya joined them shortly, and President McMorris politely steered the conversation away from the important issues facing them. Christie wanted to know about the rescue. Katie wanted to know how Renée's people were faring. Everyone wanted to know about the Méridien home world – the climate, the people, their society.

In one of Christie's more adventurous moments, and there were several, she leaned over to Alain and whispered quietly, "Are you two twins or do all men on your world look like you?"

As Alain mulled over her question, Étienne chose to respond. "We are twins and crèche-mates. There were two other sets of twins, one male and one female, in our crèche."

Christie turned to look at Étienne and then back at Alain, a look of pure confusion spreading across her face. "Alex, I whispered to him," she said, pointing to Alain, "and *he* answered," and she pointed to Étienne.

"Well," the president stepped into the conversation, "this is the part where I talk about state secrets." He looked pointedly at Christie, "Do you understand about state secrets, young lady?"

"Yes, Mr. President, I do."

Alex was surprised by the maturity of his sister's response. He detected his parent's fine hand in her recent education.

"To answer your question, Christie," Renée explained, "we receive implants as children and are trained to use them over the course of several years." She sought the president's gaze. "My people can communicate with one another in many ways."

Christie's response was laced with a few choice slang expressions that registered her delight, none of which translated well for the Méridiens, though they had the rest of the table laughing. Undeterred, Christie launched into a flurry of questions about the implants. *Did they hurt? Could they feel them in their heads? Could she get one?* The latter question evoked more laughter from everyone except Alex. He smiled at first, enjoying his sister's exuberance, then his expression turned thoughtful.

Lunch ended too soon for the Racines, but the day was passing quickly and there was still much to do. At the central rotunda, the family said their goodbyes to Alex and delivered another round of hugs and handshakes to the Méridiens.

The hugs had an element of simple human warmth that Renée found herself enjoying. But it was Katie's parting words that pleased her the most. "When you come to visit, you can bring Alex too," she was told, and the two women shared a quiet laugh.

Alex watched his mother whisper to each of his friends, the conservative and polite Méridiens responding warmly to her hugs and words. His mother was intuitive like that, knowing just what people needed.

Christie offered a final wave to the twins, and Alex chuckled when they returned the gesture in an exact and coordinated replica of her wave, which threw his usually overconfident sister off her step.

* * *

They were guided to the conference room, where President McMorris and the Negotiations Team awaited them. McMorris laid out his immediate plans. All their service needs: their hover cars, drivers, shuttles, and security would be provided by General Gonzalez's TSF.

He challenged them to produce a detailed agreement, or contract, as Ser had called it, demanding that two points be addressed. "One, I need advice on how *not* to ruin our economy with the technology transfer; and two, how we can tie the *Rêveur*'s weapons development to some advancement for New Terra. I don't want us to be standing around with our pants down if those aliens come knocking."

He turned to look at Alex and said, "And I relieve you as ambassador." The sudden stillness at the table caused him to hurry on. "It's obvious to me that you care greatly for your new friends. You should be free to ensure their well-being. If they approve," and he nodded toward Renée, "you will be their official spokesperson."

Renée nodded her agreement. "We would accept no one else, Mr. President."

"Fine," the president beamed, standing up. "Let's get you all on your way back to the *Rêveur*, where you can focus on your negotiations. If you stay any longer, you'll be incessantly stalked by newsy vid drones."

-17-

At the shuttle terminal, General Gonzalez introduced Major Tachenko, another woman who intrigued Renée. She'd first seen the commanding, blue-eyed blonde at the news conference. What fascinated Renée was that she spoke to her people with complete authority, as a Méridien House Leader would, and her troopers were attentive to her every word. She discovered she would be seeing much more of the major, who was in charge of their security and transportation.

Upon their return to the *Rêveur*, the guests were ushered to their cabins, prepared as best they could, and settled in just before evening meal. After they had eaten their fill, they convened on the bridge.

The first two items in the agreement were simple – the New Terrans agreed to the repair and resupply of the *Rêveur* and the retrofit of the *Outward Bound*.

Julien had compiled his master list by combining his internal survey, Alex and Claude's exterior and interior analysis, and the Méridien's inventory accounts. Tara had possessed the *Outward Bound*'s schematics, which Julien had used to plan the retrofit, adding the needed items to the requisition list. To his audience, he described the manufacturing steps, facilities, and personnel required to produce the needed parts for their ships. His list detailed 925 items and the president's team members, scanning the vid display, were mesmerized by the thought of what they'd be able to produce for themselves after taking care of the Méridiens' needs.

"I would like a copy of this list forwarded to my Chief of Projects Derek Sanders. When will you be able to compile this information and send it to him, Julien?" Minister Drake asked, still getting used to conversing with a computer that wasn't a computer.

"Ser Sanders has a copy on his reader now, Minister. I've included some time variables that he should find most helpful, as there are some unknowns for me, such as how long you'll require to assemble the requisite staff."

"That's ... umm ... very efficient of you, Julien," Drake managed to say.

"It's a pleasure to be of service, Minister."

Alex covered his mouth and feigned a frown, as if deep in thought, hiding his grin while Drake composed himself.

The next topic of discussion wasn't so easily resolved ... the weapons. After Alex laid out his concept of creating shields and beam weapons to fight fire with fire, they struggled with how to proceed. In the quiet, Minister Jaya offered the sentiment that he'd hoped this day would never come – building destructive, large-scale weapons.

Uncharacteristically, it was Julien who responded to the minister's sentiment. "I am in agreement with Captain Racine. Our people are proud of their efforts to eliminate aggression and protect all beings. And while we lived alone in our corner of the galaxy, we could indulge our fantasy that all intelligent entities would be like us. Now we know that's not true. And while the truth is painful, we must accept this pain and change. These plans are the first step in that transformation."

There was no ship-to-ship weapons expertise among them and no one had a concept to propose. All they had were questions. So their progress ground to a halt.

As an alternative, Renée suggested that they work on the president's other key point, the methods by which Méridien technology could be introduced to New Terran society without destroying the economic base. But by now, the day's hectic events had caught up with them. The team decided to retire for the evening. Pia met them at the accessway and guided them back to their cabins.

Alex remained on the bridge, lost in thought. He barely acknowledged Renée as she left for her cabin.

"You need your sleep as well, Captain," Julien advised.

"There was an old saying about the blind leading the blind, even though we have no more blind," he murmured.

"An appropriate sentiment in these circumstances, Captain. But without data, we *are* blind despite our desire to explore this new field. I've searched my records and it appears I was never given information regarding weapons. I would suspect this omission was purposeful."

Julien dimmed the bridge lights while Alex sat in the command chair pondering the problem. The view of the stars and the planet below provided a quiet background to his thoughts. It was more than an hour later when he suddenly sat up. "I wonder if we have it?" he exclaimed and then raced off the bridge.

Geneviève and Terese squeaked as the captain barreled past them with a hurried apology. They queried Julien on the nature of the emergency and received, <Do not be concerned. Our captain is just excited.>

Alex had Julien guide him to Jaya's cabin, where he pounded urgently on the door. It slid open, revealing the minister dressed in his sleepwear and holding his reader, "Yes, Captain?"

"Minister, do we have the colonists' records – the ones they downloaded from their ship? It just occurred to me that they might include Earth's military weapons."

"Captain Ulam's logs state that the first mate transferred the entire ship's library to portable memory cores. I know for a fact that the early colonists depended on much of that knowledge and made backup copies to preserve it. How much of that library survives today, I don't know. But I know who has the archives." He grabbed a robe and they dashed back to the bridge.

* * *

At 7.88 hours, Julien notified Renée, Alex, and the team of the shuttle's arrival. Alex and Jaya were ecstatic, while the others were puzzled since no delivery had been scheduled. Responding to Renée's query, Julien cryptically replied that the captain and Minister Jaya had been quite busy last night.

When the *Rêveur*'s inner airlock door slid open, Major Tachenko extended a sealed case to Alex. "Hope this is what you need, Captain," she said. "We shook a great many people out of bed to get these records. It appears the colonists' cores were dispersed to several universities and none of them knew if they had the entire original library."

As Renée arrived at the airlock with the remainder of the team in tow, Major Tachenko delivered a quick salute. "Ser, we loaded a double-ended, flexible docking tunnel this morning. We can secure one end to your airlock hatch and leave the other end sealed. That way the shuttles won't have to deploy docking collars to transfer personnel. We just require your permission, Ser."

"Permission granted, Major Tachenko." As the airlock sealed, Renée heard the major ordering her people to begin the installation. The part where she referenced a New Terran animal was lost in translation.

Alex hurried off to the bridge with the package. Jaya ran after him, rubbing his hands together and chuckling all the way. Forewarned by Julien this time, the Méridiens cleared the corridor as the two men raced past, offering apologies.

"Where do you want them, Julien?" Alex asked, rushing onto the bridge, Jaya right behind him. Julien directed him to a lower cabinet, and Alex opened the carrying case and extracted a stack of memory cores enclosed in their own casing. "These will need power as well as data access," he said.

"I understand, Captain."

Alex placed the cores in the cabinet. Following Julien's directions, he took a cable from the cabinet and slotted one end into a bank of connectors and held the other end against the core's data port. He heard Jaya's *wow* over his shoulder as the cable end morphed to accommodate the casing's connector and glanced over to see a huge grin plastered across the minister's face.

Renée and the other two team members arrived on the bridge to witness the two men on their hands and knees with their heads buried inside a cabinet.

"We understand you two have been busy." Drake said.

"The connection has been made," Julien announced. "Allow me one moment, Captain, while I review the organizational structure." They all waited in silence for Julien to continue. "My analysis is complete and I'm transferring data." Moments later, "I'm ready, Captain. I can review the files or we can query the data together, as you desire."

Alex climbed to his feet alongside Jaya. "Query, please. Images, Earth, war ships." He said excitedly, ignoring the people behind him.

An image of an ancient, ocean-sailing vessel with rows of protuberances along its hull appeared on the central screen. Alex, confused by the image, said, "Uh, let's work from the most recent years." Then he caught on. "Very nice, Julien," he chuckled. "Perhaps I was remiss in not complimenting you on your inimitable skills accessing foreign data modules and integrating the records in such an expedient manner."

"One never goes wrong with a well-placed compliment, Captain."

A spate of snickers followed from the others as they caught the joke.

"Yes, well it goes without saying that you are a superlative individual where the manipulation of data is concerned."

"Yes, Captain, I can see where this conversation is heading, so I'll return to your query."

Julien began displaying images across all three bridge screens. "These are Earth *fighters*, as they were called. Some traveled in space and directed their flight through engines spread on extended booms. They employed a host of offensive and defensive armaments – missiles, machine guns, flares, and many more items. The library has details on each of these items such as how they were employed and their manufacturing specifications."

Out of the corner of his eye, Alex noticed Renée had come to stand beside him. They all continued to watch as Julien filled the huge screens with images of Earth's fighters. Overjoyed with their find, Alex couldn't contain himself any longer. He whooped, picked Renée up, and twirled her lightly around. "We found it," he crowed and then belatedly set her down with a contrite grin on his face.

She laughed. "It would seem so, my Captain."

Minister Jaya updated his teammates. "Alex knocked or, rather, pounded on my door last night and asked about the colonists' archives. I told him they were at the universities. So we contacted Major Tachenko, who contacted the university presidents, archive administrators, and techs to compile their archives."

"You did this during the night ... I mean you woke these people up during the night?" asked Drake.

"It seemed most expedient," Jaya apologized.

"How many universities responded to the request?" Maria asked.

"Why, all of them."

"That probably made the major popular," she commented.

"That's what the major delivered this morning," he said, gesturing at the screens. "She is a most impressive and efficient woman, the major." It was quite a compliment coming from the minister who oversaw technology development for the entire solar system.

"Julien, perform a quick search for energy weapons and shields for large space vessels," Alex requested.

"Searching, Captain ... there are no energy weapons, and the shields are only for protection from space dust. They'd be insufficient against the silver ship."

"Okay, so plan A is out. What about one of these fighters? Could you adapt one of these designs with Méridien technology?"

"It should be quite feasible, Captain, but I would need to monitor test results at every stage of development."

"What about their dimensions? How many could we fit in the *Rêveur*'s bay?"

"We would have to remove at least one of our shuttles to allow room for up to two fighters, Captain, depending on the final specifications."

Maria interceded. "So, say Julien designs you a fighter. Who's going to fly it when the Méridiens return home?"

Renée turned to the general, "Why, he intends to fly it," she said, pointing a finger at Alex. "Don't you, Captain?" This created a flurry of conversation, in which Renée and Alex took no part. She stared at him while he pretended to listen intently to the others.

Finally, Alex cleared his throat to get their attention. "Let's just focus on the fact that we now have an answer to the next aspect of our agreement. And while the *Rêveur* might only have room for one or two of these fighters, New Terra can build as many as it wishes. I suggest we leave Julien to review the data for other concepts that might be of use while he works on a fighter design. In the meantime, I'm headed for morning meal." And as no one else had eaten yet, they trooped after him willingly enough.

Alex was grateful Renée didn't return to the subject of who would pilot the fighter once they sat down to eat. She was quiet for most of the meal, but toward the end, she said, "One of President McMorris' requests was that we devise a means by which to transfer our technology to New Terra without destroying its economy, but it's outside this group's expertise …" Minister Drake started to speak but she raised a hand to forestall him, "but not outside Julien's expertise. I've requested that he develop economic models for the transfer. He needs more information on your financial systems before he can get started and I've relayed this request to Major Tachenko, who is gathering the information Julien requires. When he's finished, we'll forward the models to you for your consideration."

The ministers and the general sat there stunned, absorbing the enormous problem-solving power of which a SADE was capable. Minister Drake finally spoke up. "And I expected to be up here for at least thirty days."

Minister Jaya inquired, "What would it take to get our own SADE?" his expression hopeful.

-18-

Eight days later, Alex and the Méridiens were riding to a second emergency session of the Assembly in a TSF convoy of hover cars. Renée found she was more nervous about this presentation than the last one, even though much of the burden would be carried by President McMorris.

Major Tachenko's troopers guided them into Assembly Hall and onto the dais, ensuring there was no interference from Assembly security.

After the president's opening remarks, greeting the representatives and his guests, he got to the heart of his presentation. "My purpose here today is to present the agreement that has been negotiated with the Méridiens and ask for your approval. We won't debate it today. What I want is to demonstrate why I support this agreement and place the full weight of my office behind its approval."

"First, you will view a tour of the *Rêveur* taken by five of our own. And please keep in mind that the technology you'll see is only what was left after their ship was nearly destroyed." At his request, the Méridiens had edited out Downing's blunder. He wasn't about to embarrass the conservative faction for political gain. This was too important. He wanted ... no ... he *needed* the Méridiens to continue to make a good impression.

He turned to Renée, who signaled the holo-vid projector affixed to the lectern. Once again the Assembly was awed by the power of the tiny projector as it displayed the visitors' tour compiled from Julien's vid pickups and the Méridiens' implants. They witnessed the grav-pallets and grav-belts in action; heard how medical nanites repaired traumatic injuries and manipulated genetic material; witnessed an imaging display of an embedded implant; and watched Renée's belt harness protect her from Étienne's stun weapon.

The holo-vid ended there and President McMorris picked up the narration without missing a beat. "And you should know that our own Assemblyman Downing volunteered to test the efficacy of the stun weapon himself, although at its lowest setting." He chuckled and the Assembly responded appropriately, several associates near Downing patting him on the back. "We've prepared a live demonstration for you to witness the power of the Méridien technology that our people could have today."

Above the president, a vid screen activated, displaying a hospital emergency room. A patient lay in the bed surrounded by a doctor and two nurses. "Our demonstration is of the Méridien medical nanites," the president continued. "Due to the sensitive nature of this information and the potential medical liability, we chose not to test these nanites on an injured citizen, but rather on a TSF volunteer, Sergeant Thompson. His lower right arm was deliberately broken by a surgeon. How are you, Sergeant?"

"I would say I'm in pain, Mr. President."

"Yes, well, thank you for volunteering, Sergeant. Doctor Oberon, the arm appears to be quite swollen and broken, but have you confirmed the break through your imager?"

The vid drone shifted closer to the doctor. "Yes, Mr. President, it's a compound fracture of the right ulna."

"Has anything been done to treat the injury, Doctor?"

"No, Mr. President."

"And under ordinary circumstances, Doctor, how long would this take to heal?"

"About thirty days, Mr. President, with cellular boost injections. He would need another thirty before he could apply maximum leverage to the arm."

Renée took up the narration. "We've become familiar with New Terran physiology through our contact with Captain Racine and your Negotiations Team. At the cellular level, we are amazingly similar despite our hundreds of years of separation."

The drone rotated to Terese, who had been standing out of sight of the camera. The gathered Assembly had just seen her in the prior vid and her striking red hair, bright green eyes, and pale face were immediately identifiable. She accessed her medical tablet and pulled a small device from its side.

"Terese will employ a cranial wave modulator against the sergeant's temple," Renée explained. As the shiny metal disk, only 1.5 centimeters in diameter, was applied to the sergeant's temple, his grimace disappeared, replaced by a calm expression as he slumped back into the emergency ward's bed.

"Doctor," the president requested, "can you verify the patient's state?"

The doctor reviewed his med-tablet. "All vital signs are strong. His brain waves indicate that he's in a deep sleep."

"That's correct," Renée continued. "Terese's device blocks sensory input to the brain without interrupting the autonomic nervous system. Since this is an artificial state, the patient will remain asleep, unaware and without pain, until the device is deactivated."

Terese loaded a small syringe and placed it in a holder beside her tablet.

"Terese is now programming some of our stock of medical nanites, which she will inject into the wounded area," Renée explained as Terese applied the aero-syringe. "And now we must wait."

During the next hour, Renée told the Assembly of some of the other technology her people had developed. At the end of her summary, she explained that, per the agreement, all Méridien technology would be given to the New Terrans. It created such uproar that the Hall monitor had to call for quiet three times before the commotion subsided.

Major Tachenko received a quick comm. She caught the president's eye and nodded toward the screen. He took the podium once more as the screen was activated. Terese turned to the vid lens and nodded.

"Doctor," the President said, "would you please use your imager to view the break? And may we have it on screen while you view it?"

The doctor positioned the imager over the sergeant's arm and tapped the controller screen. The vid drone hovered in front of the imager's screen. He mumbled, "Just one moment, Mr. President." Then he started tapping the screen again.

"Is there a problem, Doctor?" the president asked with a trace of humor in his voice.

"Sorry, Mr. President, I was told the nanites would accelerate the healing. But there's no evidence of a break," the doctor said incredulously. "There's not even a shadow of one."

"Terese, if you could remove the device from the patient's head, please," the president requested. The drone pulled back to cover the emergency room bed as Terese did as asked.

The sergeant came to with a confused expression on his face. "How long was I out?" he asked.

"You were asleep for a nearly an hour, Sergeant. How do you feel?" the president asked.

The sergeant carefully lifted his arm and slowly rotated it. The noise level in the Assembly ratcheted up considerably, and the Hall monitor requested silence again.

The sergeant looked at the doctor, at Terese, and then back to the screen. "I feel fine, Mr. President. And I don't mean fine for just having broken my arm; I mean fine as if it was never broken in the first place, although the skin looks a little worse for wear."

Terese leaned over the sergeant, who smiled up at her, and smeared a light gray, jelly-like substance, which quickly disappeared into his skin.

"Hello, Sergeant," Renée called out, since he was no longer focused on the vid drone but on the red-haired Méridien standing next to him. When he finally looked into the drone's lens, she explained, "Terese has just applied a nanites compound that will heal the skin."

"That's fine," he said distractedly as he turned his attention back to Terese. More than one sympathetic chuckle rippled through the audience.

"Sergeant, your attention please," the president commanded. "Thank you for volunteering, Sergeant Thompson. Your participation in this demonstration was most commendable," the president assured him and received a sharp salute in response.

"It's been my honor to be the first New Terran experiment for alien technology, Mr. President," the sergeant piped up. "One request, Sir. Can we keep her?" he asked pointing to Terese, which evoked a round of laughter and stomping from the Assembly.

"That concludes our presentation," the president said as the Assembly's applause died down. Your readers are receiving a copy of the agreement as we speak. At my request, this Assembly will stay in session until you are ready to vote, though that period will not exceed seven days. Accommodations have been made at several nearby establishments for the entire body at the government's expense. You'll find that information in your readers as well."

The Assembly was stunned into silence by the president's words. Not in many, many years had they been unable to control their own calendar. They'd need several days just to analyze the agreement.

The president and his guests exited while bedlam broke out among the representatives. They examined their readers for the relevant files, contacted staff members to relay the news of the mandatory session, and ordered food. Most important, they started making comm calls to key constituents.

Powerful representatives supported by captains of industry were shocked to find that the government would control all the astounding Méridien technology – first, for the manufacture of parts for the *Rêveur* and the *Outward Bound*; second, to build fighters; and finally, for dissemination to the public and industry.

Assemblyman Downing and his faction, who were the primary opposition to President McMorris and his Cabinet, applied all the pressure they could to sway other representatives to reject the proposal. They wanted control of the new tech without any government interference.

Downing's dynasty founder, Clayton Downing I, a Canadian billionaire, had made his fortune from mining and probably did as much as any man to pollute the face of Earth. His mining concerns were what ultimately got him killed. During a visit to upper Mongolia, Chinese separatists attacked the mine, and he was killed in a mortar explosion.

Rather ironic since that was what his companies did to Earth – blew it up – as they strip-mined huge swaths of land.

His son, Clayton Downing II, inherited his father's fortune and chose to sink billions of credits into the colony ship, the *New Terra*. The caveat was that his son and family received reserved seats. His daughter chose not to go.

Following the *New Terra*'s disastrous accident, Clayton Downing III was removed from his sleep module by crew members and loaded into a shuttle with his wife and two children. It wasn't, as some later groused, that he was privileged. He was a mining engineer with multiple disciplines in geology, hydrology, and construction, and his wife was a renowned doctor specializing in transplant surgery. Clayton III suffered the drudges of the new colony along with everyone else for eleven years and died after being bitten by a poisonous, lizard-like animal.

Representative Downing had been irritated throughout his life that his family was never given its fair due. His ancestor had been the largest individual contributor to the colony ship, and Clayton wanted New Terrans to acknowledge his family as the movers and shakers who helped deliver them to their new home. To make matters worse, President McMorris was an egalitarian, a man who would definitely not pay tribute to his betters, which was how Clayton perceived himself.

But two points worked against the conservative elitists led by Clayton. First, the proposal contained a foreword from the president that it would be the only version of the agreement offered to the Assembly. Second, Julien disseminated the economic models for the distribution of Méridien technology. In each scenario, they heard him narrate the initial suppositions, the technology distribution method, the economic modeling employed, and the results from day one to ten years out. They watched as some companies went bankrupt overnight while others weathered the change and grew enormously rich. Unemployment often spiraled out of control as automation took over; government support services were inadequate to meet the needs of the unemployed. In several scenarios, companies sought out the Méridiens for trade deals, forgoing upgrades to their own manufacturing plants.

The outcome was the same for every model in which technology was controlled by private industry – New Terran society, as it existed today, would come to an end. Only controlled distribution over time would allow their society to retain its essence. Toward this end, Julien recommended the new technology be fed into social entities, such as the government's health services; power and communications infrastructure; and the government's habitat experiments.

The conservative opponents argued the economic models were invalid since the SADE's predictions would inevitably be biased toward the government's position.

But the majority didn't agree, saying it didn't matter how they got the technology. Didn't they trust their elected president and his ministers to manage this marvelous bounty? And that was the crux of the argument – who could be entrusted with their people's future – the industrialists or the government? This was New Terra, not Earth. When the representatives reached out to their constituents to discuss the agreement, the people overwhelming supported the government.

New Terra was a world where voter turnout averaged over 91 percent. The people carefully researched their candidates, and the media devoutly published a candidate's background, voting history, and major supporters. The public kept a close eye on the government.

One day before the deadline, the Assembly majority called for a vote and the agreement was approved, as submitted, by an 83 percent majority.

-19-

Within the hour following the Assembly's vote, the president placed a comm to the *Outward Bound.* The Negotiations Team had returned to the *Rêveur* with Alex and the Méridiens to await word of the Assembly's decision. They used the time to develop a list of contractors for the manufacturing sites that met Julien's specifications.

The president outlined the steps he'd set in motion. A location adjacent to Prima's space shuttle terminal would be the first manufacturing site. The team's contractors, who had signed stringent security agreements, were being mobilized to modify the site – power, comm cabling, environmental systems, network and security systems, dormitories, and meal facilities – in expectation of Julien's requirements. Major Tachenko was responsible for site security.

"The Negotiations Team is hereby disbanded," the president said. "You are now my Technology Transfer Team. Congratulations on your promotion!"

Alex placed a comm to Major Tachenko for transport only to discover she was on approach to the *Rêveur* and would be arriving in hours to collect the team. They used the university's memory core to transfer Julien's master plan: building layouts, infrastructure, and schematics with tech manuals for the machines that would produce the tools, circuitry, crystals, nanites, and supplies the Méridiens required.

The team waited with Alex and Renée for Major Tachenko to cycle through the airlock. She greeted Maria with a sharp salute. Maria motioned the major over to her and addressed everyone. "I'm ordering two shuttle flights a day at 10 and 20 hours, until further notice. This will prevent transfer delays of personnel or material. But I want you two," she said, indicating Alex and Renée, "to notify Major Tachenko if either of you are riding so that security is prepared."

"Understood, General," Renée said. Then, much to Alex's surprise, she leaned forward to hug Maria and shook hands with Drake and Jaya, who carefully carried the memory core.

* * *

The new manufacturing location, Transfer Station One (TS-1), was a flurry of personnel hiring and orientation – engineers, fabricators, techs, support personnel, and security.

Julien was in constant contact by comm and shuttle with TS-1 engineers during the fabrication of the first generation or GEN-1 machine. Each new part or circuit had to be flown up to the *Rêveur*, plugged into Julien's diagnostic network, and then sent back to TS-1 as approved or failed.

Even with personnel working in shifts around the clock, it took thirty-three days to assemble the first GEN-1 machine. And that milestone was only achieved because a SADE was driving the manufacturing process and quality inspection. The first machine, which Julien had designed as a master, was dedicated to fabricating other GEN-1 machines, whose built-in diagnostics allowed components to be checked for errors, eliminating the need to transport the parts to the *Rêveur*.

With the newly fabricated parts, GEN-2 machines were assembled, which were immediately engaged in creating the parts for the first GEN-3 machine. The TS-1 site had doubled in size and staff in just fifty-two days.

Alex, Renée, and the twins had flown planetside the day before. Security woke them when the engineers completed their final assembly. At 6.50 hours, everyone who wanted to witness the event had gathered around the GEN-3 machine. The lead engineer powered up the machine. Its sophistication was such that it was completely self-adjusting, able to compare its circuit and mechanical responses to its required specifications and make any necessary adjustments. When it completed its internal diagnostics, the machine's voice emanated from speakers, "All parameters are met. Ready."

The techs had already loaded the required components, so all that was required of the lead engineer was to verbally request the first item displayed in Julien's list. A quarter of an hour later, the machine produced a flawless Méridien circuit board. Four hours after the first board was produced, a bundle of boards caught the scheduled shuttle flight to the *Rêveur.*

Edouard and Claude stood ready to receive the package. They were walking to the bridge before the airlock transfer hatch was even sealed behind the shuttle's copilot.

* * *

In TS-1's dining room, Alex and Renée were enjoying New Terran fruit juices, celebrating the milestone that had been achieved that morning, when their comms activated, "Good day, Ser and Captain."

Both shouted, "Julien!" The other diners turned to look for the person Alex was addressing, Renée having responded via implant.

"The new boards are working within the expected parameters," Julien said. "The ship's local comm transmission is now online. I'm able to communicate directly with either of you so long as you are within range of TS-1's comm station."

As they expressed their joy at the achievement, Julien delivered even better news. "In addition, I can now control the GEN machines. I'm directing engineering personnel to produce Méridien ear comms for all TS-1 personnel. Soon, we will have comm stations and ear comms for the offices of the president and the team. In three days, we will be able to conference in any manner you choose."

Renée covered Alex's hand with hers. She sent him a message via Julien, <Home! Our journey back has truly begun.>

-20-

"Captain, we have an intrusion at TS-1," Julien said, simultaneously sending the message to Ser via her implant.

The two of them left their meal half-finished and raced to the bridge.

"What particulars do you have?" asked Alex as they navigated the corridors.

"TS-1's master database has been copied. I queried Ser Marion Delbert, the station manager, as to the reason for the copy, suspecting a problem with the storage material. Ser Delbert reported that she'd received no request for a data transfer and there were no maintenance issues."

"Who accessed the data?" Alex asked as they arrived on the bridge.

"One moment, Captain." Then an instant later, "The access code belongs to Engineer Sebastien Velis."

"Do we have the location of Major Tachenko?" Renée asked.

"Ser Delbert has alerted station security, who contacted the major. She will be at TS-1 within a quarter hour. Security is working to relay our comm to her."

Renée asked, "Captain, what does this unauthorized copying mean?"

"It means that someone has stolen the data for their own use."

"But if they make a Méridien product, it will be known immediately."

"Anyone can use the data to design a product's endpoint years down the road and then slowly introduce *improvements* over time until that goal is reached."

"What will happen when they're caught?"

"*If* they're caught, they'll face trial; and if they're convicted, they'll go to prison."

"They will be incarcerated?" Renée asked incredulously after Julien explained *prison*.

"It's what they deserve," Alex growled.

"I have Major Tachenko on the comm," Julien announced.

"Major, Captain Racine here with Ser. What do you know?"

"The engineer and data are gone. According to my staff, surveillance shows him leaving TS-1 and getting into a hover car just moments after the copying was complete. He left his reader on his desk, so we can't use that to locate the man, and the hover car's auto-tracker was disabled. This was a well-planned theft. You have my apologies, Ser. I've been remiss in my job."

"Major, I believe you do your job very well. I, for one, would not have believed one of the staff would do this."

"Do we have anything that would help us find him?" Alex asked.

"We're researching him now. In the meantime, I've sent troopers to his residence, his parents' home, and we are contacting his known acquaintances. General Gonzalez has been updated and is notifying the president and the team. We'll know more in a couple of hours."

"Thank you, Major. *Rêveur*, fini," said Renée.

"Captain, Ser, we do have an option," Julien said. "My data has a unique signature that I can detect when it crosses any network that I can access."

"Which networks would those be?" Alex asked.

"All New Terran networks, Captain, but I think it would be wise to keep that private."

"Uh ... does that include government networks?"

"If the network has access to your comm infrastructure, I can access it."

"Black space, Julien."

"Precisely, Captain."

"Do you need anything from us?" Alex asked.

"Negative, Captain. I will disseminate watchers to each infrastructure node. I will receive a signal the instant the data crosses a node, allowing me to track its server destination."

Over the next few hours, few facts came to light regarding the theft. Velis did not go home. His parents and his friends heard nothing from him, and his financial accounts were not accessed. One critical piece of information did come to light, volunteered by his latest girlfriend.

"Sebastien has developed a big problem," she told the TSF investigator. "He's become an inveterate gambler, and he's an inveterate loser. Over the past year, he's sold just about everything we've acquired. He can rot, as far as I'm concerned."

Days later, Major Tachenko's report to the president, which was disseminated to key personnel, stated that Sebastien Velis had accumulated extensive gambling debts, which were probably used to leverage him to steal the TS-1 database. No trace could be found of the engineer.

He had disappeared.

* * *

One day after two men had picked up Sebastien outside TS-1, they eased their hover car deep into the woods, 126 kilometers from Prima. In the sandy soil near a stand of guriel trees, they dug a deep hole, laid the naked body of the engineer in the pit, and doused it with an industrial solution designed to dissolve organic tissue. They carefully reconditioned the ground to disguise their tampering.

The men had disabled their vehicle's auto-tracker, and they took pains to wipe the car's GPS memory after every trip. Back in Prima, they returned to their reader sales and repair service in a small industrial building.

The stolen data was transferred to a new storage device. To avoid being tracked they destroyed the original. The directive they'd received from their contractor stated, "Under no circumstances, review the data or connect the storage module to a networked device. Otherwise, you will jeopardize your final payment and possibly your lives."

But the problem with larcenous men is that they'll steal from anyone and the Frasier brothers were no exception. The following evening, after a jaunt to a private club, enjoying too many drinks and a shared woman, they returned to the shop and convinced each other that the more they knew about the data, the better they could *value* the deal.

After connecting their storage device to a reader and paging through several diagrams and tech manuals, they realized the designs were of advanced technology – Méridien. A celebration ensued. Dancing around their shop floor, they laughed and yelled, reveling in the mountain of creds they would soon possess.

After several more drinks, they hatched their ill-fated plan. The data was uploaded to a private memory account, the storage device destroyed, and a ransom message sent to the contractor. They demanded fifty times the original price to deliver the data. At the end of their message, they typed *alien* to announce that they knew what they had.

* * *

Alex awoke to a pounding on his door. He grabbed his ear comm. "Julien, what's the problem?"

"Your pardon, Captain, for the intrusion. Ser is at your door. We require your immediate attention."

"Let her in, Julien." Both of his doors slid open and the lights blinked on as he heard her rush through his cabin into his sleeping quarters.

"Come to the bridge, Captain," she ordered. "Julien has detected the stolen data." Then she ran back out.

Alex climbed into his ship suit as fast as he could, hopping down the corridor while pulling on his boots. "Where's the data, Julien?" Alex asked as he entered the bridge.

"It's been uploaded to a private security company's memory storage account. I have the address of the building for Major Tachenko."

Alex checked his chronometer. At 3.91 hours, few people would be available to them. "Who can you reach, Julien?"

"Neither the major nor the team members are available, Captain. We have two choices: TS-1 night security or the president."

"Make it the president." Once the comm station had been installed at Government House, the president had ordered it staffed day and night. "Relay a message to him that we have an emergency requiring his authority," Alex requested.

Renée curled up in the command chair and resisted the urge to go back to sleep. In contrast, Alex paced the bridge.

Nearly a quarter hour later, the president answered the comm in a gravelly voice, dulled with sleep. "What's the nature of the emergency, Captain?"

"The stolen data has been located, Mr. President."

"Located? Where? By whom?" he asked, his voice clearing quickly.

"It's in a private memory account. We have the address."

"Why didn't General Gonzalez contact me directly? Why are you telling me this?" When dead silence followed his question, he answered it himself. "Because her people didn't find it ... Julien did."

"Affirmative, Mr. President." Alex responded.

"That's going to have to remain between us," he grumbled. "Julien, send me the particulars … the account number, account holder, company, and address to my private reader. I presume you can reach it."

"Yes, Mr. President, you have the information. I've included the account password."

"Of course, you have, Julien."

Everyone, Julien included, winced at the president's tone. They were not only guilty of breaking countless New Terran laws, but they'd just demonstrated that the planet's best encryption, private or government, was child's play to a SADE.

"I don't have to tell all of you that this comm never happened, and you never discovered the data. I'll turn it over to General Gonzalez and allow her to devise a means of dealing with the thieves."

Julien was hesitant to ask his question, but knew that there might be unforeseen consequences if he didn't. "Mr. President, would you recommend I remove my block now or when the general is ready to enter the premises?"

"You blocked the account?"

"In a manner, Mr. President, I blocked data access to the security company … all accounts."

"May we be saved from ourselves," the president sighed into the comm. "Remove the blocks at once, Julien. There must be no sign that you've been in the system."

"Understood, Mr. President, it's done."

"Mr. President," Renée said, "for the record, Julien requested permission to seek out the data. And while it might have been stolen from your facilities, it belongs to us until the terms of the agreement have been satisfied."

"Ser de Guirnon," said the president, slipping on his political shoes, "neither of us wishes to see this data in the public domain. I'm very grateful that you located it and I'm chagrined that our security procedures didn't prevent its theft. That having been said, I don't want the public-at-large ... let me rephrase that ... I don't want *anyone* knowing what the four of us know … that our data security encryption is useless against Méridien technology, particularly against Julien. Good night."

McMorris cut the comm before anyone could speak. Renée was now wide awake, and Alex slumped into a command chair, his desire to pace curtailed.

In the quiet, Julien asked, "Captain, have we endangered the agreement?"

"No, Julien, the president will keep our secret."

"He's not obligated to inform your Assembly?" Renée asked.

"Yes and no, but that's a discussion for a later time. Let me commend you on locating the data copy, Julien. Now, let's see what TSF does with the information. Good night, you two."

* * *

At 6.32 hours Major Tachenko delivered her presidential writ to the owner of the private security firm where the informer indicated the data was being stored. The owner woke the general manager, who in turn woke the lead engineer.

The staff was gathered around a network control monitor with Major Tachenko and two TSF troopers hovering over them. When the lead engineer opened the account log-in screen and entered the user name on record, Major Tachenko shoved her reader in front of his face. He looked back and forth between the text and her angry face then quickly entered the passcode.

Once the account was accessed, the TSF sergeant tapped him on the shoulder, and the engineer slid out of his seat. The major ordered the owner and employees to wait in the GM's office.

With a few keystroke entries, the sergeant accessed the Méridien data and copied the information to a portable storage device. Dummy files were substituted, including a network tracking file. The account's registration and payments were made anonymously, but the TSF corporal was a network specialist and able to trace the node through which the data was uploaded. The sergeant cross-referenced the addresses of known criminals within a half-square kilometer of the node's service area. One address stood out – the reader sales and service center of the Frasier brothers.

When the major and her two troopers broke through the shop's door, they found the brothers passed out in a back room. Bleary-eyed and nearly incoherent, the hung over men were restrained and transported to a TSF garrison holding cell. Later, stimulants were used to revive them, and they were read their rights and charged.

With its damaged side, the brother's hover car was easily matched to recordings made by TS-1 security cams. It was transported to a TSF warehouse and examined by forensic techs, who determined Sebastien Velis had occupied the vehicle's back seat and, most tellingly, the rear carryall.

After hours of interrogation, the brothers confessed to the murder of Velis and the theft of the government property in exchange for sentencing leniency. Their confession yielded two key pieces of information – there had been only one copy of the data and the person who'd hired them remained unknown. They had dealt with the contractor only by etherware, anonymous, untraceable messaging.

* * *

Late at night, Alex was sitting in the dimly lit bridge and mulling over Major Tachenko's report on the Frasier brothers.

"You're thinking of the major's report, are you not, Captain? And you're dissatisfied by the outcome," Julien said, hazarding a guess.

"You're correct on both counts."

"It's easy to surmise, Captain. I am of the same opinion."

"This was done by someone who had inside knowledge, someone with power and money. And, failing the first time, he will try again."

An inside job – the term harkened back to the detective stories Julien had absorbed. When he catalogued data, it was rarely reviewed again until required. But the old English detective novels, especially those of Agatha Christie and Sir Arthur Conan Doyle, found in the colonists' archives, were different. At night, when all was quiet, he would read through a few novels slowly, for a SADE that is, absorbing the cat-and-mouse games of the master sleuths and the evil villains.

"If these individuals succeed in their infamous ways," Julien predicted, "it will undo the intent of the pact. The New Terrans responsible would become incredibly rich and powerful."

"And what do you think we should do about that, Sherlock?" asked Alex, aware of Julien's penchant for the old detective novels.

"Do we not risk the ire of your president and Ser if we were to proceed?"

"Yes ... if we were caught by either one."

"That would mean we would have to practice deception if found out … a trait possessed by New Terrans but difficult, if not impossible, for a Méridien to imitate. An individual who develops such faculties and possesses few scruples becomes a dangerous person."

"True, but good people must often adopt devious means to stop dangerous ones."

"Is that not the beginning of moral corruption, Captain … the adoption of your enemy's ways in order to defeat them?"

"So, I take it you decline to follow the evidence."

"On the contrary, Captain. I'm eager to start. I just wanted us to be clear about the nature of the ground we will be treading on."

"Muddy and treacherous, I would say, my friend."

"Precisely, Captain. Tally-ho."

-21-

TS-1's theft was never made public. Marion Delbert, the station manager, loved her new job and was happy to comply with Major Tachenko's request for silence. And the security company owner certainly wanted no one to know his systems had been used for such a crime. The major continued to plug every possible leak until she was satisfied word wouldn't get out.

Production had continued at full pace during the search for Velis. GEN-2 machines produced raw nanites while GEN-3 machines processed them into differentiated classes – medical nanites, cable repair nanites, and an injectable liquid for hull and bulkhead plate molds.

As the supplies were produced, New Terran personnel moved aboard the *Rêveur* to take on the expanding repair work, getting their first taste of life with the Méridiens. Major Tachenko assigned a few specially chosen troopers, mostly women, to maintain the good behavior of the New Terrans.

EVA teams buttoned up the remaining hull interiors; repaired the internal bulkheads; reconnected severed comm, power cabling, and lift tubes; and reinstituted environmental systems.

Each evening was a novel experience for the New Terrans. They indulged their taste buds with Méridien food and, one by one, told their stories. More than one individual experienced a cathartic moment when a deeply personal story, locked inside for years, was finally shared.

Twenty-seven days after the New Terrans first boarded, the Méridiens had access to every location on the ship, except the engine space. However, they were still dependent on the power supply from the *Outward Bound*'s generators.

* * *

After evening meal, Alex and Renée retired to the bridge, where they sat alone.

"Julien, is there any concern for our power supply?" Alex asked. He'd never operated the beam generators for such an extended period of time. There was no reason to suspect a problem would develop. He was just anxious for the safety of the Méridiens.

"There is no concern, Captain, I've been monitoring your generators since we installed the intership link and your equipment remains within operating parameters. You have, as you'd say, gotten your creds worth."

"Good to know," laughed Alex.

"Captain, Ser, I have an update from Minister Drake. The president has authorized the funds for Transfer Station Two and located a site. Purchase of the site will be concluded tomorrow."

TS-2 would manufacture the Méridien crystals. For safety, the site was located far outside Prima. Crystal growth was innocuous, but even Méridien tech hadn't devised a sure means of testing the electrical pathways of a power-crystal as it grew. Once a crystal fully matured, it was placed in a reinforced containment facility and powered up slowly over two days. If it reached full charge without exploding, it was deemed stable, discharged, transferred to its new location, and installed in a power bank.

All Méridien crystal varieties – power, navigation, and communication – were produced at TS-2 for the *Rêveur* and the *Outward Bound* as well as the new smaller crystals for the fighters that Julien had designed.

Medical nanites from TS-1 were the first tech transfer to the New Terran populace. Since New Terra practiced socialized medicine, the nanites were quickly integrated into hospital procedures and employed by emergency wards in life-threatening situations.

Following the distribution of medical nanites, the Ministry of Technology announced electrical companies could purchase power-crystals at cost from TS-2 to replace worn transformers or to install them at new facilities. The Méridien crystals were rated for 300 years, eight times the life of New Terran transformers. Their companies' contractual agreements with the government required they pass the maintenance savings on to the populace.

Nano-cables were next, right behind power-crystals. They were also purchased at cost and used in backbone comm and power cabling. Again, savings were to be passed on to the populace, a decision generating widespread public approval. Of course, the fact that the distribution scheme was the plan of a self-aware digital entity from another star system wasn't published.

-22-

When TS-2 began growing its first crystals, construction began on Transfer Station Three. Located on a rocky outcrop off the coast of Prima, the government-owned strip of land was aptly named Barren Island.

The *Rêveur*'s engines and support structure along with the new fighters would be built there. In the future, a second orbital station would be built to construct fighting ships to protect the New Terran system and sail between the stars. The island's future naval academy graduates would fill the ships.

Barren Island's craggy terrain was transformed into a complex complete with admin and engineering buildings, testing and supply warehouses, manufacturing structures equipped with GEN-3 machines, a flight terminal, and two landing strips. The TS-3 station manager worked hand in hand with the president's new naval appointee, Commander Jerold Jameson.

* * *

Late in the evening, Alex and Renée were reviewing the latest TS-3 update. "Julien," Alex said, "I need a conference call in the morning with Commander Jameson. Please schedule that when he is available."

"I'll take your request under advisement, Captain," Julien rejoined.

Alex and Renée were speechless. But before either could respond, they heard, "I believe levity relieves the pressures created by continuous work."

"You see," Renée laughed, striking Alex on the shoulder hard enough to hurt her hand, "Look what you've done to our SADE. You've ruined him."

Alex grinned back at her, pretending to rub a hurt shoulder, "I don't know about that. I think he's much improved."

But Julien had the last word. "Alas, there's no pleasing the two of you. I fear the strain on my circuits might become too much to bear," and he basked in the laughter of his favorite people.

The initial reports from Commander Jameson were encouraging. There was no shortage of volunteers for fighter training and many had solid experience as shuttle pilots. To aid their training, Julien mocked a fighter cockpit on the bridge holo-vid, then transferred the program to a dedicated GEN-3 machine on Barren Island. This particular machine was the prototype for the fighter's controller, an extremely sophisticated computer that could compensate for the lack of a Méridien SADE, the one item Julien couldn't create.

Renée took the opportunity to broach a tender subject that had concerned her ever since their discovery of Earth's military weapons. "When our repairs are completed and we leave for home, what will you do, Alex?"

"Do you mean will I come with you?"

"No, we know you will come," she said quietly. "All of us have come to rely on that fact. The question is what duty you will perform on the *Rêveur.* Will you serve as one of the fighter pilots?" she asked.

"Yes," he answered.

"And you think you can help us in this manner?"

"I think I can keep you safer than anyone else."

There it was – the heart of the dilemma. She'd see him safe, but he was willing to risk himself first and foremost to protect them all. So Renée relied on what she knew best – negotiation. After all, she was a daughter of House de Guirnon. "Well, then let us discuss our personnel requirements. We will need a ship's crew for our return trip, which means New Terran volunteers. And if you're going to be a fighter pilot, who would you recommend as the *Rêveur*'s captain?"

And just like that, she exposed his quandary. He'd considered asking for both positions but coordinating the efforts of Julien, the T-managers, the Technology Transfer Team, and Commander Jameson had taught him about the demands of command and the value of delegation. He knew he couldn't hold both positions, and he knew only one person who was qualified to be captain, even if the term *qualified* was being generous. And now Renée was asking him to choose.

When Alex failed to respond to her question, Renée signaled the command chair into a horizontal position and turned to face him, dangling her legs over the side. "Alex, we have need of you but not as a fighter pilot. Your skills are needed on the bridge."

"Captain of the *Rêveur*," Alex whispered into the darkened bridge as New Terra rotated below them.

"Yes," she said and reached across the gap to slide a hand under his. "Whatever awaits us, I want to meet it with you as our captain."

* * *

The next day, after morning meal, Renée stood up at the head table. "The day approaches when we will depart for Méridien. To safely manage our flight or, more critically, to deal with whatever might have happened in our absence, we will need New Terran crew. Toward that end, I've taken the first step by asking Captain Racine to be the *Rêveur*'s captain, and he has agreed."

As Renée finished her announcement, the seventeen other survivors jumped to their feet and, in unison, pumped a right fist into the air and shouted a Con-Fed phrase over and over.

In his ear, Alex heard Julien. "It's a traditional Méridien phrase to celebrate a new captain and to wish him safe voyage. And may I add my congratulations, Captain?" Alex bowed his head to acknowledge their tribute and whispered a *thank you* to Julien. Each Méridien came up to him, either shaking his hand or bestowing a kiss on each cheek as they had done on their first evening together.

Alain and Étienne were the last to congratulate him. As Étienne shook his hand, he leaned close. "Alain and I have agreed. He will protect Ser. I'll serve you, Captain, and I'll keep you safe as your mother asked of me."

-23-

The following day, at 15.75 hours, Alex was headed to meet the next shuttle delivery at the midship airlock. He had hoped to have been able to repair the bay doors and accept deliveries there, but offloading the damaged shuttles for transfer to the Joaquin orbital station had taken a full day, several grav-lifters, and lots of manpower to manually lever the bay doors open and then close them again. Normal operation of the bay would have to wait until the ship was docked at the orbital station where workers would replace the bay door motors and tracks.

On the way to the airlock, Alex stopped Renée in the corridor to tell her there was no need to continue with the retrofit of the *Outward Bound* since he would be leaving with them.

"Nonsense," she replied. "It's in the contract, and New Terra is being well compensated. Consider it a gift from my people to do with as you will." Then she abruptly turned and walked away, ending the conversation. He stood there with a reply on his lips before shrugging and continuing on to the airlock.

The shuttle was delivering power-crystals, deemed Security Level-1, critical or dangerous materials, so Tatia accompanied the shipment and took the opportunity to board the *Rêveur*, stretch her legs, and see if her persona grata Méridien was available.

Tatia had first met the twins when they accompanied Alex and Renée to the Assembly. Her initial reaction was one of dismissal. Despite their otherworldly beauty, they appeared too delicate to qualify as a casual liaison. She had a mental image of a dalliance with one of them resulting in their considerable pain if not their hospitalization. And, professionally, she doubted their capability to perform their jobs adequately. Later, she revised her initial opinion, having been impressed by the manner in which they shadowed their charges – understated and professional. An incident at TS-1 did even more to sway her opinion. A heavy-set engineer seeking Renée's attention had, without thinking, reached out to grasp her shoulder from behind. Alain's speed and execution in blocking the beefy arm was extraordinary. It revised her estimation of his *delicateness*.

In the early morning hours following that incident, Tatia found herself alone in the canteen with Alain. They shared hot drinks and talked shop, which led to conversations about their families and eventually their relationships. Neither of them had found that special someone – dedication to the job, relationships with the wrong people, and the other hurdles facing singles had limited their opportunities.

After that first conversation, Tatia and Alain would often steal a little time to talk, walk, and enjoy each other's company. Several days later, Alain had returned to his ship, but they continued to see each other whenever Tatia came aboard the *Rêveur* with shuttle deliveries. She was about to say goodbye to him one day when he leaned in to kiss her. His kiss was tentative until she returned it; then it became passionate. When she finally pulled back, he had a beatific smile on his face that mirrored her own. After that, the pair always found an evening's hour to chat via the ship's link to TS-1, and Tatia rarely missed a shuttle visit.

As Tatia watched Alex attach trace-tags to each container, enabling materials to be located within the ship, she was reminded of a nagging question.

"Captain, do you have a moment? There's something I've been meaning to ask you."

Alex finished tagging the shipment, then two Méridiens attached grav-lifts to the containers and guided the delivery away. "Certainly, Major, accompany me to the bridge."

"How are the repairs going, Captain?" Tatia asked.

"They should take another forty to fifty days at most, and we will still need to recruit a crew, which I don't have a timeline on yet. Now what was your question, Major?"

"Good day, Julien," she said.

"Good day, Major Tachenko."

"Actually, my question was for you *and* Julien. I received information on the Frasier brothers' memory account from the general, who got it from the president. But the president doesn't have any immediate resources capable of obtaining that type of information. He would have had to use our services, but he didn't."

Deciding Alex would be better at this game, Julien kept quiet.

"My apologies, Major," Alex said, "I don't understand the question."

"I wonder how the president managed to obtain information that would have been protected by very stringent security protocols."

"Did you ask the president?"

"Me, question the president how he received the information?" she said, laughing at the very idea. "I like my position. I might make colonel in four or five years." After a moment she added, "Still, I wonder how he got the information. He even had the account password."

Alex, searching for a way to change the subject, realized he had the perfect excuse. "Major, now that you're here, I could use your expertise."

Tatia recognized equivocation when she saw it, but was curious enough to accept the diversion.

"Julien has completed his fighter design, which you've probably heard is our best option for offense. I'm working on the weapons system."

The holo-vid displayed a narrow fuselage craft with four rear boom-mounted engines that revolved in front of her. As a subject change, she had to admit it was quite good.

"How far have you gotten?"

"That's the problem. I'm still at the strategy stage."

"Well, I like to attack problems in small steps," she said, fascinated by the challenge. "In your case, what would you say is the easiest weapon to develop?"

"Of our choices, that would be a missile, a small missile that mounts on the fighter. Julien can design any type of mount and control we need."

"So, number one, best choice is a missile. What's the next issue?" she asked.

"We've reviewed the encounter a hundred times. That alien craft was agile, its beams were powerful, and it could fire frequently. Even if we mounted missiles on the fighter, they wouldn't be many. One silver ship could easily destroy all of them before they got close, making our fighters vulnerable."

Tatia began pacing and made an entire orbit of the bridge while she considered Alex's problem. "One of our crowd-control tools fires a single shot that breaks into multiple sleep canisters. They can be fired from drones or a shoulder launcher."

"A single shot that breaks into multiple shots ... a second stage?" Alex mused. "We could use a high acceleration first-stage missile that fires a second stage of multiple heads to overtax the enemy's energy weapon."

Tatia stopped to regard Alex, who had also begun pacing the bridge. "Can you make an explosive device?"

"They're called warheads," he explained. "Yes, we have several choices. But there are other complications. First, we don't know what defenses that ship might possess."

"So, you can make missiles with multiple warheads, but you don't know if they'll do any good."

"Accurate summary," Alex replied, circling the bridge in one direction while Tatia paced in the other. "And, second, most missiles are designed to target the engines or any strong heat signature. Julien's spectrographic analysis shows the alien ship is as cool as a refrigerated vita-drink. It has no heat bloom at all."

"No heat bloom?"

"None at all, which begs the question of how they move around. Julien surmises that they might use gravitational fields. But, there's no evidence either way."

Alerted to their discussion, Julien focused his attention on them. Despite the gravity of the subject, he was amused by their actions – motion to focus thought. The more motion, the better the focus, apparently. For an entity that lived in crystal, it was an alien concept.

"So, you face a superior foe," Tatia continued. "In our self-defense courses, women trainees are taught that males, 8.4 times out of 10, will be the opponent, and, since males often outweigh them, they must use superior strategy."

"So you're saying we must be clever. But where does that lead us?" he asked, the vagueness of her response not eliciting any ideas.

"You're facing an unknown and superior foe, Captain. You need to be sneaky. Discover their weakness and hit them where they can be hurt!"

Alex rolled her concept over in his mind, his analytical skills kicking into gear. "So, if their defensive weapons are unknown, then we have two choices … we discover them or we ignore them."

"Why would you ignore them?" It was her turn to stop pacing and stare.

"Well, what can you do about something you know nothing about?"

"What if they have superb defenses?"

"I've been thinking about that," said Alex as he resumed circling the bridge. "That silver ship was small, but it didn't hesitate to attack two comparatively enormous ships. My guess is that it expected to win."

"So you think it's the bully on the block."

"Either a bully or willing to sacrifice itself, which seems highly unlikely."

"Well, bullies are all about aggression, which means they might not have bothered with defenses."

Alex looked at her intently, her idea connecting with one that had been lurking in the back of his mind. "What was your impression when you first saw that ship in the vids?" he challenged her.

Tatia replayed the images in her mind. "I see an anomaly … something that shouldn't exist as a single entity."

"Yes,,that was my thought. I think where there's one, there's many."

"But how does that help you? If you're right, it makes your chance of surviving an encounter even worse."

"That just means I have to get this right," Alex replied. "I'm thinking that if they *are* the bully on the block, they depend on that beam weapon.

In addition, I think that silver ship has to go home to a bigger ship or some place called home. It didn't come from a void."

"And this is leading you where?" Tatia asked, feeling as if she was losing the thread of the conversation.

"We swamp its beam weapon with second-stage missiles, launching so many warheads at it that it can't possibly get them all."

"You're betting an awful lot on your assumptions, Captain."

"What is the alternative, Major? Doing nothing?"

Tatia had to admit he had a point. She'd always preferred to stack the odds in her favor, maximizing her chance of success. Right now, she didn't envy him. He was taking a passenger ship populated by only a handful of survivors back to a world where one or more alien ships probably awaited them. *How did you stack the odds in your favor, under those circumstances?*

"All right, so you overwhelm the alien ship with your missiles," Tatia stated, resuming her pacing. "But is their hull like our hulls, the *Rêveur*'s hull, or something entirely different?"

"We would have to find out," Alex replied. "Though, I can't see it hanging around while we sample it."

"Yes, Captain, we sample it!" Julien exclaimed.

"Welcome to the conversation, Julien," Alex replied with a touch of sarcasm.

"Your pardon, Captain, but I believe Major Tachenko's *sneakiness* has merit."

"I'll take that as a compliment, I think," she said dubiously.

"In this case, Major, that's exactly what we need." Julien replied. "You've indicated we face a superior foe, and the key to success is discovering their weakness and using it against them. To accomplish this, we will need several missile types, the last of which would be warheads."

"Explain," Alex requested.

Tatia would have stayed to hear the answer, but just then the bridge accessway opened to reveal Alain. Most New Terrans couldn't tell the twins apart, but the difference was obvious to her, and he was just the Méridien she was hoping to see. She signaled for him to stay silent with a finger to her lips, motioning to Alex, who was deep in discussion with Julien. Then she strolled up to him, a smile on her face, linked an arm through his, and guided him back out.

As the accessway closed, Alex wore his own smile. Tatia tried to keep her relationship with Alain low-key, but everyone was aware of the liaison. And more than one New Terran–Méridien pair circled each other, which gave him another idea … but one mountain at a time.

* * *

The following morning, Renée and Terese strode to the bridge. According to Julien, the captain had been there throughout the night. They came through the accessway and staggered to a halt. Alex was striding around the bridge in conversation with Julien, his arms waving around energetically. The vid screens displayed hundreds of colored dots with streaks of light indicating their flight paths, consuming nearly every centimeter of their surfaces.

Alex stopped his pacing, leaned his head back, and closed his eyes. He stood that way for several moments then said, "Okay, Julien, cancel scenarios 133 and 135. Keep scenario 134. That's our best case for series-2. Combine it with scenario 92, for series-1. Display it."

Julien sent a quick comm to Renée. <Please, Ser, our captain is attempting to solve our primary dilemma of a weapons system. It would be most imprudent to interrupt him at this time.>

Renée signaled Terese and the two women quietly backed to the rear of the bridge and settled into observer seats accessed from the bulkhead.

The screens blanked. Then the central screen displayed two ships approaching each other. Two icons launched from the ship labeled the *Rêveur* and streaked off toward the second ship. Lines of trajectory emanated from the two icons, aimed at the smaller ship. The view magnified, spilling the images onto the other screens. Soon, the myriad trajectory lines overwhelmed the casual viewer's ability to understand the martial dance.

"Outcome," Alex requested, his voice strained as he stared at the screen.

"Probability of alien destruction is 42 percent. Probability of fighter destruction is 98 percent."

Alex's anger boiled out in a stream of expletives, which the two women didn't receive in translation.

Terese hid a smile while Renée frowned.

Alex stalked over to the command chair and slumped into it. He remained there for a while – one hand drumming a slow cadence against the side of the chair, the other cradling his head. Suddenly, he launched into a standing position and ordered another scenario. The screens continued to blaze and then clear again as Alex ran more and more scenarios.

The extent of his frustration was evident. Tendons and blood vessels stood out on his thick neck and his fists were balled. He stopped his pacing and stared at the overhead as if seeking inspiration, letting out a groan of exasperation. When his anger finally dissipated, his exhaustion was evident.

"It looks like we must have an intelligence transfer, even though it will take up missile slots. Remember the earlier scenario I discarded, calling it … um?"

"Your expressions were *a child's musings* and *too stupid a concept to take credit for,*" said Julien, his amusement evident.

"Yeah, that one," Alex barked a laugh. "We have to guarantee the fighter controllers can pick up enough data from the small amount of nanites we'll be able to deliver. So we need the relay. If we take my *child's musing*, which was …?"

"Scenario 48, Captain, the comm buoys."

"Right, so assume each fighter has two comm buoys to deploy to transfer the nanites-1 intelligence off the hull to the fighters' controllers. Then, in the remaining missile slots, use four nanites-1 missiles, two nanites-2 missiles, and four warhead missiles. Employ both fighters in the attack. Combine the new parameters and display."

Again the screens filled with a blinding set of trajectory lines then froze at the apex of the fight. "Probability of alien destruction is 68 percent. Probability of fighter destruction is 81 percent."

Julien thought a break was long overdue, but he chose to forgo the suggestion. Alex appeared to be reaching an answer, and his biorhythms were quieting as he retreated from the tension that had been building throughout the night.

"Time for some radical thinking," he mumbled, leaning over the bridge consoles, his arms bracing himself while he thought. "What parameters most severely limit our probability of success? And, if those parameters are within our reach, would they give us a 90 percent probability of success against the alien ship?"

"What fighter survival probability do you wish me to use, Captain?" Julien inquired.

Alex rubbed his face with his hands. "No parameter, at this time," he said finally.

For a moment, there was quiet on the bridge while the screens went blank. "All scenarios are limited by one common factor, Captain. We have insufficient fighter and missile resources to ensure a win against a single silver ship."

"Assume three, then four fighters. Same missile loads for each additional fighter. Run the scenario."

After the blaze of screens froze again, indicating the end of the three-fighter scenario, Julien announced, "The desired outcome can't be achieved with three fighters. I'm running a four-fighter scenario now." The screens blanked again and lit again with the display of points and lines. "Probability of alien destruction with four fighters, given our assumptions, is 93 percent. Congratulations, Captain."

"And the fighters' stats?"

"Probability of fighter destruction is 41 percent."

"Display the scenario on the holo-vid." Alex walked around and through the holo-vid display, examining the action in minute detail. He had Julien rock the timeline back and forth for nearly a half hour. When he was finished, he rubbed his face with his hands. "Yes, Julien, this is a good start, but we can do better, much better."

The women watched as Alex lowered himself into a command chair, leaned back, and covered his eyes to ease the glare of the lights. Terese signaled Renée with Julien's medical update of Alex. She indicated several parameters for Ser to note: low blood sugar, severe adrenalin drain, low cellular ATP levels, and several more negative indicators. Renée signaled her, then Terese rose and left the bridge.

Renée approached Alex and touched his shoulder. "Captain ... Alex ..."

He swiveled his head to regard Renée, a soft smile on his lips. "I think we have the last piece of the puzzle."

"As I knew you would, Captain. But now you need to rest. And Julien should have his power-crystal recharged or replaced. The two of you would need an inexhaustible supply of energy if you continue on at this rate."

Alex climbed to his feet as the holo-vid and screens winked out. "Sorry, Julien, I didn't mean to drain your lifeline."

"I've been honored to play my part, Captain."

"Rather than wait for a recharge, please have Claude swap out your power-crystals. I want a refined solution, with the *Rêveur* loading four fighters. Keep a shuttle onboard, if you can."

"I'll be ready when you are, Captain."

"You're a good man, Julien," Alex said as he and Renée left the bridge.

Created 116 years ago, having served his wards and citizens faithfully for every tick of that time, Julien experienced one of his proudest moments.

* * *

Renée accompanied Alex the short distance back to his cabin. He walked straight to the sleeping quarters and sat heavily on the bed. "We're going to have a chance, Ser." And with that he closed his eyes and fell back onto the bed, exhausted.

She had rarely heard her honorific from Alex's lips. As a House daughter, she'd expected the term of respect from him when they first met. And his insistence on calling her by her first name, an honor only allowed family, had annoyed her. Over time, though, it had become familiar and then valued. Now she wondered if something had changed between them without her realizing it.

Terese joined them as Renée had requested and pressed a hypo with a mild soporific to Alex's neck. He barely twitched in response to the injection and was soon unconscious. Together, the two women worked to remove his ship boots. They heard him mumble something unintelligible.

<What did he say?> Terese sent. <I didn't receive a translation.>

<Julien says he's still directing scenarios,> replied Renée. They shared a concerned look as they tried to straighten him out, struggling to lift the considerable weight of his legs. <Perhaps we should have the captain wear a grav-belt.>

<Perhaps we should have a grav-lift standing by on the bridge,> Terese quipped and they chuckled quietly together.

As they sought to remove his uniform jacket, Terese sighed. <I finally have an opportunity to undress the captain and he's sound asleep.>

When they finished, Terese slipped out of the cabin. Renée stayed by the bed and commed Julien for an update. He'd already ordered the replacement power-crystals from Claude and sent an order to TS-2. The station manager had promised to redirect the delivery of two power-crystals destined for an electrical company. Once Renée was satisfied that the captain's orders were being fulfilled, she stopped to regard his sleeping form. <We chose well, Julien.>

<Yes, Ser, we are well served.>

She watched Alex continue to mumble and twitch in his sleep. "Relax, Alex," she said and laid a hand on his bare arm. Soon his limbs stopped twitching and his mumbling ceased. He took a deep, shuddering breath. She looked at her hand on his arm and his now quiet form. Succumbing to impulse, she pulled his arm away from his body to make room and lay down on her side next to him, scarcely contacting him, watching his chest rise and fall. Hoping the soporific would prevent him from waking, she wriggled up against him, resting her head on his shoulder and laying an arm across his chest. She felt his arm reflexively tuck her close to him, then his breathing deepened and he passed into a deep slumber.

Hours passed before Renée stirred. There was a moment of panic when she realized where she was, but it was quickly banished. She rested her head back on his chest and relaxed, enjoying a few more moments of quiet with him. His heart beat was strong – the same deep sound that had lulled her to sleep. Finally, with regret, she eased out of bed and tiptoed from the cabin.

Julien detected Renée's return to consciousness and signaled Étienne to abandon his post at the captain's door, where he and Alain had stood to ensure their privacy. He restored her comm access and released her message queue. Terese was signaled as well.

As Renée walked to her quarters, she passed Terese, who was headed to the captain's quarters with hypos full of electrolytes and nutrients. Terese's nod was polite, but her smile was tinged with mischief.

-24-

Nine hours after falling into bed, Alex abruptly came to and sat up. To his surprise, his jacket and boots were missing, and he couldn't remember removing them. He found them stowed in his wardrobe and hurried to use the refresher and dress, anxious to return to the bridge for another planning session with Julien. However, two things puzzled him. *Why did he feel like he'd recently eaten a full meal? And what were those intense dreams of Renée about?*

Alex strode onto the bridge calling out, "All charged up, Julien?"

"New power-crystals have been installed, Captain. Spares were ordered and are scheduled to arrive with Major Tachenko in two days."

"Excellent, so how do we stand on our weapons scenario?"

Julien triggered the holo-vid display and went through the attack scenario with four fighters step by step.

Alex was pleased to see that Julien had made several improvements. For one, he'd simplified the missile's design to allow interchangeable second stages. Also, each primary stage could now deliver more stage-2 nanites, which would be fired ticks apart. It would minimize the possibility that a single beam might destroy them all at once. And he'd refined the buoy design so they could fit within the missile housing's second stage. Finally, he had coopted a controller and telemetry scanner to guide the missile heads at the silver ship.

"You've been busy, Julien," Alex marveled. "If you were standing here, I'd hug you."

"Sentiment accepted as intended, Captain."

"We have one critical item to work on later, Julien. Since we can't see the beams of the silver ship, we have to find a means of detecting them.

Otherwise, our fighters don't stand a chance. Okay, so what's the big picture? How do we accommodate this strategy?"

"Two more fighters will require an additional thirty-four days to build and test. The design and manufacture of the munitions, if expedited, will occupy all TS facilities for twenty-eight days with no production for New Terran use. The greatest challenge is that we must add an additional bay to the *Rêveur.*"

The holo-vid displayed a translucent *Rêveur*, allowing Alex to see the ship's bulkhead frames. Julien highlighted a section of portside compartments and cut them from the ship. Then he cloned the starboard landing bay, rotated it to form a port landing bay, and slotted it into the opening.

"Two bays will also give us additional protection in the event of a strike on one of the bays. Two fighters will reside in each bay. You will notice I've removed the shuttles to make room for each bay's missile silos and reaction mass tanks for our fighters."

Alex walked around the model, placing his hand into the view, spreading his fingers to enlarge it, as he had learned to do. "Okay, I like it, and the time delay is something I can sell to our people." Alex heard his words *our people* to describe the Méridiens and wondered when he might make that slip in front of New Terrans. "But we have to keep one shuttle. It's a necessity."

"And I've considered that, Captain. I was wondering what your intentions were for your ship after the retrofit."

"Well, I anticipated Joaquin would complete the retrofit after we left. Due to its Méridien technology, I can't sell it, except to the government. If they want it for Barren Island, I'll have them put the proceeds in my account, and if we don't … um, return, my parents will get the creds."

"Please view this image, Captain." He played a historic vid on the central screen. A huge-winged craft was accelerating down a runway for liftoff. Its four engines hung below extensive wings located amidship. Attached to its dorsal hull, centrally located, was a smaller craft. "They called this piggybacking," Julien explained. "Although the reference to a Terran animal consumed for protein escapes me."

"And you're thinking of *piggybacking* the *Outward Bound* on the *Rêveur*?"

"Yes, Captain, although I haven't solved the problem of the added mass reducing our maneuverability by over 22 percent."

"Let me think on that. But the first problem is that my ship is not a shuttle."

"No, Captain, it's not. Here's my solution," and the holo-vid changed view. "With the circumstances of our return to Méridien unknown, it seems to me more prudent to have a shuttle capable of greater range and passenger capacity. And some offensive capability would not be unwarranted."

The explorer-tug was unrecognizable in its new configuration. The tug's massive boom-mounted engines were replaced by sleeker Méridien designs mounted directly on the stern. The hub wheel was gone. The narrow spine was now a fully encased fuselage. Two extrusions were noticeable amidship, and the expanded view revealed missile carousels that extended into the interior. The space-eating beam engines and their generators were gone, replaced by row after row of 280 planetfall ready seats, an extended galley, and a new refresher. The bridge's advanced telemetry equipment, which Alex had spent a fortune acquiring, was replaced by Méridien designs, many times more effective and a third the size.

Despite his personal feelings about the massive transformation of a ship that had been his dream for years, Alex didn't hesitate. "How long will the rebuild take, Julien?"

"We will need to communicate with the team members to determine how they might accommodate these requests before a timeline can be established."

"Get me a conference comm. I need Renée, Claude, Edouard, the Technology Transfer Team, the T-managers, Commander Jameson, and the president."

When did I begin directing the president, Alex wondered.

* * *

When Alex joined the Méridiens on the bridge for the conference, he was surprised to find Major Tachenko present.

"The major was making a shuttle delivery," Renée explained, "so I invited her to join us for the conference comm. She and her crew are also invited to evening meal."

"Ready, Captain," Julien signaled.

"Mr. President and everyone, thank you for taking time out of your busy schedules for this call," Alex said. "Mr. President, we are about to disrupt production schedules for about thirty-four days, absorbing most T-resources and curtailing heavy tech production for New Terra during the period. We need your support."

"Go ahead, Captain," President McMorris said. "Explain what you need."

Alex outlined the new offensive solution he'd designed with Julien, which would require two additional fighters and a second landing bay for the *Rêveur*. "The good news is that we've finalized our offensive solution for the fighters." He went into a brief description of the two-stage missiles with their alternate heads: comm buoys, two loads of nanites, and warheads.

At the end of the explanation, Minister Jaya exclaimed, "Captain Racine, do you mean to tell me your attack scenario depends on splattering nanites against this silver ship's hull, programming a second attack of nanites in moments based on the information you receive, then following up with warheads aimed at small weakened areas on a maneuvering starship?"

Alex's confident voice cut through the dead silence that followed Jaya's question. "That's exactly correct, Minister Jaya. Julien gives us a 93 percent probability of a successful engagement."

"Your pardon, Captain," Julien interrupted, "that was my previous calculation. With the newest updates, particularly adding relay targeting to the warheads via the buoys, my estimate has increased to 95 percent."

"Ninety-five percent?" was echoed by several voices on the comm.

Julien continued, "The estimate is based on two assumptions. One, at least two fighters close the range with the alien craft to score with the nanites-1 missiles. And two, one of the four fighters must remain active long enough to deploy warheads when hull deterioration has been achieved."

No comments followed his announcement. Julien was describing the life and death of the fighter pilots in cold, hard numbers. It was a chilling prospect for everyone.

"Proceed with your requests, Captain Racine," said the president.

"We'll require two construction bays on the Joaquin, simultaneously. My ship will be transformed into a long-range shuttle with some offensive capabilities, and it must be completed at the same time as the *Rêveur*. The good news is that Barren Island gets both Méridien shuttles."

"Well, I approve," Commander Jameson was heard to say.

"Captain, how will you fit the *Outward Bound* in your shuttle bay?" Minister Jaya asked.

"Julien's suggestion is to piggyback it on the *Rêveur*'s dorsal hull.

"Excuse me," General Gonzalez interrupted, "what's a piggyback?"

"A piggy is an Earth animal," Alex explained.

"Ah, and this animal carries its young on its back," Maria concluded.

"No," Alex said, frustrated, "we've found no evidence of that in the archives."

"Captain Racine," the president interrupted, "perhaps you've been too busy to monitor the local news. Two days after we distributed the medical nanites, the news media ran a story about the miraculous reconstruction of a young girl's crushed legs. In the days since then, we've had hospital reports of over 121 cases of medical nanites either preventing permanent damage or saving a life. As far as this nation is concerned, so long as you don't disturb the distribution of medical nanites, you and the Méridiens can have anything you want."

"Thank you, Mr. President. Julien will transmit all relevant data, reschedule production, redirect shipments, and coordinate the repair and retrofit on both docks."

"And I'm sure he will do so admirably, Captain. McMorris out."

After the comm ended, Julien followed up with Alex on an open issue. "As we discussed, Captain, our maneuverability with the *Outward Bound* attached to our hull will be reduced to unacceptable levels."

"Apologies, Julien, I have an idea that I haven't shared. We will approach the alien's position with the shuttle attached. Then we'll launch it with its own crew, to be picked up afterward, if there is an afterward for the rest of us."

"The shuttle won't be FTL capable, Captain," Julien reminded him.

"I'm aware of that, Julien," Alex responded. Silence greeted his pronouncement.

"Then, Captain, I believe we have all the pieces of the solution."

"I'm starved," he announced and headed for evening meal. Julien updated the Méridiens on the news. They wanted to return home as soon as possible, but not if it might cost them their lives. And if the captain and Julien thought they had found a means of protection, it was a moment to celebrate.

Alex turned to his food with a vengeance. The emotional release of finally discovering an offensive solution powered his appetite. The Méridiens glanced at their captain and hid smiles. They had grown accustomed to eating at a slower pace, lingering over a dish here and there, so that they might finish when their captain did. This evening they severely misjudged it.

After all had finished their meals, including the shuttle crew and visiting workers, who had their own New Terran appetites, Renée and Tatia leaned back in their chairs and watched Alex as he polished off his last two serving dishes.

When Alex finished, he turned to look at Tatia. "It's your turn, Major." Then he explained the ritual of storytelling.

Tatia lifted her eyes overhead to consider her choices and decided to share the story that had pained her the most. She'd been in love with a young man, but he had loved space more than he did her. An EVA accident had claimed his life, and his family's grief had been doubled upon learning the body couldn't be recovered, having drifted into Seda's gravity well. She told them of her greatest regret. They had argued, an angry, mean-spirited argument, before parting. When it appeared she would end on this sad note, she said, "But each and every one of us should never give up hope, not for ourselves and not for one another. Someday, you and I will find others to love."

As the Méridiens stood and offered their thanks for her story, Alex and Renée didn't miss the significant glance Tatia and Alain shared.

-25-

On a cold and windy winter morning, a shuttle from the *Rêveur* landed on Barren Island's runway. Service personnel hurried out to offload Alex, Renée, and the twins and bundle them into a transport. They crossed the landing field to a sealed hangar and disembarked into a heated climate. Their visitors doffed their heavy winter coats, supplied courtesy of the TSF.

TS-3 personnel got their first look at the newly appointed captain of the *Rêveur*, resplendent in a Méridien uniform of deep, dark blue with gold captain's pins at the collar and a shoulder patch for the *Rêveur*.

Commander Jameson met his guests in the hanger. Waving his arm at the craft behind him, he announced, "Ser de Guirnon and Captain Racine, may I present your first Dagger."

"Did you say *dagger*, Commander Jameson?" Alex asked.

"Yes, Captain, the first time one of our test pilots saw it, he said, 'Looks like a dagger.' The name has stuck."

"I see," said Alex. It did look like a dagger, with its long, lean, black fuselage; a cockpit that barely disturbed its sleek lines since telemetry was relayed to the pilot's helmet; and four engines set on rear struts for maneuverability. A thin slit of plex-crystal shielding allowed visual sight for the pilot in the event of a manual landing. Every attempt had been made to minimize the fuselage's silhouette to reduce the targeting opportunity for the alien ship, although nothing could be done about the boom-mounted missiles and engines.

Renée, with Alain following, walked forward to examine the fighter more closely. She stepped over cables running from tech control consoles into sockets on the fuselage. "Is our Dagger ready to fly, Commander?" she asked.

"Yes, Ser, word from Julien is that all systems are ready. Here comes our test pilot now."

They watched as a young man in a TSF flight uniform crossed the bay floor, carrying his helmet under his arm. He had short, dark hair curled tight to his head, dark eyes, and light brown skin.

"Lieutenant," said the commander as he managed introductions, "Ser Renée de Guirnon and Captain Racine of the *Rêveur*. Ser, Sir, Lieutenant Jason Willard."

"Lieutenant Willard," Alex inquired, "any relation to a Willard who rescued that shuttle crew last year just before the ship entered atmosphere and burned up?"

"An intimate kin, you could say, Sir," replied the lieutenant, grinning at his own joke.

"Do we need to review the test flight procedures today, Lieutenant?" asked Alex. Jason was reputed to be one of the best shuttle pilots, but word had it that he was just as likely to stray when it came to following orders. "The fighter's flight capability won't be the only thing that's judged today."

The lieutenant's expression sobered immediately and he straightened to attention with a crisp acknowledgement. "Message received, Sir."

As the lieutenant climbed into his canopy, Alex circled the entire craft. He'd studied the vid representations, but it was nothing like the real thing. The thought of sending pilots to their death in these deadly crafts put an acrid taste in his mouth. It was difficult to absorb how dramatically his life had changed from that of a solitary explorer-tug pilot.

A small vehicle hauled the fighter from the warehouse onto the runway, which was swept by a blustery wind. They listened in as Julien stepped Lieutenant Willard through the final flight procedures. Then, with engines flaring, the fighter shot down the runway for its brief sojourn into space before returning to the runway, the lieutenant carefully adhering to the flight plan. The real surprise to everyone was that the flight telemetry was near perfect. The craft flew as expected, handled exactly as it had in the simulator, and was within operating specifications, as in dead-in-the-middle of operating specifications.

As Alex listened to the awestruck exclamations of the pilot, flight crew, and operations personnel, he whispered into his comm, “Damn, Julien.”

“Thank you, Captain.”

-26-

Production work was nearing completion. The *Rêveur*'s engine frames were being shipped to the Joaquin to be preassembled in the bay. The engine components would follow and be assembled onboard the *Rêveur*. The Joaquin station manager notified Alex that his ships were scheduled to enter the bays in twenty-one days. The station's dedicated tug, *A Little Shove*, would assist him.

After morning meal, Alex addressed Julien on the bridge. "I'd like you to draft a list of crew positions with their responsibilities. We've had a number of New Terrans aboard. Let's see where they might fit into the crew. In the meantime, I need a star chart with distances."

"Certainly, Captain, I'm ready when you are."

"Please plot these points: the New Terran system, the Méridien system, the origination point of the *Rêveur*'s last trip, and its course and destination when the attack occurred."

Alex walked around the holo-vid as Julien dimmed the bridge lights and labeled the systems. The *Rêveur* left from Méridien. A red line denoting its course led to a far system called Hellébore. "Add the star systems that make up the Confederation."

"Black space," Alex whispered as twelve more additional blue lights were added, surrounding the Méridien home system. The *Rêveur*'s course extended to the farthest limit of Confederation space. "Julien, where were you going? Was it common to travel to such a distant colony? I mean, you're a premier passenger ship with a House representative aboard, not a freighter or a common liner."

"One moment, Captain," Julien requested and immediately switched to the subject of FTL mechanics while he summoned Renée to the bridge.

* * *

Renée couldn't help but wonder why fortune had deserted her. She had been hoping this subject never arose. Alex was seated in the command chair when she gained the bridge.

"Hello, Renée, I believe I've touched on something outside of Julien's purview. I was asking him where you were going when you were attacked."

Renée examined the holo-vid and was transported to, what was for her, the recent past. She recalled the well wishes of her family and the sense of joy and celebration of a new adventure. So many close House associates had chosen to accompany her, and most were gone.

"The *Rêveur* was transporting me to the Hellébore system for my marriage," Renée said, choosing to be frank. "When I turned twenty, I was pledged to Ser Antoine Bassani, of House Bassani. Antoine's father is, or was, the Cetus colony governor in the Hellébore system."

"An arranged marriage? Is this a common practice among your people?" Alex asked.

Renée shrugged. "Yes, it is our custom, Captain. When I was awakened and told seventy years had passed, I felt as if I'd been robbed of my birthright and my marriage."

"Do you think your husband-to-be is still alive?"

"If no accident has befallen him, he should be. He was 38 at the time of our attack, so he'd be 108 or 109 years now, middle-aged," Renée said, watching Alex pace.

"I'm sorry, what?" Alex came to an abrupt halt, but his mind was racing. "Middle-aged … 108 years is middle-age? How long do your people live?"

"Life expectancy for us is about 200 years." She watched Alex make his way to a chair and sit down in a stupor. "Captain, we understand your people live about half our lifespan. It's the nanites that constantly repair and maintain our bodies. They allow us to appear much younger than we actually are throughout our lifetime."

A thought suddenly struck Alex. "Renée, the medical nanites we've distributed and used in our emergency wards. How will they affect New Terrans?"

"Captain, the medical nanites released to your people have a fourteen-day lifespan," Julien explained. "They continue to replicate, repairing and maintaining the health of the patient during this time, then they inactivate and the body removes them as waste."

"I should have guessed you had the issue covered. If the people ever learned what nanites could do for them, they would storm Government House."

"Alex, I'm not pleased we withheld this information from you, but your people were unknown to us. We thought, if you knew the truth, it would place you in a dilemma with your own people." She watched him for a sign, something that would tell her she hadn't irreparably damaged their relationship.

"How old are you?"

"I'm thirty-four Méridien years. And I'm the youngest Méridien on this ship."

"So you could live for another 160 years."

He didn't seem to require an answer, so she said nothing.

"When you return, will you seek him out?" Alex asked.

"He deserves to know what has happened to me. I hope to find him content with a wife and children," she said. "My life is elsewhere now."

"Then what will you do when you return?"

"I don't know. Since awakening, there has been so much to do and so little time to think. But all these things … our rescue, your people, our pact … have made me realize that having choices, something rarely afforded me before, is a wonderful thing."

"So if you could have anything you wanted for yourself, what would it be?"

Renée closed her eyes. For the first time since she'd reached adulthood, someone was asking her what she wanted to do with her life. The feeling was intense, liberating, and frightening.

<Now, Ser,> Julien sent to her, <is where the weak prevaricate and the strong are forthright.>

She opened her eyes, took a deep breath, and let it out slowly. "I want to know that my people are safe. And, if they aren't safe, I want to do what I can to help them. If we fail, it won't matter what I want. If we live, I'll choose my own way, my own life."

Alex leaned close to her, looking into her eyes, and said, "Then what you want for yourself is what I want for you," and walked off the bridge.

-27-

At Alex's request, there were no guests at evening meal that night. When all had finished, he stood to draw their attention. "Méridiens, three of you are trained crew members. The rest of you were passengers. Yet, all of you have helped in the repair of the *Rêveur* and you've done well." Nods of appreciation followed his comments.

"But, you have a decision to make. Tomorrow morning, I'll interview all of you. For those who were passengers, I need to know if you wish to remain a passenger or will train as crew. If you choose to become crew, what skills can you offer? To complete our crew, we'll need New Terrans. Some of them might be in positions of command over you. For each of you who crew, I need to know that you can accept this."

Alex sat back down, taking a sip of water. He recognized the unfocused looks around the tables as the people employed their implants.

Then Alain stood up. "Captain, would you accept our recommendations for New Terran crew?"

Alex's heart sped up. He'd been dreading the possibility that no other New Terrans would be willing to undertake the journey. "I'd be pleased to hear your recommendations. If the person is qualified for a position, he or she will be given first consideration." Alain's smile as he sat down was Alex's answer. Major Tatia Tachenko was as good as onboard. "If there are others who have recommendations, would you please raise your hand?" He was taken aback when every hand rose. It appeared there was more Méridien–New Terran interaction than he'd suspected. He turned to grin at Renée and saw her hand in the air as well.

Alex arranged the schedule and had Julien send it to everyone. His first interview was with Alain, but at 9 hours Julien announced Pia at his cabin door.

"Good morning, Captain," Pia greeted him, "If you'll permit, I'll speak with you first and, perhaps, save you some time."

He welcomed Pia into his sitting room, offered her a seat at the table, and took one across from her. She requested that he examine a document Julien had just sent to his reader and he opened the latest item in his download queue.

"The list you are viewing, Captain, shows our qualifications for crew positions. However, we will be honored to serve in whatever position you ask of us."

Alex examined the list. "All the Méridiens volunteered for any crew position?" he asked, looking up to Pia.

"Our preferred crew position follows our name," Pia pointed out. "But you should realize that it is just a matter of practice, Captain. Julien can guide us in fulfilling almost any new position."

And if we lose Julien, we will be nothing more than a flying rock, Alex thought.

As she tapped his reader, scrolling down the document, she said, "Below the first list are our recommendations for New Terran crew, Captain."

Alex thumbed down the pages. Each Méridien's name was followed by at least four names, with a summary of their skills. Many of the New Terran names were familiar to him and were highly qualified. Under Pia's name was Mickey Brandon, the senior engineer of the EVA hull repair team, who would also be the construction team leader on the *Rêveur* while they were in dock.

Pia was often seen talking to the engineer during breaks. Alex had wondered if Mickey was taking advantage of the younger woman. Now, in light of Renée's revelation about their lifespans, he had to adjust his assumptions. Mickey was probably in his early forties. Pia was one of the older of the youthful-appearing Méridiens. Using Renée's age as a guide, he guessed her to be anywhere from forty-five to fifty-five. He considered the distinct possibility that this wouldn't be the only misjudgment he would make about the Méridiens.

"Pia, I see you're recommending Mickey, and I don't want to question your judgment, but …"

"Captain," Pia interrupted, "you asked for recommendations. None of your people would dishonor you by recommending unqualified personnel. These individuals are aware of the potential dangers of this trip, are willing to deal with them, and have requested a recommendation to you."

Alex felt like a vid on a loop, "These are all volunteers? They asked to be recommended?"

Pia took pity on him, laying a hand over his. "Is it so difficult to accept, Captain, that there are others among your people who would follow your example? It's a special person who can lead, but there will always be many who choose to follow a leader."

Alex felt overwhelmed, but he saw a major hurdle fall down in front of him.

After Pia left, it took Alex a moment to mentally shift his priorities. Staffing the rest of the *Rêveur*'s crew appeared to be a matter of interviewing and hiring. *Hiring?* "Julien, how do we pay the crew?"

* * *

Alex required one more piece of information before he interviewed the New Terrans, and his answers were in Medical.

Terese welcomed him into her office with her usual enthusiastic smile. "Captain, how may I be of service?"

"Good morning, Terese. I need to ask you about medical nanites for the New Terran crew."

"I presume you are referring to our cell-gen injections, not the limited lifespan nanites that were distributed to your people."

The reminder of the subterfuge grated on his nerves, but he packed away his irritation. "I understand that your cell-gen injections will be offered to anyone who wishes to crew with us."

"With certainty, Captain, do you wish to receive them now?" she asked

"Tell me about them," Alex requested.

"The nanites work at the cellular level, using the genetic code of an individual's healthy cells as a template to identify and remove malformed and diseased cells. The effects are that a person appears more youthful and is much healthier than their years."

"What would be the effects of cell-gen injections on a forty-two-year-old New Terran male?"

Terese was puzzled that the captain didn't appear to be asking about the injections for his own benefit. She made a mental note to discuss this with Renée. "The nanites don't reverse the aging process. The male will be forty-two years old, but after thirty to forty days, he'll appear to have the appearance and health of a male ten years younger."

"Would he live to be as old as most of your people?"

"No, Captain. With regular treatments, he should live, barring an accident or death by alien," she said, chuckling at her own joke, "to about 140 years. Those years would be spent in very good health. We don't suffer a gradual decline associated with aging … arthritic conditions, blood diseases, or hormonal imbalances … as do your people."

"Are there any negative effects or warnings we should give the new crew should they receive the injections?"

"Oh, yes, Captain! As their health is restored, vigor is also restored. It's highly recommended that the newly restored find a healthy and vigorous partner."

Alex could still hear Terese's laughter as he left Medical.

* * *

The Méridiens' list of recommended personnel nearly equaled Julien's list of required crew. The similarity of the two lists was a glimpse into the power of the implants – a group of people sharing knowledge with amazing efficiency to achieve a common goal.

Alex had Julien send a comm to everyone on the list. The message was simple, "Passage to the stars awaits you. You are invited to interview for a seat." Appended were the shuttle flights that would originate from four locations to facilitate transport to the *Rêveur*.

To a man and woman, the New Terrans showed up. The Méridiens, dressed in their new, dark blue crew uniforms, without rank or insignia, greeted them at the airlock and guided them to the meal room. The New Terrans had all worked on *Rêveur* projects, so they carried their own ear comms, although, those who had worked only at the T-stations were seeing the *Rêveur* for the first time.

As their guests found seats, the Méridiens arranged themselves along the walls. Alex waited at the front of the room, sipping water and attempting to appear confident, even though he felt anything but. As he looked around the room, his eyes met Renée's. Unexpectedly, she gave him a slow wink, causing him to spill his water cup.

Renée had requested Julien to send her New Terran dramas portraying strong, young women. She found one actress who was particularly well-known and well-liked, and Renée had studied her behavior in depth. Considering Alex's reaction to her wink, she thought there was much to be said for emulating a well-respected role model.

Alex faced his peers and, in many cases, superiors in terms of experience. "Thank you all for coming. In less than forty days, our work will come to a close; then we'll be returning these good people to their homes." He held up his arms to encompass the Méridiens, who turned to face Alex and rendered honor. It was a powerful statement as to where their allegiance lay.

"You know the story of the tragic attack on their ship nearly seventy-three New Terran years ago. What we don't know is what we'll find when we arrive at Méridien. I've tried to prepare for the worst. We're adding a second landing bay to accommodate four new fighters, called Daggers, and we're manufacturing missiles with several different payloads to arm these crafts."

Alex was tempted to start pacing, but he held still trying to project the image of a competent captain. "You're here because a Méridien trusts you, believes in you, and knows you want to be part of this journey. We need crew. I hold the captain's position at the pleasure of Ser Renée de Guirnon, representative of House de Guirnon. Until she chooses to relieve me, my word is law on this ship as it would be for any captain."

"Before I interview each of you, Terese and Ser de Guirnon will address you. You will receive confidential information today, and I remind you that you've signed nondisclosure agreements. You will be held to those agreements."

Terese walked to the front of the room and stood with Alex and Renée. "You're aware of the medical nanites distributed by your government to hospitals. What I am about to discuss are not those, but what we call cell-gen injections. These injections are given regularly to Méridiens to maintain our good health. They also extend our longevity to an average of 200 years." She had to wait until the audience's exclamations died down before continuing. "I am sixty-two of your New Terran years." The power of the cell-gen injections was evident in Terese's trim figure, poured into her snug uniform, and attractive, youthful-appearing face. In response to the whistles from the audience, she held her arms out at her sides and turned in a slow circle, a knowing grin on her face.

Renée spoke next. "One of the concessions your government has made in exchange for our technology is to support the cost of our crew. Salaries, requisite to your position on the ship, will be paid into an account of your choice. These salaries will be paid for up to two years or until such time as you leave your position. I can tell you that these annual salaries range from 58K to 95K of your creds and are unencumbered."

There were murmurs of surprise from around the room as Renée sat down. The salaries were generous, particularly given the tax exemption and the zero cost-of-living aboard the *Rêveur.*

It was Alex's turn again. "There is one more important item to announce before the interviews begin. You know that Méridiens communicate in a unique way via the implants in their heads. These implants are quite small, but they enable direct comms with other implants, even over the length of the *Rêveur.* Through FTL relays or a SADE, such as Julien, individuals might connect with one another anywhere within the Confederation."

Alex waited while his audience absorbed the astounding concept of communicating their thoughts across the stars. There was no conversation. Instead, they were dumbfounded. Projecting his voice to gain their attention, he said, "You have an important choice to make. The implants and cell-gen injections won't be an option but a requirement to join the crew." He held up his hands to forestall their questions. "Once in Confederation space, we might be welcomed or we might be in for a fight. Either way, we need to have these tools. Failure to embrace them would be nothing less than shortsighted on our part, which is why I'll be the first to receive both of these gifts when I leave this room."

Renée's comm flooded with queries. Julien's priority query overrode them all. <Ser, were you aware of the captain's decision?> Renée ignored Julien's comm and looked across the room to Terese, who shook her head. She hadn't known either.

"The procedures, so I'm told, will take less than a quarter hour and are completely painless. But, most important, we will have to return to school. Méridien children have years to adopt their implants. *You* will have about forty days. If you have any difficulty, the implants can be removed and the cell-gen nanites deactivated. In a quarter hour, I'll be in my office. Anyone who wishes to join the crew, please give your name to Julien. He will arrange the interviews. Once accepted, you'll be escorted to Medical for your implant and first cell-gen injection. Your implants will remain off until you've received your basic training. Those choosing to leave, please enjoy our hospitality. A shuttle will depart as it is filled. I, for one, won't judge you as to your decision. It's a tough one to make. Good fortune."

Everyone seated jumped up and braced to attention as he left. It was an eerie sensation for a young man who had spent much of his working life with just three family members and a computer named Tara.

Terese glanced at Renée then hurried after the captain. She caught up with him as he entered Medical.

"Do I need to remove my jacket, Terese?"

"While it would please me, Captain, it's not necessary." To her surprise, he laughed and removed his uniform jacket.

"I wouldn't want your first New Terran to be an unpleasant experience."

Then it was her turn to laugh. It was a pleasant balm on the pain she had kept at bay since awakening.

* * *

Alex was waiting in his cabin. The aftereffects of the operation and injection were negligible. Terese reminded him that he would require the use of his ear comm until he received the implant's preliminary training.

"Captain, the first interviewee is ready," Julien relayed.

"Give me the bad news. How many did we lose?"

"None, Captain. All have requested interviews."

While wrapping his mind around that stunning fact, Alex signaled the door and in walked Major Tachenko. He'd noticed her in the front row while he was addressing the New Terrans. She stopped at his desk; her eyes were focused on the far bulkhead. Her cap was held under her arm as she rendered a perfect TSF salute. Alex returned the salute and offered her a seat. She sat impassively, waiting on him.

Alex had queried records of Earth's various military and merchant naval organizations, but none of them fit the present circumstances. In the end, he realized it was up to him to create an organization from the bottom up. He was reminded of what his mother had said to him after a particularly difficult day of taunting at primary school: "Alex, you can't be what others want you to be; you can only be who you are." It had taken him years to puzzle out what she meant.

He smiled broadly at Major Tachenko. "It's a pleasure to see you, Major." The tension visibly eased from her shoulders as she returned his smile.

"It's a pleasure to be here, Captain."

"I haven't figured out an organizational structure yet, Major. So I don't know whether we will be military or civilian, but I'm looking for a first mate or an XO, as the Terrans called them. Would you like the job?"

"That's the interview?" Tatia asked, shocked by Alex's abrupt offer. "Sorry, Captain, excuse me. Yes, Sir, I want the job."

He stood up. "Congratulations," he said and extended his hand to her. "You're hired."

She pumped his hand enthusiastically, barely catching his next words as he indicated a chair over at the table.

"For now, we have readers for lists and notetaking. In the near future, it appears we will be retaining information internally," he said, tapping his temple.

She paused for a moment before taking her seat and said, "I suppose we will, Captain." A phrase from an ancient Earth story came to mind. *A brave new world* seemed most apropos.

"We don't need to define the crew positions today," Alex continued. "My intention is to accept them, choose their departments, and send them to Medical. Later, we will choose department heads, and they can form their own departments and assign pay grades. Everyone leaves the ship today to organize their affairs. When the department heads return, they will call their crew aboard as they need them. As announced, all implants will remain off and turned on in stages as Medical approves each individual. According to Terese, beginners might suffer ill effects if they are progressed too rapidly."

"So we're not interviewing anyone," Tatia confirmed. "The Méridiens have vetted us and you've accepted their recommendations." She made it a statement and he nodded his agreement.

"Julien, please send in the next volunteer," Alex requested.

Word spread among the New Terrans that all were being accepted and many came through the captain's door smiling. The crew roster ended eight short of Julien's list, not counting the Dagger pilots and flight service crews, positions reserved for the New Terrans. He wouldn't ask any of the innately peaceful Méridiens to service the offensive weapon systems. It would probably happen one day, but not today. Not just yet.

-28-

The last shuttle of New Terrans departed at 20.65 hours. After the evening meal, Alex asked Renée to accompany him to the bridge. "I need to learn to use my implant," he told her.

"Captain, Terese is more qualified to guide you through the initial steps," she objected.

"But you can do it too, right?"

"I can, Captain."

"Good, let's go."

On the way to the bridge, she relayed Alex's request to Julien and Terese. She expected Terese to object on medical grounds, but she said, <It's best this way, Ser. His training will proceed faster with you.>

Julien and Terese decided that they'd hover in Renée's background, offering advice while monitoring the exchange.

Renée stretched the command chairs into lounge positions. She and Alex sat on the sides in order to face each other.

"You won't need your ear comm, Captain." She waited while he slipped it out and pocketed it. "My translation program will handle our language needs. We'll start with simple sending and receiving then turning your implant on and off for privacy." She signaled Julien to turn on the program and slid her hands under his.

"Close your eyes, Captain. Think of me. Continue to think of me. For each person the initial access of their implant is slightly different, but you will sense when I'm present. Don't worry if it takes a while to accomplish these first steps." A moment later, she received a comm signal from Alex.

Terese chuckled in her background. <A quick one, our captain.>

Renée sent him a simple greeting. <Hello, Captain.> He twitched and clenched her fingers tightly then quickly relaxed his hold.

<Hello, Renée,> he replied, his words tinged with wonderment. <I apologize if I gripped your hands too hard.>

<You didn't. Continue to hold me. The touch is important. It grounds you while this new sense is developed. Now, when I say *begin*, I want you to deny me access. Some people think *no*; others think *black* or *dark*. We will see what works for you. *Begin*.>

She sought his implant and connected. She was about to request he try another blocking technique when she realized she sensed a *nothingness*. It was different from any connection she'd ever experienced with a Méridien.

<Julien, Terese, have you seen this before?> she asked. Then she received, <I hear you speaking with others,> and gasped. She hadn't erected any barriers due to Alex's novice state, and somehow he'd detected her background links. <Hello, Julien, Terese,> he sent through her link. All of them could hear Terese's laughter and clapping hands.

<Julien, I hear him, but I don't have access. Do you?>

Momentarily, Julien responded, <Ser, while I detect the implant, I have no access either. My apologies, but I didn't activate his override routine when I turned on the program. Under no circumstances has it ever been necessary with a beginner.>

Before she could become concerned, she received images of herself, Terese, and an odd silhouette of a man in a long coat and a strange hat, which she took to be Julien, each floating in a soft, liquid bubble. Their access hadn't been blocked, but accepted then isolated by Alex's technique, allowing his comm to suppress theirs.

It was Julien's turn to chuckle, but all he said was, <the Sleuth.>

Alex sent images of their bubbles popping, followed by the message, <This is wonderful.>

After his remarkable beginning, they moved through new programs as fast as Alex could adopt them. Once informed of an application's purpose, he often manipulated it before Renée could instruct him. Hours later, a spike of pain accompanied his thought, and he dropped her hands and grabbed the sides of his head.

"Enough for now, Captain," Julien announced, resorting to the bridge speakers. "You have covered more tonight than the brightest Méridien children do in their first half year. I've switched off the program so you can rest. Otherwise it will interrupt your sleep until you acquire more control."

Alex opened his eyes as he stood up. He was weaving slightly, and his vision was blurred as if seeing the world through a new and strange view.

Renée slipped under his arm to steady him. "It will pass, Captain, after a night's rest," she said and guided him back to his cabin.

Terese slipped in behind them as Renée steered Alex onto his bed. She pressed a hypo to his neck, and his grimace faded as he fell back. As they struggled to remove his ship boots, Terese quipped, <We keep meeting like this, Ser.>

<I fear this might become a habit. Our captain's greatest adversary seems to be himself. Any of us would have admitted we were tired long before we experienced pain.>

<Our captain has an agenda and a timetable,> Julien chimed in, <and it doesn't allow for his own frailties.> After a pause, he continued. <I must admit that his talent is most impressive, Ser … adopting the applications in advance of your training.>

Renée felt out of her depth. <Terese, I'd like your advice on this matter.>

<As children, we wait to be introduced to each application, foregoing active exploration, but we are dealing with an adult New Terran. I'd recommend that we let him explore his implant's applications at his own rate. But we must monitor him closely and prepare to rendezvous in his sleeping quarters at night,> she said, laughing softly as she left the cabin.

Renée knew Terese's injection would allow Alex to sleep through the night. She was pleased he had his first cell-gen injection. The nanites would work to repair his stressed neural connections. She touched his bare arm, his dense muscles warming her fingertips. Ignoring any thoughts of self-reproach, she climbed onto the bed and curled up next to him.

-29-

To create the missile components, fuels, explosive compounds, and signal buoys, Julien created a new line of GEN-3 machines that were installed on Barren Island. Since the machines were vital to their militaristic plans, they decided to take a duplicate set with them.

When the stage-1 missiles were ready, Julien requested daily test flights from Commander Jameson, and Lieutenant Jason "Jase" Willard happily flew each trial, much to the exasperation of Lieutenant Andrea Bonnard, who was aching to have her turn. But with the completion of stage-1 tests, flights were scheduled twice daily, and Commander Jameson assigned Andrea to Dagger-2 for the day's second flight.

Andrea had not been born to well-to-do parents. After public school, she had enrolled in TSF, which had provided her with a salary, room, and board. But, best of all, TSF offered her the opportunity to fly. She qualified for shuttle pilot's school and graduated top of her class. At the end of her five-year enlistment, she left TSF for a job flying for the Ministry of Space Exploration. But within two years, the bloom wore off as the repetition of the job wore on. Then the aliens arrived and Barren Island announced it wanted fighter pilots. Her dream job had arrived.

Julien had the pilots practicing what he anticipated would be real-world conditions. Their Daggers twisted and flipped as they sought to evade the imaginary beam shots he programmed into their controllers. Even with their inertia compensation systems, the pilots were adding bruises on top of bruises by the end of each flight.

When the first chase trial was scheduled, Andrea found herself paired against Lieutenant Robert Dorian, pilot of the newly tested Dagger-3. Her fighter was armed with loads of two-stage missiles. Jase, having piloted the previous, single-fighter test, fumed as he watched the action from the flight terminal, the concept of pilot rotation grating on his ego.

The two pilots ran through several chase scenarios while Julien tracked Dagger-2's ability to hit Dagger-3, which stood in for the silver ship. When the trials were completed, Julien adopted a lesson from Alex, who had a penchant for experimentation. He sent new coordinates to the controllers and switched off the pilot's helmet telemetry. It was a test of nerves for the pilots to sit blind in ships controlled by the advanced Méridien computers. Some pilots argued that they were just backups for the controllers, but Andrea knew it wasn't so. The trick was to discover the right balance. But at the moment, sitting in the dark, her Dagger shooting through space, it was downright scary, to say the least.

Her fighter decelerated and then stopped. She heard Julien say *begin* and her helmet display lit up, telemetry fully restored. Her controller immediately located Dagger-3, and she launched into attack mode, flipping her fighter around, and accelerating under full power.

Lieutenant Dorian located his adversary and went into evasion mode. He slid behind a freighter, which was pulling out from the orbital station, and earned the captain's displeasure via a complaint to TSF.

Andrea fought to tag Robert's fighter, and, inevitably, her stage-2 missile caught Dagger-3 in the fuselage, splattering a dollop of nanites on the hull.

The encounter was an epiphany for Julien when he compared the results of his planned encounters to the pilots' unfettered competition, realizing just how inventive New Terran minds were when circumstances demanded it.

* * *

Commander Jameson reported to Alex that four Daggers were operational, and the base had trained ten fighter pilots, six crew chiefs, and twenty-eight service personnel. Missile production would be completed and ready for loading before the Joaquin finished their repairs.

Alex decided it was time to put his next enlistment step into action and requested Tatia, Terese, Pia, and Geneviève join him in his cabin. When they were assembled, he said, "I have a job for the four of you. I would like you to spend two or three days at Barren Island entertaining the pilots and crew."

Pia twigged to it first. "Ah ... are we recruiting or culling, Captain."

"Culling, Pia," he said, sending the list to their implants. "This is the commander's roster of trained pilots and crew."

"Captain, isn't this rather sexist on your part?" Tatia's voice rose with indignation.

"Sexist? Considering the fact that you are all women, perhaps," Alex replied, not attempting a defense.

Tatia turned to the Méridiens for support but found only smiles on their faces. When they were dismissed, she remained behind, asking for a moment of his time. "Captain, what am I missing here? I want to feel indignant, but the women look as if you told them they're going on a holiday."

"They *are* going on holiday. This is their first trip off the *Rêveur*. I'm only sorry that it's winter on Barren Island."

"But what do you expect from them, Captain?"

"I expect them to do whatever they want. They aren't children. They know what I need to know. In terms of recruitment, the Méridiens have been ahead of me since day one. And I might point out to you that you have benefited from that process as much as anyone."

Blood flushed up Tatia's neck. She stood up, clenching her fists. "Are you saying that Alain deliberately …"

Alex cut her off. "Don't attribute New Terran behavior to the Méridiens. They'll do what comes natural to them … meet people, get to know them, make friends. So, when they recommend someone, it's someone they trust. End of story."

Tatia sat down heavily at the table, chagrined at her outburst.

"I expect in your mind I'm sending these women to sleep with the crew. If so, you don't understand them yet. They will engage the pilots and crew in conversation, recording and comparing notes the entire time. That's the power of the implants. When they're done, I'll have a psychological profile on each of these people complete with vids, should I wish to review the footage."

"Reconnaissance at its best," Tatia acknowledged, mulling over what Alex said. "My apologies, Sir, I didn't give them, or you, due respect. But then why am I going?"

"I've told Commander Jameson that my first mate is conducting a readiness inspection."

Understanding dawned on Tatia. "So the base will be concentrating on me, worrying about the inspections, and the crew will be happy to chat with our Méridiens, selling their side of the story as to why they should receive high marks. Captain, I do believe you have become an aficionado of sneakiness." With that, she stood, saluted, and requested to be excused.

Later, Terese sent Alex a vid. Tatia had apologized to the Méridien women, her demeanor of self-control, usually first and foremost, was not in evidence.

Alex had watched Tatia's friendship with Alain bloom into a love affair. The two stole moments together whenever they could. Alain never shirked his duties, but in his free time he could often be found in his cabin, on a comm connection to TS-1 and Tatia. He was pleased that Tatia was starting to realize Alain was not an exception to the Méridiens but was typical of them.

-30-

In the end, Alex decided on a civilian organization for the crew, since they had no authority to operate as anyone's military. And there was always the distinct possibility that they'd arrive in orbit around Méridien, the hull full of weapons, only to find the entire Confederation at peace, the attack on the two Méridien ships an anomaly committed by a passing rogue. The thought kept him from being too presumptuous.

Julien relayed the Joaquin's message that the construction bays were ready. The primary bay wouldn't fully accommodate the *Rêveur*. A third of the ship would extend outside its structure, preventing the bay doors from closing and requiring all exterior hull and engine work be performed by EVA crews.

To provide a second bay for the *Outward Bound*, President McMorris ordered a partially constructed shuttle be moved and parked on a holding arm of the station. Compensation was paid to the Purity Ores mining company for the delay. The CEO, Samuel B. Hunsader, was outraged, but he kept his opinions to himself. At the moment, the president was a very popular man. Méridien medical nanites were saving lives and healing crippling injuries, and the news media coveted the stories, frequently crediting the pact and McMorris in the same line.

In concert with *A Little Shove*, Alex, piloting his tug, positioned the *Rêveur* bow-first into the bay's opening. He released his beams and repositioned his ship at the *Rêveur*'s stern to act as a brake while the other tug stood off. EVA crews in powered exoskeletons attached cables to eyelets Julien had propagated on the hull's bow and amidship. The cables slowly inched the multi-decked ship into the bay until the crew boss called "all stop."

Alex released his tether and slid his ship into the assigned construction bay. Several of the crew had journeyed with him to prepare the ship for its transformation, cleaning out the galley and removing his personal belongings. As bay services were attached to the hull, Alex ordered Tara to shut down, his voice thick with emotion.

"System shut down in progress," were her last words.

TSF troopers met Alex and his crew outside the bay's airlock and accompanied them through the station back to the *Rêveur*. The Méridiens' heads swiveled at the sights and sounds of restaurants, clubs, retail shops, and people crowding the corridors. And the civilians reciprocated by stopping and staring at the Méridiens.

By the time Alex and company returned to the *Rêveur*, the majority of the crew, except for some department heads and much of engineering, had left on holiday. New Terrans would visit with family and introduce them to their Méridien friends and lovers. Each Méridien had wrestled with the awkward task of choosing among the several invitations offered by their New Terran crewmates. While on holiday, the Méridiens and their hosts would enjoy specially planned festivities – music concerts, holo-light shows, museum tours, and a visit to the spectacular Corona Mountains.

The Corona Mountains were a potent symbol to the New Terrans. The colonists had landed their shuttles near the mountains, which were heavily laced with monazite crystal causing the exposed cliffs to glow with soft yellow light at sunset on certain days of the year. The luminescent display had become a beacon of hope for the struggling colonists.

Tatia and Alain were waiting at the airlock for Alex. <You sure we're not needed, Captain?> Tatia sent.

<You two go and enjoy yourselves,> Alex replied to both of them.

Wearing huge smiles, the two quick stepped down the gangway. They'd be staying at her father's farm. Her parents would meet her Méridien lover and say goodbye to their only child, who would be leaving for the stars.

The remaining crew members moved their possessions into the foremost berths, often doubling up. The ship was sealed aft of them since the possibility of catastrophic decompression outweighed any potential discomfort. It would take six, full, thirty-hour days, with three shifts of crew working around the clock, to remove the damaged FTL engines, cut away damaged frames, and excise the hull and internal sections to make way for the port bay.

Alex joined Renée and Étienne on the bridge. His attempt to convince Étienne to join the crew on holiday had failed. His *shadow* refused to take leave unless ordered to go, which seemed counterproductive to enjoying a vacation. So Alex had relented.

Senior Engineer Mickey Brandon was delegated as officer in charge of the *Rêveur*, and with TSF security in tow, Alex, Renée, and Étienne caught the next shuttle. Both of his guests had made several trips planetside, but those had been official State visits, T-site inspections, meetings with ministers, and conferences with scientists. This was their first New Terran holiday.

Two hover cars waited for them at the shuttle terminal, one for them and one for the troopers. In the more than 100 days since Méridiens first set foot on New Terra, not a single negative incident had marred their time on planet. Then again, no one had told the public of the attack on the *Rêveur* lest fear run rampant through the population that dangerous aliens might have followed the Méridiens to New Terra.

An hour outside the city, their hover cars parked on a landing pad in front of a home nestled deep in the woods. Tall trees surrounded the two-story, gray-stone house. Christie dashed pell-mell down wide stone steps, passing her parents, and jumping into her brother's arms. She hugged both Renée and Étienne, quickly taking charge of Étienne, hooking an arm through his and pulling him along. "You have to see our home," she exclaimed. Alex felt a twinge of regret for inflicting his little sister on his escort.

After the round of greetings, the family and their guests walked into the quiet warmth of the house. Two troopers took packs from the hover car's rear compartment and followed them inside. The other two took the second hover car and left for a nearby inn.

Renée loved the home's furnishings. Heavy wooden furniture covered in natural textiles was arranged around an inviting fireplace in which soft flames, emanating from gas pipes, danced around carved stone logs. A natural wood floor, something unseen on Méridien except in the oldest of houses, was covered with woven rugs of subtle tones. The furnishings were comfortable and personal, which seemed to her to describe Alex.

But the new home, courtesy of the family's lucrative earnings from Alex's g-sling program, hadn't proved to be sunshine for everyone. Christie felt isolated in the country just as she had during the years in space. She was a gregarious person. The one balm to her tortured existence was her newfound fame as the sister of Captain Racine, the hero of the *Rêveur* rescue and the discoverer of New Terra's first aliens. Half a year ago, her comm center had filled up, and it remained full today. Now, her brother's guests were going to make her even more popular. She'd accepted a major news producer's offer to interview a Méridien from her home. It would be the planet's first Méridien interview, a great coup for the network ... and for Christie. Now, she only had to ask Étienne's permission, the part she'd neglected to mention when she'd sold the idea to her parents.

When she did ask permission, her ruse was exposed, and a family conference quickly ensued. Christie was about to be comm restricted, when Renée sent to Alex, <Does this have value for us?>

For the next few moments, Alex, Renée, and Étienne discussed the pros and cons of an interview. Alex and Renée could not decide either way.

Étienne offered the deciding opinion. <Christie is of the captain's family. She has made an obligation, and her failure to deliver will reflect badly on the family. I suggest we go forward with the interview. In the meantime, I will speak to Christie of the discredit that might have been befallen her House.>

Alex made a mental note to forewarn the president and the team prior to the interview. Finishing their exchange, they returned their focus to the family, who were staring at them with bewildered expressions.

"Alex, you have one of those things in your head!" Christie exclaimed.

Alex ignored her statement and said pointedly, "Étienne will participate in the interview with you." As Christie smiled, he continued, "But not because you deserve it," which instantly deflated her. "We've discussed the matter, and we believe it's too important to cancel. We can't afford any negative press about the Méridiens."

"Alex, we apologize," Duggan said. "Christie made it sound as if you had approved it and Étienne had volunteered." All eyes turned to Christie, who shrank into her chair, guilt written all over her face.

"This might be a case of too much attention having gone to someone's head," Alex suggested. "After the interview tomorrow, you can handle her punishment." He turned to stare at his sister. "But before the interview, sister of mine, Étienne de Long of House de Guirnon, wishes to express certain sentiments to you, Ser Christie."

Christie had watched Étienne stand as Alex announced him. He stood beside her and gave her a slight bow of his head. She knew her mouth was hanging open. Somehow the fun of having her own alien interview had morphed into a hard life lesson, of that she was sure. She stood, took the arm he offered, and walked with him through the double doors leading to her father's study.

In the living room, the others watched as the two talked, Christie seated in a broad armchair and Étienne on the chair's ottoman. Christie's legs were tucked under her and her arms were crossed tightly against her chest. She was frowning, but she was listening intently to Étienne.

Renée watched the parents as they glanced back and forth between Christie and Étienne and Alex and her. She commed Alex, <You should explain to Duggan and Katie that we don't eat young girls,> and he burst out laughing.

"Wait, wait," his mother demanded, having forgotten to worry about her daughter for the moment, "You two have been talking."

"Yes, you did it before, the three of you, didn't you?" Duggan jumped in.

"Yes," Alex admitted, "I have a Méridien implant that allows me to communicate directly with my crew and Julien."

His parents stared at him, concern written all over their faces. "It didn't hurt, did it?" his mother asked.

"No, Mom, I barely felt the entire operation, which was very quick."

Renée sought to deflect their concerns. "Méridien youth take years to master the implant programs. Your son has mastered much of this same material in only twenty-six days."

"He was always a quick study," his father admitted.

Soon after, Christie and Étienne emerged from the study. Christie apologized to her parents, Alex, and Renée for her subterfuge and to Étienne for not treating him with the respect he was due as a visitor to their world. Then she walked upstairs to her room.

His parents stared agape at the stairs Christie had just vacated. Then they turned to look at Étienne, warm welcoming smiles spreading across their faces.

"Étienne, how would you like to stay with us forever?" Katie asked.

* * *

The interview turned out to be a resounding success. The producer had brought a veteran news anchor out of retirement to guide the vid comm with Étienne and Christie. Alex and Renée had coached Christie on appropriate questions to ask, and, midway through the allotted time, the anchor had lapsed into silence, allowing Christie to conduct the remainder of the interview. The result was a net hit. A favorite excerpt, displayed on almost every reader, was the manner in which Christie ended the interview. She had placed her right hand over her heart and tilted her head slightly, saying, "Étienne de Long of House de Guirnon, you have honored the House of Racine with this interview, and it is well and truly appreciated."

Christie was ecstatic that she had found her calling. She planned to become a media personality, much to her parents' dismay.

-31-

Once back aboard the *Rêveur*, Alex found the construction prep complete. Installation of the new frames for both the FTL engine and the port bay had begun. Assembly was proceeding quickly as it was a simple matter of placing a frame, confirming its alignment, and sealing it in place with nanites. The EVA crew used portable hoods to surround the joints, trapping the oxy-torch heat to energize the nanites.

Three days after Alex's return aboard ship, Tatia and her three Méridien companions arrived from their visit to Barren Island. Terese, Pia, and Geneviève had charmed the entire base. Their recordings were uploaded to Julien, and he compiled the vids, remarks, and recommendations for Alex, Tatia, and the new second mate, Edouard Manet, the Méridien navigation specialist.

When Tatia joined Alex on the bridge, she observed a patchwork of vids on the screens chronicling the ongoing construction work. The view would often rotate to follow crew and enlarge for more detail. Then the frames would change.

<What are you monitoring, Julien?> she sent, not wanting to disturb Alex.

<All the construction projects, First Mate,> Julien replied

<No, I mean the views on the screen. Are you looking for something specific?> she clarified.

<The captain is controlling the screen views and the external cameras.>

The extent of the image manipulation was astounding. She had assumed only Julien could manage that degree of complexity. <Can I do that, Julien?>

<In time, you will be able to do this and more, First Mate.>

Tatia had not been receptive to the idea of an implant in her head, but she'd refused to relent to her fear. She accepted it as the price to pay to be with Alain and a journey to the stars. Watching Alex manipulate the vids, it struck her how much she'd resisted adopting it. That would change today, she vowed, and left for Medical.

* * *

Life aboard the *Rêveur* was a cramped affair. The crowded cabins might have become intolerable, but everyone was too busy day and night to notice. After their work shift, they filed through a pair of tiny meal prep compartments, which were converted storage lockers, to collect food to eat in their cabins. Then they played implant games. It was a Tatia–Terese invention.

In Medical, only moments after her witnessing Alex's control of the monitors and vids cams, Tatia had explained to Terese her reluctance to embrace the implant, suggesting others might be having similar issues despite Alex's easy success. "These training regiments are too tedious," she had said. "We need something our people might enjoy. They need to learn without realizing they're learning."

Now the crew played games at night. It started out slow and simple. One Méridien held an image in his or her mind with open access, while the other Méridiens held theirs in privacy mode. On Julien's signal, since his duties now included referee and scorekeeper, the New Terrans raced to contact each Méridien to discover the image.

The first night they had played for barely an hour before the New Terrans became mentally exhausted. By the time the landing bays were completed and the engines were being installed, they were playing for hours, and Julien was calling a halt to the games to allow everyone sufficient time to sleep.

The games progressed until the Méridiens were using their full capabilities to compete with the New Terrans. At that point, mixed teams were formed.

An interesting side effect of the games was the transference of New Terran word and image associations that initially baffled the Méridiens. The Méridiens reciprocated or, as the New Terrans termed it, *retaliated*, by using images of animals and fruit from Confederation colonies. This required the mixed teams to share background information quickly – an unintentional, though very valuable, exercise in bonding.

The game increased in complexity as New Terrans employed satire and witticisms in game play and the Méridiens adopted these techniques as well. One team would pose a riddle then divide clues to the answer between several minds. The other side would assemble the clues before posing a guess. The winning team was the one that solved the riddle the quickest.

One evening, Tatia's team cried foul, frustrated after not finding a critical clue.

Renée, who had observed the games, enjoying the fun but never taking part, commed Tatia's entire team, <Have all players been checked for clues?> Tatia sent her a list of the other team's players, doing so with no lag time, which made Renée smile. In return, Renée asked, <Did I understand the rules of tonight's game correctly? Tatia was appointed captain and Julien assigned a team to her. Is this correct?> She received a flood of affirmations. <Were you given an official list of the other team?> She thought she knew what had been done, but wanted to guide them to discover the answer.

Tatia sent her a player's list. She'd highlighted her team's players in one color and the others in another color, with each clue that had been discovered beside the relevant opponent's name.

Then Renée dropped the final point. <So all participants are accounted for?> she asked. There was the briefest pause. Team Captain Tatia queried the referee on open comm and received a list of eligible participants. Renée and Julien had permanently excluded themselves from the games. All players watched as Tatia ran a matching program and one name popped up that was not on her list but still on the eligible player's list, the captain. Jeers, hoots, and images of New Terran and Méridien animals, mostly considered pests by their respective cultures, all wearing the captain's face, flooded the comms.

The only response was the captain's laughter, long and loud.

* * *

Widespread use of the implants did not come without pitfalls. Images of Pia, writhing in ecstasy beneath him, woke Alex one night. But it wasn't a dream. It was an implant stream from Pia's partner, Mickey. Alex immediately blocked Mickey's signal and erased the vid.

First thing the next morning, Alex received an abject apology from Mickey. In his excitement, Mickey had broadcast the event to the entire crew. He walked around the entire morning with a face flushed with embarrassment. Pia, on the other hand, was in a joyous mood.

After the games were well underway, Alex had Julien monitor and rate the crews' implant adoption, using a scale from 1 to 100. Daily frequency and complexity of an implant's use added points; use of the voice deducted points. The first time Alex reviewed the daily summary, he was surprised to discover he headed the list, especially since the Méridiens were included.

Terese, who had been copied on the list to monitor stragglers, had remarked, <Captain, you understand it's entirely possible you aren't a New Terran. But then again, maybe you aren't a long-lost Méridien either.> She had sent him an image of a man in a captain's uniform with a yellow query symbol over a blank face.

-32-

<Captain, we must discuss my recent sleuthing,> Julien sent cryptically to Alex, who was preparing for bed.

It took a moment for Alex to figure out what he meant. <Oh, yes ... any progress on your investigations?>

<Unfortunately, yes, Captain. As your people say ... are you sitting down?>

Alex experienced a sinking sensation. He'd hoped they were dealing with an isolated incident, but now he feared otherwise. <I am now.>

<According to the Frasier brothers' confession, they used ether-ware, as your people call it, to text their client via an anonymous message drop.>

<Wait, what? That confession was on the secured TSF network.>

<Yes, that's correct, Captain.> Julien waited for Alex's response, but received nothing. <The brothers stated they received a down payment on acceptance of the task. Although they never specified the amount, their business financial account shows a deposit of 100K creds six days before the theft. I traced the deposit back to the originating financial firm, then to the firm's customer, a private security firm. Within the security firm, a lead investigator's reader showed she had opened an anonymous drop-box account the day before the brothers received their initial payment.>

<How did you deduce it was her reader?>

<I didn't, Captain. I checked every reader in the firm.>

Once again, there was a quiet moment before Julien continued. <I accessed the firm's accounting records and searched for client payments of 100K prior to the opening of the anonymous box.>

<Client payments ... you believe that the security firm was hired to front this transaction.>

<Yes, Captain, a go-between as it is called.>

<Any success in finding the 100K source?>

<Yes and no, Captain. There was no deposit of 100K.>

<So it was a dead end?>

<How little you think of my skills, Captain.>

<My mistake, continue your tale, oh mighty one.>

<Two payments, greater than 100K, were made within three days of the anonymous account setup. Both were credited to numbered accounts, with no additional details. I discovered the chief financial officer's reader contained a list of numbered accounts with names and contact information. One payment of 125K was an annual retainer for security services. That one could be disregarded. The other payment of 150K was a transfer from the account of a Gregory Hinsdale.>

<And who is Gregory Hinsdale?>

<He is head of security for one of your planet's largest mining concerns, Purity Ores.>

<Oh ... black, black, black space!> Alex swore as he stomped around his cabin.

<I take it you have information to share, Captain.>

Besides being the buyer of his family's first g-sling efforts, Samuel B. Hunsader, the CEO of Purity Ores, was a powerful supporter of none other than Assemblyman Clayton Downing. Alex sat down on the edge of his bed and attempted to parse the news.

<Well, this can't get any worse.> He explained to Julien the relationship between Hunsader and Clayton, adding in some history of the Assembly's ultraconservative faction and their support from industrial leaders, who wanted to see their agenda furthered. <And you should understand that Assemblyman Downing is President McMorris' greatest detractor.>

<What should be done with this information, Captain?>

<And I thought our warheads were powerful,> Alex groused. <Julien, preserve all details of your investigation until I can figure out what to do with it. By the way, that was extraordinary work, even if it has turned our lives upside down. Good-night.>

<Good-night, Captain,> said Julien, wondering if the detectives of the old novels felt like this when they delivered bad news to their clients.

* * *

All the *Rêveur*'s repairs were finished. Crew members who had endured the confined spaces were thrilled to move into their new cabins, now restored to Méridien passenger liner quality.

To prepare for launch, specifically for the transition from station power to ship's power, all supplies, equipment, and personnel were restrained. When station power was cut, they would be in zero-gravity. The engines needed to be online before power could be returned to the grav-plates and inertia compensators.

At precisely 5.95 hours, Alex walked onto the bridge, where Edouard waited. As the navigation specialist, his experience, along with Julien, would ensure a successful launch, or so Alex hoped. They seated themselves in the command chairs, and body restraints formed over them.

Alex eyed the four empty seats at the bridge's control panels. <Julien, I've always meant to ask. Why does this ship have bridge positions when you do everything better and faster?>

<The positions are for navigation, engine control, environmental, and comm, Captain. They are there in the event of my demise or if I am unable to perform my duties.>

Alex sat wondering how either of those two possibilities could come to pass and was only reminded how much more he still had to learn about his cousins and their world.

Julien confirmed that all bay doors and hatches were sealed and maneuvering thrusters were operational. He announced their impending departure to the crew and reduced or cut power to unnecessary items to save the drain on the energy banks.

Alex commed the crew boss and ordered all service lines released. After confirmation, he ordered the release of the massive docking bay clamps.

The crew boss confirmed "all clear," but Alex waited for Julien's affirmation that the *Rêveur* was free of all attachments and their path was clear before he ordered them out of the bay on thrusters. *A Little Shove* stood by in case assistance was required.

When the ship cleared the bay by several hundred meters, Alex ordered the engines online at minimum power.

<Engines are online and operating within parameters,> Julien responded. <All systems are ready, Captain. The *Rêveur* is yours.>

Alex's heart swelled in his chest. An advanced, technological starship was at his fingertips, and he was the captain. The thought that he was also responsible for the safety and lives of everyone aboard doused his elation with cold water.

Employing the ship's thrusters, Julien slowly spun the *Rêveur* to come about to their new course.

As the bow swung past the orbital's viewing platform, Alex enlarged the central screen and spotted hundreds of workers and citizens standing and waving through the station's viewing windows. <Julien, do we have running lights?>

<Exterior ship lights, Captain? No, but I am able to send electrical impulses through the hull.>

<We have an audience at the station windows. If you could send them a thank you, I'd be pleased.>

<It would be my pleasure, Captain.> He quickly designed an algorithm to vary the hull's sensor feeds from bow to stern and around the circumference. When he activated the program, it sent fluctuating signal waves down and around the hull's length. This effort exemplified how his life had changed since meeting Alex. He didn't regret his previous century of service, but moments such as this one gave him cause to celebrate his existence. And if anyone were to ask, he was particularly pleased to be the referee of the implant games.

As they cleared the orbital complex, Julien relayed a vid to the port view screen. "Captain, I have intercepted a vid transmission to a New Terran news station." In the vid, the sleek silhouette of the *Rêveur*, barely visible in the Joaquin's exterior lights, suddenly blazed with streams of color traveling in waves across the hull. The reporter's voice-over said, "The *Rêveur* signaled her exit from the Joaquin station this morning in a dazzling show of Méridien technology. It was a wonderful salute to the hundreds of workers and civilians who had turned out to watch the launch of the starship."

<That was a wonderful display, Julien! You're an artist!>

<Thank you, Captain.>

<Please send the vid to the crew.>

Alex kept everyone in confined conditions until their sub-light and inertia compensation tests were completed and Julien was satisfied. After these systems checked out, FTL engine power-up sequences were successfully run as they orbited New Terra.

Alex announced to the crew that all the system tests had been successful, and they were released to move about. Julien relayed to him the cheering that broke out throughout the ship.

After several more orbits, the *Rêveur* was stationed, once again, beside the Joaquin. Engineers staffed the starboard landing bay, ushering in one of the ship's repaired shuttles.

* * *

Tatia, as first mate, had responsibility for department requirements and day-to-day issues, one of which was the question of fraternization. Knowing full well she was putting herself and Alain in jeopardy, she broached the subject with Alex.

From behind his desk, Alex smiled up at her, knowing the effort it took her to ask the question. "Tatia, we aren't a military ship. We aren't even a company ship. We are an invention, the first in over 700 years in this corner of the galaxy. The rule book is ours to invent. So if it's broken, we will fix it; if it isn't broken …"

Tatia gave him a soft salute and a smile as she acknowledged his decision. "Aye, aye, Captain," she said, whirling about and barely containing her excitement as she exited the cabin.

Another of her responsibilities was monitoring the implant progress list. Both she and Renée noticed when Alex's score changed from 99 to 102. They retired to Renée's suite and linked with Julien so they could explain their concerns. Alex's score rising above 100 … how was that possible? Alex holding a conversation with multiple people and manipulating vids on screen simultaneously … how was that possible?

<There is no need for concern,> Julien replied. <The captain is adopting the implant much the same way as our mathematicians and code engineers have always done. He acquired the implant's programming language to design his own applications. I calculate he will require more application space in approximately thirty-two days, if not sooner.>

If the two women were amazed by this news, Julien's next words astonished them even more. <You should be aware that Alex isn't running his translation program anymore. He speaks to Méridiens in Con-Fed.>

Tatia laughed with abandon. When she finally stopped, she said, <Just when I hoped I might catch the captain's implant score someday.>

And Renée, as astonished as Tatia, added, <And now I have to ask the captain for lessons.>

-33-

Alex sent Tatia, Terese, and the twins to Barren Island to recruit the pilots and flight crew. Tatia chose not to reinvent the wheel and had Julien edit Alex's original speech to the first batch of recruits.

The commander's candidates, minus those who hadn't been recommended, were assembled in the mess hall. Tatia sent a comm to Julien, who played the edited vid over the hall's screen.

When it was over, she opened the floor for questions. The candidates asked about their destination, about the implants, the cell-gen injections, and how long they'd be gone, the latter of which had no answer. Then she and the Méridiens waited. Slowly, first one and then a few others got up and left the room. Their names were pulled from consideration, and Tatia was pleased to note she had more than enough volunteers to fill her crew list.

One bright individual, Lieutenant Andrea Bonnard, seated up front, had noticed Tatia's momentary unfocused look. "What did you just do, Major, I mean, First Mate Tachenko … just then as the crew members left?" she asked.

Tatia repeated the question to the group in her command voice, adopting the parade-rest position she often used in front of her troopers, and explained her manipulation of the recruitment list. Someone at the back voiced a comment about a computer in her head, and it was easily heard in the quiet of the room.

"Exactly, people!" she agreed, warming to her subject, "Imagine you're in an emergency situation. The captain orders the landing bay evacuated, but you have a stuck airlock hatch. You comm the chief engineer or Julien, and you receive a vid of how to manually override the hatch controls. You play the vid and replay it, if necessary, in your head until you are able to clear the airlock. Then you signal the captain that you're out, and you're back in action."

"And that's possible with these implants, First Mate?" Lieutenant Bonnard asked.

"That and much more, Lieutenant."

Tatia got her crew; everyone they wanted. But there would be a twist on the pilot hierarchy. While the recruits lined up at Base Medical for their implants and cell-gen injections, Tatia met privately with Lieutenant Bonnard.

"Have a seat, Lieutenant," she said casually. "You're presently flying Dagger-2, as wing for Lieutenant Willard, correct?"

"That's correct, First Mate."

Tatia had intended to just announce the decision, but she took a different tack, one influenced by Alex's style of leadership. "I'd like your opinion on the best organization of the Daggers."

"How does the captain intend to deploy them?" she asked.

Tatia was pleased by the strategic question. She explained the captain's intention to pair the Daggers and use one pair at a time.

Andrea considered her response, not bothered by keeping her superior officer waiting. "It seems to me," she said finally, "that the first Dagger out the gate needs to be the best flyer. It's critical the first fighter tag the target to start the ball rolling. That would be our squadron ego, Lieutenant Willard, but I'd prefer to keep that comment private."

Tatia responded with a conspiratorial grin, and Andrea continued, "And although I've been Dagger-1's wing, I think Dagger-3, Lieutenant Dorian, should be his wing.

"And you, Lieutenant Bonnard?"

"I'd take the lead for Flight-2."

"Please explain yourself, Lieutenant."

"The strategy is a two-shot offense. Each pair of fighters represents a single shot, and each shot has the task of sticking the goo on the enemy, receiving the findings, updating the second payload, hitting the target with updated goo to dig a hole, and finally punching through the hull with a warhead."

Tatia nodded her agreement, smiling inwardly at the lieutenant's representation of the Méridiens' sophisticated nanites as *goo.*

"Since the pairs are operating independently," Andrea continued, "you need the best two pilots in the lead positions of each flight, Jase as lead for Flight-1 and me as lead for Flight-2."

Tatia sat back and reflected on Andrea's analysis. She had described the strengths of her fellow pilots and herself accurately, but, more important, honestly. The captain's faith in his Méridiens appeared to be quite well placed.

"Thank you for your evaluation," Tatia said, standing up behind her desk, "Squadron Leader Bonnard. You're receiving our pilot and crew lists on your reader now. Coordinate with Commander Jameson to have our flight crews and missile loads shuttled to the *Rêveur* tomorrow morning at 12.50 hours. All Daggers are to be flown to the *Rêveur* the following day to arrive at 10 hours. Julien will control any shuttles or fighters within 10K km of the ship, managing all landings, until otherwise ordered. Congratulations, Squadron Leader!"

Andrea was still processing her promotion while attempting to retain her orders and gave a quick thought to the value of an implant. Then, she snapped to attention, delivered a sharp salute, and a firm, "Thank you for the promotion, First Mate. Orders received!"

"Report to Medical for your cell-gen injection and implant, Squadron Leader. Dismissed," Tatia responded and smiled as Andrea flew out of the office.

-34-

"Captain, I have control of the Daggers," Julien reported.

The flight service crews had arrived the day before and spent the day moving into their cabin berths and becoming familiar with the ship's layout. They knew the landing bays intimately. Commander Jameson had built mockups of the bays, per Julien's specifications, for flight crew training.

In addition to the flight crews, the shuttles had delivered the missile silos. Aboard the last shuttle was an auxiliary crew, who flew the *Rêveur*'s remaining shuttle to Barren Island to make room for the fighters.

"Holding all Daggers at 500 meters, Captain, ready for landing."

"Starboard bay, stand by to receive Dagger-1," ordered Alex over the flight crew's ear comms, since the bay personnel were not trained on their newly embedded implants.

"Bay-1 standing by," replied Flight Crew Chief Eli Roth.

Sensors relayed to Julien the moment Dagger-1 touched down on the deck, but he allowed the crew chief to reply.

"Dagger-1 down and locked," the chief called out.

Alex walked the crews through the rest of the landings, satisfied with the steadiness of the new crew chiefs and their comm protocols. When the chiefs reported the bays secured, Alex left the bridge watch to Tatia and retired to his cabin.

Renée sent him an urgent message, moments later. <Captain, you appear to have a very distraught pilot, who has asked for directions to your cabin.>

Alex took a seat behind his desk and picked up his reader. He knew who was coming. When the loud knock came at his cabin door, he waited before signaling it open and calling out, "Enter."

Lieutenant Willard stalked through the door and demanded to know why he wasn't squadron leader. No salute. No decorum.

"Lieutenant Willard, we meet again," Alex said quietly.

Before the pilot could reply, Alex held up his hand. "One moment."

The lieutenant was forced to stand there, his control wavering, until another knock came at the door, followed by, "Captain, reporting as requested."

"Come in Squadron Leader Bonnard. I was about to answer Lieutenant Willard's question as to why he doesn't have your position."

The two pilots exchanged hard stares as Andrea took a stance beside the captain's desk.

"I chose the best strategist and tactician for squadron leader, and that's not you. Now, Lieutenant, I have a simple question for you. Can you or can you not operate under this command organization?" He watched Jase fume. The pilot wanted to argue. That was clear.

Jase had hoped to receive some signal that the captain might waver in his decision when challenged, but the other man just sat there staring at him, his expression fixed in stone.

"I'm waiting for your answer, Lieutenant."

"Yes, Sir, I can accept the position," Jase said, deciding a retreat was in order.

"I see. Let's test this, Lieutenant." Alex pitched his voice deep and authoritative, copying the tone Tatia used with her troops. "Please exit my cabin and approach again as it should have been done." When Jase hesitated, Alex added, "This will determine whether you serve with us, *pilot*," hitting hard on the common term, no title offered. Alex watched the lieutenant's eyes flick between him and Andrea. Then, apparently having made up his mind, he saluted and strode out the door. With an about-face, he knocked quietly on the door.

Alex glanced at Andrea.

She took up the cue. "Yes, Lieutenant?"

"I request permission to speak to the Captain, Squadron Leader."

"What is the subject of your request, Lieutenant?"

"The lieutenant owes the captain an apology, Sir."

"Captain, Lieutenant Willard wishes to address you."

"Admit him."

"Step forward, Lieutenant."

Lieutenant Willard stepped to Alex's desk and saluted, holding his arm locked to his brow.

Alex continued to examine his reader. Finally, he looked up and didn't have to pretend the cold anger he felt. He snapped a quick salute. "What is it, pilot?"

"Sir, I wish to apologize for my behavior. My question was out of line. I believe I'm a good pilot, Sir, and would like the opportunity to prove it."

Alex eyed the lieutenant, who kept his eyes trained on the bulkhead. "Your piloting skills were never in question, Lieutenant. It's your judgment that is suspect. Squadron Leader Bonnard, you've heard the pilot's apology. Do you wish to retain him in your squadron? If not, he can be on the shuttle that's docking in two hours. It's your choice."

"Sir," she said turning to face Alex, "Lieutenant Willard might be a pain in the ass, but he's also our best pilot. If he says he can conduct himself properly, I'm willing to give him one more chance." Then she turned and stared hard at Jase, "But just one more chance."

"You heard your squadron leader, Lieutenant. You have one more chance. If I were you, I'd be careful. Once we set course for Méridien, another insubordinate act on your part and you'll have one fine long walk back to New Terra. You're dismissed."

"Yes, Captain." Jase saluted him. "Thank you, Squadron Leader," he said, nodding to Andrea as he exited the cabin.

Andrea turned to look at Alex, a little unsure of what to say or do next.

"Is there anything else, Squadron Leader?" Alex inquired of her, which galvanized her to snap to attention. "No, Sir," she said, and when dismissed, left almost as quickly as Jase had done.

Afterward, two stories circulated among the crew, one from Jase and another from Andrea, but the messages were similar. Don't cross the captain or you will be walking back to New Terra.

-35-

Since it was third watch, Edouard was on the bridge when Alex joined him. They were still in a geosynchronous orbit around New Terra, holding position next to the Joaquin station.

<Good evening, Captain,> Julien greeted Alex. <By the late hour, I take it we're about to have an important discussion.>

<And you'd be correct,> Alex said, taking a seat in a command chair.

<Excellent. I look forward to these challenging moments. What's to be the topic this evening?>

<You, Julien, you're the topic.>

<Now that's a subject I wouldn't have predicted,> Julien responded, halting several subroutines to focus on the forthcoming discussion. It couldn't be said that he was nervous, but he was anticipatory.

<I'm concerned about you. The *Rêveur* has a defense, four Daggers, if we get them out of the bays in time. Otherwise this ship is just as vulnerable today as it was seventy-one years ago. You're the operating heart of the *Rêveur*, yet you're housed on this bridge, very exposed. I'm sorry that I didn't think of this before now, but we need to find a means to protect you and do it fast.>

<The mechanics of my protection are quite easily accommodated, Captain. Don't concern yourself. Senior Engineer Brandon and his team will receive comms in the morning to begin the necessary preparations, and I'm ordering the materials as we speak. I calculate it will take four days to complete an alternate, central location with reinforced hull plating. My data storage will be duplicated at all times and I can shift my kernel from one location to the other within moments.>

<That's what I've come to expect from you, Julien, answers and action.>

<It's my pleasure to be of service, Captain.> After a brief pause, he continued, <And if I may say, Captain, I'm humbled that you considered my well-being.>

<I need to worry about the safety of every crew member, Julien.>

* * *

The following days marked the delivery of the *Rêveur*'s final supplies. Two shuttles arrived requiring offloading via their rear ramps. Tatia coordinated with Andrea, and Flight-1 cleared the starboard bay for a short training run. Once the shuttles were safely down, their ramps were dropped and their precious cargoes of GEN-2 and GEN-3 machines were offloaded and stored amidship. The shuttles also brought ship supplies, personal items for the crew, and Julien's alternate site materials.

Alex was surprised to receive a gift from his parents. It was a small, wooden carving of a New Terran tree-dweller seen frequently in the woods outside his parent's home. It was carved from a fragrant wood, and holding the little carving close, he could smell the forest.

In the midst of midday meal, Alex nearly choked on a bite of food. While he understood the concepts of Méridien food stocks, nanites, and a controller to fabricate recipes, he'd never before wondered about the available food supply and immediately queried Julien.

<Captain,> Julien replied, <a ship such as the *Rêveur* launches with a two-year food supply for 300 people. Rest assured, I'd have mentioned it if it had been a concern. One would think you were required to think of everything, Captain. Then what would I do?>

Soon afterward, Julien passed a comm to Alex from the Joaquin station manager. The *Outward Bound*'s retrofit was complete. Alex ordered a station shuttle for the transfer crew, which consisted of Second Mate Edouard Manet as captain; a Dagger pilot, Lieutenant Miko Tanaka, as copilot; two engineering techs, Lyle Stamford and Zeke Krausman; and Pia Sabine as medical support.

From the bridge, Alex monitored their new shuttle as it slid out of the bay. If he hadn't known it was his ship, he wouldn't have recognized it. Gone were all the earmarks of an explorer-tug. It now had the streamlined hull of a super-long passenger shuttle with small but powerful Méridien engines and ventral hull struts that would allow it to land planetside.

Julien controlled the shuttle's final approach. With sensors embedded in both the *Rêveur*'s newly installed dorsal hull shoes and the *Outward Bound*'s struts, he was able to mate the two ships with minimal vibrations. The shoes extruded over the struts, securing the ships together.

With all preparations finally complete, Alex announced to the ship's crew that they'd be underway the following morning at 8.50 hours. Then he placed a conference comm to the president, the team, Commander Jameson, and the T-managers.

When Julien signaled Alex that everyone was ready, the president spoke first. "So it's time, Captain Racine."

"Yes, Mr. President, tomorrow morning. Everything that you and I have worked for has been realized. And for our efforts, the Méridiens have rewarded New Terra beyond measure. Now it's time to return their generosity and take them home. I wanted to thank everyone personally for their efforts on behalf of the Méridiens."

"Captain," then the president corrected himself, "Alex, it's us who should be thanking you. Your courage and loyalty to these new cousins of ours have served this nation as few have done since Captain Ulam first landed our people here. You have made us very proud."

"Captain Racine," General Gonzalez added, "we will be waiting for your return."

"Maybe you will bring more friends," Minister Jaya added hopefully.

"And, Captain Racine," Commander Jameson chimed in, "try not to bang up my Daggers. I was hoping to get them back."

Alex laughed and let the call end on an up note. He placed a last comm to his parents, getting Christie on the pickup. Her comm punishment had ended days ago, much to her delight. He spoke to his family for a while and was about to sign off when his mother gave him some last words of advice.

"Alex," she said, "your name derives from Earth's ancient Greek, Alexander. I wonder if you knew it means the *defender of humankind.* You have a good heart, my son, and I know you want to help others first. But remember this … not everyone can be saved. Please come home safe to us."

* * *

In his quarters, Alex sat at his desk pondering the choices he'd made, wondering if he'd done everything possible to protect the crew and ship. And in reverse, he worried he was overreacting, taking his own nation down the path of weapons building that had aided in Earth's decline. In the end, hunger finally chased him from his cabin.

The evening meal was subdued, even with the entire crew present. At its end, Alex stood and said a few words, telling them he was proud of them and they'd face the future together ... come what may. Then he suggested an early evening for all. The nightly implant games were suspended by mutual agreement.

After leaving the meal room, Alex headed for the bridge and the quiet of the stars. He sat in his chair, not even greeting Julien, who kept his own counsel. Soon, he heard the opening hiss of the accessway doors. Renée climbed into the second chair and reached out her hand to him. He took it in his and they watched the stars together in silence.

-36-

At 8.50 hours, Alex ordered the *Rêveur* underway, and Julien engaged their sub-light engines. Instead of a direct course toward Méridien, they circled deep toward Oistos. Eventually, the ship arced passed the second planet of the Three Sisters, the system's most inward bodies – rocky, barren planets.

Alex and the Méridiens stood on the upper view deck of the starboard bay. Many of the New Terrans waited respectfully silent behind them.

The bay had been vacated for the memorial. Julien played the Méridien's traditional eulogy, an Ancient's poem set to music, "Lament for the Dead."

Utilizing the bay's beams, Julien launched a large crate out through the bay doors, aimed at the New Terrans' star. In the Méridiens' memory, none had attended star services for more than two or three of their people in a single occasion. To witness so many of their comrades launched starward in a construction crate, instead of enclosed in crystal covers as befitted the dead, was difficult for them to accept.

As the poem ended and the strains of music faded away, silence held the audience. Alex reached to hold Renée's hand, and she squeezed his in return. Then in small groups, the memorial audience faded away, returning to their duties. Alex and Renée stayed for a while longer. Julien kept the bay doors open for them, holding the view of Oistos.

"So many lost, Alex," Renée whispered. "My hope goes with them that they will be the last of our people sacrificed to the silver ships."

Alex couldn't imagine what the Méridiens were feeling. Their society fervently believed in the sanctity of life and had built layers of protection for each and every individual. In one day, a silver ship had torn apart the façade of their safe society.

* * *

After the memorial, Alex appeared to settle into his watch with Renée as company, but his link with Julien was active. <Julien, I've decided to send President McMorris the data on the Frasier brothers and the money trail, despite the trouble it might get us into, but only if you agree.>

<I concur, Captain. The president has dangerous adversaries, and he has been an honorable man in all manner of things with us.>

<Send it anonymously to his private reader. Add this comment, 'Mr. President, this is a gift from your friends. Be careful with whom you share this dangerous information.'>

It had taken Alex forty-seven days after tethering the *Rêveur* to reach New Terra, arcing out and back into the ecliptic. Within an hour, the *Rêveur* had surpassed Alex's incredible velocity of 0.02c, and now, just four hours later, they had reached 0.1c. According to Julien, they'd pass through the ice asteroid fields in just four days at a velocity of 0.71c.

The crew's time was filled with daily training and nightly implant games. For Alex, Tatia, and Edouard, it was occupied by comm protocols, department regulations, and tactical training games, Andrea joining them for the latter subject.

Alex was commed in his cabin soon after they cleared the ice fields. It was second watch and he joined Tatia on the bridge. <Status?> he sent and was pleased when she responded via implant, having overcome her natural tendency to respond to a New Terran with her voice.

<We're clear of the ice fields, Captain. Our velocity is holding at 0.71c. Julien has set course for a white, G-type star we call Mane. The Méridiens call it Oikos.>

<Yes, the Morning star,> Alex said and observed Tatia's puzzled expression. He watched her eyes defocus and knew she was querying Julien, reminding him she was a grounder not a space explorer.

<Yes, Captain,> Tatia responded, <Julien said the Méridiens renamed their star Oikos, an Earth term for *home*. Distance is 23.6 light-years. Julien reports that everything is ready for FTL drive.>

They had been briefed by Julien on the transition effects of entering and leaving FTL as well as the flight oddities. Alex had spent many nights reviewing aspects of the process with Julien. The universe was always in motion, Julien had explained. Stars and planets weren't fixed. Their positions relative to other celestial bodies, once known, were fixed in databases with time stamps, directional courses, velocities, and orbital trajectories, if necessary. Then courses were calculated integrating the time difference from the original time stamp to project where the celestial bodies would be at the expected time of arrival. SADEs were quite accurate at calculating the intricate equations, but they still erred on the side of caution.

According to Julien, the greatest danger lay in the FTL exit. The starship's hull could manage space dust and small rocks with its electrostatic field. But anything larger, when exiting at 0.7c, he'd explained, would be catastrophic. With their high-quality sensor suites, fast maneuverable ships, and superbly tuned inertia systems, the Méridiens simply evaded obstacles before they became a problem.

But you couldn't steer around an alien energy weapon, Alex thought.

<Engage FTL engines, Julien,> Alex ordered. He felt an odd twisting in his head, a touch of vertigo that passed quickly. Julien blanked the view shield and screens, having explained that the twisting of space would overwhelm a human's optical senses.

Tatia, on the other hand, looked as if she'd tasted something rotten and steadied herself against the bridge console. She regained control, straightened up, and flashed Alex a crooked smile. <Oh, that was fun,> she announced.

<According to Julien, the effect is about the same whether it's entering or exiting FTL.>

<I can't wait.>

Alex checked in with Terese who was monitoring the crew's reactions. Two of the Méridiens, who knew from experience how hard the FTL transfer was on them, had preferred to be in a state of unconsciousness. The New Terran crew had a range of responses and Alex requested a list of people who would need to be debilitated for future transitions.

Alex queried Julien. <What's our time to Oikos?>

<Eight days, ten hours, Captain.>

Eight days and seventy-three years, for my Méridien friends, Alex thought. He kept the crew busy, practicing emergency drills of all types. Up until now, the Méridiens had relied on their SADE and their stasis tubes in emergencies. Now, they were well aware of their vulnerabilities and took to the drills with a passion, especially since the GEN machines and additional supplies had supplanted their stasis tubes. It was of no consequence to the Méridiens. Come what may, not one of them wanted to use the stasis tubes again.

The crew practiced manual hatch operation, isolating ship compartments in case of decompression, operating fire-suppression equipment, and the ship's intercoms. They practiced operations with the department heads incapacitated, emergency medical procedures, and, most important, flight bay support.

* * *

Eight days and ten hours later, they exited FTL just outside the Oikos system. The crew was anxious to download vids from Julien, but there was little to see at this time. Alex waited on the bridge while Julien compiled sensor data from his active telemetry. Renée dispatched a lengthy comm to House de Guirnon, summarizing the events of their attack, rescue, and return.

Méridien was the fourth planet outward from their star. As they closed at 0.71c from outside the heliosphere, Julien reported no signs of the silver ships and everyone breathed a sigh of relief. He did detect extraordinary outbound traffic from Méridien's orbital stations. Shuttles filled the sky traveling from the planet to the stations and back, and the vessels leaving the planet's orbit were headed primarily on one of two courses.

"The holo-vid, Julien," Alex requested. "Place the Oikos system in the center. Draw a red line from the system to the point of your attack. Draw a blue line for our direction of approach and add yellow lines to indicate the courses for the exiting ships."

Their blue line was about 100 degrees out of phase with the *Rêveur*'s original course, represented by the red line, and about 20 degrees off the system's ecliptic. The yellow lines were nearly opposite to the trajectory of the red line.

"That can't be a coincidence," Alex commented to Renée and Tatia, marking the holo-vid's opposing yellow and red lines.

"No, it can't be," replied Renée.

<Ser, there is a private comm for you,> Julien sent to Renée.

<Captain,> Renée interrupted, <I've received an encrypted comm from House de Guirnon. Please retire with me to your cabin.>

Alex turned the bridge over to Tatia and followed Renée back to his suite. He queried Julien on the quick response and was reminded that the *Rêveur* and all Confederation systems had FTL comm. In his cabin, Renée took a seat at the table, an earnest expression on her face.

"Captain, I'm concerned as to why I've received a private comm from my House. It's voice only and will unencrypt after reading my brain pattern. It will play only once then the accompanying application will delete it. I'll link with you so that you can hear it as it plays. Don't communicate with me in any manner until it ends."

She held up a finger to silence him and the message began. <Renée, my sister,> a man's voice said, <House de Guirnon is overjoyed to hear of your miraculous return. If father had only lived to greet you once again, our rejoicing would be complete. We owe gratitude to these New Terrans for their assistance, but it must be paid another day. House de Guirnon has urgent need of the *Rêveur* to support the exodus of our House. Station coordinates and docking-bay clearance are being sent to your SADE. Most

important, sister, tell the New Terrans only that we welcome their arrival and will arrange passage for them to the planet. Ensure all of them board the shuttles. We will send security escorts to aid you. Welcome home, sister. House de Guirnon fini.>

Alex sat still as he replayed his copy of the message for himself. When it finished, he reached out for her hands. "I'm so sorry, Renée, for the loss of your father."

She looked up, offering him a sad, tentative smile. Having heard that her brother was preparing to lure his people planetside, probably to abandon them so he could commandeer the ship they'd worked so long and hard to restore, his first thought had been for her and the loss of her father.

Julien broke into their conversation. <Captain, Ser, I've received House orders to proceed to the Barden Orbital Station, docking bay E-43.>

<Julien, disregard those orders,> Renée retorted hotly.

<Julien, disregard Renée's request. Please standby,> Alex countermanded.

"Captain, my people are planning to betray you! You must turn around. Take the *Rêveur* and return to New Terra."

"Renée, your brother is only one person." he said, gripping her by the shoulders. "Your people are fleeing from something, probably the silver ships or whoever or whatever sent them. If that's what's happening, then we have a job to do. Sooner or later, this menace will come for New Terra, and my people don't have the resources or tech to vacate our planet. And, not to put too delicate a point on this, but aren't your people just running to the far end of the cage after the beast has crashed through the door?"

"You'd still defend my people without their support?"

"We need information. I say we go where we can find it. The question is what will you do?"

Her eyes narrowed as she thought furiously. "I'll talk with my people on *this ship*," she said with fierce determination, then spun around and hurried from the cabin.

Alex strode toward the bridge, comming his first mate. <We have a problem, First Mate. Clear the bridge.> Once on the bridge, he included Tatia in his comm to Julien. <Renée's private comm was from her brother, Albert. Her father has passed, and her brother is head of House de Guirnon. He wants this ship, and it appears he wants us marooned planetside … *us* being all the New Terrans on this ship."

<What?> Tatia exclaimed.

<It was a momentous day, Alex, when I first saw your face in the hull sensors,> Julien said. <Since then my world has expanded in unique ways, and I like the new view. What are your orders, Captain?>

<Thank you, my friend,> said Alex. His implant picked up Renée approaching the bridge, and he admonished Tatia to wait before saying anything.

Renée entered the bridge and said, "I've shared my brother's message with my people, Captain." Alex had relayed his unencrypted copy back to her as she left his cabin. "We are of one mind. The Méridiens of this ship will follow our captain, wherever he chooses to go, whatever he chooses to do. We will not dishonor the sacrifices he and his people have made for us."

Alex was grinning at Renée, who smiled back at him.

"You heard her, Julien. I need information." he ordered.

"Ready, Captain," the glee apparent in Julien's words.

"I want you to operate in the open as the SADE of a House liner returning to the system. Gather all the intelligence you can on what this panic is about and summarize it. Where's the problem? How big is it? How long has it been happening? And when you have that information, I want you to find us some allies. Some Méridiens have to be trying to fix this problem. Locate them for me. Until then, maintain course and acknowledge the House comms as expected.

"Tatia, you have the bridge," Alex ordered. "Renée, may I see you privately?"

Alex commed the entire crew to bring them abreast of the dilemma. He heard angry rumblings from the New Terrans when he explained Albert's betrayal, but they ceased when they learned of their Méridiens' declaration. His plan, he told them, was to gather information on the nature of the panic, locate the danger, and, if possible, test their weapons.

In his cabin, he turned to look at Renée. "I need to understand what your decision means to you – refusing to obey your brother."

"Our betrayal places us outside our House, and no one stands outside their House. It's how order is kept."

"Someone, sometime, must have disobeyed his or her House before you. What happened to them?"

"They are declared as *Independents* and are relocated to a system near here, where our government provides for them. They are allowed to live as they chose, without House allegiance, and form whatever industries they wish to support themselves, but there is no transport off planet for them."

"You mean it's a penal colony?"

"I wouldn't have considered it so, Captain. But in light of my recent decision, perhaps it is. And my people and I have now joined its ranks."

Alex could sense her loss. She'd returned home after an absence of more than seventy-one years only to find it in turmoil – her father dead and her brother ready to betray her newfound friends. On top of it all, disobeying her House was apparently a criminal offense, even if it wasn't called one.

"Perhaps you just need a better House?" he told her.

She laughed out loud, taken by surprise. "You can't change Houses, Captain. Even if it were possible, who would have us under these circumstances?"

"Then you need your own House," he told her.

"There hasn't been a new House in hundreds of years."

"Perhaps it's time," said Alex, holding her gaze with a steady expression of his own.

Her eyes held his and her brows closed in a frown. Suddenly, she commed Julien, linking Alex in. <Julien,> she said, <a list of Méridien Houses, please.>

Julien responded with the list, which included their functions. Alex scrolled through it and spotted what he suspected would be missing. <No military house.>

Renée's heart was pounding in her chest and she felt dizzy. Raised as the daughter of a House Leader, a traditionalist, she was abandoning her House and had the temerity to consider starting her own. She knew she could never do this alone, but she could do it with Alex.

<Julien, please record this comm for the Confederation Council and House de Guirnon records,> she sent. She regarded Alex with an impassioned gaze. When he nodded to her, encouraging her with a smile, she dived into some dark deep waters.

<I, Renée de Guirnon, a self-proclaimed Independent of Méridien, in joint tenant with Alexander Racine of New Terra and Captain of the *Rêveur,* do establish this day a new Confederation House. Said House, to be responsible for the Military Affairs of the Confederation and to be called House …> She paused searching for a name.

Alex picked up on her thoughts as she rejected name after name, her frustration evident. He recalled his mother's last words to him. Slightly embarrassed, he nonetheless played his recording for Renée, who listened to Katie describe Alex's namesake, Alexander, the *defender of humankind.* <Probably a little, if not a lot pretentious,> he sent.

Renée's response was a huge grin and she announced, <To be called House Alexander. We so petition the Confederation Council for approval and will operate as such until the Council approves or denies our petition. Our charter of responsibilities and the assets we possess to perform our function, as required by Confederation law, will be forwarded within two days.>

<It has been duly recorded and dated by the SADE, Julien, aboard the starship *Rêveur* for Captain Alexander Racine and Ser Renée de Guirnon,> Julien stated officiously. Then, off record, he asked, <When would you like it filed, Ser, Captain?>

<Hold it for now, Julien,> Alex responded. <We'll send it before we exit the system. Until then, we continue to play dumb.>

<Understood, Captain, and I have a personal request. Having chosen to disregard House de Guirnon directives, I am also an Independent. Therefore, I formally petition for admission to House Alexander.>

<Granted!> Alex and Renée shouted in unison.

<Then I'm honored to be the first inductee,> Julien replied.

<And no better first could be found,> Alex responded.

Renée and Alex settled into a discussion of the finer points of establishing a new House, possible responses to her brother, and required communication with the Confederation Council. Alex requested a synopsis of Council structure and procedures from Julien, attempting to understand what he'd gotten himself into with Renée. In the midst of their discussion, they received a signal from Julien.

<What is it, Julien?> Alex asked.

<Captain, Ser, I might have made a mistake.>

<Julien, you don't make mistakes,> Alex retorted.

<Then, Captain, I might have done something that could be interpreted as a mistake. I announced to the crew that I have joined the newly created House Alexander, formed by the Captain and Ser, to operate as the military arm of the Confederation Council.>

<A little premature on your part, wasn't it?> replied Alex.

<As I said, Captain, perhaps it was an error.>

<And what happened?> Renée entreated.

<You have requests from all to join the new House, Ser.>

Renée jumped up and clapped her hands. <All the Méridiens?> she asked.

<No, Ser, the entire crew has requested to join House Alexander, Méridiens and New Terrans, to the last member.>

Renée's hands flew to her mouth as if to prevent something from exploding from her. She whirled around in a circle – once, twice, three times – her arms stretched over her head. Alex laughed, enjoying her delight. Then she flew into his lap, wrapping hers arms tightly around his neck. "And such a good heart," she whispered, quoting his mother. She planted a long kiss on his cheek, disentangled herself, and gave him a brilliant smile before hurrying from the cabin.

"It's getting to be a very memorable day," Alex mused to himself. "I hope we survive it to see a few more."

-37-

No more House directives came their way and they continued to play dumb, withholding their own announcement as they maintained their heading toward Méridien. Julien gathered data as quickly as he could. Their intent to disregard the House orders would be discovered when they failed to begin deceleration to dock as directed.

Alex was finishing a conference with his squadron leader and her pilots when Julien signaled his summary was ready. He sent a request to Renée to join him on the bridge.

Edouard, who had bridge duty, vacated a command chair for Renée, and Alex settled in beside her.

Julien used the entire bridge display for the pertinent images he'd culled from Méridien media stories going back over seventy years. The attack on the *Celeste* and the *Rêveur* was only the beginning. The Confederation lost more ships over the next ten years, the riddled hulks always found near industrial outposts in barren systems. No evidence of the perpetrators was ever found. Then the most far flung colony, Cetus, in the Hellébore system, only forty-two years old, sent a Confederation-wide signal that an enormous spherical ship over 4 kilometers in diameter had arrived in system. When the ship passed the outer planet, strange ovoid ships with dark silver hulls exited the huge ship and surrounded it. The flotilla was headed directly for them. Cetus' last communication, originating from Governor Bassani, announced they were attempting to communicate with the alien ships.

Fourteen days later, a House passenger ship exited FTL into the Oikos system, broadcasting an emergency comm to the Council. They had arrived at the Hellébore system from Bellamonde in time to witness alien ships destroying the colony. Using intense energy beams, emanating from their bows, the silver ships burned buildings, structures, and people into cinders. Confederation ships, liners, freighters, and orbital stations were rendered into dead hulks, riddled with holes.

The Council sent ships to investigate. Their vessels recorded some of the small alien ships circling the planet as well as the giant spherical ship. Several more of the small ships were seen patrolling the system. However, the total number of ships did not match the multitude seen by the first House ship. Close magnification of the colony planet revealed domes, resembling the top portion of the silver ships, buried in the ground.

According to the records, nothing more happened for years. Council ships continued to monitor the system. Around the domes, resources were harvested – flora and the occasional cave-in marking the mining of mineral deposits.

Occasionally, a dome erupted from the surface, revealing itself as a silver ship, and flew to the mother ship. Often a silver ship emerged from the giant sphere and rather than return to the surface it relieved a fighter patrolling the system. Then that craft landed on the planet and buried itself in the soil.

Eleven years after the Cetus colony was subsumed, the monitoring Confederation ships witnessed the eruption of the remaining domes. The flotilla of silver ships returned to the mother ship. Then the behemoth, accompanied by its brood, journeyed to the heliosphere and entered FTL.

The monitoring ships attempted to track the horde, but several silver ships broke out of formation and gave chase. Only the ship commanded by the captain who ran first survived; the others took the full brunt of the aliens' energy weapons.

And so it had gone for the next fifty-nine years. The Confederation lost colony after colony, one about every eight to twelve years depending on the richness and size of the overtaken planet. The last colony subsumed, Bellamonde, was one system away from Méridien and the chronometer was counting down. It had been seven years since that planet was overtaken.

At the conclusion of Julien's summary, Alex stood up and walked the length of the bridge. Renée followed his pacing. She thought of Antoine, her husband-to-be, and his family, who were probably still on Cetus when it was attacked.

"Julien, edit the package down to a short summary and send it to the crew," Alex requested.

"Yes, Captain."

After a few more moments, Alex stopped his pacing and looked at Renée. He wanted to feel sympathy for the loss of her people, especially her husband-to-be. But what he felt was anger – anger over the sheer waste. "So for decades, your people have watched these aliens take over colony after colony, killing their people and harvesting their planets, and they've done nothing?" he asked, throwing his arms wide in exasperation.

"My people have worked hard to remove aggressive tendencies. We've chosen order over independence."

"So when it came time to fight back, there's no one with the will or the means to do so? Is that what you're saying?" Alex challenged her.

Renée hung her head, unable to find the words to answer him. She'd suffered through nightmares of this scenario. But, in the light of day, she'd managed to convince herself that, at most, the aliens might have attacked a single colony. This worst-case scenario was one she hadn't let herself believe was possible.

"Captain, I have information regarding your second request." Julien said. "House Bergfalk has made repeated requests to the Council to be allowed to investigate the alien ships. They petitioned for permission to capture one for analysis, but the Council refused the request, stating that such actions might incite the aliens to retaliate against the Méridien home world."

"Have they taken any independent action against the aliens?"

"I can detect no signs of that, Captain."

"Who is this House Bergfalk? What does it do within your society?"

Renée collected herself and rejoined the conversation. "It is responsible for the Independents. It gathers them, transports them to Libre, and maintains the colony as well."

"Tell me more about the Independents. Are there any commonalities in their backgrounds?" he asked her. "And Julien, research this House. Seems to me that if you have a House dedicated to managing troublemakers and this same House is begging for a chance to take on the aliens, all is not as it seems."

"What are you suggesting, Captain?" Renée asked, confusion written on her face.

"I'm suggesting that you don't manage people such as your Independents for hundreds of years without some of their tendencies rubbing off on you."

"Julien, you have one hour of research time." Alex ordered as he hurried off the bridge. "Come back to me by then."

"Aye, Captain. The master Sleuth is at work."

Renée asked her Méridiens if any had personal experience with Independents. Pia and Terese responded, and she requested they join her in the captain's cabin. Pia had lost a niece and Terese a younger brother. They sat at the captain's table describing the transition their family members had undergone that led to their status as Independents. Their relatives had started by questioning House traditions. Later, they professed unhappiness with society's rules, and, finally, they graduated to outright rebellion.

What amazed Alex was that they didn't exhibit antisocial behavior as he defined it. To him, they had simply dared to express their opinions, choosing to disregard the status quo. It was apparent from Pia and Terese's stories that their family members had become anxious to join the Independents' colony, the sooner the better. Their families lost their loved ones forever. Once transferred, the Independents were never allowed off Libre, and only House Bergfalk ships staffed with their personnel were permitted to travel there.

Alex's chronometer app chimed one hour and simultaneously Julien came through his implant, <Ready, Captain.>

<Julien, relay to Renée, Pia, and Terese as well.>

<House Bergfalk transport records reveal an interesting trend, Captain. Your suggestion of an interaction might be accurate. Prior to forty years ago, their transport logs indicate a small, steady, linear increase in ships to Libre, as one would expect with a growing population. Then, several decades ago, continuing on through the present, the number of transports increased on a scale inconsistent with the population.>

<So fear of the aliens caused more Méridiens to rebel against their Houses?> Pia asked.

<A logical assumption, Pia,> Julien agreed, <but the increase in Bergfalk ships, journeying to Libre, wasn't in passenger ships but in freighters.>

<What's your analysis of the change, Julien?> Alex requested.

<Freighter transports to Libre occurred twice yearly for many decades, Captain. Then, they increased in plateaus correlating with the alien advancement. When the silver ships took over their sixth system, seven years ago and only fourteen light-years from Méridien, House Bergfalk sent a freighter to Libre on an average of every thirty-seven days.>

<Any idea what the freighters were carrying?> Alex asked.

<Their shipping manifests, normally available to the public, are not online.>

<Julien, do you have images of the freighters and the orbitals they exited?> Renée asked. As a daughter of the House responsible for Méridien passenger liner service, she was anxious to contribute her knowledge.

<Excellent thought, Ser.> He supplied images of the freighters, the orbitals, and the docks. They only made sense to Renée, who sat with eyes closed, making soft sounds as she examined the vid images. Finally, she opened her eyes and looked at Alex. <I can tell you what they weren't carrying. Those aren't grain or food containers along those spines. Not consumable liquids either. And they aren't transshipping ores or raw materials, which leaves finished machinery, manufactured metals, electronics, and the like.>

<I concur with Ser,> Julien added. <Manufactured components are the most probable supposition, Captain.>

<Could the material be employed to build ships?> Alex asked.

<Yes, Captain, that's within the realm of possibilities.>

The three Méridiens regarded Alex, trying to discern his thoughts. <Do you think they're transporting the Independents away from the aliens, Captain?> Terese asked.

Alex was about to reply to her but changed his mind. <Julien, what's the feasibility of building sufficient transports to move the Independents?>

There was silence while Julien pulled data and ran calculations. <Given the passenger manifests of Independents transported over the last 200 years, the population growth from the estimated family bonds, and comparing the capacity for passenger liners if all the material from the freighters was used for that purpose, it's estimated only 42 percent of the population could be moved.>

<So they aren't building ships?> Pia asked.

<Not necessarily,> Alex replied.

<Captain, your enigmatic style might be the death of you. Don't worry about the aliens,> Renée challenged him.

Alex grinned at her and pursed his lips in a kiss. Renée frowned; Pia and Terese politely hid their grins. <Ser, I was thinking that,> he held up a finger, <one, Libre's population of banished Independents has been increasing and they're in control of their own industries. Two, the Independents must be aware of the advancing alien horde, against which they stand no chance since they have neither a method of escape nor any weapons. Three, those Independents are kept by a House, whose Leader has pushed for a forceful stance against the aliens. You have all the ingredients for an aggressive mix. I think, at least I hope, they're building warships.>

The Méridiens stared at him aghast. <Not possible,> Renée said, doubting her own statement even as she uttered it.

Julien added, <I believe this is referred to as *thinking outside the box*, and while I myself admit I wouldn't have come to that conclusion, the probability of the captain being correct is equally as high as that of them building passenger liners.>

<So let's say that your suppositions have merit and that's what's happening on Libre,> Renée agreed. <Do you think they would have developed weapons for their ships? Better weapons than ours?>

<Those, my dear Ser, are excellent questions,> Alex responded as he stood up from the table. <I'm starved. Let's continue this over food.> Then he walked out. The women exchanged glances and then hurried after him.

* * *

Within moments of streaking past the deceleration point for Méridien, Julien received a House de Guirnon encrypted comm requiring the ship's status. He queried Alex and Renée, requesting instructions. Alex told him to send their House announcement to the Confederation Council and House de Guirnon.

<Ser, do you wish to make an announcement to your brother before he receives word of your new affiliation?> inquired Julien.

Renée started to say no, when a thought occurred to her. <Yes, please send this: 'Albert, dear brother, I can't accede to your ignoble request. We are committed to protecting our people as you should have done decades ago. And, be aware, the *Rêveur*'s Méridiens, to save their honor, which is owed the New Terrans, have declared as Independents. With our New Terran brothers and sisters, we have joined House Alexander.'>

<It will be my pleasure, Ser,> said Julien, his delight evident.

In the meal room, Renée observed Alex and Tatia. The two were sitting across from each other. Plates of food sat untouched in front of them. Once she'd asked why he had chosen Tatia as first mate. Alex had replied that everyone needed an ace. She'd needed Julien to puzzle out his words for her. Now, watching the two stare into space, their food going cold, she was glad Alex had his ace.

<Attention, crew,> Alex announced after meal, <we are proceeding to Bellamonde, the latest site of alien infestation. We will exit this system in under eight hours, and Bellamonde is fourteen light-years or about five

days FTL for us. We'll arrive outside the system, wait and watch, pick our moment, and test ourselves against a patrolling silver ship. Then we will get our collective rear ends to a planet called Libre, home of Méridien malcontents – just the sort of people we need. Make all preparations for resuming FTL in seven hours.>

<Captain, Ser,> Julien sent, <I've received an encrypted comm with instructions to override bridge authorizations and pilot the *Rêveur* to the predirected orbital bay. House de Guirnon maintains that this ship is House property. The term *thief* was mentioned in conjunction with Ser's name.>

Alex laughed. <I suppose that might be true,> he returned.

<Except the duration for recovery of lost ships per Confederation law is fifteen years,> Renée challenged in return. <Afterward, salvage laws apply to the individual or company who recovers the ship.>

<But you can't be considered salvage since you were still aboard,> Alex protested, <and a Méridien ship didn't find you. I did.>

<Technically, you're both correct,> Julien clarified. <Salvage law concurs with Renée. The ship cannot belong to House de Guirnon since neither it nor any Méridien ship recovered the *Rêveur*. As we were recovered in your system, Captain, it would be your laws that govern the disposition of the ship, whether you granted rights to the survivors or not.>

<Under New Terran law,> Alex replied, <you're a rescue. So I suppose, Renée de Guirnon, you own the *Rêveur*.>

Neither Alex nor Julien heard a word from Renée. Alex swung his head around to locate her at the front of the meal room. She was staring off into space. He walked over to her and placed a hand on her shoulder, which, after a moment, she covered with hers. Alex understood well the challenges of dealing with overwhelming changes, having experienced so many since meeting the Méridiens.

Renée relaxed and reopened her comm, responding to the anxious queries she'd received.

Terese, a couple of tables away, eyed the captain looming protectively over Ser, his hand encompassing her shoulder. *It appears the captain's therapy eclipses that of our medical solutions.*

<Ser?> Julien anxiously queried.

<I'm fine, Julien.> After a moment, she replied to both Alex and Julien, <So, I own a starship.>

<Technically, Ser, you own half a starship,> Julien replied.

<Half?>

<Yes, Ser,> Julien responded, <you have formed a House and have a Co-Leader, after all.>

The crew jumped in their seats as the captain's explosive boom of laughter echoed throughout the meal room. He was still laughing as he left.

<Oh, so now you want half my ship,> Renée sent after him. She followed it up with a vid of a Bellamonde wild cat hissing at him.

Before Alex could respond, Julien interrupted, <I still require a response to the House directive to override the bridge controls, if you two could halt your pillow talk.>

Renée sent Julien her vid of the Bellamonde wild cat cornering a frightened Méridien vermin. She could still hear Alex laughing down the corridor. He chimed in on their exchange, telling Julien he was free to respond as he wished.

Later Julien updated them. <The message has been sent, Captain, Ser.>

<And you said …?> Alex asked.

<I sent them an encrypted message directing them to the salient points of the law in the attached Confederation Compendium of Salvage Law. The House SADE should decrypt my code by the time we exit the system.> He sent Renée's cat–vermin vid back to her. Only the vermin morphed into a giant predator and ate the cat.

-38-

In the intervening time to their FTL exit point, the pilots joined Alex on the bridge. Julien projected scenarios on his holo-vid, connecting each pilot's implant to the icon of his or her Dagger.

Alex studied the pilots' responses as the scenarios changed. He ordered twin-flight launches, single-flight launches, and single-Dagger launches, one after another. They gamed until Alex halted practice for a meal then resumed as soon as they were done, running increasingly complex scenarios.

Preparations got underway across the ship. The flight decks prepped the Daggers for launch, loading missiles and confirming flight readiness with Julien. This time, as the *Rêveur* passed the Oikos heliosphere, the transition to FTL was easier on the crew. Terese notified the vulnerable crew members to report to Medical, who were awakened moments after the transition with no ill effects.

For the next five days, the crew continued to train and practice drills. At night, the entire crew continued to play implant games. The fighter pilots proved especially adept at adopting their implants.

Julien brought them out of FTL at 0.71c, hours from the system's outer edge and four degrees down from the system's ecliptic. A gas giant, the farthest planet outward from Bellamonde's star, approached an intercept point with their course. Viewed from above the ecliptic, its orbit was counterclockwise.

Examination of the Confederation ships' extensive records had revealed that the alien vessels on patrol never ventured far beyond a system's last planet, which supported Julien's theory that they used gravitational waves to drive their ships.

Alex and Tatia waited anxiously for Julien's telemetry update. Both were hoping the silver ships stayed true to their patterns.

"Single contact, Captain," said Julien and activated the holo-vid, populating the display with the near planets, the *Rêveur*, and the lone silver ship.

Alex studied the holo-vid. The gas giant loomed in their path. The silver ship was heading out toward the huge planet and had probably detected them at the same time they'd detected it. Soon, he suspected, it would change course to target them.

"Julien, I need a quick analysis of Confederation footage of encounters with the alien ships. I'm looking for tactical trends."

"What are you thinking, Captain?" Tatia inquired.

"I'm wondering if this species has any intrinsic tactical habits. If they are a species ..."

Alex was working on his sixth orbit around the bridge when Julien replied. "Captain, footage indicates a preference for maneuvers that remain within the ecliptic and port turns around planetary bodies."

"Yes!" Alex shouted, his fist striking the air. "Well done, Julien. You are a stellar body unto yourself."

"One is pleased to be of service and to be challenged to such a degree."

Alex received a vid of Julien's crystals and circuit boards framed in a halo of flames.

"Julien, advance your display's timeline, maintain our present course and velocity, until we are within one hour of the planet. Assume the silver ship has turned toward us and will maintain course and velocity." Julien moved the holo-vid's timeline and Alex noticed they would be in line-of-sight. With his implant, he pinned a point in the holo-vid. "I want to be in this position, Julien, at that one-hour mark. Make your course change now so that ship sees where we're going. I want it to anticipate our position even as we disappear behind that gas giant."

Tatia studied the holo-vid "Are we playing hide-and-seek, Captain?"

"Yes, First Mate, we are."

* * *

Alex ordered Edouard, Andrea, and the Dagger pilots to the bridge to study the holo-vid with him.

When everyone was assembled, Alex indicated a tagged position on the holo-vid. "This was Point Alpha when I started the plot and made a starboard turn with an inclination of a few degrees to gain the ecliptic. This silver ship," Julien highlighted the craft, "was traveling outward when it made a turn to intercept us. In an hour, we'll disappear from its view behind the planet, Point Beta." And Julien tagged another point on the advancing timeline. "When the alien ship has picked up our course change, it will project our end point to a spot on the opposite side of this gas giant. They will be forced to circle one way or the other around the planet to attack us."

"At Point Beta, we'll launch Flight-2 to circle in front of the planet." He could see Jase draw in breath to object, but his squadron leader's glare was heated enough to stop him in his tracks.

Julien advanced the timeline again and Alex marked another way point, "At Point Gamma, we'll launch Flight-1 to circle behind the planet. Immediately afterward, we'll release the shuttle.

"To make this plan work, Julien will preset your controllers. Don't go to manual until contact with the enemy or unless necessary. Based on Julien's research, these silver ships have habits we can use against them. They have a distinct preference for staying within the ecliptic and passing around planets on a port turn. Flight-1 should meet them head on."

Jase's posture straightened as he realized he would be on the front line after all.

"Flight-2," Alex continued, "you aren't there for insurance in the event they make a starboard turn around the planet." He eyed his squadron leader. "Andrea, your path will be the longer one, so you will be under heavy acceleration and must use the planet's gravity to accelerate even faster. My intention is to catch the silver ship in a pincer. Point Delta," he said.

Julien advanced the holo-vid timeline, showing the ships and the gas giant moving in concert. Red trajectory lines traced the fighters' paths as they circled the planet, the two flights pinching the silver ship between them.

"Julien, slow play from the start."

The holo-vid reset and, in moments, they watched what would take hours to complete. Edouard, Andrea, and the Dagger pilots all nodded in comprehension of the captain's plan.

* * *

Julien monitored telemetry, ensuring the silver ship's course and velocity held to Alex's plan until the planet obstructed their view.

In the port bay, the Dagger pilots were arranged in a semicircle in front of Alex. "You've seen the vids of these silver ships," he said to them. "Don't underestimate them. You face an incredible challenge, one I don't envy …"

"Says the man who whipped his tug around a gas giant to snatch an alien ship zipping through the system," Jase joked, and the pilots' laughter filled the bay.

"He's right, Captain," Andrea said. "This is your fault. You're the one who set the bar so high that we're only trying to catch up." The pilots broke out in laughter again.

Alex took their cue. They needed the banter to chase away the fear. His somber tone wasn't helping. "Well, if you're all so anxious to prove yourself, go bag me an alien." They responded with wild cheers, and Jase and Robert left for the starboard bay.

While Lieutenant Sheila Reynard, wing for Andrea, readied Dagger-4, Alex addressed Andrea. "You have the tough job, Lieutenant. That's why I made you squadron leader. You can't be late to the party and I'm counting on you to drive the tactical fight. We won't be of any help. We'll be blind at the interception point."

"I won't let you down, Captain." She saluted him and walked over to her fighter.

Alex sent a message to the pilots. <Hey, people, I want my Daggers back in one piece.>

They recognized their old commander's good-luck message to his pilots and all of them sent back signals of *thumbs up*.

It had always been Alex's intention to launch one pair of fighters at a time, reserving the second flight for the next encounter. Catching the alien ship in a pincer movement, with the planet allowing them to play hide-and-seek, was fortunate. But then fortune had always been his friend.

In a curio shop, Duggan Racine had discovered a set of ancient playing cards. Hundreds of years ago, someone had carefully sealed each card. He bought them for the children, along with a download of the games that could be played. It became a family tradition to play cards after evening meal. Their favorite game was called poker and they played for ship's duties. Christie, usually a loser due to her impetuous bets, claimed Alex, usually the winner, cheated. His father patiently explained to Christie that Alex could memorize the cards played and calculate the chance of new ones being received. While Alex knew this to be true, it didn't explain why, when the odds favored him losing, he often received the cards he needed. To Alex, it was fortune.

Squadron Leader Andrea Bonnard settled into her cockpit seat and hooked up her flight suit's maintenance lines, letting the cool air circulate over her body. She commed her pilots and repeated her caution, <Let your controllers guide you. We back the captain's plan,> and received prompt affirmatives, even from Jase.

Alex ordered the *Outward Bound*'s flight crew to board. He met them at the dorsal lift that was installed as part of the *Rêveur*'s repairs. Four of the five crew members arrived – Lyle Stamford and Zeke Krausman, the two engineering techs, Lieutenant Miko Tanaka, the copilot, and Edouard Manet, the captain. They took the lift up after receiving Alex's well wishes.

Alex still wrestled with his conscience. So many lives were at risk and now this decisive moment had arrived. Days ago, Tatia had cornered him during a strategy session to communicate her concern.

"I have one question, Captain," Tatia had asked. "What are our priorities for our exit, if our fighters are unsuccessful?"

"You mean, what do we do if we lose our fighters? We grab the *Outward Bound* and run."

"And what if the silver ship has significant velocity over us, how will we get clear of the system's gravity well and jump to FTL before it catches us?"

This was why he'd made Tatia his first mate. She asked the hard questions and kept asking them until she was satisfied with the answers.

So Alex, who had planned to release the *Outward Bound* early and keep its crew out of harm's way, had changed their mandate. They would cruise abreast of the *Rêveur* and, if necessary, intercept the alien ship. And, while they were outfitted with two carousels of warhead missiles, they had nowhere near the maneuverability of a Dagger. If Captain Manet launched the warheads in a continuous stream, he might buy the *Rêveur* time to escape, before his ship succumbed to the alien's weapon.

When Pia arrived at the lift, he stood still, unable to give voice to the emotions roiling in his mind and heart.

She embraced him in a long hug, whispering in his ear, "You are our people's best hope, Captain. We believe in you."

Alex watched her enter the lift and fought the temptation to call her back.

-39-

Alex commed the crew in priority mode. <We are 0.35 hours from Flight-2's launch. You've seen the vids of these alien ships. There should be no doubt that, if nothing is done, the Confederation will cease to exist. And in time New Terra will be next. We must learn how to destroy these ships. Do your best. That's all I ask.>

The flight crew, kitted out in lightweight, Méridien environment suits, had sealed the pilots in their Daggers, depressurized the bays, and opened the giant bay doors to reveal the deep dark, lit only by distant stars. As the chiefs received each pilot's ready response, the fighters' skids were released.

Alex ordered Flight-2's launch when Julien signaled their arrival at Point Beta. Andrea and Sheila's controllers eased their fighters out of the bay on maneuvering jets and pointed them toward the gas giant's forward edge. Then, initiating their preset course, they fired their engines, hurtling the Daggers to maximum acceleration. Pressed into their seats, the inertia compensators reaching their limits, each pilot sat alone with her thoughts. Sheila replayed the crushing defeat of the Confederation ships, large and small, unable to imagine how they would succeed where so many others had failed. Andrea was hoping Julien, the designer of their fighters, was as good as the captain believed him to be.

The countdown reached Point Gamma and Flight-1 was launched, Jase and Robert on course for the planet's trailing edge.

Alex commed his old ship. <Captain Manet, don't expose yourself unless absolutely necessary. I wish you good fortune.>

<Trust in us, Captain Racine. We will do what needs to be done. *Outward Bound* fini.>

On Alex's command, Julien released the shoes holding the shuttle's skids. With his maneuvering jets, Edouard eased the armed shuttle away from the hull before he engaged his primary engines. He headed for a position forward and port of the *Rêveur*, prepared to intercept the silver ship, if it got past Flight-1.

Alex, Tatia, and Julien monitored Flight-2 until it curved around the planet's front edge. Later, Flight-1 disappeared in the planet's trailing haze.

* * *

Jase's helmet displayed the diverging lines of the present trajectory from Julien's preset course as the Daggers delved deeper into the planet's gravity. He hadn't been able to resist overriding his controller to gain the added velocity.

Robert, his wing, was biting his tongue, refraining from challenging Jase on their deviation from orders. He missed flying Sheila's wing. She was a solid pilot and he knew what to expect from her. Jase was an unknown, a big question mark ... perhaps even a liability.

The two pilots waited anxiously for enemy contact. According to Julien's original projections, their target should be within 90K kilometers, coming at them through the gas giant's infrared radiation, which was playing havoc with their telemetry. It didn't dawn on either of them that Julien would know that the planet's radiation, generated by frictional heating from raining liquid helium, would interfere with their telemetry and had programmed a wider circle for their course.

Suddenly, their controllers located the alien ship off their port quarter at 10.6-degrees declination and switched into attack mode. The alien craft detected their presence as well and angled to meet them. They were closing on one another at over 1,100km/sec.

Before they could reach missile range, Jase's controller, anticipating the beam's firing, yanked his fighter in a starboard spiral out of the path of the energy weapon.

This was the edge Alex had sought for his fighters against the enemy's beams. Without it, the Daggers would have had no chance to evade them, invisible as the beams were. Julien had discovered the answer in a monitor ship's telemetry. A Confederation captain had the foresight to record a silver ship's attack on his fleet across a broad range of electromagnetic frequencies, and Julien had identified an energy surge that built across the hull just prior to the weapon's firing. He had programmed the controllers to detect the energy buildup and initiate evasion before the beam's release.

Both fighters were jinking and rolling. The silver ship was forced to divide its shots between its two adversaries. Jase felt his fighter shudder as his controller launched two nanites-1 missiles, but they were still in stage-1 acceleration when a beam vaporized both of them. He didn't even get a chance to swear before his Dagger swerved up and out of the path of another beam. Then they were past the silver ship without having scored a single missile strike.

As they flipped their fighters over, the silver ship mirrored their maneuver. The enemy ship targeted Jase's fighter first, since he'd turned quicker to reengage, breaking the formation flying that the pilots had practiced. While the alien ship concentrated on Jase, Robert, who kept his fighter in Jase's shadow, was able to fire two nanites-1 missiles, which ignited their second stages before detection. Twenty stick-heads launched from each missile. A single beam immediately destroyed eight of them.

With stick-head missiles deployed, the controllers shifted priority. Two buoy missiles launched from Jase's Dagger and arced away to take positions around the combat area. Just before his ship rolled hard to port in a double spiral, his controller launched two nanites-1 missiles to join Robert's. Both missiles achieved stage-2, and forty more stick-heads raced at the enemy fighter.

Jase switched his controller to manual flight mode to relish the personal defeat of the enemy. His controller signaled the charging of the silver ship's hull, and Jase yanked his fighter into a starboard roll, but his reactions couldn't match those of his controller. The beam cut through his port missile pod, igniting his remaining armament. The detonated missiles, now a mass of hot shards, tore through his fighter, exploding it in a fiery ball.

Of the eighty stick-heads launched from their four missiles, only nine struck the alien ship, splashing on its hull. The impacts kicked off reactions in their viscous payload. Embedded in an oxygen-rich, slow-burn, gel, the nanites began interacting with the silver ship's hull.

Julien had loaded a variety of nanites in each stick-head, not trusting to one design. The nanites, which integrated with molecules in the alien hull, would coopt the other nanites. Once a critical level was reached, the nanites would form a chemical signature. It was the job of the buoys to relay that signature to the controllers.

Robert registered the disappearance of his leader's signal. He pushed his emotions aside as his fighter rolled again, first one way, then another, pushing the envelope of his inertia compensators. His cell-gen nanites worked diligently to treat his bruising.

Once more, Robert and the silver ship shot pass each other, and his controller executed an about-face to reengage the enemy. He tried to calculate how far ahead of Flight-2 they had arrived, but found he couldn't concentrate on the task. Instead, he tried to slow his breathing and concentrate on surviving. It crossed his mind that he wouldn't be giving Jase the tongue-lashing for disobeying orders.

A buoy pinged and his controller uploaded the chemical signature from the nanites on the silver ship's hull, revealing a crystal composition with an embedded metal amalgam. With the buoy information in hand, he realized their first goal had been achieved.

Their fighters were closing again when his controller signaled completion of the nanites-2 programming. Simultaneously, his helmet displayed Flight-2's arrival. Relief shot through him. Help had arrived. Abruptly, his fighter jerked straight up into a twisting spiral, but the alien ship seemed to have anticipated his movement. Its energy weapon cut through his fuselage, slicing his fighter in half.

* * *

The gas giant's gravity had boosted Flight-2's velocity. Andrea and Sheila, arcing around the planet's 91K-km radius, came in high on the alien ship in time to witness the strike on Dagger-2. Their controllers detected the buoys, uploaded the data, and programmed their nanites.

The alien ship flew past the remains of Dagger-2 and flipped over to engage them. As they closed within 20K km, their controllers fired four nanites-2 missiles. The silver ship targeted the fighters, ignoring the missiles, which allowed all of them to reach second stage. The nanites-2 missiles splattered against the alien's hull, with only two misses.

Andrea signaled her wing. <Break off, Dagger-4, head below the ecliptic. Give the nanites some time to do their work.> In turn, she headed up above the ecliptic.

<Understood, Dagger-3,> confirmed Sheila, grunting as her controller activated evasion mode and spiraled her fighter down and away from the enemy.

The evasion programs were based on the best of the fighter games – not mathematical algorithms, but human ingenuity. The fighters twisted and danced away from the silver ship in an asymmetrical ballet with the pilots along for the rough rides.

<Leader, that ship ignored our missiles.>

<Saw that, Dagger-4. Probably ignored them since they weren't doing any damage. Maybe it will ignore the warheads too.>

<May we be so fortunate,> offered Sheila.

The silver ship chose to dive after Sheila. <Oh, fortunate me,> she groused, leaking her comment over the comm.

<Max acceleration, Dagger-4. Remember, Julien thought the ships use gravity waves. They need the planets.>

Sheila signaled her controller for maximum acceleration. With the combined onslaught of acceleration and her fighter's twisting and turning, she couldn't maintain consciousness and soon blacked out. This was the balance that Andrea had argued with her compatriots that could exist between a controller and pilot. After she lost consciousness, Sheila would have died if her controller hadn't continued to evade the enemy fighter closing in on her.

As it was, the silver ship detected the compromise of its hull's integrity and flipped end over end to return to the safety of the inner system.

When the enemy fighter had pursued Sheila, Andrea had flipped her fighter over and given chase. She was pushing max acceleration as well when the silver ship reversed course, abandoning its chase of Dagger-4, and headed straight for her. During the split moment that the two fighters faced each other, the silver ship fired a near point-blank beam shot, and Andrea's controller violently twisted her fighter out of the way.

As Andrea fought the inertia overload, her display flashed a temperature spike on the tip of her port weapon's boom. It had been a near miss. She flipped end over end and launched four warheads after her fleeing enemy. As her missiles chased the silver ship, Andrea urged them on with a whispered, "Go. Go."

The buoys directed the warheads toward the strongest pools of nanites. But, the four missiles wouldn't have struck the craft's weakened areas. The pools were on the forward half of the ship, and the warheads were closing on its aft end.

Unexpectedly, the fleeing ship flipped over again, and its beam weapon took out three missiles. It missed the fourth one, which was rearward of the others, its release being slightly delayed due to the damage on Andrea's weapons boom. Boring in on the strongest nanites pool, the warhead struck the weakened hull, slamming through the metal-exhausted crystal, and exploded. The entire force of the blast was projected inward.

* * *

Alex sat in the figurative dark and continued to second-guess himself even though there was no opportunity to change the strategy. But he did make one tactical change. Trusting in the aliens' penchant for their port maneuvers, he'd directed both his ship and the shuttle to move under the ecliptic beneath the gas giant in a port turn. If the alien ship defeated his Daggers, he expected it to continue on to where he was expected to be. So, he was taking their ships to the pincer point, where the silver ship had been. If they had to run, their ships would be on opposite vectors and he would have time to accelerate and gain FTL before the alien ship could catch them.

"Contact, Captain," Julien sang out. "I have three images in close proximity. Two are under power. They're our Daggers. The silver ship is drifting."

"Julien, rendezvous immediately!" Alex ordered, decisions playing out rapidly in his head. "Show me the system, all ships, and the vectors to Libre and Méridien." As Julien updated the holo-vid display, Alex zeroed in on a point far below the ecliptic. "There, Julien, send the information to Captain Manet." It was a course that created a third axis to the two vectors for Libre and Bellamonde.

"Still playing hide-and-seek, Captain," Tatia commented.

"We don't know if that alien ship sent an emergency signal, and if we follow the shuttle on this heading we won't be leading the silver ships back to either Libre or Méridien."

<*Outward Bound,*> Alex commed, <Captain Manet, our Daggers have bagged a silver ship and we're intercepting them. Proceed immediately to the coordinates you've just received. Monitor for any ships closing in on you and keep us posted. We'll pick you up later.>

<Orders received and acknowledged, Captain. *Outward Bound* fini.>

"Julien, can you identify the two fighters and locate our other ones?" Tatia asked.

"That data is unavailable, First Mate. The emissions from the planet are overwhelming comms, and the signal buoys are out of range. At this time, I have limited telemetry."

Julien displayed the local system on the holo-vid, color-coding the display as Alex preferred. The gas giant appeared in a swirl of red, orange, and green gases. The *Rêveur* was a blue dot, its red trajectory line curving to intersect yellow dots, the three ships emerging from behind the planet. The shuttle was in green and heading down and away from the system.

Examining the holo-vid, Alex's immediate concern disappeared. The three fighters were headed above the ecliptic, away from patrolling ships. *Fortune*, Alex thought.

Julien attempted to relay a comm call but it was garbled. They proceeded to close the distance on the three fighters, which were leaving the envelope of the gas giant's emissions. Then a comm came through. <*Rêveur*, Dagger-3,> then repeated, <*Rêveur*, Dagger-3.>

<Dagger-3, *Rêveur*,> Alex replied.

<Captain,> Andrea's comm came through in the clear, <we have your silver ship … a little worse for wear. And, Captain, I'm sorry to report that Dagger-1 is gone. Dagger-2 is out of action, but Lieutenant Dorian might be recoverable.>

<Message understood, Lieutenant,> Alex sent. <Stay with the silver ship. Once we rendezvous with you, come aboard via the port landing bay. Julien reports you are both without injury and craft are operational. Please confirm.>

<Both pilots and Daggers are good to go, Captain.>

<Understood, Lieutenant, we'll see you soon. *Rêveur* out.>

<Dagger-4, did you copy?> Andrea sent to her wing.

<Affirmative, Leader, I'm very happy to be able to say so,> Sheila returned. When she had come to, she discovered Andrea had signaled her controller to reverse course and close with her fighter. She was still trying to puzzle out why the operation hadn't come together. <What went wrong, Leader? Why did we arrive late to the party?>

<Hard to say, we kept to our controller's flight path. But someone reached the pincer point early … either the silver ship or Flight-1 or both. Let's see what Julien says after he analyzes the data,> Andrea cautioned, peering at the silver ship floating just forward of her Dagger, its once pristine hull marred by the missile strikes.

They sat quietly. Both were haunted by the loss of Jase's fighter. He might have been an egotistical pain, but he was their comrade.

Sheila's thoughts turned to Robert, wondering if he might have survived. He had become a good friend. *A sweet man*, she thought.

Julien focused his prodigious processing power on locating Dagger-2. As the *Rêveur* reached the buoys, he transferred their data and received the trajectory and velocity of the fighter's two halves just after the fatal strike. Once he determined the direction and distance that Robert's cockpit had drifted, he focused the ship's telemetry on that section of space, sweeping the area until he found the fighter's nose section.

"Captain, Lieutenant Dorian's ship was cut in half by a beam strike. The tail section is entering the gravity well of the planet; the cockpit is drifting inward and above the ecliptic. I can't communicate with the Dagger's controller."

"Okay, Julien, plan B. Get to Lieutenant Dorian, immediately. Let's see if we can recover three pilots today. Send an update to Captain Manet and Lieutenant Bonnard on the change in plan."

* * *

Robert sat in his Dagger or, at least, what was left of it. The controller's last signal of *engine separation*, before he lost all power, had shocked him to his core. Absolute quiet had followed – no engine thrum, no helmet telemetry, and no controller. Stars slowly tumbled past his plex-shield's narrow view. *Not too damn good*, he thought.

His flight suit would keep him alive until his oxygen ran out, which he calculated should last about two days. He wondered if they even knew to look for him. Cold, dark fear crowded his thoughts and he desperately tried to focus on something else. He played a recorded vid of Sheila telling him a joke and played it over and over. Later, he tired of the joke and froze the vid on a frame of Sheila smiling at him after the punch-line.

* * *

In need of human contact, Sheila broke the comm silence. <Do you think Robert is still alive, Leader?>

<It looked like his fighter was cut clean in half, Sheila,> Andrea sent sympathetically. She knew the two liked each other. <There was no explosion.>

<He won't have any power, which means he has no comm or telemetry. He doesn't even know help is coming,> Sheila returned, worry tingeing her thoughts. She imagined herself alone and without power, drifting in the debris of her fighter. The thought chilled her to her bones. Her one comfort was her faith in the captain, who was attempting to rescue Robert. Not wanting to dwell on her fears, Sheila changed subjects. <Leader, like it or not, it appears we're now Flight-1. Not a great way to move up in the organization.>

<I think there's going to be a lot of opportunity for promotion in our future, Dagger-4,> Andrea prophesized. <These aliens are accustomed to taking what they want. It's going to take a lot of work to disabuse them of that notion.>

<After the crew services our fighters, the first thing I'm going to have them do is paint our hulls, Leader.>

<Paint them with what?>

<On Barren, I saw a vid of an Earth fighter called a jet. It's similar to our fighters except it never left the atmosphere. The tag said the American pilot was an *ace*.>

<An ace? Like one of those playing cards the captain has?>

<Same word, different meaning. Like the ace is the game's top card, this captain was a top fighter pilot. But the important part was the text. It said he'd destroyed fourteen enemy fighters,> Sheila said excitedly.

<And, so …?>

<Well, I noticed there were fourteen silhouettes of fighters painted on his ship's hull.>

Guessing where she was going, Andrea said, <So you want an image of a silver ship on your Dagger.>

<Absolutely,> Sheila confirmed, <and since it takes multiple missile strikes to bring down a silver ship, I thought you would want to share your victory.>

Laughing at her wing's enthusiasm, Andrea replied, <We'll see what the captain has to say about your paintings, Lieutenant. I, for one, will be happy just to make the bay.>

-40-

The *Rêveur* closed within 220 meters of Dagger-3's tumbling cockpit. Julien signaled Alex that they were within range of Robert's implant.

<Lieutenant Dorian?> Alex sent and received a jumbled stream of jubilant sobbing in reply.

Alex had Julien orient the ship for a starboard recovery and readied Chief Roth. As Julien eased their ship closer to the bow fragment, Alex worked to calm the distraught pilot. Tatia coordinated with Julien and the chief to align the bay opening with the tumbling chunk of fighter.

<Standby, Lieutenant, we're bringing you aboard.>

<Thank you, Captain, thank you.>

The flight crew slowly powered the bay's twin beams, installed as part of the repairs, to stop the cockpit's uncontrolled spinning. A third beam, at the rear of the bay, drew the wreck inside.

Once the bay was repressurized, the crew extracted Robert from the remains of his fighter. When he reached the deck, he hugged every crew member, including his surprised chief. Then he stood beside the crew to stare at the metal hulk that was once Dagger-2.

<Julien,> Robert sent, <you have my deepest thanks, Sir, for building a craft so well that I could survive in less than half of it.>

<You're most welcome, Lieutenant Dorian. I'm pleased to see you safely aboard and will endeavor to build you a better fighter next time.>

As soon as Alex received Chief Roth's confirmation of Robert's safe retrieval, he ordered Julien to retrieve the other pilots. Their detour to catch the damaged fighter had taken them system inward and time was wasting. While he waited, Alex paced the bridge, throwing a glance every now and then at the holo-vid, worrying another silver ship would appear.

When Julien closed on the three ships, he commandeered the Daggers' controllers and, one at a time, landed them in the port bay. As the fighters settled to the deck, the flight crew locked their skids down, then sealed and pressurized the bay. Cockpits were opened and the women were guided to the deck, where they were met with back slaps, hugs, and a whole lot of cheering. Andrea and Sheila were grinning so hard, they feared their expressions would be permanent.

As Sheila cleared the crowd, she came face to face with Robert. She smiled at him, and he seized her in a hug that took her breath away. When they separated, she could see he was embarrassed by his actions. She grabbed his face, pulled him close, and said, "I'm happy to see you too."

* * *

Perhaps it's wrong to be cheering, considering we lost Jase, Andrea thought. But she decided to mourn later; right now, it felt too damn good to be alive. She broke through the ranks of well-wishers, comming Sheila and Robert to follow, and headed for the bay's upper deck, cycling through the airlock and crossing to the starboard bay view deck. If the captain was going to bring the silver ship aboard, and she was betting creds he would, she wanted a front-row seat.

With the pilots safely aboard, Alex directed Julien to orient the ship to present their starboard side to the drifting alien ship. "Can you detect any activity, Julien?"

"Scanning, Captain. There are no external power emissions, but there might be active internal systems."

Alex studied the mottled, dark silver ship on the screen. He had to decide whether to take it onboard, perhaps risking their lives, or leave it behind. That the hot-headed Jase had given his life for its capture was a factor, but it didn't sway him. In the end, he decided that what they could discover through examination outweighed the risk.

"First Mate," Alex ordered, "lead a security detail to the starboard bay with environment suits and stun-weapons. We'll bring the alien ship aboard when you're ready."

Tatia saluted and dashed off, comming her team.

<Chief Roth,> Alex sent, <ready the bay to receive the silver ship. Then vacate the bay. We'll manage the bay door and beams on remote. The bay will remain unpressurized until further orders.>

<Understood, Captain.>

Renée, who had been ready to assist Terese with crew emergencies, left Medical to join Alex on the bridge. The central screen was filled with an image of the alien hull. She shook her head in disbelief and linked with Alex. <For sixty years, these ships have destroyed our colonies. According to Julien's research, not one silver ship has ever been captured or even damaged by my people. It took you less than a day to capture one,> she said, anger underlying her words.

<Renée …> Alex began then received Tatia's priority message.

<Captain,> Tatia sent, <starboard bay is clear. Security is standing by.>

"Julien," Alex directed. "You have control. Get me that ship." He studied the screens as Julien employed the bay's three beams to capture and draw the craft aboard.

<Terese,> Alex sent, <report to the starboard bay airlock, lower deck. After security checks the ship, I want you to examine it for any dangerous organic residue.>

<Understood, Captain,> Terese replied, smiling to herself while she finished sealing her environment suit outside the bay's airlock.

"Julien, signal Captain Manet with rendezvous instructions," Alex ordered. "I want them picked up as soon as possible. Ensure they have the latest information on events."

"Proceeding, Captain."

Alex received the image of a sharp-winged raptor launching itself skyward. <Julien, you're becoming as bad as the crew,> sent Alex, shaking his head with a slight smile.

<As a full member of House Alexander, and, one might add, the *original* member, I wish to enjoy all member privileges.>

And, once again, Alex received a vid. This one was of an overweight matron in an archaic dress walking away in a huff, her exaggerated rear end swinging to and fro.

* * *

Everyone wanted to watch, and Alex decided he couldn't object. They were safely leaving the system behind to catch the *Outward Bound*, and he knew this was a momentous occasion for the entire crew.

The pilots and flight crews crammed the starboard bay's upper view deck. Flight Crew Chief Stanley Peterson nudged Andrea's elbow and passed her a small flask. The sip of New Terran alcohol, distilled from an imported cactus, burned down her throat. She nudged Sheila's elbow and passed the flask along.

The alien ship settled to the bay's deck, a smooth and symmetrical shape. Its silvered nose was marred by the nanites and a dark circle surrounded the warhead's point of impact.

Julien carefully scanned for any sign of nanites activity and, much to his relief, found none. By design, the nanites had a short lifespan, but Julien wasn't about to risk letting loose an uncontrolled, metal-hungry, self-replicating menace aboard the *Rêveur*.

The bay doors slid closed and the airlock hatch opened, admitting Tatia and the de Long twins. Bright lights illuminated every inch of the bay as they carefully approached the ship.

Alex had Julien relay Tatia's implant view to the port screen. She had reached the hull and was extending her hand toward it.

<Don't touch!> Alex and Julien warned simultaneously and she snatched her hand back. <Security,> Alex commed, <don't touch anything until Terese has analyzed the hull and interior for pathogens.> He had

Julien split the views from Étienne and Alain on the starboard screen as the twins walked around the craft.

<Captain, can you believe this?> Tatia asked as she completed her second revolution of the craft. <No hatches. No windows. No engine cowls. No sign of any opening whatsoever.> Tatia studied the craft for a moment then sent, <Captain, we can't give you an all clear. We have no idea what's inside and no way to access the interior.>

Alex was pondering his next move when he saw Étienne's view shift to a corner of the bay. The twin activated the grav-base of a service ladder and towed it to the ship's nose. He climbed the ladder and examined the 12-centimeter hole in the center of the missile's scorched circle. <Captain?>

<Understood, Étienne.> Alex conferenced Julien, the security team, Terese, and Mickey. <Mickey, I need an optics cable to slide into the missile's hole. It needs to be controllable and linked to the bay's comm console.>

<No problem, Captain. I'm on my way.>

<And Mickey, have the tech take it in when Terese enters the bay. Remind the tech. No touching the hull and the optics cable stays in until Terese gives the all clear.>

<Copy, Captain.>

As they entered the bay, Julien switched the central screen's view to feeds from Terese and Mickey's implants. The engineer was connecting a vid cable to the bay's comm console and unrolling it toward the ladder.

<Was the expertise of my chief engineer required to operate an optics cable?> asked Alex.

Mickey's deep chuckle came back, along with the image of a man standing proudly atop a hill. <On momentous occasions, only the best will do,> he responded.

Terese replaced Étienne on the ladder. She ran a small probe over the hull, both the silvered portion and the mottled areas, and examined her reader. <Captain, there's nothing. All material on the hull is inert. There are traces of residue on the edge of the missile opening, but the compounds are crystalized and no danger to us.> She attached a long, thin reader line to Mickey's optics cable, and he fed the entwined lines into the opening. The interior of the ship was dark; the optics cable provided the only light. Mickey rotated the cable end to touch Terese's reader tip to a dark substance thickly coating what appeared to be a console.

<Captain, it's picking up crystalized material,> Terese sent, <a great amount of it. It's the same material I picked up at the opening. It's inert, possibly cooked by the explosion. Based on the amount coating this console, I would surmise that the material came from organisms in the ship.>

<So we did have occupants,> Alex sent to Julien. <Were they participants or cargo?>

<An excellent question, Captain. An examination of the organic remains and the operational positions of the crew should give us some indication.>

<Can you determine whether it was a single individual or more?> Alex sent.

<I'll need samples to determine the nature of the organics and attempt to detect if there were distinct individuals, Captain.>

<Can you collect samples and safely quarantine them?>

Terese replied with a vid of a child, fumbling a collection of toys from her clumsy grasp. <Most assuredly, Captain.>

<Apologies, Terese,> Alex sent. <Collect your samples. I'll also need a decontamination procedure for the people and equipment exiting the bay. Tell Mickey what you need. Everyone gets tested, and keep medical personnel on duty to test anyone and anything exiting that bay.>

<Your instructions are clear, Captain,> Terese acknowledged.

Alex left the bridge and headed for the bays. He located his three pilots, still dressed in flight suits, intently observing the silver ship's investigation. Alerted of his approach, Terese, Sheila, and Robert turned to him and snapped to attention. "Squadron Leader Bonnard, Lieutenant Reynard, and Lieutenant Dorian," he greeted them. "It's good to see you safe."

"It's good to be seen, Captain," Andrea agreed.

"Congratulations to the three of you. I know the loss of Jase hurts, and we'll remember his sacrifice. What you've demonstrated today is that the enemy is vulnerable and can be defeated. You have my personal thanks." He snapped a salute to the three of them, holding it until they returned it.

-41-

Engineering built a decontamination unit outside the bay's air lock and a medical quarantine station just beyond it for testing. The airlock's environment was ventilated to space for the immediate future. When Terese exited the landing bay, Renée met her in the airlock and checked her before allowing the air to be evacuated. Then she checked the security team one by one, but no active organic residue was detected.

Meanwhile, the *Rêveur* and the *Outward Bound* successfully rendezvoused. Immediately after the five crew members safely entered the lift, Alex sent, <Julien, proceed at top acceleration for two hours along our present course. If no pursuit is detected, jump to FTL on this vector for two light-years. Warn the crew.>

<Understood, Captain,> Julien affirmed.

Alex greeted the shuttle's crew, shaking the hand of each one as they exited the lift. While he gripped Edouard's hand a little tighter than was comfortable, the Méridien's grin indicated he didn't mind in the least.

Pia ignored the offered handshake, choosing to hug Alex. "I want my hug back since you didn't die," she said. When she released him, there were tears in her eyes.

"Pia, the custom is to give a hug, not take one back," he said, his own voice thick with emotion.

She laughed at him. "You have your customs, Captain, and we have ours, even the new ones." And as she walked away, she turned her head and threw a cocky grin at the young captain she'd thought, for many terrifying hours, she'd never see again.

Alex's next stop was Medical. A second decontamination chamber had been erected in front of the suite. Julien had notified him of the activation of Medical's sealed environment protocols to prevent air exchange with the ship's system. He stopped short of the temporary chamber, not wanting to waste time on a decontamination procedure, and sent a query to Terese.

<There is little left to analyze, Captain. I might suggest less explosive next time, except I know that the cost of capture was too high.>

<Yes, it was a poor exchange,> Alex agreed as he leaned against a bulkhead. He was realizing the toll the day had taken on his energy and nerves. <I hope to do better next time.>

<I can tell you that what we believe to be the organics is a form of carbon-silica-metal. Méridien manufacturing produces similar compounds through a process of hydrosilylation. Nothing in Julien's databases indicates these compounds occur naturally, much less that they could constitute the basis of an organism.>

Alex sunk down to the deck as the conversation continued, leaning his head back against the bulkhead and closing his eyes. <Julien, what does the buoy data from the controllers tell us about the alien hull?>

<Nanites targeted metals in the hull structure, which was a metal-crystal matrix, Captain. The buoy data is insufficient to recreate the hull's full matrix. There was insufficient time. Controller and buoy priorities concentrated on identifying and communicating the hull's weakness.>

<Understood, Julien, it wasn't a criticism,> Alex replied. <If anything, we should be congratulating ourselves on a successful offensive design.>

<There is that, Captain,> Julien said. <In hindsight, it is always easier to be critical of one's efforts. Mickey will be collecting unblemished hull samples for analysis.>

<Are there any biological concerns to consider if we keep the ship in our bay, Julien, Terese?> asked Alex.

<The composition of this lifeform is incompatible with human physiology,> replied Terese. <Any of the organisms or their micro-biota, if they could have survived the detonation's heat, wouldn't interact with us at a cellular level.>

<Okay, that's good news. Rescind the quarantine notice, Julien. When the hull analysis is complete, I want a conference with you, Mickey, and Terese.>

* * *

Renée located her captain outside Medical, resting on the floor of the deck. She waited beside him without comment until Julien signaled the completion of their conversation. "Captain," she finally said, touching his shoulder, "it's time for evening meal. I think you should eat and get some rest."

Alex levered himself up, and they walked to the meal room together. He didn't realize how hungry he was until dishes were set before him and Renée. He dived in as if he had been starved for days.

<Good!> Geneviève sent Renée. <We were concerned when we didn't see the captain at morning or midday meal.>

<Perhaps it's time to dispense with some traditions … this custom, for one.>

<But, Ser, meals are our time of sharing,> Geneviève objected.

<Geneviève, these are dangerous times. We must support the captain and ensure that the weight of his responsibilities don't bow those wide shoulders. If this means food must be brought to him in his cabin or silence granted to him to think or rest, then that's what must be done.>

Geneviève's comm was quiet as she mulled Renée's suggestion. <Ser, apologies,> she responded, <you teach me wisdom.>

Renée received the image of a small child, her head lowered. <Think no more of it. Our ways are being shattered by these aliens in their silver ships. I believe the New Terrans will help us save our people. But rest assured that it will be a different world when all is done. And I, for one, believe it will be a better one.>

Those serving the evening meal made additional trips to the food dispensers. Even the Méridiens were taking extra portions. It had been a long, hard day for all. When the last utensil was laid down, the company waited in respectful silence.

Andrea rose up. Implants were signaled to record, including those of the New Terrans. "Today was my first fight," she began. "But I wasn't alone. I piloted a Dagger in the company of three brave pilots. We won the fight, but one shipmate did not return. I wish to honor Lieutenant Jason Willard, who gave his life for all of us." In memory of Jase, she told the story of the fight against the alien ship – the heartache she'd felt over the loss of the two Daggers, the fight she and Sheila had waged against the alien ship, the long wait for rendezvous with the *Rêveur*, and the joy of discovering Robert had survived. She paused and her audience waited. "When I enrolled in fighter training on Barren Island, I joined as a foolish young woman who sought adventure. It's not an adventure when you face death and lose a companion. Today, I returned to the *Rêveur,* grateful to be alive and humbled by the death of Jase Willard. Your fight," she said, singling out the Méridiens with her eyes so they knew who she meant, "is now my fight, until we win or die trying." As she sat back down, the entire crew rose in salute, the Méridiens with crossed arms and bowed heads, the New Terrans clapping and cheering.

When the crew returned to their seats, Alex said to the assembly, "We will miss Jase. Others will follow him before we defeat this enemy. Today was just the first step, but it was a great one. Julien tells me that in over six decades, there is no record of the destruction of one of these alien ships. Yet, today, this crew, this group of humans, did just that. At this time, we're headed away from Confederation space. When we know for sure that we aren't being pursued, we will turn for Libre. I believe we'll find allies there." With that, he exited the room for the bridge.

Alex chatted briefly with Julien then sat in companionable silence with Edouard, who had the watch. In the quiet and comfort of his command chair, he closed his eyes and laid his head back. <Come, Captain,> he received and opened his eyes to find Renée standing beside him. A half hour had passed since he'd closed his eyes. He climbed down from his chair and walked to his cabin with Renée beside him.

"You push yourself too hard, Captain. You shouldn't exhaust yourself so."

Once inside his cabin, he signaled the door shut and asked her, "Are you planning to tuck me in?"

She ignored his question. Instead, she said, "I am ensuring you go to bed and don't start working again."

Alex ignored her comment in return. "The first time I woke without my jacket and boots, I was confused because I couldn't remember removing them, and I thought I had dreamt your presence. But there was this lingering scent in the morning," he said as he stepped close to her. "I was in a hurry that first morning and forgot about it."

Her heart beat faster as Alex entwined his hand in her dark curls. He was close enough that she could feel the warmth of his chest.

"But the next time it happened, I realized I wasn't imagining it. And the scent in the morning ... that wonderful scent was yours." He leaned close to breathe in the aroma of her hair.

Now, her heart was racing and the cabin seemed short of oxygen.

He whispered in her ear, "Would you like to tuck me in again?" And when she could only nod silently, he kissed her. She wrapped her arms around his neck and returned the kiss. She wanted to take him to bed immediately, but he continued to kiss her lips, stroking with his tongue, teasing one lip then the other, playing with her, and she wasn't about to interrupt him. When he finally pulled back, softly cradling her face in his hands, he sent, <I told myself that when I found the woman I wanted I'd kiss her so that she'd know it.>

Renée looked into his eyes, brimming with intensity. <She knows it.>

Alex picked her up in his arms and held her close to him. She buried her face against his neck as he carried her to bed.

* * *

In the morning, Alex woke with Renée pressed to his side, her slender arm across his chest. "It takes an alien invasion for me to find the woman I want," he mumbled to himself. He reached out and caressed the line of her shoulder, the edge of her ear, and her slender neck. When she didn't wake, he pulled his hand back from the swell of her breast, allowing her to sleep.

<Don't stop,> he received. He smiled and returned to stroking her not-so-sleeping form.

Renée stretched her body out against him, wrapping a leg over his and sighing in pleasure. She had fought to keep Alex at arm's length, not wanting to endanger their greater goal. For some time, she had known that he was attracted to her too. The intensity they felt that first day, rather than fading over time, had grown in strength, was still growing, and she had tired of waiting and denying her own desires. She wanted Alex, and now that she had him, she was going to hold on to him, come what may.

Easing over on top of him, she reveled in the feel of his hard muscles against her body. Cupping his face in her hands, she kissed his lips, his cheeks, and his forehead, finally resting her cheek against his. She whispered, "Good morning," in his language. When he quickly sat up, she straddled him, laughing at his shocked expression. <You aren't the only one who can learn a new language,> she sent.

Alex laughed and hugged her close, pressing her to him.

"Tighter," she whispered.

He gently increased the pressure, and she felt him stir against her.

"Again," she whispered in his ear.

He eased his embrace and kissed her softly as she started rocking her hips slowly against him.

Two hours later, they awoke and chatted in Con-Fed, still holding each other, until Renée heard Alex's stomach rumbling. "Oh, no, I'm failing to care for my captain."

"Yes, I think he's about to waste away to nothing," Alex moaned, teasing her. "We've missed morning meal."

"Ah, my brave Captain, I've made other arrangements," she said, giving him a wide grin as the cabin door chimed.

"Well, let them in, Captain," said Renée.

"Who's out there?" he asked as he signaled the door open.

Renée rolled off him and walked to the door, which she slid open enough to reach through, retrieve some garments, and close again.

As she walked back to the bed, Alex admired her naked body. She tossed the garment in his face when he failed to pay attention to what she was saying.

"These are New Terran-style lounging robes, like the ones your mother lent us, so that the captain might be comfortable in his cabin," she repeated.

Alex climbed out of bed. The robes covered each of them from neck to mid-calf. While he was belting his closed, she came to him and kissed him gently.

"I don't know what the future holds for us, Alex, but we will make the most of it. Now come. Morning meal waits," she said and left for the cabin's main salon.

The center table was laid out with covered meal dishes and a pot of the Méridien thé Alex favored. Terese, Pia, and Geneviève stood against the far wall, all three of them beaming.

"Good morning, Captain," they chorused in singsong.

"Morning," he greeted them in return. "It's very kind of you to serve us after meal time. I know how important your custom of taking meals together is to you."

"Our customs are important to us, Captain," Geneviève replied. "But we've learned that it's important for our people to embrace change for the good rather than resist it to our detriment." She sent a *thank you* to Renée.

"Again, thank you all," Alex said, a little embarrassed to have an audience in his cabin this morning, of all mornings. "But did it require three of you to carry the food?"

"Why, yes, Captain," Pia volunteered. "A man with such a hearty appetite requires a great deal of servicing," and the three Méridiens beamed.

"You've been corrupted by the New Terrans," Alex grumbled.

"Oh, no, Captain," Terese objected. "We believe it's only Ser who has been corrupted." They squealed with laughter and ran out of the cabin before their captain could either throw them out or throw something at them. Instead, it became a war of rude images fired rapidly back and forth.

Renée was laughing as Alex signaled the cabin door closed. Both sent their own quick queries to Julien, who replied that all was quiet.

"Alex, I believe that you have done more than save us and our ship. I think you have saved our hope. It's good to see my people smiling and laughing again. It's even better to see them join your people in their love of life." She leaned over and kissed him long and sweet. When they broke apart, she ordered, "Now eat, you have much to do."

-42-

After their meal, Alex donned his uniform and set off on a tour. He checked in with Chief Peterson in the port bay since his two remaining Daggers had both taken minor strikes.

The crew, under Julien's guidance, had employed a vid-laser to detail the damage on Andrea's fighter. A GEN-2 machine was unpacked to create raw nanites for the repairs while the crew created molds for the missing section of her missile boom. The raw nanites would then be programmed by a GEN-3 machine and poured into the molds.

Alex cringed as he reviewed the damage done to Andrea's fighter. The melted edges reminded him of the *Rêveur*'s holes. "That was close," he commented. And the chief, looking over his shoulder, nodded his head in reply.

Outside the starboard bay, Alex saw that the quarantine station had been removed from the airlock, but security stood watch to restrict casual visitors. Alain, who was on duty, gave him a respectful nod and a bright smile. "Good morning to you, Captain."

"Morning, Alain," he returned. It hadn't escaped his notice that everyone was especially cheerful this morning. He thought the crew's buoyant mood stemmed from their success, but he had a feeling it might be something else. His chief engineer confirmed his suspicions. Mickey and his techs were arranged around the alien craft, an array of equipment spread out around them.

"Ah, good morning, Captain! How are you feeling this morning?"

"Fine, Chief Brandon, thank you."

"That's great, Captain. Every man needs his … his rest."

"Yes, well, thank you for your concern, Chief. What have you got for me?"

Mickey led Alex through their progress. His team had managed to cut samples out of the hull, which were in the Engineering Lab, a space carved from the original stasis suite. His techs were running a series of spectrographic tests to determine the makeup of the hull. It was hoped it might provide some insight into how the aliens entered and exited their ship.

"Captain, I've the strangest feeling about this," Mickey said.

"Well, Chief, all of this is strange, so don't hold back. All ideas are welcome."

"Last night, I was telling Pia that this ship doesn't make sense to me. She said I shouldn't prejudice my thinking with human expectations ... to let my imagination run free. So that's what I did and the oddest thought occurred to me. I'm thinking this ovoid seed is a home … not in any human sense, but the way certain sea mollusks carry their homes around with them."

Mickey stood in the bay, a few cables in his hand, and waited for the captain to laugh at him, but he was frowning instead. Without warning, he received a recording of a subsumed planet taken by a monitor ship. The vid was from the later stages of alien occupation, the ground pockmarked by the ubiquitous holes. He realized he was linked into a conference between the captain and Julien. Imagery assaulted his implant as a variety of monitor ship vids were compared and contrasted. Finally, a vid froze on a single frame of the domes. Straight lines were connected to the domes from areas of bare ground. It was a push-and-pull process between the captain and Julien as they traded ideas faster than Mickey could follow. Later, when the image froze, Mickey found he was hyperventilating. He would have been embarrassed to know that his crew had stopped working to watch the two officers frozen feet apart, their eyes staring into the distance.

Alex's requests were a blur to Mickey, but not Julien, who returned library lists of Earth fauna from the colonists' database. Alex directed Julien's search, first to insects, then ground insects, and finally ground insects with nests. Then the two resumed their pattern matching. This time, the lines were irregular and followed subtle depressions in the terrain.

When they completed their mapping, the perspective sank into the ground, the image morphing from 2-D to 3-D as it rotated on a horizontal axis. Translucent shading was added to indicate variations in the substrata as gleaned from exploration surveys. Seen from underneath, the ovoid domes occupied the center of subterranean tunnels that branched and reconnected as the aliens located and harvested mineral deposits, trees, and shrubs.

Mickey took his first step from observer to active participant as he revolved the 3-D image. The concept unnerved him. It appeared that the aliens were subterranean. His comm pinged and he focused on the captain, who was grinning at him like a man who'd lost touch with reality. And maybe he had, because the captain grabbed his face, planted a smack on his forehead, and made for the bay's airlock. His parting message was, <Tell Pia she's a jewel!>

Mickey turned back to the alien ship and found his team staring at him with dumfounded expressions. "Well, this nutshell isn't going to give up its mysteries by itself. Get back to work!"

As fortune would have it, he wouldn't have to struggle to share with Pia what had transpired. Mickey had developed the habit, whenever he worked, of running his implant in record mode. He could play the entire event for Pia that evening. When finished, a pleasant smile would engulf her face, her eyes lighting with warmth. She'd pull him close and send, <It was a fortunate day, my love, when we found your people.>

* * *

Alex ended his tour in Medical, where Terese and Pia were testing samples under Julien's supervision. He linked to Julien and the two Méridiens. <Any more progress on your sampling?>

<A fascinating development, Captain,> Julien sent. <Terese's organic samples and Mickey's hull samples are similar in nature.>

<How similar?>

<The similarities are sufficient to indicate a relationship.>

<A relationship?> Alex mulled the concept over in his mind. With his implant still open, he started assimilating various pieces of information quickly – Mickey's concept of sea mollusks; the asymmetrical, underground tunnels that might connect the domes to their plunder; and now the similarities between the organic remains and the hull. His thoughts raced ahead. <Black space!> Alex exclaimed.

<It would seem to follow from the evidence, Captain,> Julien sent.

<Wait? What?> Terese and Pia interjected, confused by the comms exchange.

<There's a distinct possibility that the aliens in the silver ships built their hulls organically. We think in terms of a mechanical opening, a hatch or bay door. What if the aliens in these fighters can organically open and close their hulls?> Alex replied.

<They might have used nanites technology to accomplish that,> Pia sent.

<Did you find any evidence of them in the hull samples, Julien?> Alex asked.

<No, Captain, there's no evidence of nanites or even a construction process. For all intents and purposes, the hull seems to have been grown, much like our crystals.>

Alex considered that information against his theory. <After they burrow into the soil, someone or something is exiting the hull, below ground, and foraging for resources. We grow our crystals slowly, under pressure and heat, doping them with metal gases. There is no evidence of that type of industry here. No ... the simple answer is biology.>

Julien considered Alex's idea and researched the colonists' data records. He selected vids of Earth insects, wasps and bees, creating nests with their own saliva and sent them to the three in Medical.

<Exactly, Julien,> Alex replied.

<And how does this information help us, Captain?> Pia wondered.

<If we can decode their biology at the molecular level and use it to understand the hull matrix, then we will better understand their weaknesses. Learning to destroy their ships is just the first step. Unless I'm wrong, extermination appears to be the only end game for either of our species.>

Julien updated Alex. Following their two light-year jump from Bellamonde, they had begun backtracking on their exit point to watch for any pursuers before they laid a course for Arno.

It was a cue to Alex that he had important business to conduct before they turned for Libre.

-43-

When Renée, Tatia, Andrea, and Edouard were seated around his cabin table, Alex linked them with Julien to share the newest data. <This started with an idea from Mickey. Then Julien and I added our own spin. Now, this is only conjecture. Just watch and keep an open mind.>

Julien replayed the original exchange and Alex narrated. <We started with an overview of the domes and attempted to find a pattern between the domes and the resource harvesting. An interesting note is that no Confederation vid has ever captured above-ground movement. So we posited we were dealing with subterranean organisms and patterned ground-nesting insects as the template to connect the depressions.> On the vid, the asymmetric lines on the surface sank into the ground and the view rotated to reveal a network of connecting lines leading out from the domes. He finished and waited as each individual played with the model, struggling to come to grips with the inhuman nature of their adversary.

<It's something for everyone to think about,> he offered offhand. <It's only a theory at this point.>

They came out of their fugues to stare at him.

<I don't think he's New Terran at all,> Tatia said.

<Well, I don't think the Méridiens want to lay claim to him either,> Renée added. They chuckled in response to Alex's scowl.

<Okay, enough fun at your captain's expense,> said Alex, feigning hurt. <Is this how you show your respect for my position?> He raised a hand to silence them before anyone could respond and they held their comments.

For all of them, Alex's transformation had created a duality with which they still struggled. One moment, he would be the shy, soft-spoken, generous, young man they'd first met. The next, he would be their captain

– the man who led them in the capture of the first silver ship and had sent five crew out to sacrifice their lives, if needed, to save the rest of them.

<On another note,> Alex continued, <similarities have been discovered between the organic material inside the ship and the hull itself. It's very possible, once the ship is buried, the aliens create an exit and close the opening biologically.> Then he shared the vids of the wasps and bees making their nests.

He gave them a moment to absorb that supposition, then proceeded with his immediate plans. <I'm also making an educated guess as to what we might find at Libre.>

<Are you referring to the Independents or House Bergfalk, Captain?> Edouard asked.

<Both,> Alex answered. <I hope they're working together. If they are, the manner in which we present ourselves will be critical. We are after all, House Alexander,> he said, adding a jaunty grin, <the Méridien military arm, which means, as of today, we're adopting a military structure. It will give us more authority than a bunch of civilians with weapons. This means we must change our organization: assignments, ranks, uniform insignias, and protocols. Furthermore, we'll expect anyone who joins us to participate in kind.>

His audience exchanged glances. Based on their blank looks, more than one message was being passed, but no one raised an objection. <First order of business, the *Outward Bound* needs a permanent captain. Yes, it's an auxiliary ship, not capable of FTL flight, but on Libre, the ship, with its weapons and our fighters, will play a significant role. In this regard, I'd like to officially offer the captain's position to Edouard.>

A huge grin spread across the Méridien's face before he regained his composure. He stood, adopting a serious expression, and delivered a New Terran salute. Alex rose and returned the salute, then shook his hand. <Congratulations, Captain.> The others sent their compliments, and the closest to him touched his arm as he sat back down.

Edouard had been in the employ of House de Guirnon as a navigation specialist for twenty-two years, a position he'd expected to hold until his retirement. The time lost in stasis had angered him. Then Julien had delivered the news that his people were being exterminated, which wiped away his anger, replacing it with determination. He vowed to make House Alexander proud of his captaincy.

Alex observed Edouard's face as it reflected his thoughts, moving from pleased to pensive then determined. The last expression gave him confidence that he'd chosen well. <The next item in this reorganization is that of the *Rêveur*'s captaincy. Renée has advised me that it's weak to play the part of House Alexander's Co-Leader from the position of captain. Therefore, I'd like to offer the position of senior captain of the *Rêveur* to you, Tatia.>

Tatia's expression didn't mirror Edouard's. It wasn't that she didn't want the promotion. She was flattered when Alex asked her to be first mate, giving her the opportunity to be with Alain and see the stars. But the adventure had changed when their worst fears had materialized. And while she could follow him, she knew she couldn't lead. Not yet. <Captain, I'm not right for the position. I respectfully decline the offer.> Stunned expressions surrounded her, but Tatia sat quietly observing Alex, hoping he'd understand. He smiled at her, and she smiled back at him. He knew. Somehow he knew, but he'd wanted to show everyone his faith in her, so he'd offered her the position anyway. This gave her the courage to demonstrate what she'd learned from him. <I believe there is a better candidate among us, Captain.>

<And who would that be, First Mate Tachenko?> His conspiratorial tone was her cue, and the two of them turned to fix their stare on Andrea, who sat frozen like prey in front of two carnivores.

<She's an experienced fighter pilot,> Tatia stated.

<That she is,> Alex agreed.

<She has demonstrated leadership ability.>

<That she has.>

<And she has demonstrated courage in the face of the enemy, risking her life for her fellow crew members.>

<Agreed,> said Alex continuing to play along. <Not to mention that she's successfully captured an alien ship, an accomplishment that has eluded an entire civilization for six decades.>

<Yes, there is that,> Tatia added, enjoying their repartee.

Andrea looked around the table for support, but found none. They waited with bemused expressions on their faces.

It was Edouard who offered her a few comforting words. <I can sympathize with you, Andrea. It takes a moment to absorb. Look on the bright side, the captain's cabin is so much nicer than yours.>

<Captain,> she said, <I'm flattered, if not shocked, but I don't believe I'm qualified. I can't be the senior captain, the ranking officer. I don't have the overall, strategic vision. I was a shuttle pilot not more than 130 days ago.>

<I quite agree with Andrea,> Renée said and heads turned to regard her, surprised that she was ignoring the captain's wishes. <Not your refusal of the senior captaincy, Andrea,> she continued, <but regarding the position of senior officer. I have been reading about Earth's military. Julien, if you would please.>

Julien presented on organizational chart, titled "North American Space Force."

<You will notice that when two or more ships operated in concert, it was common to provide a higher ranking officer called an admiral,> Renée explained. <This admiral usually resided on the greater of the ships and was the senior-ranking officer. The captains guided their ships per the admiral's orders. Now, Méridiens wouldn't have heard of an admiral, unless they studied Earth's military history. Most, if not all, wouldn't have any knowledge as to whether or not it was appropriate for a House Co-Leader to be called admiral. And, since our House is a new formation, of a heretofore unknown function, the admiral would be accepted as the way our new House does business.> She turned a satisfied smile on Alex.

Silence reigned for a long moment while Alex privately "discussed" Renée's suggestion with her. Then he turned to Andrea. <Is that your primary objection to the position of senior captain?>

Though she had other concerns, many of them, this was the one that frightened her the most. Her days as squadron leader had taught her something about herself. She had discovered she could be a leader, but she wasn't yet the strategic thinker they needed, not with so much riding on her decisions. Finally, she relented. <Yes, Captain. It is.>

<Then congratulations, Senior Captain Bonnard, on your new position.>

As she stood, she responded, <Thank you, *Admiral* Racine,> and snapped a smart salute, which Alex returned with a sour expression on his face.

Andrea remained standing. She'd found what she needed in Julien's organizational chart. <And I'd like to congratulate you,> she said, staring at Tatia, <*Commander* Tatia Tachenko. I look forward to working with you and returning the favor you've granted me today.>

Tatia rose and saluted her new captain. Andrea returned the salute then offered her a handshake and a cheeky smile.

<Well, Admiral, now that we're all a little overwhelmed, except for Ser,> Edouard quipped, <what are your orders?>

Alex laid out his plans for the crew's ranking system based on their new organization. They had less than five days to create a new House insignia, department insignias, and ranks to be affixed to the officers' uniforms before they made a vid connection to Libre. Within two more days, the entire crew had to be outfitted in preparation for the expected guests. He dismissed them and waited for them to leave before addressing Renée.

"Renée, I'd hoped to minimize my responsibilities for military decisions. Tatia was a TSF major. Andrea was a TSF lieutenant and a trained fighter pilot, not to mention, she successfully captured that enemy fighter," he said, the roughness in his voice betraying his emotions.

She walked around the table and put her arms around his neck from behind him, resting her chin on his shoulder. "I know you don't want the responsibility, Alex," she said, "and we would take it from you if we could, but we can't. You're our leader and we run to keep up with you. Without you, we'd stumble and our best opportunity to stop the madness that's decimating our people might be lost."

She stepped around him and slid into his lap. They held each other until evening meal.

-44-

In the evening, Alex sat on the bridge with his newly promoted officers, Captain Manet, Senior Captain Bonnard, and her executive officer, Commander Tachenko. Julien had disseminated the "North American Space Force" regulations to them. Later, they would have to decide what to adopt from the manuals. For now, they were discussing tactics to try against the aliens.

"It would seem most advantageous, Admiral, to strike while they are on the ground. Static targets, as the pilots say," Tatia proposed. "But, we would have to find the means to attack them soon. They've been on Bellamonde for over seven years and they've swarmed as early as eight years after the initial infestation."

"So we have less than a year's time, but possibly more," Alex mused.

"If the admiral is correct about the Librans building fighting ships, they might be prepared to fight now," Edouard added hopefully.

"And if they aren't, then we need the Librans to offer us a manufacturing base, or we have to return to New Terra. Either way, it will take time to produce an enormous supply of nanites, missiles, and fighters," Alex said.

"Whichever way we go, our fighters are non-FTL. They will need carrier transport to Bellamonde," Andrea added.

"And crew ... a captain, engineers, techs, flight crew, pilots ... all trained," said Tatia, adding another blow to their hopes of taking the fight quickly to the enemy.

"Well," Alex said, interrupting the dark mood that had descended, "as my uncle used to say, 'the bigger the problem, the smaller the bites.' Let's see what Libre brings us. Get some sleep."

As they left the bridge, Alex requested Andrea stay for a moment. "You need to own your new role, Andrea. I'll move my gear out of the captain's cabin tomorrow."

"Excuse me, Admiral," Julien interrupted, "an update is in order."

"Yes, Julien?" asked Alex.

"Captain Bonnard's possessions have already been moved into your cabin, Admiral."

"Ah ... and what, may I ask, has become of my possessions?"

Julien hesitated in his response. Just then the bridge accessway opened to admit Renée. "Ser is here to offer more details, Admiral."

Alex sent Julien a vid of a thin, lanky man in an oversized flapping coat running away while glancing over his shoulder in fright.

Julien sent back the words *the better part of valor.*

"Captain Bonnard," Renée greeted Andrea, "your cabin has been prepared for you, and if you have no other business with the admiral, I'd like a word with him."

Andrea glanced at Alex, who nodded his approval. She offered him a quick salute and left the bridge.

"Good evening, Admiral," Renée said in a business-like tone. Then, after they were alone, she slid her arms around his neck and looked into his eyes. "How are you this evening?'

"Better now, I think."

"You think?" she murmured as she started to nuzzle and kiss his neck.

"Well, this is nice, but why do I detect subterfuge?"

She stopped kissing him and stepped back. "Well, as House Co-Leader, I took charge of some of your directives. Personnel are at work on the fabricators, which will transform the crew's wardrobe into military uniforms, and I managed some cabin changes to befit the promotions you made. As you heard, Andrea has been transferred to the captain's cabin. Edouard has been moved to a suite behind the captain."

"And what has become of my meager belongings?" Alex asked, "Where do they reside? On the deck of the landing bay, perhaps?" he teased. He could tell Renée was struggling with what to say next.

"Well, of course, their final destination would be the admiral's decision," she teased in return. She turned away from him to hide her face and added, "Temporarily, your belongings were placed in my cabin."

Alex turned her back around to face him, enveloping her in his arms. "Only temporarily?"

"Well, again, that would be the admiral's decision, temporarily or permanently," she said as she buried her face in his shoulder and held her breath.

"I think that's the perfect place for them," he whispered.

* * *

The next morning, Alex woke spooned behind Renée, his arms cradling her. He smoothed the curls from her face and kissed her neck, receiving a soft moan in return for his efforts.

"Busy day, Ser de Guirnon of House Alexander. It's time to rise up and greet the day,"

She wriggled back against him. "Are you certain it's time to rise up, Admiral?" she said with a throaty laugh. Just then, the cabin door's chime sounded, announcing crew members, and interrupted their banter. "Argh, I should learn some of your New Terran expletives," she exclaimed. "There are times when they would be most appropriate." She groaned in dissatisfaction as she watched Alex leave the bed for the robe she had fashioned for him. For a moment, she was tempted to stay behind and replay her recording of last night, but Alex was hurrying to the main salon, and she knew there was too much to do.

The salon's door slid open and the inveterate triad entered. Terese and Pia carried morning meal trays, and Geneviève carried a uniform.

"The admiral appears to be in a good mood this morning," Terese quipped. "Perhaps the new accommodations agree with him?"

Alex ignored her goading as Renée joined them, wrapped in her robe.

Geneviève laid out the uniform. "If the admiral would care to try this on for fit and give us his approval, it would be appreciated. We have much to do to fabricate all the uniforms."

"You want me to do it now?" Alex asked.

"If you would, Admiral," Geneviève said politely. Alex took in their expectant faces then took the uniform and left to change.

"Pity," Geneviève said, as the door slid shut.

When Alex stepped back into the room, wearing his new admiral's uniform, Terese and Pia began fussing with it. The color was the Méridien dark blue. Instead of the ship's patch on the left shoulder, Alex's uniform bore a House Leader emblem, a staff with a curled head over an image of the home world. On the right shoulder was the new House patch, a slender circle of gold surrounded a golden Dagger blazing across a field of blue white stars. Four gold stars adorned each side of the short, standing collar. Renée turned Alex toward a mirror.

"Are you pleased, Admiral?" Geneviève asked anxiously.

"Beautiful work," he commented. He queried her on the stars and she relayed their list – four stars, admiral; three stars, captain; two stars, commander; and one star, lieutenant. "The House patch is inspired."

"Thank you, Captain," Pia replied.

"Very handsome, Admiral," Terese commented. Then the three left to continue the work on the crew's uniforms.

"Yes, very handsome," Renée repeated as she stood beside him, leaning against his arm as she admired him in the mirror.

"Well, let's hope your people on Libre are impressed as well," Alex commented. <Julien, what's our status?>

<Since exiting FTL, I've made a wide loop, Admiral. We've crossed over our exit point, and there's no pursuit.>

<That's good news. Announce FTL conditions. Let's go make some friends at Libre.>

<Your wish is my command, Sire!> Julien sent.

Alex received an image of a dark-skinned man in baggy pants with cloth wound around his head. He bowed and sketched a ritual flourish with his hand. Alex laughed to himself. At one time, he'd thought to flush all the colonists' ancient vids from the databases. But then he'd thought better of it. His people needed all the respite they could find before the long fight to come. *In four days, Libre*, he thought.

* * *

Eric Stroheim, Leader of House Bergfalk, sat in his finely appointed office aboard an orbital station, floating in a geosynchronous orbit over Libre. His personal treasures, collected over generations of his House's Leaders, decorated his office. They had been carefully transshipped with him when he fled Méridien for Libre a year ago. He was deep in contemplation, dwelling on their ships' failing construction schedule, when the Drei Orbital Station director interrupted him.

<Leader Stroheim, a ship has exited FTL and is entering the system,> sent Director Karl Beckert.

<A silver ship?> asked Stroheim, fearing the worst.

<No, Leader, I beg your pardon,> replied Beckert, realizing the enormity of his error. <Those should have been my first words.>

<Then they're Méridien,> Stroheim sent. <They should know this system is forbidden to them. What type of ship is it?>

<That's the problem, Leader. It's the oddest thing. It ... it appears to be two ships stuck together.>

Glossary

Méridiens

Alain de Long – *Rêveur* security escort for Renée, twin and crèche-mate to Étienne
Albert de Guirnon – Leader of House de Guirnon, brother to Renée
Antoine Bassani – Son of Governor Bassani of Cetus colony and former husband-to-be of Renée
Claude Dupuis – *Rêveur* engineering tech
Edouard Manet – *Rêveur* navigation specialist, later the *Outward Bound* captain
Eric Stroheim – House Bergfalk Leader, responsible for Libre colony
Étienne de Long – *Rêveur* security escort for Renée, twin and crèche-mate to Alain
Geneviève Laroque – *Rêveur* passenger
Jacque de Guirnon – Renée's grand-oncle and *Rêveur*'s original captain
Julien – *Rêveur*'s SADE, a self-aware digital entity
Karl Beckert – Station director on Drei Orbital Station over Libre
Pia Sabine – *Rêveur* passenger
Renée de Guirnon – House de Guirnon representative aboard the *Rêveur*
Terese Lechaux – *Rêveur* medical specialist

New Terrans

Alex Racine – Captain of the *Outward Bound*, an explorer-tug for ice asteroids, later Méridien leader
Amy Mallard – Ulam University professor and Alex Racine's mentor
Andrea Bonnard – Lieutenant, Dagger-3, Flight-2 leader and squadron leader, later *Rêveur*'s senior captain
Arthur McMorris – President, resides at Prima's Government House
Christie Racine – Alex Racine's younger sister
Clayton Downing XIV – District 12 assemblyman

Clayton Downing I – Canadian billionaire killed in Mongolia by separatists, founder of dynasty

Clayton Downing II – Founder's son who sank billions into the colony ship, *New Terra*

Clayton Downing III – Mining engineer and survivor of the *New Terra*'s catastrophic accident

Damon Stearns – Colonel in TSF and outpost commander on Sharius

Darryl Jaya – Minister of Technology and member of president's Negotiations Team

Derek Sanders – Minister Drake's chief of projects

Duggan Racine – Alex Racine's father

Eli Roth – *Rêveur*'s starboard bay flight crew chief

Frasier brothers – Criminals hired to spirit away Sebastien Velis after the engineer stole the TS-1 database

Gregory Hinsdale – Head of security for Purity Ores

Jason "Jase" Willard – Lieutenant, Dagger-1, Flight-1 leader

Jerold Jameson – Naval base commander, stationed on Barren Island

Jonathan Davies – Aerospace senior engineer and a member of president's visitor team

Katie Racine – Alex Racine's mother

Lem Ulam – Captain of the colony ship, *New Terra*

Lyle Stamford – *Outward Bound* engineering tech

Maria Gonzalez – Terran Security Forces general and member of president's Negotiations Team

Marion Delbert – TS-1 station manager

Mickey Brandon – *Rêveur*'s chief engineer

Miko Tanaka – Lieutenant, Copilot of *Outward Bound*

Osara – Captain of the fuel tanker, *Thirst Quencher*

Paulo Oberon – TSF emergency room surgeon

Prima – New Terra's capital, named after the first colonist baby to survive one year

Robert Dorian – Lieutenant, Dagger-2, wing for Jase

Samuel B. Hunsader – CEO of Purity Ores, a mining company

Sebastien Velis – TS-1 engineer who stole the Méridien database
Sergeant Thompson – TSF trooper and volunteer for medical nanites demonstration
Sheila Reynard – Lieutenant, Dagger-4, wing for Andrea
Stanley Peterson – *Rêveur*'s port bay flight crew chief
Tara – *Outward Bound*'s bridge computer
Tatia Tachenko – Terran Security Forces major and the *Rêveur*'s first mate, later commander
Terran Security Forces (TSF) – New Terran police force
Timothy Greene – General manager of Purity Ores on Cressida
Ulam University – University in Prima named after Captain Ulam
William Drake – Minister of Ministry of Space Exploration and leader of the president's Negotiations Team
Zeke Krausman – *Outward Bound* engineering tech

Ships
A Little Shove – New Terran tug dedicated to Joaquin space station
Celeste – Confederation freighter attacked by silver ships
New Terra – Colony ship from Earth, survivors named their new planet after the ship
No Bounds – Explorer-tug, leased from the government by Duggan and Katie Racine
Outward Bound – Explorer-tug owned by Alex Racine
Rêveur – Méridien House de Guirnon passenger liner, Jacques de Guirnon was the original captain
Thirst Quencher – New Terran fuel tanker, commanded by Captain Osara

Planets, Colonies, and Moons
Bellamonde – Sixth and latest Confederation planet to be attacked by the silver ships
Cetus – Last Confederation colony established, first colony attacked by the silver ships
Cressida – One of New Terra's metal-rich moons circling Ganymede

Ganymede – New Terra's sixth planet outward, a gas giant with metal-rich moons
Libre – Independents' colony in Arno system
Méridien – Home world of Confederation in the Oikos system
New Terra – Home world of New Terrans, fourth planet outward of Oistos
Niomedes – New Terra's fifth planet outward and site of the Habitat Experiment
Seda – New Terra's ninth and last planet outward, a gas giant with several moons
Sharius – Moon circling Seda and TSF support outpost for explorer-tugs

Stars

Arno – Star of the planet, Libre, home of the Independents
Cepheus – Original star destination for the *New Terra*
Hellébore – Star of Cetus colony, first Confederation colony attacked by silver ships
Oikos – Star of the Méridien home world
Oistos – Star of the planet, New Terra, Alex Racine's home world
Mane – Original name of the star, Oikos

My Books

The Silver Ships series is available in e-book, softcover print, and audiobook versions. Please visit my website, http://scottjucha.com, for publication locations. You may also register at my website to receive email notification about the publish dates of my novels.

If you've been enjoying this series, please consider posting a review on Amazon, even a short one. Reviews attract other readers and help indie authors, such as me.

Alex and friends will return in the upcoming novella, *Allora*.

The Silver Ships Series

The Silver Ships
Libre
Méridien
Haraken
Sol
Espero
Allora (forthcoming)

The Author

I've been enamored with fiction novels since the age of thirteen and long been a fan of great storytellers. I've lived in several countries overseas and in many of the US states, including Illinois, where I met my wonderful wife thirty-seven years ago. My careers have spanned a variety of industries, including the fields of photography, biology, film/video, software, and information technology (IT).

My first attempt at a novel, titled *The Lure,* was a crime drama centered on the modern-day surfacing of a 110-carat yellow diamond lost during the French Revolution. In 1980, in preparation for the book, I spent two wonderful weeks researching the Brazilian people, their language, and the religious customs of Candomblé. The day I returned from Rio de Janeiro, I had my first date with my wife-to-be, Peggy Giels.

Since 1980, I've outlined dozens of novels, but a busy career limited my efforts to complete any of them. Recently, I've chosen to make writing my primary focus. This, my first novel, *The Silver Ships,* was released in February 2015. It was to be the first installment in a sci-fi trilogy and was quickly followed by books two and three, *Libre* and *Méridien. Haraken, Sol,* and *Espero* the fourth, fifth, and sixth novels in the series and *Allora*, a novella, continue the exploits of Alex Racine and company.

I hope to continue to intrigue my readers with my stories, as this is the most wonderful job I've ever had!